BLOOD WORLD

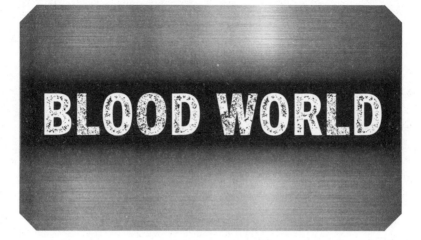

CHRIS MOONEY

BERKLEY

New York

BERKLEY
An imprint of Penguin Random House LLC
penguinrandomhouse.com

LIBRARY OF CONGRESS CATALOGING-IN-PUBLICATION DATA

Names: Mooney, Chris, author.
Title: Blood world / Chris Mooney.
Description: First Edition. | New York : Berkley, 2020.
Identifiers: LCCN 2019057674 (print) | LCCN 2019057675 (ebook) |
ISBN 9780593197639 (hardcover) | ISBN 9780593197653 (ebook)
Subjects: LCSH: Psychological fiction. | GSAFD: Suspense fiction.
Classification: LCC PS3563.O565 B56 2020 (print) |
LCC PS3563.O565 (ebook) | DDC 813/.54--dc23
LC record available at https://lccn.loc.gov/2019057674
LC ebook record available at https://lccn.loc.gov/2019057675

Printed in the United States of America
1   3   5   7   9   10   8   6   4   2

Jacket image by Aleks Ivic Visuals / Getty Images
Jacket design by Tierney and Wood LLC
Book design by Katy Riegel

For Jackson,

the greatest gift

BLOOD WORLD

Thy Kingdom Come

CHAPTER 1

WHEN ELLIE BATISTA turned the patrol car onto Montclair, a quiet street in Los Angeles's Brentwood neighborhood, she spotted a big Secret Service–looking dude in slick mirrored sunglasses and a black suit ushering a boy dressed up in prep school clothing to a Chevy Suburban with tinted windows parked at the top of the driveway of a spacious, contemporary ranch house. The guy holding open the SUV's back door was bigger and taller than his partner, but the thing Ellie noticed right away was how both men were looking around like a sniper was lurking somewhere nearby, in this neighborhood where the greatest danger was living next to someone who hadn't paid their parking tickets.

Ellie was close enough now to see the anxiety on the kid's face. She hit the lights but not the siren. Her partner looked up from his smartphone, saw her shooting up the driveway, and rolled his eyes.

"No," Danny said. "No, we are *not* doing this again."

"Relax, Pops. I'll take care of everything."

Ellie parked at an angle so the SUV couldn't escape—at least down the driveway. She couldn't see the driver—the SUV's windows were tinted, almost black—but if there was someone behind the wheel, he might decide to make a break for it, tear across the lawn.

Danny sighed as he unsnapped the holster of his sidearm. "You're doing all the paperwork—*and* you're picking up lunch."

"Where?"

"Jimmy J's taco truck."

"The place where you got food poisoning?"

"I think it was a stomach bug."

"Still," she said.

"That's the deal. What's it going to be?"

"Your funeral," she said, opening the door.

At five feet eight, Ellie was tall for a woman. The guy holding open the SUV's back door stood six feet six and weighed probably close to three bills. He looked, Ellie thought, like vanilla pudding poured into a cheap suit. He had a tiny pug nose and small hands for a man so large, but there was no doubt in her mind that he could swat her away like a fly.

The driver had rolled down the windows. He knew the drill, and he rested his hands on top of the steering wheel.

"IDs and permits," Ellie said.

Vanilla Pudding sighed. "We've been stopped three times by you people just this past week alone. You're seriously screwing with our, you know, productivity."

Ellie looked to the driver. "Sir, please cut the engine and step outside." Then, to the group: "Put your hands on top of the car roof so I can see 'em."

As Danny frisked them, taking their licenses, gun permits, and handguns, Ellie studied the boy from behind her sunglasses. He looked to be eleven, maybe even as old as thirteen, and had a sweaty pie-shaped face and stringy blond hair, and there were dark circles under his eyes. He kept swallowing nervously and his eyes skittered across the ground in front of him as if it contained hidden land mines.

Carrier, Ellie thought. Had to be, given all the security. If this kid had the gene, he was worth big money. The rule of thumb in the blood world was the younger the carrier, the more potent their blood, the more he or she was worth. Blood didn't discriminate. Boy or girl, black or white, mentally challenged or potential Mensa candidate, a single child could be worth several million dollars over the course of his or her life—unless the kid was drained and dumped, the blood sold for quick cash. That seemed to be the norm these days, at least here in California, with everyone looking to make a quick buck.

"What's your name?" Ellie asked the boy.

"Christopher."

"Christopher what?"

"Christopher Palmer."

"Nice to meet you. Do you know these men?"

The boy nodded. He wore dark gray pants with loafers and a navy blue suit jacket with a school crest on the lapel, over a white shirt with a red tie. Prep school kid, lots of money.

"I need to hear you say it," she said.

"I know them."

"Are you in danger?"

"From what?"

"From anything. Are you a carrier?"

Vanilla Pudding, standing with his hands splayed on top of the SUV's roof, turned his head and spoke over his shoulder. "Don't answer that, Christopher." Then, to Ellie: "Look, kid's already late for school, and we've got to get him there before noon. He's got a big test today he can't miss."

"I'm not through with my questions."

"All due respect, Officer, what you're doing, LAPD—it's harassment."

"So, if I'm hearing you correctly, sir, you don't want to cooperate."

"How about you take our licenses and gun permits, our weapons, do the background checks, whatever, while you follow us to his school? We drop him off, and then we can play question and answer for as long as you want. I'll give you the numbers for his parents, too. You can call them along the way, make sure everything's copacetic."

"Give me the numbers."

The parents' names were Cynthia and Francis Palmer. After she wrote down the numbers, she showed them to the boy. "Are these your parents' phone numbers?"

"Yes," he replied. "Can I sit in the car, please? It's really hot out."

Ellie opened the back door for him. Then she looked at Vanilla Pudding and said, "Lead the way."

Danny took over driving duty so she could work the laptop installed in the car. As she checked the licenses and permits, she thought about the steroid-laced goons playing rent-a-cop and wondered if someone, maybe even a group of people, was watching the boy right now, shadowing his movements and working on a plan to abduct him. She doubted anything would happen on the way to school, but something might go down *at* the school. Last month, a group of masked men armed with assault rifles stormed their way into a fancy private high school in Van Nuys to abduct a pair of teenagers who carried the blood gene. The gunmen were killed, along with two students and six school employees. There was a lot of talk in the state about teachers arming themselves.

The bodyguards checked out. Their gun permits all checked out. Ellie called the numbers Vanilla Pudding, whose name was Trevor Daley, had given her. She got the boy's mother on the phone, but the woman refused to answer any questions until Ellie gave her own personal information.

Ellie didn't blame her. Families of carriers had to worry about people posing as police and federal agents. You couldn't trust anyone these days. Anyone.

When the boy's mother called back fifteen minutes later, she seemed more relaxed. Ellie asked the woman a series of personal questions, comparing her answers with the information listed on the computer screen. Everything seemed to be in order.

St. Devon's Academy looked more like a maximum-security prison facility than a private school. Its sleek modern buildings sat behind tall concrete walls that had barbed wire installed along the tops. Almost all schools these days had fences or walls, but this was the first one she'd seen that had its own guard tower. Seeing a guy armed with a high-powered rifle and a scope looming above a bunch of little kids kicking around a soccer ball or just hanging out, acting like this was all normal, made her heart sink.

When it came to carriers, the police were subject to the same checks as ordinary citizens. Ellie and Danny had to wait several minutes while two men armed with assault rifles checked and rechecked their IDs. Forms were signed, fingerprints scanned, and after the gate was unlocked, Danny pulled up against the curb of what appeared to be the main building. Another pair of armed men guarded the door. Others were stationed at various checkpoints and roamed the perimeter and parking lot.

Vanilla Pudding pulled up behind them. Ellie got out and again asked the boy if he felt safe. He assured her that he did, and off he went to the front door to submit his hand to the portable fingerprint scanner one of the guards was holding.

"You happy with your job?" Vanilla Pudding asked.

"Is anyone?"

Vanilla Pudding smiled. He had tiny, baby teeth. "Reason I'm asking is, my company has a lot of clients who are young girls. They'd feel more comfortable in the presence of a woman." He reached into his coat and came back with a business card. "If you want to make some real money, with real health benefits, call me."

Ellie thanked him, handed him back his documentation and weapons, and headed back to the patrol car.

"Your stop-and-frisk routine back at the house," Danny said as they drove away. "You mind telling me what that was about?"

Ellie shrugged. "We saw something, so we stopped."

"We?"

"The kid looked scared shitless, so I decided to check it out."

Danny's gaze cut to her; he wanted, she knew, to call bullshit. And he'd have been right, of course.

Ellie had been a patrolwoman for a little over a year, but her real goal—her future—lay in the LAPD's newly formed Blood Crimes Unit. Admittance was extremely competitive—only the best and brightest. She considered herself reasonably intelligent, knew she was a hard worker, and, for the most part, had good people skills. What she had going against her was lack of investigative experience—and BCU looked for two years minimum, even for lowly data analyst positions.

The way she figured it, the more information she could collect on the blood world during her stop-and-frisk routines, as Danny called them, the more knowledge she would accumulate, and the more attractive she'd look when she reapplied to the BCU.

There was another, more personal reason she didn't want to get into it with Danny—with anyone.

Ellie was about to change the subject when Danny, thankfully, did it for her. "You ever wonder what it's like?" he asked.

"Being a carrier?"

"Getting an infusion."

Ellie shrugged. "Don't really see the point."

"You can say that 'cause you're young and good-looking. How old are you, again? Twenty-four?"

"Twenty-six, which is a whole two decades younger than you, Gramps."

"Yeah, wait until you hit middle age. Your body starts changing without your permission. Everything begins to wrinkle and sag, and everything hurts. It's depressing as hell." Danny sighed. "You do know this is one massive government conspiracy, right?"

Ellie drew a slow, deep breath through her nose as she shifted in her seat.

"No," he said. "No, don't give me that look. I'm not some conspiracy nut. Carrier blood is a real thing. It's a fact. It's got that circulating protein there, that enzyme called eNAMPT that makes cells produce these unbelievable amounts of energy, which is why carriers look like they don't age, why they seem to be able to fight off disease. I mean, that's a legitimate medical thing, right?"

Ellie sighed. "Yes."

"Okay, and we also know a full-body transfusion of carrier blood alone doesn't erase wrinkles and burn belly fat and increase muscle tone and all that other wonderful stuff—which is why, back in the day, scientists and biohackers started experimenting with carrier blood mixed with other medications. They found one that worked, that chemo pill that's now off the market because it's supposedly carcinogenic, Vira-something."

"Viramab."

Danny snapped his fingers. "That's the one. So, all these megawealthy one-percenter types start flocking to these holistic centers that are springing up like warts all over the East and West coasts, and they're paying *mucho dinero* to get these carrier transfusions mixed with Viramab, and, *voilà*, the *shit actually works*."

Everything Danny had said so far was 100 percent true. *Now here comes the crazy curveball.*

"This goes on for about a year," Danny said, "and then suddenly the government shuts everything down because people getting these transfusions allegedly die from them."

"Allegedly?" Ellie chuckled, saw that he was dead serious. "Danny, people actually *died*. They were on the front pages of major news sites. Their immune systems eventually broke down—"

"That's what the government wants you to believe."

"You're saying that all those well-known actors and actresses and titans of industry and rich folks from all over the world who died from these blood transfusions were targeted by the CIA or some such bullshit? Please don't tell me you believe that."

"I'm talking about the Illuminati."

"Okay, we're done here."

"You read that article last week in the *Times*, the one about Senator

Baker from Ohio? Guy was showing early signs of dementia, right? People were urging him to retire. Now the dementia's gone—"

"According to an anonymous source," Ellie said. "There's no direct proof—"

"Oh, please. Pull up the side-by-side pictures. There's no doubt he's using carrier blood. And that's my point. Wealthy people, people in power—you know they're getting carrier blood from someone who has perfected the recipe. Could be an underground supplier, could be big pharma. Who knows? Point I'm trying to make here is that the law and rules of society only apply to common folk like you and me. The wealthy and the elite—these are the people who can get their hands on this stuff. These are the people who will continue to live and reproduce, and in time they'll create a new world order."

Danny had a point. Not about the whole new-world-order bullshit, but the fact that the privileged and the elite had access to things that regular people didn't. She wasn't naïve about the way the life worked, especially when it came to crime—the one person with the best political connections and the best lawyer, sadly, had the chips stacked in their favor. But when it came to carrier blood and whatever chemical cocktail worked—if there actually was one—so much was still unknown because the whole process had all been driven underground, made illegal. Younger carriers had blood that was "fresher" and, it was believed, more powerful and longer lasting—which was why kids were being abducted in record numbers not only in California but across the country, imprisoned and forced to live out their lives like golden geese.

At least that was the operating theory. No one had ever found or seen one of these mythical "blood farms," as they had been dubbed by the media, so no one knew for sure if they existed. The blood world in LA consisted of two main factions: Armenian Power X was a cartel that, on the surface, seemed more organized than the second faction, the Mexicans, who seemed to favor draining and dumping carriers.

"The blood I'd want to try," Danny said, "is Pandora."

You and everyone else, Ellie thought.

"Bye-bye, wrinkles and belly; hello, smoother and tighter skin, thicker hair, more muscle tone, and less body fat. But wait—there's more! Order now, and we'll throw in, free of charge, *the* most intense orgasms you will ever experience in your entire life."

"If Pandora actually exists," Ellie said.

"Blood Unit believes it does."

"But there's no proof. No sample has ever been found, and no one has ever been caught using it. For all we know, we could be chasing a unicorn."

"There you go with *we* again." Danny rolled his head to her and cracked a grin. "That's what all this stop-and-frisk shit is all about, isn't it? You're doing a little R & D, hoping to find something, something big, so you can try to secure a spot on that unit."

Ellie smiled. "Look at you, playing detective. How cute."

"It'll never happen."

"You becoming a detective?"

"You working on the Blood Unit."

Ellie's throat clenched. "That's a real shitty thing to say."

"I'm just giving you the lay of the land. It's not about how good or talented you are; it's who you know and who you blow. You don't strike me as the type who—"

"Danny, look out!"

The patrol car's forward-collision warning system sounded. The vehicle automatically decelerated, Ellie's attention locked on a black Labrador retriever that had darted into the road and, instead of running away, stopped and looked at them, its tail wagging.

Danny swerved to the right. The Lab didn't move, and Ellie let out a small cry when she heard and felt the front-left corner of the fender hit the dog, the yelp it let out freezing her heart.

Ellie was already out of the car before it came to a stop. She got down on one knee beside the dog and Danny remained behind the wheel, blinking in shock, Ellie knowing he was thinking about his Bernese mountain dog, Mickey. The dog had been the most loving thing during the final months of his marriage—his anchor, he had admitted to her more than once.

"Danny!"

He threw open the door, his gut brushing against the steering wheel as he got out. The dog lay on its side, shaking and panting, its eyes closed against the bright sun. Danny looked like he was going to pass out.

"Didn't break any bones, as far as I can tell, and I don't see any cuts," Ellie told him. The Lab flapped its tail in agreement, then stopped when Ellie started rubbing its soft pink belly. "Probably just whacked Sasha here with the fender."

Danny let loose the caged breath he'd been holding. "Sasha?"

"Dog's name, according to the tag on his collar."

The dog had several tags. Ellie was focused on the one shaped like a red fire hydrant. SASHA was etched on the front, along with a phone number and an address right here in Brentwood.

Ellie held the tag along its side. "Take a look at this," she said, and flipped the tag over so Danny could see the words someone had written in black marker, beneath a bloody fingerprint:

Help Us.

CHAPTER 2

ELLIE BAGGED THE dog collar just in case this turned into something—and it had to be something; it was too bizarre *not* to be something. Afterward she placed the dog in the backseat, Sasha wagging her tail, the memory of being hit already forgotten. Ellie slid into the passenger seat, got on the horn to dispatch, and worked the laptop while Danny drove to the address printed on the dog tag.

One twenty-three Bleeker was a lot like the typical Mediterranean-style houses popular in affluent Los Angeles neighborhoods: a low-pitched red-tile roof with stucco siding and arched windows and wrought iron balconies. There was a fountain in the front, and the grounds were meticulously maintained—no doubt thanks to the abundant and cheap migrant labor.

A driveway wrapped around the front of the house. By the time they had pulled in and parked, Ellie had some background info on the home's current owners. She showed Danny the license pictures on the laptop's screen.

Louis Vargas was fifty-nine and wore every second of it on his face: dark circles under his eyes; jowly, wrinkled, and saggy skin. Sophia Vargas was fifteen years his junior but could have passed easily for late thirties: perfect complexion, black hair, and lovely dark eyes. No criminal record, either one of them. No traffic tickets or violations or citations. No children. No report of a missing dog.

Danny left the engine running. Before he got out, he cranked the AC up to its highest setting, since the dog would be staying in the back for the time being. Ellie slipped on her sunglasses, a pair of Ray-Ban Caravans, and followed Danny to the front door, a big ornate slab carved from oak. He rang the doorbell.

No one answered the door. He tried the doorbell again, and got the same response. Danny was about to knock when they heard splashing coming from somewhere out back.

"Let's go check it out," Danny said, and Ellie nodded.

They discussed the approach as they moved back down the steps. Ellie walked around the left side of the house, Danny around the right.

The fence was a custom job, made of redwood boards with a matching inset gate, the shrubbery incorporated into the fence. In the spaces between the boards, Ellie could see into the backyard. The surface of the swimming pool was still rippling from the person who had been in it: a tanned beanpole of a kid who couldn't have been any older than sixteen. He had that surfer thing going on, and part of his long blond hair was tied up in a goofy man bun.

He sat on the corner of a chaise longue, hunched forward, texting on his phone. Ellie didn't see anyone else in the yard. She opened the gate and walked across the cobblestones, underneath a roofed area off the back of the house. Floor-to-ceiling windows looked onto a good part of the downstairs—what real estate agents called "open concept." In the adjoining kitchen, a big cooler, its lid open, sat on top of a dining table. She didn't see anyone inside the house, and she gave the all-clear signal to Danny, who was moving with his hand resting on the butt of the nine tucked in his hip holster, on the other side of the yard, twenty or so feet away from the kid.

Then the kid looked up.

Saw Ellie, but not Danny.

Seeing one cop was enough. His body froze but his head swung across the pool, to the chaise longue sitting on the other side of the yard. The chaise was propped into a sitting position and faced the fence. Ellie couldn't see who was sitting on it, just a woman's tanned and slender arm hanging limply over the side, blood dripping from the fingers.

Ellie pulled out her sidearm, about to make the approach when Danny waved her back. "Stay with the kid," he said. "And keep an eye out."

Then, to the boy: "You. Keep your ass parked right where it is."

Danny lumbered across the area around the pool and stepped cautiously on the grass, eyes scanning the backyard. Ellie took up a vantage point near the corner of the pool; it offered her the best view of the kid, the inside of the house, and Danny.

"Mrs. Vargas?" Danny called out.

The woman didn't answer. Didn't move, either, Ellie noticed. Her gaze cut sideways, back to the house. The living room and adjoining kitchen were still empty—as far as she could tell. She thought about the two words written on the dog tag—*Help Us*—and wondered who was inside the house. Wondered if she was being watched.

Danny moved across the lawn, taking bigger steps. Ellie thought she saw the woman's arm twitch.

"Mrs. Vargas?" Danny called again. "LAPD."

Still no answer, and that set something off in Ellie—an uneasiness that made her move into the backyard so she could get a better look at the woman lying on the chaise longue.

Ellie had seen a lot of messed-up shit during her short time as a patrolwoman. What she was witnessing right now immediately shot to the number one slot: Sophia Vargas—and it was her, no question, the woman an identical match with her driver's license photo—wearing a pair of earbuds, her eyes closed and her mouth open and her right hand, buried underneath the tight fabric of her black bikini bottom, moving up and down, up and down, like she was trying to coax a genie out of its bottle.

When Danny's shadow passed over the woman's face, she opened her eyes. She saw the blue uniform and swallowed—not in embarrassment but in pleasure.

"Wait," she said to him. "I'm almost there."

Ellie watched, thunderstruck. She could see the still-fresh IV puncture wound in the crook of her arm, the wound bleeding, she was sure, from a recent transfusion.

"Ma'am," Danny said, "I need you to stop masturbating."

Sophia Vargas ignored him. She kept going, moving her finger even faster, trying to climax, not stopping or slowing down even when Danny leaned forward and yanked out her earbuds. Ellie had been told one of the side effects of blooding, at least in the initial hours after a transfusion, was a heightened sex drive, but she had never seen *anything* like this before.

Sophia Vargas arched her back. Her limbs stiffened and she cried out in pleasure.

Danny's face was as red as an apple. He had to clear his throat before he could speak. "What happened to your arm?"

The woman didn't respond. She relaxed back against the chaise longue, trying to catch her breath.

Again Ellie glanced at the house—all clear downstairs, from what she could see—and then she looked back at the kid, who was sitting with his forearms on his knees and acting like what was unfolding here in the backyard was no big deal. Like he couldn't understand what all the fuss was about. He was way too young to administer a transfusion all by himself, but had he assisted someone? Was that person, maybe even group of people, hunkered down inside the house at this very moment?

Ellie had never heard of blooding being performed in someone's home, but then again, this was Los Angeles, where if you were rich enough and willing to pay the price you could get anything you wanted, anytime.

"What happened to your arm, Mrs. Vargas?" Danny asked again.

"I gave blood," the woman replied between breaths. "This morning."
"Where?"
She licked her lips. Smiled. "One of those Red Cross mobile things."
Bullshit, Ellie wanted to say. And why was Danny bothering with the

whole Q & A dance? He had more than enough probable cause to arrest the woman on suspicion of receiving carrier blood.

The sliding back door slammed open. Ellie turned, saw a shirtless guy step out. He was tall and jacked with muscle, his chest and arms exploding with all kinds of shitty, colorful tattoos, like a box of crayons had vomited on him. The largest and oddest one was on his left shoulder: a gingerbread man with a bloody knife clamped between its sharklike teeth. He was a redhead—skin so pale it didn't tan, freckles, and blondish red hair that had been shaved into a military-type crew cut.

Despite his intimidating build, Ellie didn't feel threatened; his hands were empty, and she didn't see a weapon in his shorts pockets. He was smiling, too, but there was absolutely nothing pleasant about it.

"Something wrong, Officers?" Gingerbread Man asked, his tone casual and relaxed, like he was receiving guests at a party. He didn't wait for an answer, didn't even give their presence a second thought; he walked away from them, to his right, heading toward a custom-made barbecue island.

Ellie was scanning the island surfaces, looking for a weapon, when Danny said, "Sir, I'm ordering you to stop right where you are and—"

Gingerbread Man lurched forward, had his hand on the grill handle when the kid, who had been staring sullenly at his feet the whole time, reached into the canvas bag beside him.

"Stop! Hands in the air!" Ellie shouted, just as the kid came out with an Uzi, the submachine gun looking way too big in his small hand.

"Down!" Ellie screamed, locked in the Weaver stance, like she'd been trained. Only this wasn't a training exercise; this was *real* and this was *happening* and her career and life were hanging on whatever she did next. *"Put the gun down now!"*

But the kid wasn't listening, and Gingerbread Man had flipped open the wide hood of the grill, revealing the AR-15 lying underneath. Two targets, both armed, spread across the area, a civilian and her partner in the middle. No good options.

She fired a warning shot at the kid, the round going high above his head.

"Drop it!" she screamed. *"Don't make me—"*

But the words fell on deaf ears. The kid had the gun up and the safety off.

Ellie dropped to the ground, behind a waist-high wall made of blue-gray stone. The first rounds ricocheted off the stone and then more rounds cut across the grass behind her. She was trapped and she knew she had to deal with this; it was happening; it was full-on; she was in a gunfight, her first. She had to put both the kid and Gingerbread Man down. That was her only option. She said a quick prayer, begging God to keep her safe, and when she came up with her weapon, the backyard erupting in a hailstorm of bullets, she saw several rounds tearing into Danny's chest.

CHAPTER 3

SEBASTIAN NEVER MET with his blood clients. Keeping his identity secret was paramount for his continued success, and besides, he had people for that. Still, he wouldn't have minded saying a quick hello to the beautiful Italian woman in treatment room number 3, an actress he remembered fondly from his teenage years. Her name was Isabella Flores, and she had starred in a string of critically panned but monstrously successful action movies in which she played a demon hunter named Mistress Knight, who, with an old-fashioned .357 Magnum loaded with special bullets crafted by Lucifer himself, ran around at night collecting souls that had somehow managed to escape from hell. She had starred in the first nine films before committing the one cardinal sin Hollywood could never forgive, under any circumstances: she had gotten old.

Her real age, Sebastian had learned, was sixty-two, although her Wikipedia profile had it listed as fifty—and she could easily pass for fifty, maybe even for late forties. Based on what he could see, she didn't appear to have had cosmetic work done, which didn't come as much of a surprise. She filled out the black V-neck hospital smock and matching pants quite nicely, still had the thick black hair, perfect jawline, full lips, and fiery green eyes that had made her *People* magazine's Most Beautiful Whatever for several years running, even when she turned forty-two. Well, fifty-four, in all honesty.

Sebastian stood on the other side of the one-way mirror, drinking his coffee and watching her pace across the room, this woman who had played the starring role in many of his teenage masturbatory fantasies. He didn't normally hang around this long, evaluating his clients; he didn't have time for that, had a number of other places he was actively needed. The reason he was watching her had more to do with the fact that she reminded him of a woman he had dated a long time ago and still remembered fondly. Perhaps too fondly, he thought. Ava Martinez. She had been the great love of his life.

Still was, really.

His business partner, and the owner of the dermatology and laser center, Dr. Maya Dawson, entered the hidden chamber off her private office. Her expression was stern—always was, reminding him of the Catholic nuns from his youth, dour-faced, humorless women. She didn't dress like one, though—nuns didn't favor Armani business wear—and what he enjoyed about this petite middle-aged woman with brown eyes and a maternal-looking bob hairstyle was the sense of comfort and serenity she radiated, Maya the kind of person who could solve all your problems. Nothing ever seemed to rattle her.

But something had rattled her this morning. He could see it in her face, the way she folded her hands behind her back and straightened, as if bracing for an argument.

"Good," she said. "You're still here."

Sebastian always showed up on transfusion days. His clients paid a ridiculous premium for his product and he wanted to make sure everything ran smoothly. It was more out of habit now than necessity. He rarely encountered a problem, because he ran a tight operation but also because he chose his people well.

"Why isn't she sedated?" Sebastian asked, nodding to Isabella Flores.

"She *is*," Dawson replied wearily. "That's her, sedated."

That took Sebastian by surprise. When clients were picked up at their homes, before dawn, they were given anesthetic injections. Once they were out, they were loaded into a van and transported here, where they would be brought out of sedation and given breakfast before the transfusion, which took the better part of the day. They'd spend the night, the staff monitoring for any side effects, and once Dawson pronounced them good to go, they would be sedated again, loaded back into the van, and driven home, where they would wake up in their own beds, having no idea where they'd been. Phones and other electronic devices were left at home, and the clients were given special clothing to wear on the morning of their transfusion, Sebastian always concerned about an undercover cop or Fed posing as a client, wearing a hidden camera, microphone, or tracking device inside a belt or a button, the sole of a shoe. It had happened to his main competitors, the Armenians, too many times.

Right now Isabella Flores should have been acting like the other two clients: mellow or half-asleep and lounging in the surgical chair, mindlessly watching TV or listening to music as they waited for their transfusion to begin. Instead, she was frantic, pacing rapidly back and forth.

Dawson said, "She's refusing the transfusion until she speaks to the man in charge—the one who runs the whole operation. The gangster, not the doctor."

"The gangster?"

"Her words."

"Why?"

"Because she's an actress and she's crazy?" Dawson sighed as she took off her glasses and rubbed the bridge of her nose. "How would you like to handle this?"

"I'll talk to her."

Dawson blinked in surprise. "You never talk to the clients."

"This is her first time getting a transfusion. It's probably just nerves."

"Or maybe she's just another miserable narcissist who thinks the world revolves around her."

"There's that."

Dawson shook her head. "Enjoy."

The click of Maya's heels faded behind him as Sebastian took a seat in front of the console. Facing him was one-way glass looking into Isabella Flores's room. It took him a moment to find the switch for the microphone. He didn't worry about disguising his voice; the mike already did that.

"Good morning, Miss Flores."

Isabella Flores started at his voice. She looked up at the ceiling speaker directly above her.

"Can you hear me okay?" Sebastian asked. "Do I need to turn up the volume?"

The woman stepped directly in front of the one-way and straightened and squared her shoulders, looking like she was about to climb inside a boxing ring and knock someone out with one punch. Sebastian caught a whiff of fear behind her pose—the fear of being a onetime insanely popular item now kicked to the discount aisle, reduced for quick clearance.

"Tell me what's troubling you," Sebastian said.

"Are you the person in charge?"

"What's the problem, Miss Flores?"

"How *dare* you lock me inside here like a prisoner? Do you know who I am? How much I paid?" She glared at the one-way mirror—at him—demanding an answer.

Sebastian had to shut down her attitude right now. He picked up the small microphone and leaned back in his chair, grinning. "I've got this recurring dream," he told her. "It always starts out with me sitting at the head of this really fancy banquet table, right? All the food and booze I could possibly want, and there are—"

"I don't give a shit about your dream. What I want is—"

"What you want, Miss Flores, is immaterial. What I want is all that matters, and what I want is for you to stop acting like a spoiled brat and to show some manners. A woman such as yourself should know better." Sebastian paused, pleased when he saw some fight go out of her eyes—

not a lot, just some. "Now, I was in the middle of telling you a story. An important story. May I continue?"

She didn't answer—although she clearly wanted to, her nostrils flaring, Sebastian watching as she swallowed her words. Sebastian continued.

"Okay, so, the dream. Like I said, the banquet table is full of food and booze, and there are, I dunno, a dozen or more chairs around me, and they're full of dead people. I'm not talking Hollywood dead, with makeup and good lighting; I'm talking real-life dead. Rotting flesh and missing limbs and eyes—everything. I don't recognize a single one of these people, or any of the ones standing behind them, because their faces are, well, you know, gone. But I've got an *idea* of who some of them are because of the clothes they're wearing. Can't remember their names or why I killed them, yet most times I remember what they were wearing when they died. Does that make me crazy?"

Isabella Flores didn't answer. His story, which was 100 percent true, had taken a bite out of her self-absorption. He had her full attention. "The other crazy thing about the dream?" he said. "Flies and maggots everywhere. On the bodies, the food. I know it reeks to holy hell in there, but I can't smell anything because it's a dream. Have you?"

"Have I what?"

"Smelled a dead body?"

She swallowed, indignant. "Why would you ask me such a horrible question?"

"I've been around a lot of dead bodies, and it's the single worst odor on the planet—the kind that hits you in the stomach like a fist. The only thing you want to do is to run from it, find a place to throw up. But in the dream? I just keep on eating like it's no big deal."

Sebastian chuckled. "But that's not the crazy part. That happens when I wake up. Every single time I do? I'm hungry. Not 'Let's go downstairs and grab a glass of milk' hungry. I'm talking about eating-the-entire-contents-of-the-refrigerator hungry. Crazy, right?"

Her eyes cut sideways, to the door.

"Oh no," he said. "No, no, no. This isn't some shitty movie where you're going to escape. No one's coming to rescue you. This is real—this is happening—so I need you to focus, and answer my question."

"What question?"

"About the dream. What do you think it means?"

"I'm not a psychiatrist."

"You seem like a smart woman. Surely you have some insight."

"I don't know," she said, but this time her tone was softer, less hostile. She was ready to play ball.

"But you're smart enough to understand that being rude to me, my staff, acting ungrateful—such behavior isn't exactly in your best interest. You're here as my guest. If I were so inclined, I could let you starve to death, or if I were feeling more generous, I could simply make you disappear. Sure, there would be an investigation, but the fact of the matter is, nothing would come of it, because nobody knows where you are. You see my point?"

Her lower lip trembled. "Yes."

"Anything else you'd like to say?"

She nodded, chastened. "I'm sorry for my behavior."

"We'll chalk it up to pre-transfusion jitters. This is your first one, correct?"

"It is. How do I know I'm really getting Pandora and not some . . . imitation or substitute?"

"Is that what's making you nervous, Miss Flores?"

"That and a few other questions I have."

Sebastian decided to indulge her. He had plenty of time until his next appointment, in Pacific Palisades, where he'd be showing a house. His real job—his cover—was in real estate.

"How about you take a seat and I'll answer every single question you have until you're completely satisfied? How does that sound?"

"Thank you. I appreciate it."

"Of course."

She sat on the side of the surgical chair, looking a bit cowed, and gripped the edge with both hands. Her arms trembled a bit and her knuckles were white.

"Now, you asked about Pandora—specifically, how do you know whether or not you're getting the real thing?" Sebastian said. "Great question—and one that we get asked a lot. The answer is, you don't know. There is no FDA seal of approval or anything along those lines, for reasons I don't have to explain to you."

"So I'll just have to take your word for it."

"Yes."

"The medications you mix into your carrier blood—"

"All perfectly legal, all perfectly safe."

"What are they?"

Wouldn't you like to know? Sebastian thought with a grin. People would have been surprised to discover that his winning formula consisted of a generic diabetes drug and a generic used to prevent organ rejection. *Well, those and one special ingredient.* Sebastian had the medications smuggled into the US from Canada and other countries so he wouldn't raise suspicion with any of the federal watchdogs and agencies here in the US.

"It's my right to know what's going into my body," she said.

"Think of me as Coca-Cola. I can't give away my secret recipe."

"That's not an answer."

"True, but it's the only one you're getting. I assure you the medications are safe, with few to no side effects."

His answer, he saw, did little to mollify her.

"You don't have to go ahead with this," Sebastian said. "If you'd like to change—which is certainly your right—I will refund your money. But the rule is, once you say no, that's it. You don't get an invite back. And you waited a long, long time to get to this point."

"Almost two years," she said, a bit indignant. Her attitude didn't surprise him. A lot of powerful and famous women believed they should shoot up to the front of the line instead of waiting with the common folk.

"Would you like to leave, Miss Flores? If so, please tell me now so I can make the proper arrangements."

"And the side effects?"

"This wasn't explained to you?"

"It was. I just . . . I'd like to hear it again, one more time. If you don't mind."

"Not at all. The transfusion will take more or less four hours. During that time, you will most likely experience intense hot flashes, possibly even chills—like a bad flu. Your vitals will be monitored, of course, and someone will be here to assist you the entire time. By the end of the day, you'll feel tired. Worn-out. You'll stay here tonight, as my guest, and tomorrow you'll be examined and, as long as you don't have any medical issues, released."

"What about blood moles?"

"Not a single one of my clients has ever developed them, so you can put that out of your mind," Sebastian said. It was true. Blood moles— tiny red sores that developed all over the body, in hivelike clusters, usually on the face and chest and inside the mouth, sinuses, and anus—had been the telltale sign of a major and deadly autoimmune disorder caused by a chemotherapy drug that was now off the market. Those early blood seekers who had wanted to look beautiful and extend their lives and thwart disease had their blood platelet counts drop so low, they were at risk of hemorrhaging. These people had to undergo, ironically, chemotherapy— massive "shock and awe" rounds to try to escape death.

Most didn't.

Sebastian took a sip of his coffee. "What you *will* experience over the next few days is what many clients refer to as a rebirth. Your senses will feel as though they were, say, rebooted. Colors will seem particularly intense, as will tastes. You'll be very sensitive to sounds and touch. Are you married?"

"God no."

"Seeing anyone? Involved in a serious relationship? I ask because a good majority of my clients report heightened and sometimes intense sexual arousal during the first month. Nothing to be alarmed about, but we tell clients so they can inform their partner or partners. Clients who are single—we urge them not to put themselves in situations for the first month or so where they may engage in, say, sexual conduct that they may later regret.

"Now," Sebastian said, "the physical benefits—the tightening of skin and firmer muscle tone, thicker hair and more energy. Those will be noticeable in about fifteen days. Your sleep will improve, too. Of course, a lot of this depends on your lifestyle choices—exercise, diet, what have you. You smoke?"

"No."

"Great. Booze?"

"A glass of wine every now and then."

"Nothing wrong with that. We urge our clients to live healthy and active lives in order to gain the maximum benefits of Pandora. If you do that—and judging by how well you take care of yourself, I don't see that as being a problem—then you can get your next treatment in, say, five or six months. If you start smoking or pounding back bottles of wine, if you develop some disease, then we urge clients to get quarterly transfusions."

"And if I decide not to get another transfusion?"

"You will go through withdrawal. It will feel like the world's worst flu. Not life-threatening, mind you, but extremely unpleasant. Do you have any other questions?"

"The blood I'm getting . . ."

"It's the best on the market," he said. "That's why we have such a long waiting list. We harvest the blood on the morning of a transfusion so it's fresh. No chemicals or preservatives."

"I want to know about the—you know, the donors."

"What would you like to know?"

"You treat them well?"

Sebastian had assumed her anxiety had to do with fear of dying or her fear of aging gracefully into a woman who was no longer admired for her radiant youth, beauty, and sexuality. Or, as Maya had suggested, maybe she was simply a narcissist. Sebastian didn't peg her as the type to have a crisis of conscience.

"The person giving you this blood," he said, "did so willingly. Hand to God."

"But you treat them well?"

"No," he said. "I treat them *very* well."

She looked down at the floor, embarrassed.

"I want to keep living my life," she said.

Sebastian sensed she had more to say. She did.

"I have the most amazing life. I'm going to be taking a tour of Egypt next month—I'm dying to see the pyramids—and then I'm heading to France, where, God willing, I'll meet a much younger man who will enjoy the company of a much older but hopefully still vibrant woman."

"He'll be a lucky man, Ms. Flores."

"I'm completely shallow. That's the only benefit of getting older— knowing who and what you really are. I miss being young and pretty because I'm deeply shallow, and I love young and pretty things." Her gaze drifted back up to him, and she seemed incredibly vulnerable. "Does that make me an awful person?"

"No," he said. "Makes you human."

Ava was still very much on his mind later that morning, for reasons he didn't completely understand. He hadn't seen her in a good ten or twelve years, and here he was showing a beachfront home in Pacific Palisades to a bony, blue-eyed blonde named Celine Marcus and thinking about Ava's home, a modern architectural marvel of stone and glass that sat on half an acre in Hollywood Hills West, high above Sunset Boulevard. He wondered if she still lived there.

When he had been released from prison, he would often drive through her neighborhood—first at night and then, when he felt braver, during the day. He eventually found places where he could safely spy on her using binoculars, watching her for long periods of time while she was inside her house or out in her backyard, gardening or enjoying the pool. Sometimes he would follow her as she ran errands, often with her daughter in tow. He never approached her, because what was the point? She had gotten married and had a kid while he was in prison. She had moved on without him.

It had gone on for almost five years, his spying, this constant craving to punish himself for something that had been stolen from him—which, he would later learn, explained why he had turned from a heavy drinker into a full-blown alcoholic. Frank, his friend since childhood, stepped in, got him into a ninety-day detox and into AA. Frank knew about his obsession with Ava, and Sebastian eventually confessed it to the man who became his AA sponsor, and they both told him he was engaging in alcoholic behavior even though he was no longer drinking, that the only way to move forward was to stop moving backward, and that meant putting his past to rest—his prison sentence, the life taken from him, everything. It meant putting Ava behind him.

And he did.

Or at least he thought he had. So why was he thinking about her now? Why was he thinking back to the last time he'd seen her—not in person but through a pair of binoculars, something he had admitted to no one, including Frank, because he had known it would make him sound like a major-league pervert even though he had never watched her get undressed. That would be wrong. Watching was never about sex. Watching her was about—

"I love the way the natural light fills the room," Celine Marcus said, her voice echoing in the cool, cavernous space. The current owners had been forced to unload all the furniture in the house in a fire sale. "So beautiful and peaceful."

"Absolutely."

Celine turned to the picture windows overlooking the backyard, with its pool and private spa, the thick lawn and the covered patio with its ample alfresco dining space. Sebastian turned his thoughts back to the last night he'd seen Ava. He had watched her getting ready for bed, coming out of her bathroom, her hair still damp from the shower. She wore a pair of gray boy shorts and a matching tank top, her Colombian skin dark with a summer tan, her curves still there but firm with muscle. She slid into the king-sized bed she shared with her husband—the bed empty a lot, he saw, her husband, some sort of hedge fund douchebag, out entertaining clients most nights—and Sebastian thought, *I should be lying there next to her.* He would have had that life with her if the judge hadn't sent him off to prison for beating someone to death—even though it *was* self-defense *and* an accident.

"The architecture," Celine said, "is beautiful."

Ava had visited him every Saturday the first two months and then stopped when she got into a bad car accident that broke her leg and injured her spine. Prison didn't allow him access to a phone, unless he was contacting his lawyer, and he couldn't use email, but it did allow good, ol'-fashioned snail mail, and she wrote to him—long letters at first, then, by the end of his fourth month, short and vague notes featuring highlights from her life, the sort of thing you wrote to a long-distance aunt or cousin out of obligation. Five months into his life sentence the letters had reduced to a trickle, and then they stopped. No more visits, either.

His mother visited him, though, every Saturday, until the bone cancer progressed. Frank brought his mother up every Saturday. Frank continued to visit him when his mother no longer could. Frank was the one who had told him that Ava had moved in with another man. Told her she had gotten married. Was pregnant.

His phone vibrated once; he'd received a text.

It was from Frank. Two words: Call ASAP.

"Excuse me for a moment, Mrs. Marcus."

Sebastian went outside, through the front door. He could hear waves lapping in the distance as he made the call. Frank picked up immediately.

"What's up?" Sebastian asked.

"Not *what*. *Who*. Your stepson."

Sebastian bristled. He hated it when Frank—hell, when anyone— used that word. Paul wasn't his stepson—not in any legal way, Paul sim- ply being a part of the package when Trixie moved in . . . Christ, twenty-two years ago? Had it been *that* long? It had, he realized; Paul had been two, still in diapers. They had never married, he and Trixie—had just lived together until the day she died. It was coming up on a year now, her death, Trixie marooning him with her now twenty-four-year-old son, Paul, full of ugly tattoos and misplaced anger and confidence.

"How bad is it?"

"When I get through telling you," Frank said, "you'll want to order his headstone."

CHAPTER 4

ELLIE TOLD THE paramedic she thought she was going to throw up.

"Not a problem," he said. His name was Brad and he was somewhere around her age, she guessed, in his early to mid-twenties, and had a boyish, almost angelic face. He smiled, all perfect white teeth, when he handed her a good-sized barf bag. "Nausea is a perfectly normal side effect from the adrenaline dump you just suffered."

As was crying, she supposed. Ellie didn't tell him how badly she wanted him to leave the back of the ambulance and lock the door so she could break down, get it all out of her system.

She wouldn't cry—*couldn't* cry. A woman caught boo-hooing on the job, even if the reason was that she had seen her partner get wasted, was immediately branded as weak and unreliable. *Always remember to grieve on your own time,* a prominent female detective had once warned her. *If you cry, show any emotion of any kind, the boys will never look at you the same way again. They'll automatically think you don't have what it takes for when the shit really hits the fan.*

So far, she'd kept it together throughout the whole ordeal that followed the shooting. In a strong, clear voice she took her supervisor through how it all went down.

Her voice didn't break once, and it hadn't broken when she'd had to give her official statement to the pair of investigators from the "shooting squad." She didn't balk when they bagged her firearm and placed it into evidence, or when they demanded she give a blood sample for toxicology testing, to see if she had been under the influence of alcohol or drugs when she fired the weapon.

Now, though? Now she felt like she was coming apart at the seams.

Brad checked her blood pressure again. "Still a little low, but not too bad," he said. "Again, that's normal, given what you've gone through."

The back door suddenly swung open, letting in a blast of hot air and jarring noises—crackling police radios and voices shouting over one another. She also heard the sound of a helicopter, maybe more than one, hovering somewhere overhead.

A patrolman she didn't recognize motioned for her to come out. "Commissioner's here, wants to see you," he said.

"Before you go," Brad said to her, "your blood pressure and heart rate may decide to suddenly drop, so the *second* you feel light-headed? Sit down immediately, because there's a good chance you're going to faint."

Ellie thanked him and got out, surprised to see how much the area had changed during the two hours she'd spent sequestered inside the ambulance—dozens of cruisers, their lights flashing, and people, mostly reporters, she guessed, crowded behind blockades; news copters hovering in the sky, taking aerial footage of the backyard and the chaos in the surrounding streets. A patrolman was stationed at the front doors, his sole job to write down the name of every single person who entered the home. She spotted two more patrolmen, holding clipboards, standing near the gates along the fence. It was overkill, yes, but it was always better to control the chaos as much as possible—and have plenty of paperwork to prove to a jury that no one had slacked off on maintaining the integrity of the crime scene.

As a general rule, police commissioners stayed away from crime scenes and focused on the *really* important work, like paperwork and politics and making sure they looked good in front of the cameras. They were more administrators than cops, and wherever they traveled the media wasn't too far behind.

But there were exceptions, like the killing of a police officer, or if the crime had a high-profile element to it that needed to be thoroughly understood so it could be spun properly for the public. What happened here in Brentwood had both elements: a cop killed during the commission of a blood crime in one of the safest, most expensive neighborhoods in Los Angeles—a definite first. Of course the man was here.

It was easy to spot Kelly, a mountain of a man who stood six six. He paced along the grass near the side of the house where Danny had entered the backyard. As Ellie drew closer, she saw Kelly had a phone mashed against his ear. He wore a tan suit with a stylish tie and a pair of rimless eyeglasses with lenses that magnified his intense blue eyes.

She didn't know the man personally—had never met him—but she had heard he was frank and tough, with zero tolerance for bullshit. When he was deputy chief, he was given the nickname "the Pied Piper" for his ability to ferret out crooked cops.

Kelly told the person on the other line he had to go and hung up.

"Walk me through what happened," he said. Then he paused, as if reconsidering his words, and looked her over briefly. "Are you up to it?"

"I'm up to it."

"Good."

The way he said it, Ellie got the feeling she had passed some sort of test. "Have we made any progress here, sir?"

"We've got an APB out on the vehicle and the shooter, copters in the air searching, but so far, nothing."

She led Kelly through the backyard dappled with afternoon sunlight, and explained everything that had happened. Everywhere she looked she saw glass fragments and spent shell casings and blood—and three dead bodies.

"The boy over there? He's a stickman," Ellie said. "That's what they call themselves, the kids they use to find out if people are carriers."

Why did I say that? Of course he knows what a stickman is. Kelly flashed her a look that told her as much. *Dammit, Batista, get your shit together.*

"What makes you think he's a stickman?" Kelly asked.

"May I show you?"

The commissioner scratched the corner of his mouth with his thumb. "Go ahead," he said.

Ellie moved to the chaise longue where the skinny teenager with the man bun had sat earlier. His body and what was left of his head were now concealed inside a forensic tent to prevent news copters and any reporters and bystanders from viewing the carnage.

She reached into her pants pocket for a pair of latex gloves, used her other hand to wave down one of the forensic techs working the backyard. She wanted this documented and on the record, just in case. Better to cover your ass than to have your ass handed to you in court.

"The canvas bag," she said to the male tech. "Has it been photographed?"

The man checked his tablet. "It has," he said.

"What about the contents inside?"

"Just pictures of what we can see. We haven't searched through it yet."

Ellie turned to Kelly and said, "Sir, with your permission, I'd like to reach into the bag."

Kelly nodded, then told the tech to document the process—including video. The tech held up his tablet and then recorded Ellie as she carefully dipped a gloved hand inside the bag, with its neatly folded towel and change of clothes and a couple of paperback books, as well as a clear bag holding processed and ready-to-eat food like meal-replacement bars and nuts.

When she stood, she had, pinched between her fingers, what at first glance looked like the kind of small flashlight people tossed into a glove compartment or a cabinet underneath a kitchen sink. Only the black metal tube she was holding didn't have a bulb, and it was small enough to conceal in your palm.

"Do you recognize this, sir?"

Kelly shook his head. The tech didn't answer, either, too busy recording.

"This was originally developed for diabetics to get blood glucose levels," Ellie said. "The army had it modified so blood types could be determined on the battlefield, in order to speed along the process of an emergency transfusion. You press the button on the end here with your thumb and a very fine needle ejects and pierces the skin so fast that most people don't even realize they've been pricked. It only takes a few seconds to get a result. It flashes on the small LED screen right here on the side."

Kelly was looking at her with avid interest—and some skepticism, too, she thought.

"Word on the street," Ellie said, "is that these devices have been modified to identify the proteins in carrier blood—within seconds, from what I've heard." She returned the item to its original place inside the bag.

Kelly thanked the tech, his tone leaving no doubt that the man should leave and get back to work.

Then she was alone with Kelly again.

"That injector," he said. "How do you know about it?"

Ellie had learned early on that there was nothing more dangerous to a powerful man than a woman who, intentionally or not, made him feel stupid or inferior.

"I do a lot of reading," Ellie said. "And I visit a lot of blood chat rooms on the deep web. There are a lot of theories out there—"

"Thank you for your help, Officer Batista. And I'm sorry about the loss of your partner." Kelly seemed to genuinely mean it.

"Sir, the two vics inside the house—have they been identified?"

"Not yet. Thank you—you're dismissed." Kelly left toward the house.

Ellie saw her opportunity. It was risky, but she might not get it again.

"Sir, with your permission, I'd like to see them. I didn't get a close-up look the first time I was in there, when I was clearing the house."

"Did you touch them? Disturb the crime scene in any way?"

"No, sir. I did everything by the book. Cleared the house, checked for a pulse, and then radioed dispatch. Nothing will come back to bite us on the ass. You have my word on that."

Kelly's features relaxed a bit.

"The reason I asked to see them again," Ellie said. "Sir, I think I know who they are."

CHAPTER 5

POLICE COMMISSIONER KELLY was looking at her with renewed interest. Not in the admiring way you looked at someone who could help you, but in the suspicious way you looked at someone you suspected was holding important information from you.

"I only saw a quick glimpse of them when I was in the house," Ellie explained, which was true. When she had entered the bedroom down the hall, she'd found the victims, a male and a female, both in their late teens or early twenties, tucked underneath the covers as though sleeping. Her first thought was that they were, in fact, asleep—and drugged. They had to have been drugged, because that was the only logical explanation as to how they'd slept through the gunfire.

Then she saw the backs of their heads and knew what had happened to them.

"If I could take a closer look, I believe I could identify the victims."

She had a personal and completely selfish ulterior motive for not wanting to share the victims' names right here, right now, with Commissioner Kelly. If she told him, he would dismiss her and then head into the house and share the names with Detective Alves, the head of the Blood Unit. Maybe Kelly would tell him who had given him the names, maybe not. For the past few hours, she had been mulling over ideas of how she could use this information to her advantage. The way she figured it, if she could find a way to get inside the bedroom, take a look at the bodies, and then share her findings, she could show Detective Alves what a valuable asset she could be on Blood Crimes. Now that the commissioner was involved—even better. Identifying the victims might very well be her ticket into a spot on BCU.

First, she had to convince Kelly to let her inside.

"The two vics," Ellie said. "I'm pretty sure they're carriers."

"Names?"

"I need to take a closer look to be sure, but if I'm right, they've been missing for . . . well, a good amount of time."

"How long?"

"Years," she said.

Kelly stared at her, Ellie feeling the weight of his gaze. She said, "When carriers are abducted, you either find them drained and dumped or you don't find them at all. This is the first time, as far as I know, that carriers have been found inside a residence."

"You're right about that."

"Let me see if I can help you ID them."

Kelly nodded his head toward the house, signaling for her to join him.

Ellie entered the house for a second time, only now she was wearing a white bunny suit that covered her from head to toe. Kelly was wearing the same kind of suit.

The inside was cool and still reeked of cordite from the gunfire. Ellie caught the half a dozen or so forensic techs in the living room and adjoining kitchen flick their gazes between the commissioner and her, as though the two of them were invading their turf—which they were.

Kelly carefully made his way to the staircase, watching where he stepped. Ellie took in her surroundings.

The living room had high ceilings and a gray stone floor and white walls, the furniture modern—the type that was more artistic than designed for comfort. Numbered neon evidence markers sat next to each shell casing on the floor. The pattern indicated that Gingerbread Man had fired while he was inside the house, kept shooting on his way down the hall, to the door leading into the garage.

The second floor, Ellie noticed, felt considerably warmer. Or maybe it was just her nerves.

Detective Alves was waiting for them in the brightly lit hallway, standing next to a tall white wall holding an enormous painting of a nude woman crawling through a desert, toward a bloodred sun. He was a short, angry Portuguese man with gray hair that was cut close to the scalp. He looked five ten but was probably closer to five eight. She'd heard he wore shoes with lifts, to give him a couple of extra inches.

Alves's gaze screamed, *What the hell is she doing here?*

"Our two vics," Kelly said. "Have you identified them yet?"

"No, sir, not yet," Alves replied. "And it's going to take some time. Both victims, their fingerprints were burned off some time ago—acid, judging by the scarring. The tech assigned to our unit has already collected their blood samples and is on his way back to the lab to start preparing them, add 'em to the List."

The List, Ellie knew, was a new and ever-growing database containing the names of missing and dead carriers. Almost all of the names on the List were of people in their early twenties and younger.

For years, the LAPD had wanted to identify carriers living in the state, but everyone jumped all over it, citing medical privacy and possible conspiracy scenarios where officers sold the names of carriers to the blood cartels. The LAPD backed off, but the current president had recently made statements about the importance of identifying carriers within communities so the police could better serve them. There were rumblings about passing a federal law making carriers come forward and sign up, but privacy and civil liberty groups kept shutting it down.

"I've spoken to the husband," Alves said. "He's in London, visiting his daughter, Luciana. That's her bedroom down the hall, where the two vics are. His wife stayed behind—came down with food poisoning, he said." Alves swung his attention to Ellie.

Kelly addressed the elephant in the room. "Officer Batista told me she might be able to help us identify the victims. She believes they're carriers, wants to take a closer look."

"Which victim do you think you know?" Alves asked her.

"Maybe both," Ellie replied.

Alves raised his hairy unibrow at that.

"Let's get on with it," Kelly said.

Ellie approached the male. He was Hispanic and had a thick mop of black hair that covered his ears. Alves stood on the opposite side of the queen-sized bed. He looked only at the commissioner.

"No sign of a struggle, as you can see," Alves said. "Looks like they were both attacked while they were sleeping." Using a gloved finger, he pulled back the woman's long hair so Kelly could see the stab wound on the back of the neck, near the base of the skull. "My money's on a hunting knife. Blade was slid in sideways and more or less severed the brain stem. Takes a lot of strength to do something like this."

Ellie said, "One of them would have woken up, don't you think?"

Alves let go of the hair. He didn't answer her question, looked only at Kelly. "My operating theory is that our guy was inside the house when Officers Batista and Boyle entered the backyard. Saw that Officer Boyle had engaged with the woman, Mrs. Vargas, and then he panicked, swiftly executed the two vics before he went out back."

That would explain why Gingerbread Man took so long coming out of the house after we arrived, Ellie thought. He couldn't have escaped with these two, and he had killed them so they couldn't talk later to the police.

Kelly turned to her. "Did the shooter have any blood on him?"

"I didn't notice any," she replied.

Alves said, "That's not surprising. The blood pattern on the pillow and mattress indicates pulsing instead of spurting—the back of the head doesn't have arteries. And both victims had lowered heart rates, which explains why the crime scene isn't that messy." Now he looked to Ellie, his gaze telling her to hurry up.

She turned to the young man and gently lifted the black hair away from his left ear, as though afraid she might wake him.

"This is Alex Hernandez," she said. "This crease along the top part of his ear? It's called 'lidding.' It should be listed in the distinguishing-characteristic section of his file."

Alves held his smartphone, tapping the name into the LAPD Blood database through a secured and encrypted link.

Ellie said, "I think he's the one who wrote the message on the dog tag and left blood. There's a small cut on his right thumb, and there's a black ink mark on his hand. The message on the tag was written in black marker. I want to say he's been missing for three, maybe four years."

"And you know all of this how?" This from Kelly, Ellie having a hard time reading the man's tone, whether he was showing normal skepticism or being dismissive.

"His face was all over social media and news websites," Ellie said. "But the main reason I remember was the billboard on the 110. I saw Alex's face every day for almost a year when I was taking my Criminal Law and Procedure college class at LATTC." It was the truth, or at least part of it. His sweet, angelic face had, in fact, haunted her every day on her commute.

There was another reason why she knew Alex Hernandez—a reason why she knew practically every missing carrier in the state of California, one that she would never share with Commissioner Kelly.

Alves looked up from his phone. "The lidding thing is listed in Hernandez's file. And the photos we have on file look like a solid match."

Ellie turned her attention to the young woman. She had a round face, but it was lean, the skin healthy and tight. She had a small nose. Good hair. Her mouth hung open. She, too, had given blood. Ellie saw the thick bandages in the crooks of both arms.

"I think she might be Jolie Simone," Ellie said. "If she is, she'll have a small heart tattoo on her chest. Her father gave it to her."

Kelly said, "The father tattooed his own kid?"

Ellie nodded. "For her to remember him by," she said. "He was a tattoo artist, and he was dying of leukemia. May I pull back the comforter a bit?"

Alves checked with the techs, who were both huddled next to their gear near the entrance of a walk-in closet. The techs said they had taken the necessary pictures, so it was okay to proceed. The smaller one used the camera on his tablet to record Ellie's movements.

She grabbed the corner of the comforter and carefully pulled it back. Alex Hernandez had a long, lean body and wore blue sweatpants and a San Francisco Giants sweatshirt that seemed too small for him. Had he borrowed the clothes? Yes, he had; she saw his other set of clothes neatly folded on a chair by the window.

"Why is he wearing so many layers?" Kelly asked. "It's pretty warm in here."

Ellie answered the question before Alves could: "Your core temperature drops dramatically if you've given two or more pints—or, say, fifteen to twenty percent total blood volume. It's a class two hemorrhage. You have to keep your body warm or you'll go into shock—which explains why it's warmer up here than downstairs."

Kelly turned to Alves and said, "You think they brought the carriers here and gave Vargas a transfusion?"

"I don't see the point in it," Alves replied. "You don't need to bring the carriers. You just need their blood. There's got to be another reason—one that we haven't discovered yet."

Ellie hovered over Hernandez's body to get a closer look at the woman she believed to be Jolie Simone. She wasn't wearing layers like Hernandez, just a plain white tank top with a bra. A tanned muscular arm was draped over her waist, and her fingernails were freshly painted a dark red. A cotton ball was taped to the crook of her arm; she'd given blood.

Maybe the blood given to the dead woman in the backyard, Ellie thought as she hooked a finger in the neck of the tank top and gently pulled it aside.

There it was: the nickel-sized tattoo of a blue heart with a crown of thorns.

Then, as an afterthought and mostly to herself, she said, "They took good care of you."

Kelly moved closer. "What did you say?"

Ellie straightened. "Whoever kept Simone and Hernandez took very good care of them."

"Explain that."

"They're both lean and muscular. Well-fed and well-groomed. Simone painted her nails recently. Whoever had them, wherever they were being kept—they were well treated. Physically, at least."

All the eyes in the room were pinned on her. They didn't look friendly, either.

"Sir," Alves said. "What Officer Batista told us about Jolie Simone's tattoo? She's right. It's listed right here in her file." He tapped the phone's screen. "And the pictures we have bear a strong resemblance to our Jane Doe here."

"How long has she been missing?" Kelly asked.

"Just under five years," Alves replied. "Hernandez for about four."

"Officer Batista," Kelly said, sounding a bit hostile. "A word?"

Ellie followed the commissioner into the hallway. Kelly stopped just outside the bedroom and placed his hands on his hips. Ellie knew what was coming and recalled words Danny had shared with her during her first few months on the job.

Don't ever try to be helpful, Danny had told her. *And never, under any circumstances, offer advice to anyone who has a higher pay grade than you. The higher-ups don't care about you, what you bring to the table. Your job is always CYA—Cover Your Ass.*

"What's the connection between you and those two victims in there?" Kelly asked.

"There isn't one."

Kelly's eyes looked like they were going to pop out of his head. "You're telling me you just *happened* to recall all of the salient points from not one but *two* missing-persons cases out of thousands?"

His words put some starch into her posture, some heat into her voice. "I'm not lying to you, sir, and I resent the implication."

"Then how do you know them?"

"I don't." Ellie felt beads of sweat rolling down her forehead, the small of her back. This was her big chance to get on BCU and she couldn't blow it. "The reason I know about Simone and Hernandez is because I read about them. Studied them and others. Finding out as much as I can about the blood world—it's become sort of a . . . passion of mine." She paused and took a deep breath. This was her chance, her opportunity. *Go for it.*

"Sir, I can be an asset to you not only on this case but other cases. Give me a spot on the Blood Unit. You won't regret it, sir—I *promise* you."

Kelly stared at her, deciding her fate.

Either he's going to offer me a spot on the Blood Unit or he's going to tear me a new ass for overstepping.

"Christ." Alves's voice, coming from the bedroom.

Kelly joined him. Ellie didn't follow. She could see well enough from the doorway.

The forensic techs had removed the white comforter and bedsheets. Someone—probably Alves—had pushed up Jolie's tank top over her belly, revealing her stomach, the baby bump the size of a child's basketball.

CHAPTER 6

SEBASTIAN CRAWLED ALONG the crowded freeway, listening to the all-news radio station, hoping to learn actual details about the shooting in Brentwood. Frank hadn't had much in the way of specifics when he'd called earlier. He'd promised to call back when he did.

That was forty minutes ago.

The news was high on drama and low on facts. *Very* low. Police—who were in Brentwood in record numbers, according to one reporter—had confirmed that the owner of the home, Sophia Vargas, and an LAPD officer had been shot and killed in what one witness called a "gangland-style shoot-out," but so far hadn't offered up anything beyond that. A witness reported seeing a "black compact car with tinted windows" fleeing the scene. There was no other information.

But that didn't mean the police hadn't discovered things. Important, key things.

Paul owned a black BMW with tinted windows. Sebastian wondered if anyone had seen and perhaps memorized a plate number. Maybe a camera in a traffic light had recorded it. The thought made Sebastian feel sick all over.

The radio newscaster teased a possible breaking story. First, Sebastian had to listen to an interview with a witness—a hysterical neighborhood yenta who had been out walking her dog when she heard the gunshots.

"It sounded like firecrackers—*hundreds* of firecrackers going off at the same time. And then came the screaming, the awful screaming." The woman's voice caught. "I can't believe this happened," she said, and began to sob. "I cannot believe this is happening here."

Sebastian couldn't believe it, either. He was having an out-of-body experience—the second of his life. The first one he had experienced years and years ago, when he was a teenager, after the judge sentenced him to life in prison.

Which was exactly what would happen to him again if he didn't find Paul before the cops did.

Ever since Frank's initial call, Sebastian had been choking on the thought of Paul already in police custody. Paul didn't know the inner workings of Sebastian's blood operation, but he knew enough to throw Sebastian to the wolves. Paul worked with a guy who managed stickmen and acquired carriers exclusively for Sebastian's business, and Sebastian had allowed him to do some menial tasks like the one today—chauffeuring well-behaved carriers and playing babysitter. Paul knew nothing about the infrastructure or the treatment center, and he didn't know the names of actual clients and had absolutely no idea of the locations where the donors lived.

Sebastian imagined Paul wearing a shit-eating grin while asking the LAPD if they would be interested in the person behind the elusive Pandora in exchange for a reduced sentence. Or maybe the slick lawyer he would hire would bypass the LAPD altogether and go straight to the Feds, see if they wanted the info in exchange for, say, placement in Witness Protection.

Sebastian's thoughts shifted to his two donors. Paul had taken Alex Hernandez and Jolie Simone to Brentwood for a day of sun and fun. Sebastian had a special arrangement with Sophia Vargas, a long-standing client who, in exchange for free transfusions, allowed his well-behaved donors to spend a nice, long summer day outside in the privacy of her backyard, get some sun and fresh air when her husband was away on yet another one of his overseas business trips. The system, while unusual, had worked perfectly for the last few years, helped make the donors feel less like prisoners.

Had Paul taken Alex and Jolie with him, or were they dead?

On the radio, the reporter who was live at the scene broke in and said, "We've got confirmation police found two bodies inside the house—a yet-unidentified male and female. A source close to the investigation believes the victims are carriers who were abducted several years ago."

So, there it was.

The phone rang. Frank.

"Paul reached out to me," Frank said.

Sebastian felt a couple of the stones stacked on his heart slide away.

"I gave him the address of our house in Long Beach," Frank said. "I told him he could lie low there until we sort this mess out."

Paul didn't know about the house in Long Beach, what they used it for. With its sweeping ocean views and stellar sunsets, the fully furnished house was disarming—not the sort of place you figured you'd spend your last moments of life.

Which was the point. Paul wouldn't suspect a thing.

"He's on his way there now," Frank said.

A few more stones fell, Sebastian now feeling like he could finally draw a full breath. Forty minutes ago, he'd had his mind set on going home and getting his new passport and credit cards and cash, packing up some clothes, and preparing for life on the run. Now he had hope.

"You're sure?" Sebastian asked.

"If you mean am I tracking his cell signal, the answer is no. I'm not at the office at the moment. I've had bigger fish to fry."

Frank, Sebastian knew, was referring to certain business arrangements that had become top priorities. "Our other donors," Sebastian began.

"Already being moved to our new compound."

They had built a new facility as a backup, in the event the location of their current one was ever compromised. The locations of his donor compounds were Sebastian's biggest and most important secret. There was no way Paul would know where the donors lived. But with Paul, he wasn't going to take any chances.

Frank said, "The old compound is being scrubbed and shut down as we speak. Same with the house where Paul picked up Alex and Jolie this morning. There won't be a single shred of evidence to indicate they were there—I promise you that."

"What about his car? The Beemer."

"He said he took care of it."

"Took care of it how?"

"He didn't say, and I didn't ask, figuring we could do question-and-answer time later. I stuck to the script."

"How'd he sound?"

"Like he always sounds. Like we were talking about the weather or last night's box score instead of him killing six people."

"Six? I'm counting four. Vargas, the cop, and now Alex and Jolie."

"There was another kid there," Frank said. "A stickman, I'm hearing."

"One of Anton's?"

"I don't know any details yet. As for the sixth victim, remember Jolie Simone was five months pregnant. State considers that another human life."

Sebastian thought of Jolie's unborn kid suffocating to death inside the womb because her mother had been killed. The news angered him—and Frank angered him. Not Frank personally but the deadpan way Frank spoke, like he was a computer rather than a man. Frank always spoke that way, and there were times, like now, when Sebastian wished Frank shared his outrage.

"I have more news from our man on the inside," Frank said. "It appears Jolie gave blood. And Vargas got a transfusion."

Sebastian chewed on that for a moment. Jolie wasn't scheduled to give blood today, or any day, because she was pregnant—and Sophia Vargas wasn't scheduled to get her transfusion until next month.

"Why would Paul take Jolie's blood?" Frank asked.

"Must have a side deal going with someone, make some extra money, is the only thing I can think of."

"With who? The Armenians?"

Let's hope not, Sebastian thought. "What else do you know?"

"When the cops arrived, they found Sophia Vargas lying in the back-yard, in her bikini. She was having a little DIY time—you know, butter-ing her muffin—even *after* the cops arrived."

"What?"

"That's what our guy said. She ever done anything like that before?"

"No. And she's been getting Pandora infusions for years."

"So what changed?"

Sebastian didn't know. Had no idea. One of the immediate side effects of Pandora was enhanced sexual arousal, yes, and a lot of his male and female clients reported feeling extremely horny for a good couple of weeks or so after a transfusion. But he'd never had a client act the way Sophia Vargas had, if what Frank had just said was true.

"My guy also told me they were executed—his word—while they were passed out, sleeping, whatever," Frank said. "Single stab wound to the back of the head with a strong blade, like a hunting or military knife."

Instant death—at least according to Paul, who had told Sebastian about the night he used his government-issued knife to quickly dispatch a pair of Iraqi soldiers during a night mission over in camel country. Paul had brought that knife home with him—carried it with him. He even had a name for the blade: the Angel's Kiss.

"Why were the cops called to the house?"

"Because of the dog," Frank said.

"What dog?"

"Vargas's dog. Black Lab. Somehow it got out of the fenced-in back-yard, was running around the neighborhood when a police car hit it. The cops saw its tag. Someone had left a bloody fingerprint on it and written the words *Help Us*, I'm told. If I had to guess who did it, I'd say Alex."

It took Sebastian by surprise, the betrayal, how deeply it stung. Alex and Jolie had been with him since they were kids and had never given him so much as a lick of trouble—had, in fact, been appreciative of how well they were taken care of. They didn't want for anything. He had made sure of it.

No, that wasn't entirely true. He couldn't give them their freedom.

Frank said, "I'm guessing they had some plan in place to run away together, start a family."

"Run to where?"

"No idea. I'm sure it was more of a fantasy than an actual plan. You remember what it's like at that age, the stupid shit you do when you're in love. You believe anything in the world is possible."

Frank, Sebastian knew, was referring to him and Ava.

Frank, though, didn't have any personal experience in this area. Frank had never been in love—at least as far as Sebastian knew. He had no idea if Frank saw someone or got laid or if his childhood friend had any interest in sex. Sebastian had no idea about Frank's sexual preference, either, because Frank was still, after all their years together and after all the shit they'd gone through, intensely, almost pathologically private.

Still, Frank was dead-on about the stupid shit you did when you were young and in love—especially the first time you fell hard for someone, believed she was the great love of your life, your soul mate, the person God created only for you. It made the impossible seem possible.

Frank said, "Where are you?"

"I was heading home to prepare for my new life on the run. I'm almost there. Let me change out of my clothes. Then I'll meet you in Long Beach." Sebastian wasn't going to ruin a perfectly good Tom Ford suit.

"Stay home. I'll take care of Paul. You don't need to be there, see what happens to your kid."

"He is *not* my kid."

"But he *is* the kid of your former longtime girlfriend or live-in or common-law wife or whatever you called her. You don't need to be there for the particulars. Sometimes ignorance is bliss."

Sebastian's thoughts shifted to Trixie. Like his dearly departed mother, Trixie had lived her life as a God-fearing woman. She devoted her time to various charities and went to church and organized fund-raisers, many of which were devoted to helping the families of missing carriers. Trixie had had absolutely no idea of her husband's real business. Sebastian had made sure of it.

When she was diagnosed with Stage IV malignant melanoma, it was Sebastian, not her, who had brought up Pandora, explaining how carrier blood could destroy cancer cells and halt the progress of the disease, sometimes reverse it. Sebastian said he knew people—discreet people—who could acquire it. No one would ever know.

But I'll know, Trixie had told him. *It's illegal and, more importantly, immoral. An abomination. That blood will come from some child who was kidnapped and tortured. If God wants me to die, then it is his will.*

In the end, it didn't matter. Once melanoma entered the bloodstream, it became one of the most aggressive cancers. Rounds of invasive testing revealed Trixie's cancer had already worked its way past her lymph nodes and spread to most of her organs. No amount of carrier blood could reverse that. As she lay at home dying, all she thought about was God and the welfare of her son. Paul, she kept telling him, was a good man. He had served his country and deserved a good life. All he needed was some good, orderly direction. Not just from God but from the second most important person in Paul's life. Sebastian had given her his word. He would watch over Paul. Help guide him.

Paul, though, had zero interest in real estate. He did, however, have a ton of interest in Sebastian's other business.

Sebastian obliged, albeit reluctantly. The cat was already out of the bag. Better to manage Paul and keep an eye on him and where he went than to have him poking his nose around where it didn't belong.

I brought him into our thing—I allowed it, Sebastian wanted to tell Frank. *And if I'm being honest, I'm not surprised about what he did today. Somewhere in the back of my mind I knew something like this would happen.*

"Don't do anything until I get there," Sebastian said.

Traffic, finally, seemed to be moving. As Sebastian drew closer to his exit, he thought about what Frank had said, about not being there when Paul got to the Long Beach house.

He's not my kid, he'd told Frank.

Which was true. He had never adopted Paul—had never had any interest in the job, either, and, as far as he could tell, Paul had never wanted him to fill out an application. Even as a kid, Paul had never been big on talking. Sure, he'd had plenty to say about sports, movies, and his favorite TV shows, maybe the occasional book he read, but anything deeper than that? Sorry, nothing to say.

Same with his feelings. Nothing ever seemed to bother him. Whatever happened to him, good, bad, or indifferent, he never showed his true colors.

"He's just sensitive. Quiet and insular," Trixie would tell him. "Insular men are always the most private."

Sometimes, she would add, "His father was like that."

Sebastian could count on one hand the number of times Trixie had spoken about Paul's father. That was how she always referred to him: "Paul's father." Like he was a store that had gone out of business. She wouldn't tell him the guy's name, just that he split town when he found out she was pregnant, and she always ended the conversation with her mother's favorite words: *Good riddance to bad rubbish.*

On paper, everything pointed to Paul being solid. He had never given Trixie much in the way of grief beyond the usual kid shit of not picking up his room or putting away his clothes and his dirty dishes. He rarely got into trouble at school or at home, always got good grades and had plenty of friends, all of them good kids from good families, and, later, plenty of girlfriends—all pretty blondes with the same life ambition of looking good in a bikini. And yet Sebastian had always suspected there was something not quite right with Paul, something that made him different from everyone else.

An incident when Paul was ten had provided Sebastian with some deeper insight.

For Paul's eighth birthday, his mother had given him a three-month-old puppy that was part Tibetan mastiff and part chocolate Lab. With its dark brown fur and shaggy face, the dog looked like a baby Chewbacca, which was the reason why Trixie had instantly fallen in love with the mutt. Chewbacca was Paul's favorite character from his favorite movie, *Star Wars. He's my favorite because he's loyal,* Paul had explained to him once. *Loyal and protective.*

Chewie the dog lived up to his namesake. And Paul, unlike most kids, took over full responsibility, feeding and walking Chewie without having to be reminded or nagged, playing with him in the backyard. Paul had never been big on sleepovers, but the handful of times he agreed to them he had insisted Chewie accompany him.

When Chewie collapsed in the driveway one morning, Trixie and Paul still asleep, it was Sebastian who brought the dog to the twenty-four-hour emergency veterinary hospital.

When the vet gave him Chewie's diagnosis, Sebastian sobbed like a baby right in front of the vet, Chewie lying right there on the examining table after coming out of anesthesia for the X-ray and MRI, the dog wagging its tail limply, no clue as to what was happening.

While Chewie had been undergoing the tests, Sebastian had texted Paul and Trixie, telling them he had brought the dog with him to the office. When Sebastian pulled into the driveway, his eyes were no longer puffy or bloodshot.

Paul was home—out back, practicing his free throws. He shot the ball, Sebastian watching it roll off his fingertips, like he'd taught him. *Swish.* He had made the JV team.

"I've got to talk to you," Sebastian said after he got out of the car.

Paul used a forearm to wipe the sweat away from his eyes. "What's up? Where's Chewie?"

"That's what I want to talk to you about."

Sebastian told him about the cancerous tumors the vet had discovered in Chewie's brain. About how surgery and chemotherapy weren't options with this type of cancer, and even if they were, the cancer had spread. It was too late. There was nothing to do but say goodbye.

Sebastian was proud of himself for getting through his talk without his voice cracking. He was grateful for the mirrored sunglasses he was wearing, so Paul couldn't see him blinking back fresh tears.

"I'm sorry," Sebastian said, watching as Paul cradled the basketball against his hip and looked down the long driveway, as though someone were about to arrive at any second to rescue him, turn this situation around. "I'll take you to the vet's office."

Paul turned back to him, his head cocked to the side. "Why?" he asked, sounding—and looking—genuinely puzzled.

"So you can say goodbye."

"He's a dog."

"No," Sebastian said. "He's *your* dog."

Paul's expression and body language didn't change. It was as if Sebastian had been speaking another language.

He's in shock, Sebastian thought. But he quickly dismissed it because of how eerily relaxed Paul was, how the kid seemed to be waiting for more information. In that moment, Sebastian thought of his mother, an intensely religious woman who constantly quoted from the Bible, and he recalled a passage from Mark or Matthew about how the eyes were the lamp of the body, how if they were healthy your body was full of God's light.

God's light wasn't in Paul's eyes. There wasn't any light, not even a flicker of one, because his eyes were dead. And they had always been dead, Sebastian realized—*that* was the thing that was off about him, what the kid was missing.

Sebastian pulled into his driveway and stepped out of the car, the memory still fresh in his mind when his phone rang. Frank again.

"More news from our guy on the inside," Frank said. "A cop got a solid look at Paul. A female cop who was at the scene. Don't have a name for you yet, but we'll know soon, I'm sure."

"Paul's not going to come to you."

"You spoke to him?"

"Not yet," Sebastian said, staring into his backyard, at the pool. "He's here."

"Here as in your *house*?"

"Yep."

"What the hell is he doing there?"

"Judging from where I'm standing," Sebastian said, "I'd say the breaststroke."

CHAPTER 7

S EBASTIAN HUNG UP and stared at Paul, trying to process what he was seeing.

Paul had killed five people—no, six, including Jolie's unborn kid—just a couple of hours ago. He had just dropped an atomic bomb, creating the single worst cataclysmic disaster Sebastian had ever experienced in his business, and the prick decided to swing by here to take a dip in the *pool*?

Sebastian unlatched the gate, wanting to bolt into the backyard and leap into the water, on top of Paul, and then, after bashing his head in a few times, hold the stupid son of a bitch underwater until he drowned.

But Paul wasn't a skinny teenager anymore; he was a man, and he had come back from overseas with an extra twenty pounds, all of it solid muscle. Then he had gotten heavily into bodybuilding and put on more. Sebastian was twice his age and while he worked out nearly every morning at the health club, doing weights and running on the treadmill, he was a far cry from the man he was during his boxing days—and a little soft, too, carrying an extra twenty pounds from indulging in too many expensive dinners.

In terms of pure physical strength, Paul outmatched him. But in a fistfight? Sebastian was sure he could take him.

Or maybe he would just shoot the bastard. Sebastian carried a legally registered subcompact 9mm Glock in a shoulder holster. California had eased up considerably on its gun restrictions when carriers started getting abducted from their homes at all hours, from schools and on the streets. Sebastian was just another card-carrying NRA member wishing to protect himself.

Only a gunfight wasn't going to happen here in his quiet neighborhood, where the slightest odd noise would be reason enough for someone to pick up the phone and call the police. The house was neutral territory— which was exactly why Paul had come here. Paul knew Sebastian would have to behave himself.

But that didn't mean Sebastian was going to go in unprepared. *Always expect the unexpected,* he thought, removing the Glock from his shoulder holster. He slid it into his right front pocket as he moved into the backyard.

When Paul's outstretched hand touched the pool liner, instead of turning around underwater and doing another lap he came up for air. He saw Sebastian looming above him and whipped his head to the side to whisk away the water.

"There you are," Paul said. "Thought you might swing by here."

In times of great stress, Sebastian had learned the importance of keeping a lid on his anger—not because it was the right or civil thing to do, as the prison therapist had suggested, but because it was the smart play. Killing Paul out here in the open was off the table—for now. He had to put his anger on hold—for now. Put it on hold, get Paul to Long Beach, and then he would unleash his rage. Take his time.

Savor it.

Paul hoisted himself out of the pool, splashing water on Sebastian's shoes and pants cuffs. He straightened to his full height as if to remind Sebastian of his size and physical power.

"We've got a lot to talk about," Paul said, padding away and dripping water as he walked toward the opposite side of the pool.

Sebastian stayed right where he was.

Paul retrieved the towel draped over the back of a chaise longue, Sebastian looking at the ridiculous tattoos covering Paul's muscular chest, arms, and back—those decorative, brightly colored skulls, set in candy, with flowers and jewels for eyes; a gingerbread man with a mean and ugly face, and jagged teeth biting down on the blade of a bloody machete. Paul had gotten them halfway across the world, in tattoo parlors in Iraq, but as for the significance behind them, what had inspired Paul to turn his body into a nightmarish version of the board game Candy Land, Sebastian had no idea. He had asked Paul about it a couple of times, but Paul never answered, just shrugged.

Paul finished drying off and tossed the towel onto the grass and pulled out one of the chairs arranged around the patio table where the three of them had shared many meals together, as a family.

He's not my family, Sebastian reminded himself.

Paul crossed his legs. "You talked with Frank, I take it?"

Sebastian didn't answer. He didn't want to have this conversation outside, their voices carrying so the neighbors or someone walking by with their dog could hear. He walked over to the table but didn't sit, glared at Paul from behind his sunglasses.

"Care to explain just what the fuck you're doing here?"

"Was just about to ask you the same question," Paul said. "Frank told me you were meeting us in Long Beach."

"I had to stop here. Because of you," Sebastian lied. He took off his sunglasses, eyes flat as he looked down at Paul. "You're going to need cash so you can hide out until I clean up your epic cluster—"

"Relax. The police aren't coming anywhere near here."

"Yeah? And how do you know that?"

"You're not the only one with friends on the force." Paul said it like he knew, exactly, the names of those within the LAPD he and Frank had on their payroll. "Trust me, we'll be fine."

Paul suddenly reached over the side of his chair to grab something sitting on the ground, behind the table. Sebastian stepped forward, ready to lunge if needed, when Paul stopped and cocked his head up at him, grinning.

"You think I've got a gun down here? That I'm going to shoot you in our house?" Paul chuckled and came up with two highball glasses—the set of Baccarat crystal given to Sebastian as a gift by a real estate client who had no idea he was an alcoholic who had been sober for over two decades. Sebastian kept the glasses on a kitchen shelf, where they had gathered dust. Paul, Sebastian noticed, had cleaned them up.

When Paul reached down again, that shit-eating grin still plastered on his face, Sebastian looked over the tops of the neatly trimmed hemlocks, to the house sitting on the hill above them, the sun burning gold and red against the back windows. The windows were shut, always, because nobody was home. Nobody lived there anymore. Sebastian owned the property, had bought it for privacy, and thought maybe he should take Paul down right now. He had fired the subcompact Glock many times. The report was no louder than a car muffler backfiring.

Hand in his pocket, Sebastian threaded his fingers around the Glock and clicked off the safety as Paul came up with a dark bottle of something and placed it on the table. The bottle had a gold crown on the top. Paul turned it around so Sebastian could see the label: thirty-eight-year-old Royal Salute Stone of Destiny blended Scotch whisky.

"You once told me your biggest regret was not having tried this before you got sober," Paul said.

It was true. Sebastian eyed the bottle, aware that his mouth was actually watering over the thought of having one measly sip.

"This shit's rare. *And* expensive," Paul said. "This bottle cost me almost two grand."

"And you, what, decided to pick up a bottle today after murdering six innocent people?"

Paul's eyebrows rose at the word *innocent*. "Bought it a while ago, actually. Was saving it for a special occasion. And today *is* a special occasion—

it truly is." He opened the bottle and placed the little gold crown on the table between them. "Guy who sold it to me said it's important to let the Scotch breathe for a few minutes before you drink it. Why don't you go grab us some ice?"

Sebastian pulled out the chair next to Paul and sat. He could smell the chlorine wafting from Paul's skin.

"That mean you want me to go get the ice?" Paul asked.

Sebastian didn't answer. Paul leaned back in his chair and crossed his legs again, and smiled, and right then Sebastian realized Paul had very skillfully manipulated him to get him to sit down at the table, make Sebastian think that he had done it of his own accord.

But that was what psychopaths did. They manipulated. The intelligent ones, anyway.

"Right now," Paul said, folding his hands against his hard, flat stomach, "I'm guessing you want to kill me. Understandable, given the circumstances. That won't solve anything—will, in fact, just lead to a whole new set of problems, the first of which being the cops. You don't want the LAPD—or the Feds, especially—to start poking around this wonderful facade you've created. You're an ex-con who murdered one of their brothers in blue. Who knows what sort of shit they'll uncover?"

Was that a threat? On paper it sure as hell would look like one, but the way Paul delivered it—like he delivered everything, in that soft voice of his, like he cared about you and your well-being—made it seem like he was offering sound counsel, one close friend to another.

"How much?" Sebastian asked.

"Excuse me?"

"How much money do you want? That's why you're here, isn't it?"

"You think I came so I can extort you?" Paul chuckled, shook his head. "I could have done that over the phone—could have done that months ago, if I'd wanted."

Paul's smile felt like a knife.

"I don't want to take money from you, Sebastian. I want to *make* it for you. I'm talking the kind of money that builds empires." Paul poured a drink, his expression serious now, all business. "All that charity work you love to do, so you look like a pillar of the community? You can fund any charity you want, a whole stable of 'em, for eternity. They'll name buildings after you, parks and streets. You'll be immortal."

"And then what?"

"What do you mean?"

"After you make me immortal, then what? What else are you offering?"

"Whatever you want, my man." Again with the cutting smile. "Whatever you want."

You mean whatever you *want,* Sebastian wanted to say, glancing at the little gold crown on the table. Men like Paul were never content with their current status. Make them a prince, and they'd want to be a king. And when they finally managed to take the throne—always by force, by blood and deception—then they'd want to be a god, and even *that* wouldn't be enough, because with men like Paul the wanting never stopped. Their bellies were never full, their egos never satisfied.

Paul took a sip of his drink. He closed his eyes as he swallowed.

"Wow," he said. "You really, really need to try this."

Paul poured the second drink.

"Alex and Jolie," Sebastian said.

"Yeah," Paul sighed. "That was unfortunate."

"That's what you call executing two kids? Unfortunate?"

"It had to be done." Paul put down the bottle. "If they'd lived, they would have told the cops everything."

Only they hadn't known anything. Sebastian took great measures to keep the salient details from his donors in the event one of them somehow escaped. It had never happened.

He didn't need to share any of this with Paul. Sebastian said, "Your only job today was to keep an eye on them, make sure things went smoothly. Instead, you brought the cops—"

"No, sir, I did not. They just showed up out of the blue. Why? Because someone in our organization must've tipped them off."

Our organization. Sebastian wanted to reach across the table with his fist, punch that smirk all the way back to the center of Paul's sick brain.

"Vargas's dog got out of the yard," Sebastian said.

Paul narrowed his eyes at him.

"One of the kids let it out of the yard, and the cops found it—and a message," Sebastian said, pleased by how calm and reasonable he sounded. He needed to stay that way if he was going to get Paul to go with him to Long Beach. "Someone, either Alex or Jolie, wrote a message on the dog tag. It said, 'Help us.' That happened under *your* watch."

Paul stared down at his flat, hard stomach.

"Then," Sebastian said, "I come to find out that you took blood from Jolie. Only you know she's not allowed to give blood because she's pregnant. Because it's not safe, places her at risk of anemia. Because it could kill—"

"Her blood is different from all the others."

"Different how?" The words jumped out of Sebastian's mouth before he could stop to consider them.

"With Pandora," Paul said, confidence creeping back into his voice, "I know a lot of people get super horny after a transfusion—a *full*-body transfusion. But if you take the blood from a pregnant carrier, it's insane how potent this shit is. Think of it as Pandora on steroids. Pandora makes you look five to ten years younger? My shit makes you feel like a *god*. And the best thing is that it only takes a few units to get the results I'm talking about."

"Too bad you killed the golden goose."

"What're you talking about?"

"Jolie," Sebastian said. "You killed her."

Paul opened his mouth, about to speak when he snapped it shut. His face brightened. "Oh, I see. Forget Jolie. I'll replace her with one of my donors." Paul caught his expression and said, "I found some of my own carriers—for testing purposes, you understand. I wanted—"

"The stickman at Vargas's house. He's one of Anton's."

"I borrowed him, to do me a favor. He's not a part of this. Anton. No one is. I've been doing the testing on my own, and on my own time. You're the only person I've shared this with—the only one I wanted to share this with." Paul frowned. "Wipe that look off your face. I had to get some of my own carriers to test out my theory. I didn't want to approach you with some half-baked concept—and it's not. My product is rock-solid. Let's call it Pandora two point oh. Together, we can—"

"What are you mixing it with?"

"Are you asking me to share my secret recipe?" Paul shot him a sly grin. "I'll show you mine if you show me yours."

"How many donors do you have?"

"Three." Paul frowned, then said, "No, two. One of them lost the kid. She's not back in rotation yet. I've got to give her some time to, you know, heal up before I breed her again."

Breed her.

Sebastian didn't harbor any illusions about what he did for a living. When you boiled it down to its core, he abducted carriers—young kids and teenagers, more often than not—and stole their blood and sold it. He took only carriers who came from broken and shitty homes and gave them not only a better life but a safe one, where they would never be hunted or abused. He was as good to them as he knew how to be, given the circumstances—not out of guilt but because it was the right thing to do.

But what Paul was talking about—it was unthinkable.

Paul looked at him with those boyish, innocent eyes. "It doesn't matter who knocks 'em up—Jolie proved that to me today. Although, I've got to say, with her I needed to use less blood for some reason. Maybe it's because another carrier impregnated her, makes the blood a bit more potent. Maybe we should shoot for that down the road—carriers breeding with other carriers. For right now, though, anyone can— Where are you going?"

Sebastian had gotten to his feet. "I want to see it," he told Paul, masking his disgust and anger.

"See what?"

"Your farm."

"It's not really a blood farm. It's more like a holding pen, and a crappy one at that."

"Still, I'd like to view your operation. How you harvest the blood, how you store it, the medications you're using, et cetera." *And once you take me there,* Sebastian added privately, *I'm going to blow your brains out.*

"So we've got a deal?" Paul asked.

"What you've got is my interest. After I see everything with my own eyes, we'll sit down with Frank and discuss terms."

"Then a toast." Paul slid the second glass across the table.

Sebastian didn't take it, his mind seized on a string of questions: *Have any of his carriers carried a baby to full term? What did he do to the kids? What does he* want *to do to the kids? No, don't ask.*

"Just one sip," Paul said. "You can do that, right? Just take one sip?"

Sebastian felt his lunch sloshing around in his stomach. "Get up and get dressed."

Paul remained seated, squinting up at him. "You *do* realize what I'm offering you."

"And you realize what *I'm* offering *you.*"

"Capital and infrastructure."

And *that,* Sebastian believed, was the leverage he had over Paul. If Paul had wanted to launch his own operation, he would have put something together already. But undertaking such an operation took a tremendous amount of capital. Paul didn't have that, or an infrastructure, which was why he was here. Paul needed him in order to produce his ungodly product.

Which was never going to happen. After he killed Paul, he'd take in Paul's carriers and give them a good life, treat them properly.

"After the farm," Sebastian said, "we'll go to Long Beach and—"

"Why go all the way to Long Beach? Frank didn't say."

"We got a house there where you'll be safe until things cool down."

"I've got my own place. I can—"

"We purchased this place in the event something happened and we needed to lay low. It's got state-of-the-art security and, in case cops or anyone else decides to come snooping around, a well-hidden panic room. You'll be safe there. No, don't argue with me on this. One step at a time, okay? That's how I work—how *you* need to work if you want to go into business together."

Paul considered him. Sebastian saw traces of the kid buried in the man, the boy who, when his mother had asked him to finish his vegetables or to put away the cookies, would stare back at her as if to say, *Make me—I dare you*. Paul was staring at him that way right now.

His face suddenly relaxed. "You're right," Paul said. Sighing, he got to his feet, his muscles flexing as he walked over to his clothes.

Sebastian stood several feet away, near the table, his hands in his pockets. His right hand gripped the gun, just in case Paul tried something. Paul seemed relaxed—too relaxed, Sebastian thought. It bothered him. Put him on edge.

Paul slid into his sneakers. "I've got to be honest, Sebastian. You're not showing the level of excitement I expected."

"Lot of shit went down today. I'm still trying to process everything."

Paul worked his T-shirt over his head. "What if I say no to Long Beach and taking you to the farm?"

"Then no deal."

Paul sighed. "What I thought." He shook his head and stared off in the distance. "I know what you do there, you know. At Long Beach." His eyes cut back to Sebastian. "I know everything about you, Frank, and your operation."

An inner voice urged Sebastian to pull the gun, put him down now. It was the right thing to do, no question—and he could make up a story.

He could spin it for the police. Spin it in a way it wouldn't come back to bite him in the ass. *Do it now, before he—*

"I was going to make you an emperor," Paul said sadly, extending his arm above his head and performing the kind of hand signal Sebastian associated with SWAT and military special operations commands. Paul was giving a command to someone, but to whom? And to do what?

Sebastian caught a wink of light coming from the house on the hill. One of the windows facing him was now cracked open, the mesh screen gone, the sun reflecting off the glass lens of what he was sure was a sniper scope. He turned as the report of a rifle echoed through the air, the round slamming into his chest and knocking him off his feet and sending him tumbling backward, over the edge of the pool.

Sebastian sank through the cool water, grabbing his chest and thinking only one thing: *Ava.*

CHAPTER 8

Ellie was sent straight to the hospital—not that she had asked, and not that there was any need. Physically, she was okay, everything in working order. What she needed was to go home, take a long, hot shower, and then change into comfortable clothes, go sit out on the back deck with a glass of Irish whiskey, and enjoy the peace and quiet, take some time to process everything that had happened. No more talking, and answering the same questions over and over again.

Her plans, though, would have to wait until later. The procedures in place after a shooting were specific and nonnegotiable: she had to go to the hospital whether she wanted to or not, and get a full examination, everything documented in writing so she couldn't turn around later and try to milk a disability claim, maybe even sue the department down the road for some injury she suffered while on the job.

Riding shotgun in the patrol car, she stared out the side window and wondered if there had ever been a time in human history when people had simply done their jobs without trying to game the system.

"We're here," the patrolwoman said, pulling into the parking lot of St. Michael's Hospital. Her name was Toni Vickers. She was somewhere in her fifties and had white hair and smooth brown skin and a round, comforting face.

Vickers had said something. Ellie couldn't recall it. "I'm sorry, what did you say?"

"I asked if you're okay to walk, or would you like assistance? I can go inside, wheel out a chair, and—"

"I walked into the car by myself," Ellie snapped. "I sure as hell can walk out of it."

Vickers nodded somberly, lips pressed tight.

"I'm sorry," Ellie sighed. "You didn't deserve that."

"It's okay."

"No, it's not. It's just that . . . I'm not the victim here. Everyone is talking to me in this patronizing way, acting like I'm going to explode into a million little pieces. That's not going to happen, okay? I just want to get this over with."

The ER waiting room was packed to capacity. When Vickers returned from the check-in area with a young, plump nurse with rosy, cherublike cheeks, the woman led them down a series of halls and into an exam room.

The nurse handed her a neatly folded dressing gown. Ellie stared at it, the fabric thin and rough against her fingers. While computers and medicine had advanced and kept making breakthroughs, some things never changed—remained a constant—like the drab examination smock a patient had to wear backward.

The nurse left, but the room felt claustrophobic because Vickers, by no means a small woman, with her ample hips, remained. She stood against the wall, underneath a pair of taped sheets of paper advocating the importance of the HPV vaccine and handwashing.

"Let's bag your clothes," Vickers said.

"My clothes?"

Vickers nodded. "We need to collect each item of clothing separately."

"What? Why?"

"Honey," Vickers said in a soothing voice, "you're covered in blood."

Ellie stared down at her clothes, as if seeing them for the first time.

She *was* covered in blood—not hers, but Danny's. It was smeared across the dark fabric of her pants and shirtsleeves. There were splashes on her chest.

"Strip down to your bra and panties," Vickers said gently. "The doctor will collect those."

Of course. I'm covered in blood, Ellie thought. She had performed CPR on Danny. Danny was dead—she had failed to find a pulse—but she had still kept blowing her breath down into his lungs, kept using her hands on his chest to get his dead heart to start beating.

"Don't worry," Vickers said. "I have someone bringing a fresh set of clothes from your locker."

Ellie's gaze drifted to the landline phone sitting on the counter.

"You can't talk to anyone yet," Vickers said. "But he knows. I spoke with Cody and assured him you were—"

"Samantha."

Vickers, frowning, took out her pocket notebook and removed the pen threaded inside the spiral. "Is she a family member? Friend?"

"Danny's mother. Her name is Samantha. Have you spoken to her yet?"

"I'm sure someone—"

"She won't answer her phone unless Danny is calling. You can't leave her a message saying what happened. You can't do that to her."

Vickers nodded in understanding, smiled patiently. "I can assure you that won't happen. Why don't—"

"Today's Friday, right? Yes. Yes, it's Friday." Ellie felt clammy all over. Her mind raced and her heart banged so hard against her rib cage, she thought it might shoot out of her chest like a bullet. "Danny's mother will be at her sister's today—she spends every Friday with her, Danny told me. I don't know the phone number or the address, though."

"Ellie," Vickers began.

"If Danny had told me, I would have written down her number or put it in my phone. I should have asked. I should have been more prepared."

Vickers stepped up next to her. Ellie felt the woman's hand on her back.

"You've been through a terrible ordeal," Vickers said.

Ellie kept her attention on the HPV poster but wasn't really looking at it but through it, thinking of Danny zipped up inside a rubber bag and stuffed inside a refrigerated drawer while his mother was getting ready for her afternoon out with her sister, followed by the early-bird special at the Continental, the woman having no idea that her youngest child was dead.

"You're going to go through a variety of emotions and mood swings," Vickers said gently. "You may also experience survivor's guilt. The important thing is to allow yourself to experience these feelings, to talk about them, because in these situations, victims—"

Vickers stopped talking when Ellie stepped away, straightening. She blinked back the tears and said, "Yes, you're right—I need to deal with this." She began unbuttoning her shirt, her hands trembling. "I understand," she said. "I understand now."

The vast majority of the LAPD—not the elite brass or the top-level pencil pushers and executives but the actual cops who worked the streets and cases—couldn't afford to live in Los Angeles. Last year, almost 85 percent of the LAPD lived outside of the city. By the end of this year, that figure, Ellie had been told, would be closer to 90 percent, thanks to a salary cap and another round of budget cuts.

Which was why a lot of cops now lived in Simi Valley, in Ventura County. It was thirty miles from downtown LA, right next door to Santa Barbara, surrounded by the Santa Susana mountain range. The biggest selling point was that it was cheap. "You should check out the Clara Anna Woods Mobile Home Park," one of her academy instructors had told her. "It's real affordable."

Ellie had lived her entire life in small, cramped apartments. Moving into a trailer wasn't exactly a step up in the world. She had checked out several apartments in Simi Valley, and at the last minute decided to drive by the mobile home park. She was glad she did.

The Clara Anna Woods Mobile Home Park consisted of actual *homes*, not trailers, each unit a tiny yellow house with white trim and tandem parking for up to three cars. The little village—and that was what she considered it—was flat and open and had fresh, clean air and she had a wonderful view of the mountains from her back porch. Most important, for the first time in her life, she had privacy. It surprised her how badly she wanted it.

It was coming up on nine when the cruiser pulled up against the curb. Ellie wished she could have driven home herself, but regulations dictated that an officer involved in a shooting wasn't allowed to get behind the wheel. Her car, she'd been told, would probably be delivered to her tomorrow, Sunday at the latest.

It didn't really matter. She was on a mandatory five-day paid leave.

Cody's black Ford F-150 truck wasn't there—which surprised her. Maybe it was just as well. This was the first moment she had when she didn't have to talk, to answer questions. Now she had the opportunity to just *be*, and see what happened.

The last of the sunlight was still visible over the mountains when the patrol car pulled away. A gold and purplish color washed across the lemon tree planted in her front yard and the crushed white stones she had instead of a lawn. Ellie, dressed in the gray hoodie, sweats, and flip-flops brought from her locker to the hospital, forced herself to take in the beauty around her—the sunset and mountains. All it did, though, was make her feel small and insignificant.

She knew why. The reason she was standing here right now and breathing this air and enjoying this view and listening to Claire Leddy's yellow Lab, Greta, barking three doors down was simply because today she had gotten lucky. That was it, no other reason. Sparing her life wasn't a part of some divine grand plan. Things in life didn't happen for a reason or because you were good or bad or indifferent or all of the above. It all came down to luck, and didn't you know that was out of your control, and trying to sit with that knowledge and accept it, well, that was a hard thing to do when you believed you *did*, in fact, control every single aspect of your life.

She wished Cody were here. Cody, who was rock-solid, his viewpoints on life and marriage and family as unshakable as his faith in God and the greater good. Cody, who loved her unconditionally despite her best efforts to push him away at times because, deep down—let's face it—didn't she at times feel unworthy of his type of love? And wasn't that because she had deliberately chosen not to share a certain particular burden with him?

Thinking about that burden made a part of her feel *glad* he wasn't here. Relieved. That part of her said, *Call and tell him not to come.* The LAPD had confiscated her phone. She couldn't call him unless she borrowed a phone from someone.

She wanted to call him and yet didn't want to call him. Why couldn't she make a decision? *Why am I so confused?*

You've been through a terrible ordeal, Vickers had said to her. *In these situations, victims—*

"I'm not a victim," Ellie whispered into the fading sunlight. Her hands balled into fists and she shook uncontrollably. "I am *not* a victim."

Ellie marched into her house and headed upstairs. She stood in the shower until the hot water ran out. She felt scrubbed clean but cold all over, even after she got dressed.

Two glasses of bourbon fixed the problem.

Her little house, with its vaulted ceilings and clever use of space, felt like a mansion to her. After she fixed herself a fresh drink at the breakfast bar, she paced back and forth across the carpeted family room, her ice tinkling against the glass.

Her gaze kept drifting to the stairs.

Tonight wasn't a good time to take a trip down memory lane. Cody, she was sure, would arrive at any minute to check on her—and besides, memory lane always led to the same dead end.

And yet it didn't surprise her in the slightest when she stepped up to the refrigerator and pulled open the bottom drawer of the freezer and fished out the key she kept tucked underneath a carton of Ben & Jerry's Chunky Monkey ice cream. She didn't fight the urge or question it when she carried her drink up to the second floor and used the key on the doorknob lock for the spare bedroom. It certainly didn't surprise her when she flicked the light switch and felt a wave of relief wash through her. She *had* come home, back to the person she kept hidden from the rest of the world.

Cody had not stepped foot inside this room, thought she used it as a storage area for her mother's old things and kept it locked because she said she was embarrassed by all the clutter. He would have been surprised if not outwardly shocked to discover that this boxy room, with its white walls and light beige carpeting, was just as neat and organized as the rest of her house. The shades were drawn, always, to block out wandering eyes, because if someone looked inside and saw what was in there, they might be inclined to call the police. The room looked like the lair of some diabolical serial killer.

The soft white light came from a cheap plastic lamp she had owned since childhood. The desk, made of heavy walnut, had been purchased at a yard sale by her mother. Ellie could remember that lazy Saturday afternoon in May when Kay Batista had returned home and, beaming with pride, said, *I've got such a surprise for you.* Ellie, also a proud veteran of yard sales and flea markets and thrift stores, had rescued two items left out as trash on a sidewalk in Van Nuys: a dented filing cabinet and a big wood-framed corkboard.

She opened the top drawer of the filing cabinet and took out the files for Jolie Simone and Alex Hernandez. She placed a red X on each tab and then moved the files to the bottom drawer—the drawer of the dead, she called it. Touching the paper, moving the files—it was tactile. Made the victims seem real to her and not just bits of information stored in the cloud or a database.

Now she turned her attention to the corkboard. Her main project.

A strip of masking tape ran down its center.

The left half of the corkboard contained an eight-by-ten photograph she had taken herself—not with her smartphone but with a professional Canon digital camera with a telescopic lens, the same rig the paparazzi used to capture female celebrities frolicking half-naked on the beach. She had taken the picture at night two months ago, on a street around the corner from a popular club in Los Angeles. In the photo, a tall, muscular guy dressed in jeans and a tight-fitting blue T-shirt leaned against the driver's-side window of a Buick SUV, handing over the same kind of sticker device she'd seen earlier today at the Vargas house.

The man handing over the sticker was Anton Kuzmich, a Russian immigrant in his early thirties who owned a private security business that catered mostly to LA's high-end nightclubs. He was also, she had discovered on her own time, heavily involved in the blood world.

The man seated behind the wheel was another matter. Despite her best efforts, no amount of digital enhancement or computer trickery could coax the driver's face from the shadows, and she'd been unable to capture the license plate number.

What she did capture was the man's left hand on the steering wheel. It was pale, the thick knuckles and forearm as hairy as an ape's, and he wore a ring on his middle finger. The ring's design had two lions circling each other, preparing to fight. That was the only detail she knew of him.

She assumed he was an important player in the blood world, given the fact that Anton Kuzmich had handed off the sticker to him, probably telling the man behind the wheel he had identified a carrier. That was how it was done these days, by a stickman, a task normally performed by a kid like the one she'd seen at the Vargas house—a homeless teenager who could run fast, get in and out in a hurry.

Ellie drank some more of her whiskey. After she put down the glass, she took in a deep, slow breath and, squaring her shoulders, turned her attention to the picture on the right half of the corkboard.

This one was a five-by-seven of a black-haired boy a few months shy of celebrating his sixth birthday. He wore dark blue footie pajamas and sat Indian-style on a hardwood floor desperately in need of refinishing. His expression was what always drew her to the picture—the way he stared in wide-eyed rapture at the Christmas presents arranged under a small artificial tree bursting with lights and handmade decorations.

The boy's name was Jonathan Cullen. His mother called him Jonathan, always, but everyone else called him J.C., including Ellie. She had no idea if J.C. was still alive, what he might look like now. As she stared at his photograph, she hoped, as she had thousands and thousands of times over the years, that wherever J.C. was right now, he knew she still loved him and missed him and was still searching for him.

That his twin sister hadn't given up, would never give up.

CHAPTER 9

I'VE BEEN SHOT.

That was Sebastian's only thought as he sank through the cool blue water belonging, ironically, to the very same pool where he had taught Paul to swim. He had played with him in this pool, had thrown Paul and his friends into the air in this pool when they were little, and that boy had grown into an adult monster that had given a hand signal to the person aiming the rifle from the neighbor's bedroom window.

But he had been shot in the chest, not the head, and here came the question riding on the throbbing waves of pain: had the round penetrated the thin, light bulletproof vest he wore every day? It sure as *hell* felt like it had.

How much blood am I losing?

How much time do I have before I get light-headed and pass out and bleed to death?

Don't let that prick win.

Sebastian could no longer hold his breath. His body ignored his brain's order not to breathe and he found himself trying to inhale the water—not the brightest idea, since he wasn't a goddamn fish. He pushed himself off the bottom of the pool and kicked and thrashed his way to the surface. The moment he felt the air hit his face, he tried to breathe, and his lungs and body revolted. He vomited up pool water and the digested remnants of the Coke and chicken salad sandwich he'd had for lunch. His loafers couldn't find purchase on the slick bottom of the pool and he flailed about wildly in the water, his chest on fire and the pool steps directly in front of him, ten or so feet away.

His brain was locked in survival mode, and it screamed, *Sniper could still be in the window, and don't forget about Paul—where's Paul?*

A couple of quick glances revealed that Paul wasn't in the backyard or near the driveway or anywhere else. Where the hell was he? As for the sniper, Sebastian didn't bother to look as he swam madly toward the steps—although what he was doing wasn't really swimming but more like stumbling through water and thrashing his limbs as he tried to suck in air between gagging, coughing, and heaving. *Keep moving,* he told himself. *It's hard to shoot a moving target, so keep moving if you want to live.*

Moving, though, was the problem. Moving through water was like moving in slow motion, which made him an easy target. Still, he kept at it, limbs flailing. He gagged on water and, he was certain, blood. He didn't stop to check, just kept moving, the adrenaline, he knew, keeping him alive for the moment.

Sebastian's hands found purchase on the pool steps. He crawled up them, but when he went to stand his legs gave out and he collapsed sideways against the ground. The sliding glass door off the kitchen was less than twenty feet away. *Get to that* now.

By some miracle combination of adrenaline and sheer will he managed to get back on his feet and then staggered to the sliding glass door, which was unlocked because Paul had come out through it earlier, with the crystal highball glasses.

Sebastian's destination was his office. He slipped, slid, and skidded his way across the living room's hardwood floor, splashing and dripping water along the way, then moved through the immense kitchen, with its tiled floor and gleaming white surfaces, using the furniture and walls for support. He kept glancing over his shoulder, half expecting to see Paul behind him, coming to finish the job.

Down the foyer, and finally there was the door to his office. He stumbled inside and slammed the door shut. When he threw the dead bolt, his legs fluttered in relief or fear or maybe both; whatever the reason, he collapsed against the cold tile floor, wet and shivering—and safe. Paul couldn't get in here. The door had a steel core and two strike plates—no way Paul could kick it down. The pair of windows overlooking the front yard were made of bulletproof glass—no way the sick prick could shoot his way in, either.

Sebastian was no longer gagging but it still hurt like a mad bastard every single time he drew a breath. He managed to get his tie and suit jacket off, but unbuttoning his shirt was another matter; his hands wouldn't stop shaking, his fingers unable to hold on to the buttons. *Screw it.* He ripped his shirt open, buttons flying everywhere, and with a quick and silent prayer looked down at his chest.

At Frank's urging, Sebastian had purchased a bulletproof vest—a sad statement on the world they now lived in. Frank had picked out one that, according to the website, was designed with a gel that worked in conjunction with carbon nanofibers, which resulted in a vest that guaranteed police-level protection from any round on the market, without the weight and bulk.

It seemed the claim wasn't marketing bullshit. Sebastian was pleased to report that he didn't see any blood, just a mark on the fabric where the round had struck him.

Maybe I'll go online and leave a review, Sebastian thought, and was overcome with a fit of giggling. His body put a stop to that when his ribs howled in protest. *Must have cracked one—probably a whole bunch of them.* He undid the Velcro straps and pulled away the thin fabric to examine his skin. He had one *hell* of a welt, and it was located on the right part of his chest—directly opposite from his heart. The shooter had been aiming for it when Sebastian turned at the last second.

Only a trained marksman could have managed such a shot from such a distance. Had Paul hired one of his Marine buddies? How many people did Paul have working for him?

Sebastian collapsed against the floor. He turned onto his side and waited for the pain to quiet down, lose its bite.

Trixie had decorated his office—picked out all the furniture, the big walnut desk and matching bookcases and leather sofa and club chair and, leaning against the corner wall, the large standing mirror. Sebastian saw himself in the office now, soaking wet and curled up on the floor. It shamed him, seeing himself this way, looking like the scared little boy who had once curled into a ball and wanted to scream and cry at being sentenced to life in prison for a crime—

You're alive, an inner voice said. It was the voice of his Higher Power—his higher self. *Focus on that.*

Yes. That was the main thing, the takeaway: he was alive and, for the moment, safe from Paul. Paul, who had outsmarted him. Paul, who wanted to control his blood business, where the kids were safe and well treated, turn it all into a horror show where he would rape and impregnate his female carriers in order to harvest their blood. Sebastian had to prevent that.

But first, the police. Were they already on their way here? The rifle shot hadn't been that loud, which suggested the use of a silencer. That made sense; Paul wouldn't have wanted to draw any unnecessary attention to the gunman—or himself. The two of them had needed to leave as quickly and quietly as possible. Still, the report *could* have been loud enough for someone to pick up the phone and call the police about a possible gunshot. And since Sebastian lived in Whitey Town, the police would be lightning quick.

He saw his suit jacket lying in a wet ball on the floor and patted down the fabric until he found his phone. He had never met any electronic device that enjoyed swimming, but he was hoping this case would prove an exception.

It didn't. His smartphone was dead.

The safe. He had a couple of brand-new burners stored inside the wall safe, along with passports, IDs, and cash. He got to his feet too quickly and doubled over in pain so debilitating, his legs came dangerously close to buckling. Again he used the wall and furniture for support as he shuffled his way to the other side of the room and opened the closet door. He turned on the light, pushed aside his winter jackets, and faced the safe, an old-fashioned model with a rotary dial. Digital safes were notoriously easy to hack.

The burners were in there, sitting on top of neatly wrapped bundles of cash—fifty grand in total. For a brief moment he had the urge to throw everything in a duffel bag and then get the hell out of Dodge, live somewhere on a Caribbean island until he died of cirrhosis of the liver or skin cancer, whichever came first. The fantasy—and that was all it was and would ever be—quickly scattered like a puff of smoke.

Three rings, and then Frank's calm and even voice spoke on the other end of the line: "Hello?"

"It's me."

"Why you calling me from this—" Frank cut himself off. Then, concerned, his voice lower: "Why are you out of breath? There a problem?"

"Yeah," Sebastian said, his voice pinched tight, "you might say that."

CHAPTER 10

THE HANDFUL OF childhood memories Ellie had of her brother were either snapshots or brief videos attached to bursts of intense emotion: young Ellie scared and wearing incredibly bright, almost neon orange inflatable floaties around her tiny arms and fiercely gripping J.C.'s hand as they stepped together into a pool for the first time. J.C. insisting on wearing them when he took a bath, afraid he was going to drown—and also insisting on wearing a swimming mask, because he was terrified of getting water on his face. Ellie wailing when she discovered J.C. had given the doll she named Miss Bee-bee a haircut that had left her looking like something from a science experiment gone horribly wrong. Oh, here was a really funny memory, one of her favorites, that always made her smile: J.C., three, maybe four years old, sitting buck naked on the toilet and gripping the seat for dear life so he wouldn't fall in, his face a dark red from straining to crap, tears running down his cheeks as he scream-sobbed, *"Poopy, get out of my body!"*

Ellie had had no idea her brother was a carrier until after he'd been abducted. She also had no memory of that night. She had been staying at the home of her mother's friend, a woman who also lived in Westmont, a suburb of Los Angeles. Her mother had to drive out early the next morning to Children's Hospital to discuss ear tube surgery—because of J.C.'s chronic ear infections—and she couldn't do that while trying to juggle a pair of rambunctious twins.

Ellie vaguely recalled staying with her mother's friend—an older woman with graying hair who loved wearing scarves—for two days, maybe three or four. She couldn't recall the name of the friend, but what she could recall, *vividly*, was coming home and seeing the bandages on her mother's still-swollen face, her left arm in a sling because she had broken her arm. Her mother was crying, and Ellie was crying, too, even though she didn't yet know what had happened, but it had to be bad, real bad, because her mother looked all hurt and banged up, and the car was packed with boxes.

During the drive to Maryland, her mother told her that J.C. was a carrier, which meant he had very special blood that could heal people, make them look younger. Very bad people had abducted him. *You're not a carrier,* her mother explained, *but these bad people think you are and may come back for you. That's why we're moving—and why we need to change our names. We need to make sure we're safe—and we will be, sweetheart. I promise you, we'll be safe.* Her mother said it like she was trying to convince herself instead of her terrified six-year-old daughter.

Or that was Ellie's memory of it. That and feeling that the world was this great big monster that could not only bite you but devour you whole, no matter how many people loved you. She had grown up in a state of perpetual fear of not only the dark but also the light. It wasn't until she became a cop that she reclaimed herself—from that day forward she would no longer be a victim.

Life after her brother meant moving across the country every few months and being homeschooled and living under different names and having heavily supervised playdates with her mother acting like a bodyguard, constantly scanning for potential threats. *Ellie* was what her mother always called her—the middle name of some cousin Ellie had never met. Ellie was twelve, and she embraced her new identity as she'd always done, as she'd been trained to do. *Amanda Cullen*, who had lived on the first floor of a rental home in Westmont, no longer existed, except in her mind. Amanda Cullen was, for all intents and purposes, dead.

As for her brother? There were no pictures of him around the house or on her mother's phone. J.C. could be spoken about only at home, only when she and her mother were alone.

The Los Angeles police are still looking for him, her mother would say in the beginning. *Keep praying. Don't give up hope.*

That became: *He's gone. He's probably never coming home.*

Then: *We have to live our lives. Maybe one day things will change, but we need to live our lives.*

Things *did* change, at least for Ellie, when she made the decision to move from Boston, where she had settled with her mother, to attend a small college in Los Angeles, against her mother's wishes. Christ, what fights they'd had over that. Running away from your problems and fears, Ellie had learned at a young age, only magnified them, turned you into a victim. Victims ran away from their shit. Ellie wanted to run to them. *Into* them. That was how you dealt with life. After she got her degree in criminal justice, she enrolled in the LAPD Police Academy.

Now she had access to the most powerful and interconnected law enforcement databases from all over the world. Ellie quickly discovered that no one named Jonathan Cullen from Westmont had ever been reported missing. She confronted her mother, who admitted that she never reported to the police what had happened.

Why? Because, her mother explained, she recognized the voice of one of the gunmen that night. The voice, she was certain, belonged to a cop who was well-known in the neighborhood. She couldn't go to the police, because they might come after Ellie. This cop, her mother had learned, was working with other cops to abduct carriers from all over the country and sell them to blood farms.

Save your daughter or stay and try to find your son? Pick one.

She picked her daughter.

Even as her mother was dying, the body lying in the hospital bed looking more like a husk by the day, the cancer having feasted on all her organs—even in pain and on morphine she refused to share key details from that night that would help Ellie find J.C. or, at the very least, find out what had become of him, if he was alive or dead. *It's for your own protection,* her mother kept telling her. *Those men are still out there—they could find you. Promise me you'll let it go.*

Ellie couldn't let it go. She had begged and pleaded for details and asked questions—she got good and angry and walked away more than once—and her mother refused to share details, reciting the same lines over and over again, as if by rote. When her mother finally passed, Ellie remembered sitting next to her, loving and hating her equally.

Ellie wondered what her mother would say if she could see her daughter now, standing in this makeshift shrine/operations center devoted to finding J.C., wondered if her mother—

A car was approaching.

Ellie turned away from the photo, listened. The engine was loud, rumbling—the kind that belonged to a truck, not a car. The kind Cody's Ford F-150 had.

She realized she was quite drunk. Not stumbling, fall-on-your-face drunk but riding that oh so wonderful warm wave that made her feel relaxed. In control.

The doorbell rang as Ellie plodded downstairs on her bare feet. She placed the empty glass next to the whiskey bottle sitting on the breakfast bar and caught her reflection in the glass cabinet door. A normal twenty-something woman would have taken the time to look more presentable for her boyfriend, worn something other than a pair of Under Armour track pants and a frayed T-shirt that should have been relegated to the rag pile or dumped in the trash. But a normal twenty-something woman wouldn't have spent her afternoon dodging bullets and dealing with a crazy masturbating woman high on illegal blood, so screw it.

The doorbell rang again. She was glad Cody was here. She didn't need him to be here, and she wanted him to understand that. She didn't want him hovering, treating her like some bruised flower. *Screw that,* she thought, and opened the door.

Her little speech would have to wait. Police Commissioner James Kelly was standing on her doorstep.

"Evening," Kelly said. "I hope I'm not catching you at a bad time."

Ellie was too stunned to speak. Why in God's name would the police commissioner be standing on her front doorstep at—she glanced at the wall clock over the fireplace—quarter past eleven?

And alone. Kelly had come here alone—at least it appeared that way, because there was no one else standing anywhere outside. And he must have driven himself, because she didn't see a driver sitting behind the wheel of the vehicle parked in her carport, a two-door white Toyota Tacoma truck with a Santa Clara University sticker on the back window.

"My daughter's truck," Kelly said. "She's home for the weekend." He smiled. "Mom washes and folds the laundry and provides free meals while my daughter complains about how rough and demanding her schoolwork is."

Ellie wanted to say something, or at least nod in acknowledgment, but her mind was overflowing with questions, and underneath them she felt a vague sense of panic. Having the commissioner dropping in at such a late hour didn't exactly scream good news.

"This is usually the part where you invite me in," Kelly said kindly.

Ellie's face flushed in embarrassment. "Right, yes. Yes, of course." She stepped back and held the door open for him. "Please come in."

"Why, thank you."

Kelly had traded his suit and tie for loafers, a white polo, and a pair of khakis with a razor-sharp pleat. The cold and mechanical exterior he had displayed this afternoon had been replaced by something more relaxed and agreeable. Ellie shut the front door, feeling certain he hadn't come here to deliver bad news or interrogate her; he had lackeys for that. She suspected he needed something from her—something important. A favor, maybe.

Ellie felt herself relax a bit. "Can I get you something to drink?"

He eyed the whiskey bottle on the breakfast bar almost lovingly. "Thank you, but no," he said. "I'm fine."

"You sure? There's plenty."

"I'm in recovery, which is a more polite way of saying I'm a boozehound. But please, don't deny yourself on my account."

"Don't worry, I won't."

Kelly let loose a bark of a laugh. It erased a good decade off his face.

She didn't know why she had said those words; they had simply rolled off her tongue, uncensored. It probably had something to do with the booze and the fact that, whatever this was about, she had the home court advantage. She hadn't been brought to his office and called out on the carpet, and he had come here alone, all of which reinforced the notion that he needed something from her.

Ellie motioned to the sofa and took the armchair. She crossed her legs and rested her hands on her lap.

"What do you need from me, Commissioner?"

"Straight to it."

"Saves time."

Kelly considered her for a beat. Outside, she could hear the ticking of his cooling truck engine.

"Gingerbread Man," he said. "Did he get a good look at you?"

"I don't think so."

"Think about it for a moment."

"I did, while I was at the hospital," Ellie said. "I was wearing sunglasses and my cap, so no, I don't think he got a good look at me. Why?"

"Are you a carrier?"

The question surprised her.

"Yes, I know it's unethical to ask you that question," Kelly said. "But since I'm asking in the context of your job, I believe I might have some wiggle room."

"My job? I don't understand."

"Ellie—may I call you Ellie?"

"Of course."

"Today you made it a point of showing me just how badly you want a spot on the Blood Unit. I came here tonight to find out why."

"I explained that to you already."

"I think it's something more than that." Kelly's gaze felt as penetrating as an X-ray. "Something more . . . personal."

The upstairs room with the picture of her brother, the drawers stuffed with the files of missing carriers, her off-the-clock research—all of it flashed through her mind and fear raised the hammers in her heart. *He knows,* Ellie thought. *Somehow he's found out about my brother, my real life, everything.*

Which meant he knew that her real name wasn't Ellie Batista. It meant he knew she had applied to the LAPD under a false name—an alias—and that was a crime, one that could send her off to prison, her career gone. The thought of prison was terrifying, but not as terrifying as no longer being a cop. No longer having the resources to search for her brother. The panic she felt in that moment was so sudden, she felt like she was choking.

Kelly stared at her intently, waiting. Ellie remembered advice someone had given her: *If you don't like the story, change it.* She had to bear down hard.

"Your first question, about me being a carrier," she said. "I'm not one."

Kelly nodded, his features relaxed.

"As for my interest in the blood world—how can I *not* be interested? Carriers are being snatched from their homes or taken at gunpoint from cars or at school, and we lack the resources and manpower to find them. We don't know much of anything about the blood world, how it operates, what a blood farm looks like. I want to know more about this world. I want to know everything."

"But you haven't explained why." Kelly smiled, but it didn't reach his eyes.

"What I'm asking," Kelly went on, "is for you to explain what's driving you. Why you've devoted your spare time to memorizing the names of missing carriers. Someone who makes that kind of commitment—well, there's got to be a deep, personal reason, don't you think?"

In the hospital room, while being examined by a first-year resident with stale coffee breath and thinning hair, and in the silence of the car ride on the way home, Ellie had started thinking about the moment when Detective Alves and/or someone from the police commissioner's office would start asking her more specific questions about how she knew so much about the victims. She knew she would be answering a lot of questions in the days ahead, and she was prepared.

"Your older brother, Rodger," Ellie said.

Kelly's eyes widened at the mention of his brother and at the unexpected segue. Ellie continued, riding the rails of her gut instincts. "You've talked about him in multiple interviews, about how he died from a heroin overdose. He was sixteen, you were thirteen, and your parents had placed him in yet another private treatment center. Only this time he escaped. No one knew where he was for nine days, if I remember correctly."

Kelly was too much of a pro to react. He sat as still as a stone statue, letting the silence linger and waiting for her to explain her train of thought—possibly hang herself with it.

"You and your parents lived through nine hellish days before the police found his body," Ellie said. She left out the part about a homeless person finding Rodger Kelly dead in Echo Park, because she didn't need it for emphasis. "My point is, you found your brother. No matter how painful it was, you and your family got closure."

"And how, exactly, is my personal life related to your almost pathological interest in the blood world?"

"Pathological?" Ellie chuckled. "Sir, no matter where you go in the city—in the state—all you see are billboards advertising missing carriers.

Abducted carriers. They're all over the news; they're all online and clogging social media feeds. I'm *drowning* in information. I can't get away from it. I have no idea what's going on out there, or what's being done about it, and I want to know."

Ellie folded her hands on her lap. Kelly said nothing.

"Sir, I don't know you well—I don't know you at all, really—but I'm willing to bet that when you received the news about your brother some part of you felt relieved, maybe even grateful, because, when you get right down to it, you *knew*. Because there is nothing worse, no greater horror in this life, than going through it *not* knowing."

Kelly digested this silently as he stared at her from the couch.

Ellie didn't want this to be a confrontation. She crossed her legs and looked down at her stomach, pinched a strand of hair caught in the fabric of her T-shirt.

"LAPD's Blood Unit," Kelly said, "is working with a federal task force. We have a confidential informant—a high-level stickman who finds carriers and sells their names. He claims he doesn't meet the sellers, doesn't have any names for us. Yet. We can use him as your entryway into the blood world."

"You're talking undercover work?"

Kelly nodded. "How do you feel about that?"

Ellie didn't want to come across as too eager. She paused, pretending to consider the question, then said, "Sounds like a big commitment."

"It's a *major* commitment. It means giving up your life. No contact with your friends, boyfriend, anyone."

"For how long?"

"As long as it takes. The task force is after the people behind Pandora."

"We don't technically know if that product exists. We've never come across it."

"That's true. Maybe you'll find out, bring us back some hard evidence."

"Undercover," Ellie said, trying on the word and thinking about her brother. Kelly was giving her an opportunity to possibly find out what had happened to her brother. While she had no direct proof, she believed that the blood barons, as the media called them, had to have records. They had to be organized. There had to be something for her to find— there had to be.

Still, she asked the obvious question: "Why me?"

"You're young. Ambitious and smart. I need people like that. Think about it."

Kelly stood, and Ellie was about to when he said, "No, don't get up. I'll let myself out. Thanks for your time. Again, I'm sorry about what happened to Danny."

Kelly had opened the front door when she said, "No."

"There's no rush. Take as much time as you need to think it over."

"I meant no to your CI," Ellie said, thinking about the photograph of Anton Kuzmich tacked to her corkboard. "I know a better way in."

CHAPTER 11

SEBASTIAN'S MAIN COMPETITORS in the luxury real estate market were the big-box firms with main and satellite offices located inside swanky towers and strategic storefronts situated in primo locations like Wilshire and Sunset Boulevard. They paid enormous rents, had high overhead, and employed fleets of agents and support staff. They fought one another like starving orphans battling over table scraps.

Sebastian stayed out of the fray by taking a different approach to his business: a referral-based boutique agency that operated out of a three-floor, six-thousand-square-foot home in a quiet neighborhood in Beverly Hills. He owned the home free and clear, because he had no desire to build his company into a mighty global empire like Sotheby's, which was why the industry barely paid any attention to him, even when last year he sold a seventy-five-million-dollar French Palladian in Beverly Hills that had been on the market for almost three years.

Which was exactly how Sebastian wanted it, flying under the radar, so he could focus on his true business.

Operating out of a house, in a rich, quiet neighborhood, had been Frank's idea, mainly because he had insisted, even when they started out together, on living wherever he worked. Frank explained that he didn't like leaving "the kids"—his name for the computer servers he owned and operated—or any other computer equipment alone at night, vulnerable to theft and, worse, corporate espionage. Sebastian suspected the real reason had to do with the fact that Frank didn't care much for people.

Sebastian, covered in sweat in spite of his Jaguar's air-conditioning, parked in the driveway. He hadn't wanted to drive—hadn't wanted to do anything except lie on his office floor, because, oh sweet, merciful Jesus, sitting up, let alone standing, shot up his spine enormous bolts of pain that exploded like lightning inside his head, made his lungs feel like they were being squeezed to death. As much as he wanted to stay home, he needed to be gone in case the police showed up.

Sebastian parked, and killed the engine, catching his reflection in the rearview mirror. *I look like some junkie going through withdrawal,* he thought. No sooner had he pushed open the Jaguar's door than the front door of the house swung open and here came Frank bolting down the stairs, dressed as sharp and slick as a powerful Hollywood mogul—black suit and a dark blue shirt with French cuffs with a pair of gold cuff links, a Christmas gift from Trixie. Frank always wore long-sleeved shirts, even at the beach, even though he was in great shape, his six-foot frame sinewy with muscle. The reason, Sebastian suspected, had to do with the burn marks clearly left from cigarettes along his arms and back. Frank had never explained who had burned him, or why, but he took great pains to keep his scars hidden.

Frank helped him out of the car and to his feet. Sebastian lurched, his knees buckling; Frank grabbed him quickly.

"Put your arm over my shoulder," Frank said. Sebastian did, and it reminded him of the old days after prison, drinking to the point where he could barely walk or talk. A good majority of times, Sebastian had blacked out. Frank was always there to pick up the pieces.

"Still no signal from Paul's phone," Frank grunted as they made their way toward the house. "Either he shut the power off or he ditched it. But if he's still using the phone, the moment it comes on we'll get his signal and track down his location."

Provided Paul stays on the phone for at least a minute, Sebastian thought.

Frank had GPS trackers and listening devices installed on the phones of every single person who worked for them, and he conducted monthly audits of everyone's calls, texts, and emails, and even the websites they visited.

Sebastian staggered into the house with Frank, grateful for the air-conditioning. The first floor was used as the main lobby and had minimal office space, most of the exterior walls in the back of the house made of glass. Frank eased him into the modern-looking sofa, which looked uncomfortable as hell, and was. Sebastian lay back and the pain cut itself in half and he felt like he could breathe somewhat normally again.

"Just the ribs?" Frank asked.

"I think so."

"I reached out to Maya. She's on her way. I'll get you some water."

Water? I want a Scotch, Sebastian felt like screaming. *In fact, give me the goddamn bottle.* A gallon of booze followed by a handful of Percs or Oxy from Dr. Dawson's goody bag would hit the spot.

Neither Frank nor Maya would help him out that way, the two of them having been instrumental in getting him into detox and then AA to treat his alcoholism. He had never been a pill guy, but taking any kind of narcotic painkiller would free his addiction from its cage. Within a week, maybe even a couple of days, he would be back to the old Sebastian.

He had to resist the urge, no matter how great the pain. He needed to keep his mind sharp and focused so he could find Paul. Finding Paul and playing around with all the wonderful ways to torture him would be immensely more satisfying than a drink or a drug.

Sebastian licked his lips. Swallowed. "Get me some Tylenol—and some Advil."

He wiped the sweat from his eyes and then closed them, felt the pain clawing at his nerves, digging its talons into the soft meat of his brain. He tried focusing on Paul as he listened to Frank's footfalls, and then Sebastian was thinking about Frank living upstairs, alone, and wondered—and not for the first time—if Frank ever felt lonely.

Ava came to him again. Not surprising, as she had been on his mind all day. Ava had been his last thought when he sank through the water, sure he was dying. He didn't need a shrink to explain why: Ava was unfinished business. She had been the love of his life, and that life had been stolen from him because of a three-for-one taco special at the local Jack in the Box.

The two of them had gone there to eat before hitting a friend's house party in the neighborhood. There had been a lot of people there—a lot of friends—and he lost track of Ava for a while. When he finally found her, she asked him to leave; the food wasn't sitting right, and she thought she was going to be sick.

Ava lived a few blocks away. The short walk turned into a long one, Ava nauseated, sometimes stopping to catch her breath, convinced she had food poisoning. She threw up once, then twice, Sebastian encouraging her to keep walking. They were almost home when a white car the size of a boat pulled against the curb. It was a beautifully restored Cadillac Fleetwood, the paint buffed to a shine. Only one person drove that car: Paco Magic, a cholo banger who stood five foot five and always wore baggy jeans and a Raiders jersey. The door opened and here came Paco Magic, gang, occult, and astrological tats running all the way up his neck and covering his shaved head, the ink so black, he looked like he'd been dipped in paint.

Paco had another cholo with him, a tall, mean-looking dude with a big, misshapen head and a busted, scarred face that reminded Sebastian of the pit bulls he'd sometimes see guarding junkyards—scarred soldier dogs missing fur and eyes. The guy wore a crisp white tank and, Sebastian could tell, was itching to administer a beatdown, when Paco Magic said, "Hey, Ava, everything okay?" Then, with a nod to Sebastian: "This *chingado* here giving you a hard time?"

Ava said she was fine, thank you—straining to be polite and respectful because Paco was a king in training, a guy who demanded respect, and his eyes were on Sebastian when he said, "I'm gonna take your beautiful *mija* home. I know where she lives." Sebastian didn't move, said nothing, his mind stuck on Paco calling him a *chingado*, a fucker. His heart was running a marathon, not from the insult but from the awful reality of being nearly face-to-face with a guy who had killed at least a dozen people, according to the streets. Selling guns was how Paco made his money—and his name.

Paco placed a hand on the small of Ava's back and smiled at Sebastian, his teeth looking gray in the dying summer light. His smile widened as he slid his hand down and gripped her ass. Ava pulled away, and she looked at Sebastian with such terror—*Don't let them take me into that car,* her expression said. *Please don't let that happen*—that Sebastian stepped in front of her. Paco Magic snorted, and Pit Bull reached around his back and underneath his shirt.

Even now, all these years later, Sebastian couldn't remember what happened next. He had blacked out in rage, but he had fragments—hitting Paco with a solid left hook he used in the boxing ring; a jab-jab-cross that sent Pit Bull collapsing back against the car, followed by an uppercut that knocked Pit Bull sideways, off his feet. What he recalled clearly, though, even now, was Ava screaming at him to stop, Ava pulling him off Paco Magic, who lay unconscious on the ground, his face unrecognizable. Pit Bull was unconscious, too; he had cracked his head open against the curb when he fell. Sebastian learned that later. That and the fact that Pit Bull's real name was Clarence Romero—Romeo, to his friends and colleagues within the LAPD. Clarence was an undercover cop assigned to gather intel on Paco Magic's gun operation.

Paco Magic should have died, the way Sebastian had gone after him. But he survived, albeit with some severe brain injuries, and while the nearly all white jury didn't care much about a gangster who now drooled when he spoke and cried when he spilled his oatmeal, they had a much different opinion on the death of a cop. The jury delivered their verdict before it was time to break for lunch: life, without the possibility of parole.

Frank came back with a bottle of ice-cold water and some Advil. Sebastian sat up, sweat popping out on his forehead as his ribs screamed in protest, like an angry mob. He dry-swallowed four Advil tablets and then chased them down with water.

Frank's phone rang. He pulled it out of his pants pocket and glanced at the screen. His eyebrows rose, which was about as expressive as Frank got.

"*Paul?*" Sebastian asked.

Frank nodded. "Take it so I can track it." He shoved the ringing phone into Sebastian's hand. "Keep him on as long as you can," he said, and then he bolted across the room, heading for the stairs that would take him to his office on the bottom floor.

Sebastian answered the call, but he didn't speak.

"Hey, Frank, how's it going?" Paul asked, sounding calm and casual, like he was calling a store to see if a certain something was in stock. "Was hoping to have a word with you."

Sebastian sucked in air, to draw back the pain, to get some strength in his voice. "Frank's unavailable, asshole. You'll have to deal with me."

"You're alive." The words came out as half laugh, half surprise. "Well . . . shit."

"Puts a wrinkle in your grand plan, I'm guessing."

"You sound like you're in a lot of pain."

He was, in fact, although what he was experiencing right now wasn't anywhere near as bad as the first time he'd gotten beaten in jail. He was working his shift in the laundry room when a group of guys—Sebastian had no idea how many or who they were, it had happened so fast— jumped him and then took turns beating the shit out of him. It shamed him, how he begged and cried for it to stop, how he continued to cry after it was over. Eventually, he forgave himself for being a *ponocha*—he was, after all, just a kid, a terrified eighteen-year-old boy, not a man, whose life had suddenly been turned upside down through no fault of his own. He had been protecting the woman he loved—and still loved, to this day.

But he wasn't that scared little boy anymore. That kid had been dead for a long, long time. Sebastian had killed and buried him.

"How badly are you hurt?" Paul asked. "You going to make it?"

Sebastian didn't answer. A spike of pain had stolen his breath. He gritted his teeth, swallowing, not wanting Paul to hear.

"Maybe this is a good thing," Paul said. "You being alive."

Sebastian sucked in a deep breath and looked past the glass walls, to the backyard. The evening sky was the color of a bruise. A window was open somewhere, and he could hear the soft, steady gurgling of the pool filter. The calming sound of the water, the beauty of the sky—it reminded him he was alive. Knowing that allowed him to separate himself from the pain; it was only temporary.

"Here's what you're going to do," Paul said. "You're going to hand over your business, and then you and Frank can take all the money you've made and go live happily ever after together. You can stay in the real estate game, too, if you want, and you can keep your house. I'll allow that."

I'll allow that. Hearing those three words sparked Sebastian's rage, took his pain and made it small. That was the wonderful thing about rage, how it clarified, boiled everything in life down to its simple, primitive elegance.

Sebastian spoke from experience, said words he knew to be true. "I will find you," he said, his voice eerily calm. He was still sweating, and the pain was still there, roaring and clawing, but his heart was no longer racing, and his words were clear. "It may take some time, maybe a lot of time and a lot of money, but I will find you."

"Then, what, you're going to kill me?" Paul chuckled.

"I'm not going to kill you. But I am going to lock you away somewhere. And each day, I'm going to come visit you. Each and every day, for the rest of your life, I'm going to personally introduce you to a new and special level of hell."

CHAPTER 12

THE NIGHT—ACTUALLY, it was morning now, well after one a.m.—was cool and silent, the only light coming from the blue water of the community underground pool. Ellie looked out into the distance, trying to make out the mountains hidden behind the darkness. She had continued drinking after the police commissioner left and she felt good and numb, all the different voices in her head finally quiet—maybe because of the whiskey, or maybe because Cody was sitting next to her, or maybe a combination of both.

They were sitting on the back porch, in a pair of cheap white plastic Adirondack chairs. They had gone through the shared relief of her being alive and in one piece and had moved on to the part where she told him about the police commissioner's late-night house call, what Kelly had asked her to do.

Cody hadn't offered his opinion—hadn't offered an opinion of any kind. Yet. He had simply listened, intently and without interruption. Now that she was finished, he remained silent, sorting through his thoughts and feelings. She felt them brewing underneath his calm exterior, radiating off him like the heat from a fire.

Cody picked up the bottle of whiskey from the small table between them and sniffed its neck. Before coming over he had changed out of his blues, into a pair of shorts, flip-flops, and a CrossFit T-shirt.

"I don't know how you can drink this," he said, his voice toneless. "Stuff smells like gasoline."

"Put it over some ice and let it sit for a moment."

"That makes a difference?"

"Yeah. All the girls like drinking it that way."

He cracked a small, faint grin, and she sensed it melting some of the tension between them.

"Sure," he said, and got to his feet, his knees cracking. "Why not?"

He returned from the kitchen with a glass packed with ice. Ellie had studied his face during their talk, and she studied it now as he poured, saw how calm it was—how calm *he* was. Like he'd already known all the key details before she had shared them. Or was he trying to be strong for her? Supportive?

"You didn't seem surprised by what I told you," she said.

"About the shooting?" Cody looked at her, perplexed. "I told you what's-her-name, Vickers, called me. By that time, I already knew most of the details. My lieutenant had already made some phone calls for me."

"I meant Kelly coming by here."

"Oh. That."

The missing pieces came together, and she straightened a bit. "You spoke to him, didn't you?"

Cody nodded. "He called me. Told me about the shooting, that you were okay. I thought it was a bit odd, the commissioner calling, and then he explained how you helped him ID the two vics in Brentwood. Then we spoke for a bit about your remarkable ability to remember shit and your interest in the blood world."

"What did you tell him?"

"That you've been interested in the inner workings of the blood world for as long as I've known you. Then he asked me if I wouldn't mind staying away from your place until he had a chance to talk to you."

"So you knew about why he was coming here. What he wanted."

Cody nodded and leaned back in his chair.

Ellie put her glass on the floor. "When, exactly," she asked, feeling a hot coil of anger digging its way behind her left eye, "were you going to tell me this?"

He caught her tone, saw the expression on her face, and said, "I wasn't *not* going to tell you, if that's what you mean. I wanted to listen to what you had to say first—see if you want to say anything at all or just—"

"He asked you for permission, didn't he? See if *you* had a problem with me going undercover."

"He didn't use those exact words."

"Oh? What words did he use?"

"Ellie, we've been in a serious relationship coming up on, what, almost two years? It's not a secret."

Ellie shook her head as she looked out into the distance, her eyes hot with anger.

"The guy was being respectful," Cody said, like it was no big deal—and to him, it wasn't. He was a privileged white male, and still, after hundreds of years—even here, in California, the most liberal and ethnically diverse state in the nation—white men were considered the ruling class. "He just wanted to see how I felt about it. Truthfully, I thought it was a pretty classy—"

"If the roles were reversed—if *you* had been the one asked to go undercover—Kelly would *not* have called me first to see how *I* felt about it. I'd have to learn it from you." She propped her bare foot on the edge of her seat and then folded her hands around her shins. "Tell me I'm wrong."

"You're not."

Ellie sucked air deeply through her nose as she shook her head. She had been one of the best shooters in her class and, while only five foot eight and weighing a little more than 130 pounds, she had shied away from *nothing*—not a single goddamn thing the academy instructors had thrown at her. Whatever came her way, she had handled it without bitching and moaning the way some of the male cadets had. And to top it off, she had handled her shit today in a real-life firefight, done everything correctly and by the book while under pressure, and—*and*—she had helped identify two victims. And yet the police commissioner had called her boyfriend to get his permission and blessing. *Hey, Cody, it's me, Mr. Police Commissioner. Need to speak to you man-to-man about the special girl in your life. I'm going to ask her to go undercover for us, but I want to see how you feel about it first, one privileged white guy to another.*

Cody sighed. "Ellie," he began.

"You don't get it. You don't understand because you're not a woman."

"You're right—I'm not. I'm a white male, which allows me all sorts of privileges—and all sorts of blind spots. I told Kelly he was talking to the wrong person."

She turned to him.

"I told him that you don't answer to me—that you're your own person. That the decision, ultimately, is yours, and yours alone. I probably should have added that I wouldn't hold any sway in your decision, because you are, without a doubt, the most stubborn person I have ever met, which is why I fell in love with you."

"That's the only reason? My pigheadedness?"

"Pretty much, yeah." Cody grinned, messing with her, and brought the glass to his lips, Ellie feeling herself relax a bit, having what was probably the first normal moment in the past twenty-four hours.

"Whoa," he said, his eyes widening.

"How's it taste?"

"Like burning."

"Have some more. It'll help you grow hair on your chest. You could use some."

Cody leaned back and crossed his legs. "I've been thinking a lot about my brothers lately. About how all three of them married women who are perfectly content, fulfilled, what have you, staying at home and raising the kids. You're the complete polar opposite. You're . . ."

"What?"

"You're . . . uncharted," Cody said. "I could spend the rest of my life with you, and while I would never be able to discover everything about you? Every day I would discover something new, and I love that. I love the *all* of you, and I—" He cut himself off and snorted. Smiled. "You know, this sounded *so* much better in my head."

"You're doing great."

Cody shot her a look that clearly said, *Bullshit*.

"I'm serious," she said. "And I appreciate what you said. But I have a question."

"Sounds serious."

"Very serious," she said. "Want to get naked?"

"Well," Cody sighed theatrically, "if you insist . . ."

"I do."

Cody got to his feet. Ellie remained seated.

"You know," he said, "this usually works better when two or more people are involved."

"Take off your shirt."

Cody looked around the gloom to see if anyone was watching.

"We're fine," Ellie said, and picked up her glass.

Cody took off his T-shirt. He had the singular most perfect chest she had ever seen on a man—powerful, square-shaped pectorals like stone slabs, the stomach and waist ridged with muscle, everything on him perfectly proportioned, none of that freaky bodybuilder shit so many guys tried to get in the gym. He took a lot of pride in his body, but he wasn't prideful.

"Come closer," she said. "I want to get a good look at you."

He stepped up in front of her, dressed in his flip-flops and shorts. Ellie crossed her legs and took a sip of her drink. Cicadas sang all around her, and she could hear Cody breathing.

"Anything else I can do for you?" he asked after a moment.

"Take everything off. Then stand right where you are. I want to sit here and admire you while I finish my drink. No," she said when Cody opened his mouth. "No talking. Just do what you're told."

Ellie woke up to bright sunlight and the tendrils of a dream in which she had survived the shoot-out, just like in real life. Cody was there, at the house, and when she went to kiss him, he recoiled and looked down at her stomach. Then she did, too, and she saw that she was bleeding from gunshot wounds covering her stomach and chest. When she looked up, Cody was gone.

She blinked away, heard running water; Cody was in the shower. The door was cracked open, the bathroom full of steam.

"Hey," she called out from the bed, the dream starting to fade but not the cold, empty feeling it had left in its wake. "You want to grab breakfast?"

"Yeah, but not at the diner down the road."

"I love that place."

"I don't like the way they cook the bacon. Too soggy."

"Don't shut the water off. I'll jump in after you're done."

"Why not come in now? I'll wash your front and you can wash my back."

"Be right there."

As Ellie got out of bed, it amazed her that a guy who was so incredibly organized when it came to his life could be such a slob, never making the bed and always leaving his clothes on the floor—something he knew bothered her. How hard was it to fold a pair of shorts and a T-shirt? She picked up his shorts and in the front pocket caught sight of what looked like a black felt jeweler's box.

Ellie was so exhausted and hungover, the thought swam away from her. When it came back, when she realized what might be in the box, she reached inside his pocket, her mind taking her back to last night, that business about his married brothers, Cody saying how much he loved her.

Had he been planning on proposing to her?

She found the answer sitting in the small box: an emerald-cut diamond ring.

If Ellie were a different woman, she'd call the commissioner and politely decline the undercover assignment—and, most certainly, any future spot on the Blood Unit. She loved Cody and supposed, even though she hadn't given it much thought up until this moment, that she did, in fact, see a future with him. But if she went undercover, it would cost her months—maybe even a year or more—of her life.

Would he wait that long? Could their love survive that?

What if it didn't?

The ring was a choice. Cody or J.C. Pick one.

In the end, Ellie made the choice she had always made: her brother. She wouldn't abandon him again.

Thy Will Be Done

ELLIE UNPACKED HER groceries in the kitchen of her studio apartment. She had been living in it for three months.

She listened to the satellite news on her phone, the anchorman talking about the wildfires raging across the state. They had brought out the Bible-thumpers. They were out protesting in droves, ranting and raving about how God's judgment was upon them, punishing the sinners in California, the modern-day Sodom and Gomorrah.

Her smartphone chirped once. A text had been delivered. She glanced down at the counter.

The text was from the dry-cleaning-and-laundry service located two blocks from her building in Culver City. Her dry cleaning was ready for pickup.

The text was addressed to Faye.

That was her name now, Faye Simpson. Faye had an interesting back-story: she was twenty-four, born and raised in Las Vegas, and, until recently, had been a degenerate gambler. Faye's thing was blackjack. She was a good but not great cardplayer and had racked up sizable debts before deciding, nearly one year ago, to tap the remaining equity from her dying mother's small home—money her mother was using to pay for hospital and medical bills. Faye headed to the casinos, determined to win big and settle all of her accounts.

Faye lost every single penny.

Which forced her to come clean to her mother—not just about the money she'd technically stolen from the home equity line but also about the fact that she was addicted to gambling and now into the casinos for big, big money. Her mother had died heartbroken and disappointed in her daughter. Faye had hit rock bottom.

Faye had promised her dying mother she would get her act together, and she did. She religiously attended Gamblers Anonymous meetings in the basement of a Mormon church, and, working several jobs, paid off the loan from the funeral home to bury her mother and went on a payment plan with her creditors. When she had saved up a good amount of money, she packed up and headed to Los Angeles to search for a new beginning—and better earning opportunities.

Ellie's attention was locked on the last line in the text: "Have a wonderful day!" An undercover LAPD officer worked at Clean & Dry. The word *wonderful* was code for her to drop whatever she was doing and meet her handler *now*. Something critical had happened—something that required a face-to-face.

Ellie went back to unpacking her groceries, taking her time—had to, because there was a strong possibility she was being watched right now. The LAPD believed her apartment, one of several Anton owned through various shell companies, was bugged with hidden mikes and cameras. It made sense. Anton had insisted she live here, and there was also the matter of the smartphone Anton had given her—the same model he gave to all his stickmen. Her phone, an Enigma Black, a model developed by BlackBerry and Enigma, the world's top encryption company, was the same type used by spy agencies. Hers, the FBI had told her, came preloaded with special government-level covert software that turned it into a roving hot mike, allowing Anton to listen in whenever he wanted and, if he were so inclined, remotely turn on the phone's camera. Every text and email she sent or received, every single phone call and every website she visited, was captured and recorded.

And because Anton required his people to have their fancy government phones on them at all times, he knew not only where they were at a given moment but also where they traveled throughout the day, the phone providing real-time GPS tracking information. Her new friends on the combined LAPD/FBI task force had discovered all sorts of interesting things about the technology Anton used to keep a close eye on his stickmen.

Live your life as though you're on the world's biggest movie set, her handler, Roland Bauer, had told her. *Always stay in character, because someone is either watching or listening to you every single second of your day.*

After Ellie finished with the groceries, she took her time straightening up a bit; then she grabbed her purse and a light white cashmere sweater and headed out. The weather was pleasantly cool but not cold. Christmas decorations were on display in store windows.

As she walked, she thought about Cody, wondered what he was up to right now, whether she was on his mind. She hadn't seen or spoken to him in four months. No contact was allowed during what Roland called her burn-in period, to establish Faye Simpson's cover, and she realized, again, just how much she missed him.

Her destination wasn't Clean & Dry but a place three blocks away, a bar called the Alibi. Entering the bar was like walking through a time portal into the late 1990s: wood-paneled walls holding framed covers of vinyl records; autographed photos of dead actors and singers from insanely popular boy bands and the pioneers of a rock music category called "grunge"; and everywhere you looked, sprinkled on the shelves behind the bar and on the walls, these small stuffed animals called Beanie Babies. Everything old was new again, recycled like the movies, as though no one was happy with the present, everyone wanting to retreat into the past, when life had been simpler, maybe.

She was surprised to find the place so busy at three o'clock; then again, it was Friday. A pair of private security guards carrying ominous-looking Shockwave rifles, which fired nonlethal electrified rounds, manned the front door and watched the patrons to make sure no one got stuck with a needle.

The sight of the guards didn't disturb her. Like everyone who lived in LA, she had gotten used to seeing them in bars, restaurants, malls, hospitals, airports—everywhere, even libraries. Still, she couldn't escape the reality that she and everyone else in California were now living in a new version of the Wild West—only cowboys now drove cars and carried futuristic-looking shotguns and pistols.

Roland Bauer sat in his usual spot in the back, at the far end of the long bar, watching football highlights on ESPN on the wall-mounted TV directly across from him. He didn't look at her as she approached, and she didn't look at him.

What she did look at was what he was drinking: a bottle of Molson. A bottled beer meant she hadn't been followed, that it was safe to approach.

Anton's men had followed her a lot in the beginning, during those first few months when she had started working for him as a stickman. He'd had her thoroughly vetted, and while the backstory of Faye Simpson had added up, as Police Commissioner Kelly had promised her, repeatedly, that it would, it didn't mean Anton trusted her. So he put people on her, to watch as she went about sticking people, finding out if they were carriers. Crowded places that served booze—bars, nightclubs, and concerts—these places had been her hunting grounds because, Anton had explained, they were the safest, the people there often so drunk or on their way to it that they didn't feel the needle sting from a sticker. She focused on the fat ones. They hardly, if ever, even knew they'd been pricked.

Faye Simpson had collected samples without any incident, and she had discovered two carriers. The pair were undercover federal agents. Roland had supplied her with the same sticker devices Anton used, which proved they were actual carriers. She turned the devices, along with the carriers' names and addresses, over to Anton.

Roland was still lying in wait for the moment Anton would go after them. When Anton did, the agents, tagged with special biologically implanted GPS trackers, would, hopefully, lead them to the one thing no one in law enforcement had, so far, managed to find: a blood farm.

Ellie slid into the seat beside Roland and, looking inside her purse, made sure her Enigma Black phone was tucked inside the special Faraday pouch woven into a side pocket. The pouch blocked RFID and cell signals, so she and Roland could talk privately without Anton or anyone in his crew eavesdropping.

Roland kept his attention on the highlights as he spoke. "Anton's promoting you."

Ellie read the bar menu. "To what?"

"He's found a carrier, and he wants you to help collect him."

Collecting a carrier was a big step up—a way to get closer to Anton's inner circle and, hopefully, discover the names of the big players, maybe even the names of what they called the "blood barons"—the actual heads of the blood cartels. She felt excitement—and some apprehension, too.

"One of ours?" Ellie asked, referring to the pair of undercover agents posing as carriers.

Roland shook his head. "Don't know the target's name yet," he said, "but it's a guy."

She didn't ask how he'd come across this information, because she knew Roland had bugged Anton's condo and his car. The FBI couldn't bug his phone, because it was encrypted, and Roland wasn't about to try to go the legal route and secure a wiretap, because the Feds didn't know if Anton had any judges or cops on his payroll.

Roland drank slowly from his bottle. She'd been told he'd run a ton of successful undercover ops over his nearly thirty-year federal career, and everyone spoke about him with mystical reverence—Yoda dressed in Dockers, sockless in boat shoes, and the type of bland polo shirts and buttondowns you bought at buy-one-get-one-free sales at Target. Ellie thought he deliberately picked out the clothes so he'd blend into the background, look, with his rimless eyeglasses and shaved head, like a middle-aged accountant. Get up close, though, and you could see the wiry strength in his torso and the steel in his eyes.

"It's going down tonight," Roland said, placing his empty bottle on the bar.

"How are you going to track this guy?"

"I'm working on that. You up for this?"

"Absolutely."

"Might not be able to extract you in case shit goes sideways." He took out his wallet and went through his bills, still not looking at her.

"I'm ready," Ellie said.

Roland turned his head to her. When she met his gaze, Ellie thought he seemed disturbed, maybe even sad, as if he had glimpsed into the future and had seen tonight's outcome.

The carrier's name was Mackenzie Reynolds. He was twenty-three years old, a Silicon Valley brat who had been born and raised Los Angeles. Anton had supplied her with pictures and his destination. Tonight, Mackenzie was supposedly meeting up with some friends at a trendy bar in Beverly Hills called Viva, home of the fifty-dollar martini.

Ellie worked her way through the bar, searching for her target.

Not only was the place a total sausage fest, but the guys in here, most of them in their forties and fifties, judging by the looks of them, were smug corporate types really interested in rattling off their list of financial successes, where they lived, and what kinds of cars they drove, as if laying out all these details was their ticket to getting laid. Ellie supposed it worked, though, because she saw a lot of women around her age actually reacting to this bullshit, giggling and fawning and flirting, looking to trade their bodies and youth for a lifetime free of financial worry.

Finally, she spotted him. Ellie eased up next to him and sparked up a conversation. It went well—so much so that he asked if he could buy her drinks, maybe even dinner. When she said yes he called his friends and told them that he wouldn't be able to meet up tonight.

For the next two hours, over drinks and fancy appetizers, Ellie worked overtime, pretending to be dazzled by the story of how he had used a good portion of his trust fund to successfully invest in a lot of up-and-coming start-ups, Mackenzie telling it in such a way that he expected her to drop her panties right then and there. He was good-looking and he knew it, gave off that cocky frat boy vibe, like the world had been created solely for him, and when one a.m. rolled around he pretty much *told* her she was coming back to his place for a drink.

Ellie said yes. She had to get in his pants. Her job depended on it.

Mackenzie had had too much to drink, so instead of driving he ordered an Uber. She'd had a good amount of booze herself—top-shelf bourbon, all of it paid for by McDouche, as she privately called him. During the drive, while they made polite conversation, Ellie spent most of her time inside her head, strategizing the quickest way to knock him out and get him ready for pickup.

Mackenzie had been the perfect gentleman at the bar and in the car. That changed the moment they entered his house, which wasn't really a house but a mansion in Bel Air. There was no way a twenty-three-year-old dickwad could have afforded such a palatial estate. He took her to the pretentiously titled "drawing room," complete with its own bar and a pool table. Ellie saw her opening and took over the bartending duties.

"Sit," she said. "Tell me what you like."

"Right now I'd like for you to slip out of that dress you're wearing." His smile was more creepy than confident, although Ellie suspected it had worked on a fair share of women with low self-confidence and major daddy issues. "But I'll settle for a Scotch whisky on the rocks. The Glenmorangie."

"I'm seeing, like, five bottles with that name."

"Go with the 1981 Pride, the Highland single-malt Scotch whisky. And only use two cubes. You don't want to water it down. That's primo stuff—and expensive."

As Ellie poured the drinks, her hands carefully concealed from his view, she slipped into his glass the pair of white tablets Anton had supplied her. She had taken them from her purse, back at the bar, right before they left. The Rohypnol dissolved easily and quickly.

Ellie sat down next to him on a stiff sofa, the kind designed more for looks than for comfort. As they sipped their drinks, he let her in on his latest venture with some company that she had no interest in. Ellie nodded politely, keeping an eye on his glass. She needed him to drink it all for the pills to work, but all he did was keep sipping.

He put his glass down and made his move.

Shit. Ellie playfully stuck out her foot, put her stiletto on his stomach, and, smiling coyly, said, "How about we make a toast first?"

"To what?"

"To a night that's gonna blow your mind."

"I'll drink to that," he said, and did.

"I need to use the bathroom for a moment."

The one off the drawing room seemed like the size of her entire apartment, and everything in there was immaculately clean. She removed the phone from her purse and sent a text to the gangly Asian guy who had picked her up this evening and driven her to Viva. She had met him several times; he supplied her with sticks, and she supplied him with the names of carriers. She didn't know his name. Never would.

Ellie waited five minutes, making a show of flushing the toilet and running the water before she left.

McDouche was still awake, standing at the bar, waiting for her.

"One more drink," she said.

He grabbed her firmly by the shoulders and pushed her up against the wall and kissed her. The kiss was rough and sloppy, and he mashed his teeth against hers. She tensed—not only from the implied violence in it and the way he was groping at her but also because she couldn't stop thinking of Cody.

McDouche sensed her hesitation. He relaxed his grip and moved to her neck, kissing it, and when he reached her ear, his breath hot and smelling sweet from the Scotch, he whispered, "Don't worry—my mom's not home."

Ellie almost laughed out loud. "Your mom?"

"Yeah. She's in Palm Springs for the weekend. We have the whole house to ourselves."

"You live here with your mom?"

"I work out of here when I'm in town. Have my own office upstairs."

She was about to ask him another question when he kissed her hard. Not the way Cody did with care and affection but simply out of lust, like she owed him this. She decided to play along for the moment, moaning at the appropriate times, trying to act as though this were the single most exciting sexual encounter of her life.

When he reached around and fumbled at the zipper of her dress, she whispered, "Let's go upstairs and hit the shower."

"No shower." He unzipped her dress.

"Let's go upstairs, then, to your bedroom."

The dress slid off her shoulders. Ellie panicked. The kissing and the way he pawed at her—she could justify those things because she was do-ing a job. But there was no way in hell she was going to sleep with him; no way in hell was she going to allow that to happen.

The dress pooled around her shoes. He stepped back to appraise her, Ellie standing there wearing her heels, panties, and a lace bra.

"Nice," he said. "*Very* nice."

He dropped to his knees in front of her. The drugs were kicking in. *Thank you, Jesus.*

His eyes grew wide and then he started blinking rapidly as he looked around, confused.

"Everything okay, baby?" Ellie asked, cringing inwardly at the word *baby*. He struggled to his feet. She helped him.

"I've got, like, vertigo or something," he said.

"Probably drank a little too much. Let me get you some water."

She helped him out from behind the bar, holding on to his meaty bicep as he staggered and swayed. Then he dropped to his knees. She let go, and he tumbled sideways, against the floor. She rolled him onto his back so he could breathe better.

He was stone-cold out, but his erection was still standing tall, at full mast.

"Mackenzie? Can you hear me?"

He didn't answer. She hurried to her purse.

Before venturing out tonight, Ellie had collected a package from a secure drop. The package contained a syringe but no needle. She didn't need to inject him; she needed him to swallow the syringe's contents.

Quickly, Ellie shot the silvery liquid down into his throat. McDouche coughed a bit, then swallowed the latest advance in tracking: nanotechnology. Microscopic nanobots, normally used to deliver targeted drugs in the bloodstream, gave off a radio signature that allowed doctors to track their locations inside the body. The nanotechnology was currently being developed to turn people—kids and older parents suffering from dementia—into a walking biological GPS so they could be found in short time.

Currently, the range was limited. Less than a hundred feet. That was Roland's problem now, not hers. She grabbed her phone and made the call to Anton's man.

"He's all yours," she said when the phone on the other end of the line was picked up.

"Heard a lot of moaning in there," the humorous voice replied. It belonged to her direct report—Nameless Asian, as Roland referred to him. "*Papi* show you a good time?"

How the hell did he hear the moaning? The answer broke through her pickled brain: her phone. The phone Anton had given her was bugged. Someone was always listening, always tracking her movements.

"Cameras?" Nameless Asian asked.

"One by the gate, another two near the front door. You want me to see if I can find the security system?"

"No, we'll take care of it. Go unlock the front door—and kill as many lights as you can."

"What about the gate? He used his phone to unlock it, and I don't know the password."

"We'll take care of it."

Ellie got dressed and shut off as many inside lights as she could. The outside lights were a different matter. She found the ones for the front door, but the lights on the front yard were solar powered. She couldn't do anything about those.

Ten minutes later, while she was drinking a glass of water in the cool silence of the kitchen, she heard the front door open. Three men dressed in black, their faces covered in balaclavas, like they were bank robbers, stepped into the foyer and looked around, studying the layout. The tallest of the trio, a man with Asian-shaped eyes, said to her, "Where is he?"

Ellie didn't recognize his voice. "Passed out in the drawing room," she said.

"The *what*?"

"The big room with the bar and pool table." She pointed to the hall. "Last room on the right—you can't miss it. He told me he had an office upstairs."

The other two dropped their bags and rushed down the hall. After removing Mackenzie from the house, they'd go through his phone and his office computer or computers. Right now Anton had another crew at Mackenzie's Silicon Valley condo, doing the exact same thing, everyone working well into the night getting to know all about Mackenzie's online life—passwords for his banking and investment accounts, everything.

Once Mackenzie had been shipped off to his new life as a donor, Anton would assume control of all of his accounts, and electronically transfer his money through a series of sophisticated encrypted wire transfers, making it look like Mackenzie had, for reasons unknown, cashed out and disappeared. Anton had developed this side gig, flushing as much money out of rich carriers as he could.

Ellie said, "You want me to stick around and help?"

"Nah, we're good. Go ahead and take off."

"You sure? I don't mind."

"You did good work tonight," he said. "Now it's time for you to go."

CHAPTER 14

SEBASTIAN PARKED IN a shady spot near a massive rock formation that reminded him of something you'd find on, say, Mars—boulders red and orange and alien looking. For all intents and purposes, this place might as well have been another planet. Human life couldn't exist for too long here in Death Valley, the hottest and driest place on earth. Rain rarely made an appearance—maybe two inches of water per year, if that—and the temperatures could reach 130 degrees or more during the summer months. Today was a fine December morning, not a cloud in the sky, and according to the digital temperature reading on the Cadillac Escalade's dash, it was already ninety-seven degrees—and it wasn't even ten yet.

He killed the engine, and the AC with it, and when he opened the door he stepped into an oven of dead air and dry heat. He was alone. An added bonus of choosing this spot was the fact that park rangers didn't come here, the area too remote and too dangerous. The access road he'd just traveled hadn't been used in well over half a century, and during the bumpy drive across the unmaintained dirt road he'd traveled for the better part of an hour, he hadn't passed a single car or person.

Gravel crunched beneath his loafers and coated them and the cuffs of his jeans in a fine white dust as he made his way to the hatchback. He opened it and unlocked the latch for the hidden compartment used for transporting blood clients back and forth in secrecy from their homes to the transfusion center.

But the man in the compartment wasn't a client. Lincoln Miller worked for Sebastian's only supplier for carriers. Link, as everyone called him, was a "runner"; he supervised a group of stickmen and, on a handful of occasions, ran the operations to abduct carriers.

Link's eyes shut hard against the sudden sunlight. He wore a pair of long, baggy gym shorts, nothing more, and his wrists and ankles were bound with plastic cuffs, which would have made it hard for him to fight—not that the young buck had the strength. Like Paul, Link was obsessive about bodybuilding, but his three months in the dark, subsisting on a glass or two of water and a handful of almonds per day, had wasted away all his gains in the gym. Now he looked shriveled and pathetic, as harmless as a prune.

Sebastian reached inside and hefted the kid out of the compartment. He propped Link up, into a sitting position, on the back bumper. Link couldn't keep his head up, so he rested it against the side of the hatchback's frame. His lips were cracked, full of bleeding blisters, and his tongue was swollen—all a result of dehydration. Sebastian had put a stop order on the water a few days ago, and Link hadn't eaten anything solid in about a week.

Sebastian used his arm to wipe the sweat from his forehead as he went to retrieve the paper bag from Whole Foods. He placed the bag next to Link, then opened a bottle of water, glad that Frank had hosed Link down back in LA before loading him into the car. The kid had smelled ripe beyond belief.

"Drink it slowly," Sebastian said, placing the bottle in Link's hands. "If you drink it too fast, you'll throw it back up."

Link didn't gulp the water, but he held the bottle against his mouth like a baby, sucking at it, grateful. When he finished, Sebastian gave him another bottle. By the time he finished that one, almost twenty minutes

later, Link looked a bit more alert, his gaze skittering across the landscape of latte-colored mountains, the sunbaked valley floor as white as
table salt.

"Beautiful place, isn't it?" Sebastian said.

Link didn't answer.

"Ever been to Death Valley?"

Link shook his head. It seemed like a massive effort.

Sebastian reached into the bag, came back with a cellophane-wrapped
sandwich. "Chicken salad," he said. "You want?"

Link eyed it with lust. "No, thank you," he croaked.

"This isn't a trap or test or some shit. You need to eat, so eat. There're
a couple of other sandwiches in the bag—a turkey club and some Italian
or Mediterranean thing. Didn't know what you liked, so I grabbed more
than one. There's some more water in there, too. Help yourself."

"I don't know anything about Paul."

Sebastian took a bite of his sandwich. He had invested a significant
amount of money into finding Paul, and yet, with all the extra manpower, with all the resources at his disposal, had come up with only two
leads—one of them being Link, who hadn't been working the afternoon
Sebastian went for a swim in his pool.

Link, Sebastian was sure, knew *something*. Paul had worked directly
with Link, learning how stickmen worked, the ins and outs of finding
and supplying carriers—but through it all, Link had stuck to the same "I
don't know shit" script.

"If I knew anything—*anything*," Link said, some strength coming
into his voice, "I would've told Frank. I told him everything I know,
which isn't much."

Sebastian nodded, chewing, and eyed the burn marks covering Link's
chest, arms, and legs. Frank was a big fan of some electric torture developed over in Chile, had gotten solid results with it in the past. Sebastian
never stuck around to see how it worked. He couldn't stomach the way a

man lost control of his bodily functions, was reduced to a childlike state, begging for the pain to stop. Link, Sebastian saw, was staring at him that way right now.

No one's looking for you, Sebastian wanted to say. It was true. Link had no steady girlfriend and he didn't keep in touch with his parents, who lived in upstate Washington. Link had several friends in LA, but not a single one of them knew he'd been MIA for months; Sebastian knew this because he had access to Link's phone and email accounts.

The City of Angels attracted a lot of guys who had barely any ties to their families—guys who wanted a fresh start from their former lives. They made good employees, especially from an administrative standpoint. In the event that they had to disappear, not too many people came around asking questions. People floated in and out of LA all the time.

Sebastian took out another sandwich and unwrapped it. "You and Paul were tight, right?"

"We weren't, like, you know, bros or anything."

"But you hung out a lot together outside of work." Sebastian placed the turkey club on Link's lap. "Hit the gym and bars, took in some ball games."

"But I didn't *know* the guy."

"What did you guys talk about?"

"Just, you know, stuff. General stuff like workouts, broads, and baseball. Fun clubs and bars. Shit like that. I told all this stuff to Frank."

Frank had put people in and around all the bars and clubs Link had told Frank about, hoping to catch a glimpse of Paul. So far, nothing.

Link said, "Like I said, I didn't *know* the guy. Our conversations weren't deep or anything—he never shared, like, his future plans. Dreams or goals. It was, you know, all surface. You're his father—"

"I'm not his father."

The heat in Sebastian's tone made Link flinch.

Link pieced off a bit of the sandwich. When he placed it in his mouth, he looked like he was going to break down and cry in relief and gratitude.

"All I'm saying is that if anyone knows the real Paul, it's, you know, probably you."

Not true, Sebastian thought, chewing. What he hadn't fully realized until the weeks following his attempted assassination was just how little he knew about Paul and his personal life—which, truth be told, came as something of a surprise. Paul had lived under his roof until he was nineteen, when he joined the Marines, and during those years Paul had had an active social life. So when Paul disappeared after the shooting, Sebastian assumed Paul's friends and all the contacts on his phone would lead him to wherever Paul was holed up—or, at the very least, provide crumbs of information that would eventually lead to his location.

He was wrong.

Not only had Paul not been in touch with most of his old crew for months, if not years (some, Sebastian had been told, were surprised to find out Paul was back in LA), but the ones Paul did keep in touch with didn't have much to offer.

As for the people in Paul's current life, who they were, Sebastian's investigators had no idea. His people had scoured Paul's phone records, his computers and email accounts, and hadn't found anything useful. Sebastian couldn't help. Paul never talked about his personal life and Sebastian never asked, because, quite frankly, he didn't care. Up until the point when the son of a bitch tried to have him killed, Paul had been nothing more than an ugly piece of furniture—something Sebastian had to endure for living with Trixie.

Link was saying something to him. Sebastian turned to him and said, "I'm sorry—can you repeat that? I didn't quite catch it."

"I said Paul is unknowable. Doesn't tell you much in the way of what he's thinking from one moment to the next."

You got that right. "So you didn't know anything about Paul taking Simone's blood or that he might be thinking of setting up his own shop. You're still maintaining that position."

"Mr. Kane—"

"Oh, it's 'Mr. Kane' now."

"—if I knew anything—*anything*—or if I suspected something? I would've brought it immediately to Frank's attention."

Sebastian took another bite of his sandwich.

"You've been real good to me," Link said. "I love my job, and I've got a great life, and it's all because of you. First time in my life, I'm happy. Why would I want to screw that all up?"

Sebastian said nothing, chewing his food.

"I'm telling you the truth," Link said, his voice breaking. "You've got to believe me."

Sebastian looked out across the flatland, the expanse of it, and it made him feel small. Insignificant.

"Tell me about Ferreria."

"Who?"

"Sixto Ferreria. Everyone calls him Six," Sebastian said, turning to him, Link acting all *huh?* "I know you two have met."

"I don't recognize the name, I swear."

"He's one of Frank's Internet guys. Ferreria does a lot of . . . maintenance work, I guess you could call it, on our servers. He's around your age, about six feet, beer gut, shaped like a potato."

"I'm not good with names. I'm, you know, more visual. You got a picture?"

Sebastian shook his head and took another bite. "You know what's really interesting about Ferreria? He was into competitive rifle shooting back in high school. He was so good, the NRA offered him scholarship money for college. Guy was one hell of a marksman. I'm sure Paul mentioned him to you."

Link looked weary. Despondent.

"The day Paul tried to have me killed," Sebastian said. "A couple of hours later, he sent you a text that said, 'Plan went south. Meet me at the place we discussed, and we'll *all* regroup.'"

"I know. I *know* he did, but I swear to God, I had no idea what it meant. I told Frank—"

"You didn't text Paul back, though. Or call."

"Right, because I thought the text was for someone else. You know how you sometimes accidentally do that, right? You're in a rush, make a mistake, whatever. So I just, you know, ignored it."

"See, my operating theory is that Paul has to have people working for him besides that lone shooter in my neighbor's window," Sebastian said. "And Paul's text—he says we'll *all* regroup. Right there, that tells me there's got to be at *least* three guys involved in this."

"What did this Ferreria guy have to say?"

"This is about you. Paul sent that text to *you*. And Ferreria."

"I don't know him, never met him, I swear."

"But you just said you're not good with names."

"I'm not. I—"

"So it's possible you could have met him."

Link's gaze turned inward on some private thought. Or secret.

"All I want is the truth," Sebastian said.

Link closed his eyes and, shaking, took in a deep breath of air.

Sebastian ate the last bite, spoke around the food. "Give me the truth, my man, and the good Lord shall set you free."

Link began to sob, his chest heaving, but he couldn't produce any tears on account of the dehydration.

"You seem like a bright kid—a good kid," Sebastian said. "Paul is a psycho piece of shit. I always suspected he was, truth be told—and I brought him into this. That's on me. I take full responsibility for that. What I don't understand, Link, is why you're protecting—"

"I'm *not*. Don't you see? I'm the—I'm that thing there, the whatchamacallit—the herring. The red herring."

"The what?"

"The diversion," Link said. "You're focusing all of your energy on me, so you're not out there looking for him."

"Oh, we're looking for him—don't you worry. And we *will* find him. What I'm hoping is you'll come to your senses, tell us what we need to—"

Link slid off the back bumper, like he was going to faint or something, only he dropped to his knees, in the sand.

Sebastian opened a bottle of water. Christ, it was hot out here.

"Please." The kid clutched Sebastian's leg and looked up at him, squinting. "Please," he said again, and then he swayed, looking like he was going to pass out. Instead, he leaned forward and grabbed Sebastian by the ankle, Link resting his forehead on his loafer and speaking into the dirt as he cried, "I swear to God, I'm telling you the truth. You've got to believe me. I'm *begging* you."

Sebastian did believe him. Unfortunately. The kid had stuck to this story from day one, through all the torture and sleep deprivation and hunger. Coming here, treating Link like a human being again, showing him some kindness and giving him food and water while he looked out at the vast desert and, hopefully, pondered his fate—Sebastian hoped it would spur the kid into finally giving up what he knew about Paul. Maybe Link couldn't give anything because he didn't have anything *to* give.

Well, shit, Sebastian thought, and reached down and helped Link to his feet.

"My mother?" Sebastian said, propping Link back up on the rear bumper. "She was a real religious woman. I grew up with God from the Old Testament, the one who was constantly pissed off at everything that was happening in His world, and it *was* His—that grouchy ol' prick didn't let you forget it for a *second*. Still, back then? He was more in-volved, you know? Seemed to really relish playing the strict father who came home and was like, 'What shit have you done now?'"

Sebastian sat on the bumper next to Link. "Then He sends His own kid down, hoping Jesus will somehow drill it into our heads how to live our lives, and what do we do? We crucify him. Jesus is hanging there in agony, right? Looks to the sky and says, 'Why hast thou forsaken me?' but what he's really saying is, 'After all the shit I've done for you, all the sac-rifices I made—*this* is how you thank me? Really?'"

Sebastian shook his head, looking up at the cloudless blue sky. "What always struck me was that his father either wasn't listening or just didn't give a shit anymore and split, which is kind of sick when you really stop to think about it. Fathers split all the time. I get it—mine did—but if your kid's in agony and you have the power to stop it and you don't? You have to be a real sick son of a bitch to do that—am I right?"

Link, who had been sobbing quietly, wiped at his face even though he didn't have any tears.

"I'd sit there in church," Sebastian said, "listening to the priest going on and on about God's love and mercy, and I'd be staring at Jesus all life-sized and hanging on the cross and thinking, Well, I'm screwed. He let his own kid die in agony, so what chance do I have?" He turned to Link. "That's why people need to stick together, help each other out, be compassionate. Because He sure as hell isn't going to do it for us."

Sebastian stood and reached into his jeans pocket, came back with a small folding knife. He popped Link's bindings, then handed him the other sandwich and another bottle of water and said, "Maybe you're right about Paul using you as a diversion. Problem for me is that it's created, you know, reasonable doubt about your loyalties."

"Please, you've got to—"

"I do. I do believe you. But I'm still going to have to let you go. I can only work with people I trust one hundred percent. And I can't trust you one hundred percent. Not your fault, okay. But I'll always have that nagging doubt in the back of my mind, and I can't have that type of distraction, especially given everything that's going on. Stand up."

Link did, reluctantly, his attention locked on the knife gripped in Sebastian's hand.

Sebastian folded the knife, slid it back in his pocket. "This trail we're standing on? You're going to be on it for ten or so miles. I know that's a lot, especially in this heat, and barefoot, but you got water and food, so you should be fine."

Sebastian slammed the hatchback shut and took out his keys. "Keep walking until you find a white Toyota. It's unlocked. Keys are under the front mat. I put a case of water in the trunk, along with more than enough cash to get you set up somewhere. But it won't be in California, understand? Frank finds out you're alive? He'll kill you."

Link stood there, most of him covered in a fine white dusting of dirt, and eyed him nervously, his brain working overtime, trying to figure out where the trap was.

"This is where you say thank you," Sebastian said.

"Thank you, Mr. Kane. Thank you."

"You're welcome. And I'm sorry for what we put you through. I know *sorry* doesn't quite cover everything I've done, but it's all I got, so it'll have to do." Sebastian spun his keys around a finger, squinted as he looked up at the sky. "Better get moving before it gets too hot."

Sebastian started the Escalade and sighed in relief when he felt the air-conditioning. He turned around and drove past Link, heading back up the access road, and when he glanced in the rearview mirror he saw Link staring after him, skeptical and confused, like he couldn't believe he'd gotten his life back. He was God's problem now, and Sebastian knew God wouldn't look after poor Link, would let him die of dehydration. There was no car waiting for him, no trunk full of money and water, but still, he had given Lincoln Miller hope, and at the end of the day, wasn't hope the greatest gift you could give someone?

When Sebastian got a signal on his phone, he called Frank.

"Let me guess," Frank said. "He stuck to his story."

"That he did. Said he never met Ferreria, has no idea who he is."

"Ferreria said the same thing about Link."

"Are you still sure—"

"Yes," Frank said, drawing out the word, annoyed. "I'm one hundred percent positive Ferreria didn't access any critical information on our servers and give it to Paul. Like I explained to you, what, a hundred times now, Ferreria didn't have root access. He just did regular maintenance work."

"You also told me the kid was an IT whiz. One of the best. And a hacker."

"No one has accessed our servers. No one," Frank said. "Besides, our client files, test data—all that stuff is so heavily encrypted—"

"That it would take the CIA two decades to decrypt it, if they were lucky. You told me."

"And I'm telling you again, since you refuse to believe me. As for the special cocktail we use with our carrier blood, that information isn't stored on any database. Drugs we use—the only people who know about that are you, me, and Maya. We're safe—I keep telling you that."

"Link said something interesting."

"Do tell," Frank said.

"He said Paul was using him as a diversion."

"We knew that was a distinct possibility."

That we did, Sebastian thought. After Frank's crew grabbed Ferreria, Frank had had a private forensic guy perform a gunshot residue test. Ferreria's hands came back clean, but that didn't mean he *was* clean. He could have been wearing gloves. They tore up his apartment, his two cars, covered all the places he traveled—they searched everywhere for a high-powered rifle and came up empty. They searched for anything that would implicate Ferreria and came up empty.

"Ferreria and his rifle skills—I told you it was too good to be true. Too convenient," Frank said. "Still, we had to do our due diligence."

And we're still left with jack shit. "Paul's been too quiet. I don't like it. I think he's gone into production."

"Using what medications?"

"Who knows? If I were him, I'd get my hands on the old cancer drug Viramab. The Armenians still use it." The Armenians were interested in making as much money as possible, by any means possible. They didn't care about science, or the safety of their clients. *Although I'm sure as hell they'd love to get their hands on my operation.*

"Sebastian, everyone on the planet knows Viramab doesn't work."

"In the long term, no. In the short term, you can generally get good results. Paul can start transfusions, raise some money. He's going to need a shit ton of it to get up and running. I want you to break his legs."

"We'll do more than that when we find him—and we *will* find him."

"Not Paul. Ferreria. I want you to break his legs—and his arms, too, while you're at it."

"Why? For what reason?"

Sebastian told him.

After he hung up, he turned on his satellite radio and scanned through the music stations. Nothing soothed him, so he shut the radio off, went through a mental playlist of his favorite songs, picked one, and started singing, tapping his thumb against the steering wheel while praying to his Higher Power, asking for help, seeking guidance.

CHAPTER 15

EVER SINCE ELLIE had moved into the neighborhood, she had become a regular at Dinah's Café. It was here, once or twice a week, where she would meet with Jon Carlo, Faye Simpson's sponsor at Gamblers Anonymous. He had a broad back and a stringy black beard that, combined with his dark skin, made him appear as someone from the Middle East when, in fact, he had grown up in East LA, with his Cuban father and Puerto Rican mother. That was all she knew about him. That and the fact that he worked in some undercover capacity for the LAPD.

Dinah's was small, cash only, and while it had the traditional decor she associated with all the diners she remembered from her childhood—the red vinyl booths arranged around windows, the counter made of gray linoleum from another century, the thick white coffee mugs that seemed indestructible—the middle of the area, with its white chairs and tables, the fresh flowers in the center, gave the place a homier, country B and B vibe. As always, the place was packed, but there was an empty stool at the counter, next to Jon Carlo.

Before she fully agreed to undertake the undercover job, Police Commissioner Kelly had repeatedly assured her every single bit of Faye Simpson's background would come back clean. Her only job was to commit to playing the role—and she had. When she wasn't working as a stickman, she attended Gamblers Anonymous meetings, where she shared Faye

Simpson's tragic but all too familiar story. Jon Carlo attended most of the meetings, approached her, and became her sponsor, and twice a week they got together to discuss how Faye Simpson was handling her gambling addiction out in the big world. Ellie played the part 24/7, because when it came to undercover work it was critical to assume you were being watched at all times.

Ellie didn't carry a purse when she wasn't working, so when she slid into the swivel chair she placed her smartphone on top of the counter, gave Jon Carlo a quick hug, and then, for the next forty minutes, over coffee and huevos rancheros, Ellie talked all about Faye Simpson's week. Ellie made up a story about how this one time Faye got herself locked into a fantasy of driving to one of the local casinos and hitting the blackjack tables, taking the meager sum of money she had saved and using it to double her proceeds so she could pay off her creditors back in Las Vegas. It was good practice, making up these stories about Faye. Keeping the lies straight was another matter entirely.

She found she was getting good at it, though. Found how much she liked being someone other than Ellie Batista.

The bill came, and of course Jon Carlo immediately snatched it. Like her, he had to commit to the role, so he asked her—Faye—about how her part-time job was going. Faye had never specified where she worked. She had told him and the other people she bumped into at the meetings how she wanted to keep her private life private. In case Anton or anyone else had been listening or watching, she and Jon Carlo had given a good performance.

When he went to hug her goodbye, awkwardly, with one arm, he deftly slipped something into her front jeans pocket. Then he kissed her on the cheek and whispered, "Make sure you use the bathroom before you go."

The diner had one bathroom and, hanging on the door, a humorous sign that always made her grin: four stick silhouette people—a man, a woman, a man/woman, and an alien—and written underneath them, in bold black letters, the word *Whatever* and underneath that, the phrase *Just wash your damn hands.* Ellie found the door unlocked. She locked it immediately once she got inside, and as she fished out the piece of paper from her pocket she caught her reflection in the mirror. It still came as a shock when she saw herself, her long and practical shoulder-length hair gone, replaced by a trendy long, angled bob that brushed against her shoulders. She was a blonde now, too, and she used makeup on a daily basis. Would Cody even recognize her?

The piece of paper Jon Carlo had given her contained a phone number she didn't recognize. No instructions.

Has to be Roland calling with an update, Ellie thought. And it was probably about the carrier she'd helped abduct the other night, Mackenzie. Roland, she was guessing, had tracked down his location, maybe even found a blood farm. *Please, God, let that be the case.*

The bathroom had a stall and a urinal. She grabbed a wad of paper towels from the dispenser, got into the stall, and after she locked the door she removed the lid of the toilet tank and placed it on the seat. Resting at the bottom of the tank was a phone wrapped in a clear waterproof utility pouch.

Out came the pouch, and after she dried it and her hands she removed the phone. She flushed the toilet to mask the sound of what she was doing: placing inside the pouch the phone Anton had given her, sealing it, and dropping the phone into the tank. Now she could talk freely without the threat of Anton eavesdropping.

Ellie dialed the number, her brain and heart racing with anticipation.

The phone on the other end was picked up immediately. "Hey."

It took her a moment to find her voice. "Cody?"

"Yeah, it's me. LAPD arranged the phone call."

Ellie was surprised by the effect hearing his voice had on her. The two of them had talked long and hard about what the undercover gig entailed, and what she was asking him to do, which was essentially putting his life on hold for her; and on their final night together, the stark reality of what was about to happen hitting them both, she saw the pained, hopeless look in his eyes and told him he didn't have to put his life on hold. If he wanted to see other women, she completely understood. It took something out of her, telling him that, and when he didn't respond it reminded her just how fragile every relationship was, that the slightest curveball could kill it or send it on a path where it would slowly decay and then die. Cody rolled over onto his side, and his eyes narrowed in thought, maybe even anger, when he said, "I'm in this with you. The job, life, whatever comes our way—I'm not going anywhere until you tell me you don't want me around. Do you still want me around?"

She said she did, thinking about the ring she'd found in his pocket and wondering if he was going to pop the question, a part of her glad he didn't. She couldn't worry about him and their life together and do her job effectively. Yet another part was sad, maybe even a bit alarmed, Ellie wondering if he had changed his mind.

Hearing his voice now, she felt overwhelmed by a sense of gratitude so powerful, it almost made her believe in that whole Prince Charming thing she'd been sold when she was a kid. It was fantasy bullshit, but she *would* live happily because she had found someone who not only understood her but also—and this was the most important part—treated her as an equal and would have her back. A man who could be taken at his word.

"Ellie? You there?"

"Yeah," she said, keeping her voice low on the off chance someone was standing behind the bathroom door, listening. "Yeah, I'm here. Sorry, it's just . . ." *I didn't realize just how much I missed you these past few months, how important and special and rare you are.* "I didn't expect— I had no idea they'd arranged a phone call with you," she said. "No one told me."

"They wanted to surprise you. They said you're doing great. Terrific, actually."

"Good. That's good to hear."

"And you're safe, right? They told me you are, but I don't know if they're blowing smoke."

"I'm fine."

"So you're not in any danger."

"No. Not at all. They're taking good care of me."

"The LAPD, you mean."

"Yeah."

"Good." She heard his breath explode against the receiver. "Good," he said again, like he was being relieved of a great burden. "They won't give me any updates."

"Protocol."

"What did you say? I can barely hear you."

Ellie flushed the toilet again, in case someone was at the bathroom door. "Protocol," she said, a little louder. "Don't take it personally."

"I'm not. Well, I'm *trying* not to." A short chuckle, and then his voice turned serious. "I thought I'd be . . . well, better at all this. Handling it better."

Out of all the men she'd met, Cody was by far the best when it came to expressing his feelings. But she sensed the hesitation in his voice, felt him fumbling for the right choice of words, and she suspected he wasn't alone, that someone was standing close by, listening to him, or maybe listening in on their conversation.

Cody said, "I keep thinking about you, wondering if you're okay, and sometimes my mind goes to a . . . I just hate not knowing, is what I'm trying to say."

"I'm sorry."

"No. No, don't be. I'm just—"

"I realize how hard this is for you. It's hard for me, too."

"You're doing a good thing."

"I think about you. Constantly."

"I'm not trying to make you feel guilty."

Her smartwatch vibrated against her wrist. It was paired via Bluetooth to her phone, so she could be alerted to incoming texts and calls. She saw that Anton was calling and her heart jumped. Anton expected you to answer his calls ASAP—and may God have mercy on your soul if you didn't.

Cody said, "The only reason I brought it up is—"

"I've got to go."

"Is everything okay?"

"Yeah. It's fine." She plunged her hand into the tank and grabbed the waterproof pouch.

"What's wrong?"

"Nothing. Work stuff. We'll talk soon."

"Okay. I love you."

Ellie didn't answer him; she had already pulled the phone away from her ear. She heard Cody's voice echo over the tiny speaker as the burner slipped from her hand and fell into the toilet.

There was no time to feel guilty. She had to answer Anton's call *now*, before it went to voicemail. One more ring, and it would.

Anton, as usual, got right to the point: "Go to Bloomingdale's at Beverly Center. Women's section. Ask for Binx. She will—"

"Blink?"

"*Binx*. B-I-N-X."

"What kind of name is that?"

"It's a *name*. Jesus, you and your questions." He sighed, his breath exploding against the receiver. Something Anton despised, his stickmen asking questions. "She will give you clothes. Meet me tonight, at eight, place called Inge in Beverly Hills."

Click, and he was gone.

CHAPTER 16

A VA LIVED IN what the people in Sebastian's business called a "dramatic contemporary." The description was certainly accurate. Her home, a modern architectural marvel of stone and glass, sat on half an acre high above Sunset Boulevard in Hollywood Hills West, and featured dramatic and stunning ocean views. Sebastian came out here, to the spot where he now stood, because it offered him a direct line of sight to the side and back of the house, with its lower-level lounge and infinity pool and space. Because the home was constructed mostly of glass that stretched from floor to ceiling, he had a good, solid view into the majority of the rooms.

He dreamed about Ava often now, their time together and the good memories—all of it had been resurrected in the days following his attempted assassination. Sebastian felt oddly reborn, and he'd had this need to search for her. After an hour's worth of work he found out she was still living in LA. He found her address.

Finding out personal, intimate stuff was trickier. Ava wasn't on any social media, which he thought was strange until he remembered how fiercely private, like he was, she had been when they were together. When they were teenagers, she'd had no desire to use her phone to post pictures and every single detail about her life for the world to see. She was still that way now, it seemed.

Her twenty-two-year-old daughter was another story. She posted *everything* about her life. Using hacks Frank had taught him years ago, Sebastian learned Ava was separated from her husband. A search of public records revealed she had divorced Charles early this year, in January.

His mother's steadfast belief in God, and all the time he'd spent with her at church, hadn't instilled much in the way of faith. If God did, in fact, exist, He was a lot like Sebastian's father—a sperm donor who had given him the gift of life and then left, never to be seen or heard from again. Then came the miracle—and it was a miracle—of getting his life sentence overturned. Then, in AA, he learned to form a God of his understanding—sort of a Build-A-Bear approach to spirituality—and what Sebastian came to believe was that things did happen for a reason. And maybe the reason behind getting shot was to wake him up to the fact that he wasn't fully living out his true life's purpose. He didn't think it was a coincidence that he'd been thinking about Ava the moment he was shot.

Ava's black Range Rover was parked in the driveway, but he couldn't find her. He kept looking, wondering what Frank would think about what he was doing. Frank would say he was insane. And maybe he was; alcoholics, by definition, were insane. Then again, wasn't love its own form of insanity? And what did Frank know about love?

Sebastian couldn't find Ava; she had to be in some other part of the house. He sighed, disappointed, about to give up when he saw someone jogging up the road in front of Ava's house—it was Ava, dressed in tight black running shorts and a matching midriff sports top, her long black hair tied back into a ponytail. Seeing her made the fist inside his chest unclench and finally relax.

She went in through a gate on the side of the yard and he lost sight of her, spotted her a moment later climbing the stairs. He lost her again, then quickly found her in the master bedroom suite she had, at one time, shared with her husband. She had already removed her running sneakers and socks. The deep red shade of nail polish on her toes matched that of her fingernails. Now she was removing her running top.

Sebastian looked away. Even though he had seen her naked before, his twice-a-week treks to this spot weren't about indulging some pervy fetish. This was about getting to know her again, so he could take the next step.

His phone rang, its bleating sounding loud in the canyon. Sebastian started—he'd forgotten to mute the goddamn ringer. He did so, not even bothering to check the caller, shoved the phone in his pocket, and went back to waiting for Ava to return from the shower.

She did, several minutes later, now dressed in a pair of boy shorts and a tank, her long jet-black hair still damp. She propped up the pillows on her king-sized bed and then, from the nightstand, grabbed the same book she'd been reading all summer—a monstrously thick trade paperback on Winston Churchill. She picked up a pair of stylish reading glasses, got herself settled on the bed, and began to read.

She had never looked more beautiful to him.

His phone rang again, vibrating. He ignored it, thinking back to the day when he walked into court for a new trial with a new judge, who reviewed the case and agreed with his lawyer's findings. *You're free to go, Mr. Kane.*

To where? Sebastian wanted to say. *To what? You took everything from me, and I have no way to get it back.*

One of the great many tenets he'd learned in AA was to let go of the past. And he had. Took him a long time to do it, but he had said goodbye to Ava—not in person but to the Ava that existed in his mind, the Ava he had carried with him through prison and then later met doing what he was doing right now, watching her from afar. And now the past had come back to him. Demanded his full attention.

Call her, an inner voice urged.

And say what? Where would he even start?

His phone rang *again*, god*dammit*, and he pulled away the binoculars and removed the phone, wondering who was blowing it up.

The caller was Frank. "Ron's been trying to get in contact with you."

"Ron?" Sebastian asked, his mind still drunk on the image of seeing Ava lying in her bed.

"Ron Wolff."

Right, Ron. Their security guy. Sebastian blinked and inhaled, focusing his attention back on the moment. "He got something?"

A slight pause, and then Frank said, "Where are you?"

"Out and about. What did Ron say?"

Another pause. "Have you been drinking?"

Sebastian stiffened.

"You sound—" Frank began.

"I'm going to pretend you didn't ask me that. Tell me about Ron."

"He's got an update—a big one," Frank said. "He wants to meet—the sooner, the better."

Ron Wolff sat outside, under an umbrella at one of the tables. He waved, stood, picked up the two coffee cups, and headed to the car.

With his discount-warehouse chinos and bland polo shirt, Ron looked like just another middle-aged guy passing through town before heading out to play a quick nine at a public course, maybe hit a family barbecue afterward. That was one of the things Sebastian admired about Ron, how low-profile he was, dressing like Joe Average and driving a Honda Accord even though his net worth was somewhere in the neighborhood of a quarter of a billion dollars—all of it from blood profits.

No one knew that, of course. To the outside world, Ron was just the owner of yet another private security outfit, albeit a very successful one. He provided all sorts of security services to some major high-end corporations, as well as private citizens. His real talent, what made him stand out, was his success at finding missing carriers.

It had been Frank's idea, back when the three of them started out together, to turn Ron into a valuable resource for the LAPD. Over the years, Frank and Sebastian would abduct carriers and house them in private locations for a few weeks, maybe a couple of months; and then Ron, through staged investigative work, would find these carriers and contact the police. The LAPD, mired in bureaucratic red tape, was more than grateful to receive information from Ron.

Because Ron had no problem sharing information, the contacts he had made within both the LAPD and the FBI had no problem sharing sensitive and sometimes classified information on their cases, and now, after all these years of hard work and patience, Sebastian and Frank had nearly unfettered access to any blood-related crime in the country.

Sebastian reached across the seat and opened the door. Ron slid inside, grimacing in discomfort, and handed Sebastian a venti cup.

"Knee still acting up?" Sebastian asked.

"Like a mad bastard."

"I can help you with the arthritis. Just say the word."

Ron waved it away. He had no use for blood treatments—or anything else modern, for that matter. Ron was old-school. While his office had computers with Internet access, all of his case files were stored on paper. If you visited him you had to hand over your phone and any other electronic device, which he stored inside a Faraday cage that blocked all electromagnetic fields to prevent cavesdropping.

Sebastian drove aimlessly.

"Frank told me about the trip you took this morning with Link," Ron said. "He give you anything?"

Sebastian sighed. "He did not."

"What I thought. He passed the polygraph—twice—remember? Him and the other one, Ferreria."

Sebastian did remember, but what he resented right now—what was annoying the shit out of him—was the subtext in Ron's words, that "I told you so" tone. Frank spoke to him that way, too, he and Ron explaining things like he, Sebastian, was an adult toddler. Or the world's biggest idiot.

Sebastian drew in a deep breath, his thoughts shifting to Link's boss and Sebastian's quasi-silent partner, Anton.

"Anton also passed the polygraph," Ron said, as if reading his mind. "Not twice but three times."

"I know."

"But you're still thinking he might be somehow involved with Paul."

The truth was, Sebastian didn't know what to think. Paul had worked for Anton, but that didn't mean Anton had worked with Paul. The distinction was important. And there were other facts to consider. When Anton had found out about his dead stickman in Brentwood, he had contacted Frank. Anton professed to know nothing about it and immediately agreed to submit to a polygraph, guided hypnosis—anything to prove his innocence, that he, too, had been fucked over by Paul. And when Anton passed the first polygraph, he demanded another one, from someone different. Again he passed.

But polygraphs were not flawless. They could be beaten.

Ron said, "There's still not a single thing to indicate Anton knew about what Paul was going to do in Brentwood."

"I know—you've told me."

"We've kept a very close eye on Anton, listened in on his conversations courtesy of the bugs we placed in his house and car. He's still livid that Paul put him in this situation. And don't forget, Paul royally screwed him over by killing one of Anton's guys, that kid there at the house."

Sebastian already knew all this. "Frank said you had a major update."

Ron nodded and took a sip of his coffee. "LAPD has officially finished processing the Vargas home. Feds even loaned them their top lab geeks to go through it with a fine-tooth comb. I'm pleased to report they failed to recover a single fingerprint or DNA sample that belonged to Paul. We're in the clear there."

That had been a major, major concern from the very beginning, the police finding something that could link Paul to the house. When Paul enlisted in the military, he'd had, like every other potential candidate, to undergo a criminal background check. That meant submitting fingerprints and a DNA sample to see if they were related to any unsolved crimes. If something had been found at Sophia Vargas's home, the police and FBI would have come knocking, asking questions.

Ron said, "Still no activity on any of Paul's financial accounts. We know he dumped his smartphone the day you were shot. His friends are still texting and calling, wondering where he is and why he won't answer. Same deal on his emails. They keep piling up, and he hasn't answered a single one of them."

"That's it?"

"No. Pull over—I want to show you something."

Sebastian saw a couple of curbside spots in front of the Delta Cinema, Brentwood's only movie theater and the oldest in the city. He parked in front of the big art deco neon sign, which was turned off, and had flashes of memories of bringing Paul and Trixie here, the three of them sitting in the balconies and loges that had been built back in the 1930s. The kid who had sat next to him watching superhero and Disney movies had grown up into a man who had tried to kill him.

Ron dipped his fingers into his shirt pocket. He came back with a folded sheet of paper and handed it to Sebastian.

It was a color-printed photo of a lean, muscular guy dressed in a bathing suit and standing, tanned and smiling, on the beach. He looked to be around Paul's age, early to mid-twenties, and had a blond crew cut and 0 percent body fat or close to it, skinny but shredded. He wasn't big in the height department—five foot six, max eight, Sebastian guessed.

"You ever seen him before?" Ron asked.

Sebastian was pretty good with remembering faces. He shook his head. "Who is he?"

"Your sniper, I'm pretty sure."

Sebastian held the picture closer to his face, as if it contained some hidden clue. He hadn't seen the sniper, just the glint of sun off the scope before he got shot. The guy in the photo had a plain but wholesome face, like one he'd seen on those old "Milk. It does a body good" ads that were now popping up again on billboards all over the city.

"Guy's name is Bradley Guidry," Ron said. "He's thirty-three, born and raised in New Orleans, no criminal record, never married, no kids. Entered the Marines at nineteen, left at twenty-six as a Force Recon sniper. After he left the service, he did contract work all over the Middle East. That's where he met Paul. They did contract work together over there—you know, personal security shit."

Sebastian got jittery when he stayed parked in one place for too long; he couldn't get rid of the idea that that sniper was still out there, watching him through a scope. Not that the round would penetrate the windshield. It had been replaced with bulletproof glass. Still, he put the car in gear and slid back into the light morning traffic.

"About eight months ago," Ron said, "Guidry flew into LAX on an open-ended ticket and stayed at a hotel downtown for thirteen days. Normal shit on his credit cards—food and booze, some clothing purchases. Day he checked out was the same day he found a local branch for his bank and closed his checking and savings accounts to the tune of thirty grand."

"And now?"

"Now he's in the wind."

"With Paul."

"That's my operating theory. I think we should assume Guidry's involved. Keep an eye out for him. I'll forward Frank this picture."

"Your people?"

"They already have it," Ron said.

"What about Guidry's family? What did they have to say?"

"Father's been dead for roughly ten years. Cancer. Mother is still alive and seems to be a full-time junkie, says she hasn't spoken to her son since he went into the Marines. I did some poking into her email account and her phone, and based upon what I saw I think she's telling the truth. He's got a sister, too, named Clarice. She lives in Seattle. Same deal—no contact."

"Any idea why?"

"Not yet."

"How'd you find him?"

"Government records," Ron said. "That's part of the reason why this took so long. Had to call in a lot of favors to get the names of the guys Paul served with when he was in the service and later as a contractor. Once I got the names, it became a process of elimination. Guidry isn't the only sniper Paul worked with, but he's the only who has gone off the grid, at least as far as banking is concerned. Can't find any recent employment, either."

Ron drank some more coffee. "I've only spoken with three contractors so far, and they haven't heard from either Paul or Guidry for a good year or so. When I asked them questions about Guidry, about how I could get in contact with him, they all told me to talk to Paul. Nearly everyone I talked to said the two of 'em were real tight, always hanging out, doing shit together. They also said Guidry followed Paul around like a puppy dog. A couple of 'em thought Guidry had a thing for Paul."

"He's gay? Guidry?"

"I asked them that. They said they didn't know. Guidry's thing for Paul, from what I gathered, is more along the lines of hero worship. Like Paul could do no wrong. Guidry admired the way Paul carried himself, how he never seemed afraid of anything or anyone."

"That's because he's a psychopath."

"Paul was definitely the dominant one of the pair, Guidry the submissive. One guy told me this story about how they all went out to get tattoos someplace in Baghdad and Paul told Guidry what to get, one of those sugar skulls, and where it should go, and—"

"Sugar skulls?"

"Those skull tattoos he's got all over him, the ones with the eyes filled with jewels, roses, and candy, like something you'd see if you dropped acid—they're called sugar skulls. It's a Mexican thing for the Day of the Dead. The tattoos? They're used to symbolize someone who's died. Guidry got one of those, didn't even so much as question it. Paul was always telling him how and what to eat, how to train—he basically ran Guidry's life and Guidry went along with everything."

Ron was quiet for a moment, rocked his jaw back and forth. "What about Paul? He gay? Bi?"

"Not that I know. He dated girls in high school, and later he'd sometimes bring women he was seeing around the house to meet his mother."

"You ever meet them? The women?"

"A handful." Sebastian banged a U-turn.

"I've talked to the ones I found listed in his phone contacts and emails and texts. Last girl he dated, as far as I can tell, was this woman named Candice Jackson."

"She a lawyer?"

"She is."

Sebastian remembered her now: dark brown hair and a killer smile and an even more killer mind, the woman a contracts lawyer for some big-name downtown firm.

"You remember her, I take it," Ron said.

"Only met her once. One of the quick conversations in the driveway—*Hey, how are you? Nice to meet you.*" Sebastian had figured Candice Jackson was just another one in the long line of women who preferred smiling and nodding to talking. That changed quickly, the woman not only a real conversationalist but also clearly someone of substance, and after she and Paul left, Sebastian thought Paul might have met an equal, someone to call him on his shit.

Sebastian also remembered being slightly nervous. He didn't need a lawyer coming around the house, or Paul confiding in one.

"The two women before Candice had good things to say about Paul," Ron said. "You know, nice guy, smart and attractive, but things didn't work out. I met them face-to-face, so I could get a read on them, and I got the sense they were holding back something. Candice pretty much confirmed it."

"What did she say?"

"Nothing. Color drained from her face and she refused to talk to me," Ron said. "I was hoping you might tell me why Paul scared the living shit out of her."

"I'll talk with her."

"You can't. At least not now, not in person," Ron said. "She's out of the state, in New Hampshire. Her parents live there, city called Manchester. Have no idea when she's coming back, but when she does, I'll let you know."

"You're keeping an eye on her."

"Oh yes. There's definitely something there. Shortly after Paul went underground, Candice put in for a sabbatical, I guess you could call it. She went to rehab in Phoenix for pill and alcohol addiction. Place also specializes in treating addicts who were victims of sexual abuse. I can't give you any details because by the time I located her, she was getting ready to leave, so I couldn't put someone in there next to her to find out anything."

"When did you talk to her?"

"Little over two weeks ago. Team I have on her, they say all she does is stay in her house. Anything she needs is delivered."

"Anything else?"

Ron nodded. "I'm told the LAPD is working with the Feds on some sort of task force."

"On Brentwood?"

"Unclear. But it was set up *after* Brentwood, and it's definitely blood related. This is from my guy on the Blood Unit, Alves."

"So they must have found something."

"No. If they had, they would have come knocking by now. Task force isn't being run out of LAPD—it's a Fed thing—so my contacts can't get me any specific information, because they're not involved. I don't want to press, either, tip our hand."

"Should we be worried?"

"I'm not."

"And what about Boyle's partner there, the one who saw Paul, what's-her-name?"

"Ellie Batista."

"Yeah, her. What's her deal? You haven't mentioned anything about her in a while."

"Nothing has changed on that front. Like I told you, she had some sort of nervous breakdown, took a leave of absence. She broke up with her boyfriend—sent him an email that she'd had enough of LA, being a cop—packed up, and left, moved to Seattle."

"The private security company."

Ron nodded. "She's doing bodyguard work for that self-help guru who wrote that bestseller a couple of years back—you know, the one who urges women to follow their one true path or some shit. She's in Australia right now, I think. Maybe Germany."

"You talk with her, see what she knows?"

"For what reason? If she'd seen Paul, his composite would have been all over the news." Ron caught the look on Sebastian's face. "You want me to fly halfway around the world so she can tell me she didn't get a good look at him? I think we've got more pressing issues here, on the home front—wouldn't you agree?"

Ron, Sebastian admitted, had a valid point. "Okay," he said. "I hear you. What's bothering me is how quiet he is. He needs significant capital if he wants to start production."

"Could be trying to line up investors."

Sebastian nodded. He and Frank had the exact same thought.

"Or," Sebastian said, "he could be waiting for the right moment to strike."

"And you're sure he can't hurt you? I'm talking about your business operations."

"The old treatment center is closed."

"What about the new one?"

"Not open yet, and he has no idea where it is. Has no idea where *anything* is."

"Good," Ron said. "That's really good to hear. He'll poke his head out sooner or later. He can't hide forever."

CHAPTER 17

THAT NIGHT, AT a quarter to eight, Ellie stood in front of the bathroom mirror inside one of Los Angeles's most well-known (and most expensive) restaurants, touching up her lipstick and wondering what the night was all about. She was sure it wasn't a celebration for a job well done on the carrier. Anton wouldn't have made her go halfway across the city to Bloomingdale's to meet that pale waif named Binx and find out that he not only had already picked out the clothes but had also paid for them. All Ellie had to do was go into the dressing room and try everything on to make sure the sizes were right.

Anton, she had to admit, had great taste. All Chanel—a low-cut satin top with black tuxedo pants and leather cap-toe pumps. Clothes that were designed to do one thing, and one thing only: make an impression. Was tonight about another high-end job? Something that would move her closer to Anton's inner circle? It had to be. Why else would Anton have picked out these clothes and asked her to come out to this fancy restaurant in Beverly Hills?

Ellie dropped the lipstick into her clutch and checked her watch. Ten to eight. Perfect. She stepped back and examined herself in the mirror. Her new federal friends on the task force had provided her with the leather choker with the jagged-edge crystals. They had also given Faye

Simpson other pieces of bugged jewelry—a watch and a bangle bracelet—to wear when she was working with Anton.

The plunging V-neck of her blouse was a little sexier than she usually went for, Faye Simpson's tastes being more revealing than Ellie Batista's—even more so since she wasn't wearing a bra—but the double-sided tape was nicely holding the fabric in place. No danger of an accidental nip slip tonight.

Nip slip, she thought, and smiled. Something Cody would say. She left the bathroom and walked down the short, dimly lit hall and entered the restaurant, wishing she could call him back and tell him she was okay, that he didn't have to worry.

The hostess, a striking brunette named Misha, was adjusting the knot of Anton's tie and laughing at something he'd said—laughing in such a way that clearly showed she was into him. Ellie could see the appeal, in a way. Anton was built like a professional wrestler, but his face was as welcoming as a Russian prison camp. He'd spent time in one, too, he had told her once, a penal colony in Mordovia, some republic southeast of Moscow, before immigrating with his mother to the United States. His nose was slightly crooked from having been broken one too many times and he had cauliflower ears from having been punched and kicked too many times, and the left side of his mouth was slightly paralyzed, either from birth or from a fight—she didn't know which.

Anton saw Ellie approaching and smiled, giving him the full wattage of his capped teeth done in a brilliant toilet bowl white.

"Right on time, as usual," he said, spreading his arms open wide to accept her. He leaned down and kissed both her cheeks. He had a permanent case of five-o'clock shadow, even after he shaved, and she felt his stubble scrape across her skin.

"Come, come." He placed his strong hand against the small of her back and turned to the hostess. "Let us sit."

"We're staying for dinner?"

"Why else would I have invited you to such a beautiful place, asked you to dress up so nicely?"

"Drinks, I assumed."

"We could have drinks anywhere. Tonight is a celebration."

"Oh? Of what?"

Anton grinned coyly and arched his eyebrows a couple of times. His English was pretty good, but he still had a bit of an accent, Anton having arrived in the States when he was twenty-two. He was thirty-three now, and with his deep voice and accent, his solid build and the fearless way he carried himself, he looked and acted the part of Nameless Gangster Thug in a Russian mob movie—not that Hollywood made them anymore, everything now recycled reboots of things that had already been recycled and rebooted.

In the time she'd spent with Anton, she had noticed a keen intelligence at work behind the cold stare he forced on the world. He wasn't given to much emotion, but around her, when it was just the two of them, she had noticed a softer side to his personality—a man who loved his mother deeply and took care of her. A man who longed for a sense of romance and was frustrated by the constant vanity and lack of emotional and intellectual depth he found in the women he dated.

Ellie slid into a booth upholstered in fine, rich leather. Anton sat across from her, the circular table between them small, and took the elegant menus from the hostess. "Bring us two Macallans on the rocks," he told her. "The eighteen, not the twelve."

As the hostess flitted away, Anton looked the woman up and down, his fingers fishing for something inside his suit jacket pocket. Everything about this place was intimate—the dim modern lighting and limited and spacious seating to give patrons a sense of privacy and importance, which was why, according to her Google research, a lot of LA's power crowd came here. The men here this evening wore crisp suits and ties and didn't look a day under fifty. All the women were beautiful and wore fancy jewelry and stunning dresses and didn't look a day over thirty.

"That thing around your neck," he said.

"My choker?"

"Whatever. Where'd you get it?"

"My mother gave it to me on my sixteenth birthday," Ellie lied.

"Those aren't real diamonds."

"If they were, I would have hocked it a long time ago." Anton knew all about Faye Simpson's gambling problem.

"It looks tacky and cheap," Anton said. "Take it off."

Ellie didn't hesitate, took it off without a fuss. She'd started to wrap it around her fingers so it would fit neatly in her clutch when Anton reached out and said, "Give it to me."

"Won't look nearly as good on you."

He motioned for her to hand it over, impatient, his eyes dead. She placed the bugged choker in his extended hand. He got up, stuffed it in his pocket, and walked away.

Did he know the choker was bugged? That the LAPD was nearby, listening in on their conversation? If he or someone else decided to take a closer look at the necklace, they'd find the microphone. She saw Anton heading in the direction of the restrooms. He had taken his phone with him and it looked like he was either thumbing in the passcode to unlock his phone or dialing a number or possibly sending a text.

Roland and the guys who had trained her to go undercover had told her she had a pretty solid poker face. She held it in place in case anyone was watching—Anton had people everywhere—but she couldn't put out the fire inside her head, the voices screaming at her. Part of her fear had to do with Anton taking her choker, but the other part—and it was, surprisingly, much larger—had to do with the excitement of being so close to knowing something. Why was Anton looking for Gingerbread Man? And why had he invited her to this fancy, high-priced restaurant *and* picked out these expensive clothes she was wearing if he wasn't going to bring her deeper into the fold, involve her in something bigger? This dinner, she was certain, wasn't about Anton trying to get into her pants. He had shown no interest in her in that way, thank God.

What was really going on tonight?

The hostess returned. She had brought someone with her.

The man standing next to the table had salt-and-pepper hair and a pale, pockmarked face. He was in his late forties to early fifties, Ellie guessed, and what she noticed right away was how he wore his suit instead of the suit wearing him—an important distinction in LA, especially in Beverly Hills, where there were so many poseurs, guys desperately trying to look confident and powerful by wearing nice clothes and driving nice cars. One look at this guy, and she knew he belonged in that rare category of men who could have you erased from the earth. He gave off that distinct air of power and menace.

Ellie knew she wasn't imagining it; she'd caught the pinched, nervous expression on the hostess's face before she politely excused herself and walked away.

Ellie was about to slide out of the table when he said: "Please, don't get up."

But she did, anyway, because it was the polite and proper thing to do (and probably the smart thing, too). Ellie sensed that it pleased him. She extended a hand. "Faye Simpson."

"I know." He had a firm grip and rough, callused hands. "Frank."

He didn't offer his last name, and she didn't ask. The man named Frank waited until she resumed her seat before sliding into Anton's spot. He folded his hands on the table, his expression serious, maybe even dour. She caught sight of the platinum ring on his left hand—a pair of tigers or lions circling each other—and she immediately knew who he was: the man from the photo on her home office wall, the one sitting in the Buick.

He noticed her looking at it but didn't say anything. He didn't smile, either.

"Nice ring," she said. "Never seen one like that before."

"Thank you."

"Does it have some sort of special meaning?"

He shook his head, said nothing.

Ellie forced a smile. "Such a nice place," she said. "Fancy."

"You like nice things?" His glare was as intense and unforgiving as an MRI scan.

"Doesn't everyone?"

"You wear those clothes very well," he said. "They definitely suit you."

Ellie sensed a hidden meaning behind his words. "Did you purchase these for me, Mr. . . . ?"

"Frank is fine, and yes, I did."

"I'm flattered," she said. "They're beautiful. Thank you."

"I'm sensing a *but* coming."

"Well, I *am* wondering what I did to deserve such a lavish gift." The smile remained on her face as she glanced quickly to her right, across the dining area, to the hall leading to the restrooms.

"Anton won't be joining us," Frank said. "It's just you and me this evening."

Why? Ellie wanted to ask. Faye Simpson, though, simply smiled. Waited.

The waitress came with their drinks. Frank leaned back in his seat so the waitress could set them down on the table. After she did, he turned to her and said, "We'll have the prawn appetizer to start, followed by the Kobe beef. Michael knows how I like it. Thank you."

Then, after the waitress left with the menus:

"Anton has told me a lot about you."

"All good things, I hope."

"He says you're a hard worker and take direction well." His tone said otherwise. It practically screamed, *Bullshit*.

Ellie took a sip of her Scotch. It wasn't bad. Not as good as bourbon—too peaty for her taste—but she welcomed it anyway, knowing it would help relax her nerves. *Just don't get drunk,* she warned herself. *You need to stay sharp.*

Frank folded his hands on the table, his eyes searching hers when he said, "What is it you're really after?"

"Advancement."

"To what?"

"Depends on the job you're offering."

Frank smiled but there was nothing pleasant in it—or in the way he was looking at her now, a look she'd seen on detectives who were locked inside the box with a suspect, one that practically screamed, *I know who you are and what you did, so there's no point in lying.* Only the roles were reversed: she was the suspect, Frank the interrogator, and she was being questioned inside a fine restaurant and not a small, claustrophobic room.

"Anton warned me you were direct," he said.

Ellie sensed her bluntness had somehow pleased him. "Is there any other way to be?"

"He also told me he had you thoroughly vetted." Frank said it in a way that caused the hairs on the back of her neck to bristle, like he'd found something and knew who she really was.

Ellie waited for him to continue. He didn't, kept staring at her with that penetrating glare, like he could see inside her skull.

The silence grew uncomfortable—at least to her. With Frank, it was impossible to tell. She decided to wait him out, make him ask the question. Finally, he did.

"Is there anything you'd like to tell me?"

Ellie kept her tone light and pleasant. "I'm sure Anton told you about my problem."

"Gambling, yes—I know all about it. That your only vice?"

"I like to drink here and there, but it's not a problem."

"Drugs?"

Ellie shook her head. "Not my thing."

"You seeing anyone? A friend-with-benefits thing?"

"Not yet," Ellie said, raising the glass to her lips. "But I'm working on it."

"Why're you here? In LA. I'm sure there's plenty of blood work in Nevada."

"You can't reinvent yourself in the place where you were born. To get a fresh start, you need to be able to wipe the slate clean, right?"

Frank didn't answer.

"This city," Ellie said, "was built on pretending. It's its main economy, you could say. I mean, doesn't anyone who comes here want to be some better version of themselves—or, if not that, someone completely new and different? Someone prettier and smarter and richer? Isn't that why you came here?"

"What, exactly, is it you want to become, Faye Simpson from Reno, Nevada?"

Ellie decided to push back, just a bit. "Any damn thing I choose," she said.

"But there's the matter of your debt. What's the amount, again?"

"Two fifty and some change."

Frank exhaled audibly. "That's a horrible burden for someone so young. And beautiful."

"It is what it is. I'm not proud of it, but I'm not shying away from it, either. I addressed the problem way before I came here."

"Your payment plan."

Ellie nodded. "I've been making monthly payments to the casinos for over a year. Haven't missed a single payment or been late even once. I'm sure you checked."

"But what if you slip? If you do, the casinos might decide to take legal matters into their hands—which they can do, if they're so inclined. Hiring you would invite possible scrutiny into *my* life, not Anton's, and that's something I can't afford."

"Are you asking me to work for you in a . . . different capacity than what I'm doing now?"

"I'm considering it."

Ellie smiled. "I'm sensing a *but* coming."

"To work for me, you have to pay off your debt and be done with it."

"Unfortunately, I don't have—"

"That kind of money. Yes, I realize that. But I do. I could offer you a loan—a *legal* loan. I don't offer the same low interest rates as the banks, but they're certainly not outrageous."

"And what, exactly, would I have to do for this loan?"

"We can work out the parameters later," Frank said. "If you're interested."

"You do this for all your prospective employees?"

"No. Hardly ever." Frank paused to let his words hang in the air and took a sip of his drink, Ellie noticing the measured way he did it each and every time, a man in full control of his vices. "Position I have in mind, I need someone who is discreet," he said. "Someone I can trust."

"Then may I suggest a trial run?"

"This sort of job requires a full-time commitment. Once you're in, that's it." Frank's meaning was clear: once she said yes, there was no turning back. And if she screwed up, she disappeared. No second chances.

Frank dipped his fingers into his suit jacket pocket. "How long have you been working with Anton, again? Three months?"

"Closer to four."

Frank came back with a photograph. It was folded in half. She couldn't see the actual image, but she knew it was a photograph given the card stock. He placed it on the table, the picture sitting like a small tent between them.

She was about to reach for it when he said, "There's nothing I despise more than a liar."

Ellie considered him, trying to read the subtext behind his words.

"I ask questions only once," he said. "Please bear that in mind."

He motioned for her to pick up the picture.

It showed a big, mean-looking white guy dressed in military boots, khakis, and a tight olive tee with sweat stains under the arms walking across what she guessed was a desert. He had a military-issued buzz cut, his scalp gleaming underneath the sun, his monstrously developed fore-arms and biceps corded with muscle and veins and sunburned. The crazy, clownish tattoos she'd seen at the Vargas home were on full display.

Gingerbread Man.

Frank, she knew, was watching her closely, trying to gauge her reaction. Fortunately, she had been taught how to keep her true emotions from reaching her face, to keep her voice clear when she spoke. Lying, she learned, was an art form, one that she practiced over and over again in her time with Roland. Mastering the art of lying was the one thing above all else that would keep her alive.

Ellie placed the folded picture back down on the table and looked blankly at Frank, waiting for him to continue. He didn't. He stared hard at her, waiting for her to confess, to break down—to do *something*. When she didn't speak, for some reason she thought he was going to reach across the table and strangle her. Maybe she thought that way given the intensity in his eyes. She thought she saw a primal hunger there. A burning anger aimed at the man in the photograph.

"This man," Frank said. "Where have you seen him?"

"I haven't."

She could feel Frank's eyes searching her mind and heart.

Ellie had prepared for moments like this one. She radiated confidence through her body language and in her voice when she said, "I would have remembered meeting someone like that. Who is he? And what's with those tattoos?"

"Have you seen him with Anton?"

"I'm not with Anton every day."

"That wasn't the question I asked."

"During my times with Anton, no, I haven't seen him. Have you asked Anton? This would be a question more suited to him, wouldn't it?"

Frank's gaze remained on her as he picked up the picture and tucked it back inside his suit pocket. "If you see that man, you're to tell me right away."

"Who is he?"

"That doesn't concern you. I'll give you my personal number."

Ellie knew Frank wasn't going to give her any specific information on Gingerbread Man. The subject was a dead end, at least for now. She said, "How about we talk about the job you're offering? What will I be doing?"

"You'd be working for me, with high-end clients in an . . . intimate setting. Hence the need for discretion."

High-end clients. Intimate. Frank was discussing a job that would put her next to people receiving blood treatments. Was it Pandora? *Please, God, let it be Pandora.*

"There would also be some managerial aspects to the job," Frank said. "I could go over those at a later time—provided you're interested."

"Depends on the money."

"It will be a significant raise. We can negotiate later—*if* you're interested in the job."

Frank was offering her a chance to get closer to the inner circle—and, she hoped, closer to finding her brother. *There have to be records of carriers, some sort of database where they keep track of them, their blood types,* she thought, taking a long sip of her drink.

"Are you interested?" Frank asked. "Or should I look elsewhere?"

Ellie thought of the picture of J.C. on the wall. "I'm interested," she said, allowing the smile to reach her face and voice.

CHAPTER 18

SEBASTIAN PARKED IN the driveway, behind Frank's Buick. It was coming up on eleven, the neighborhood quiet and peaceful, as it always was, and Frank, bathed in the soft light coming from the porch, was standing outside, pruning a rosebush and collecting the clippings in a small plastic bucket. Frank insisted on tending to all the landscaping, his only hobby besides yoga, which he did alone. Frank preferred doing everything alone.

Frank placed the bucket on the ground, and as he walked toward the car, brushing his hands together, Sebastian looked around the neighborhood. Some of the surrounding homes were dark, the owners having jetted off to one of their other homes, maybe going on another long vacation. Sebastian couldn't shake the feeling that Paul's sniper friend, this Guidry character, was hidden somewhere in this darkness, looking at him through the crosshairs of a target scope.

Sebastian was well protected, as long as he remained inside the car. After his assassination attempt, he had brought the Jaguar to a company that specialized in outfitting cars, trucks, limos—any type of automobile—so they could withstand pretty much any type of possible security threat. The Jag's windows had been replaced with a glass designed with a special polymer that could absorb a round from a sniper rifle. The car had enough armor plating to withstand a bomb blast and still be driven. The new tires, if punctured by a round or a knife, would drive for almost fifty miles before fully deflating.

"Paul's not going to make another long-distance run at you," Frank said, after he slid into the passenger seat. "When he comes at you next, he'll use someone we don't know, do it in a crowded place where you feel safe and—"

"He, or she—you never know—will come up and plant two rounds in my head and I won't see it coming. Right, I know. Where's Ron?"

"He had to cancel. His daughter went into labor."

"You said there's a development regarding Paul."

"The LAPD finally got the toxicology report back on Sophia Vargas. They found Viramab in her system. Paul's using that in his transfusions. Now, to answer your next question, yes, I've put out feelers to the underground suppliers who are still in the business of manufacturing it."

"The Armenians—at least here—are the only ones who are still using it."

"Right. We're looking for new purchases made over the past, say, four to six months. If Paul is smart, he's covering his tracks well."

"This is the big development? You could have told me all of this over the phone."

Frank buckled his seat belt. "Let's go."

"Where, exactly, are we going?"

"Dancing," Frank said.

The address Frank had given him was in West Hollywood—WeHo, as the young kids called it now, a cutesy name Sebastian particularly despised. Or maybe deep down he just despised West Hollywood, a place that, for as long as he could remember, was the cool place for cool people who didn't have to worry about how they were going to pay for their fancy dinners and fancy drinks at the coolest nightclubs and coolest restaurants. When you grew up poor, as he had, you always carried a grudge against the rich—which was ironic given the fact that he owned an empire that was worth billions.

Their destination was on North Robertson Boulevard. Traffic was heavy on Santa Monica.

Frank pulled the phone away from his mouth and said, "Take this right up here—Hilldale. Then left onto Keith."

Frank returned to his call. He'd spent the entire drive on the phone, coordinating what Sebastian was sure was a surveillance operation. Frank, maddeningly, wouldn't provide details. No sooner had he hung up with someone than he dialed another number, telling Sebastian, "All shall be revealed, my friend."

Normally it would bother him, Frank's holding out. Sebastian, though, heard the smile in his friend's voice, which was about as expressive as Frank got when he was excited. Frank, Sebastian knew, was working on something big—something, Sebastian was sure, that had to do with Paul.

After Sebastian turned onto Keith Avenue, he took a left onto North Robertson Boulevard. "We're here," Frank said into the phone. He hung up. "You're going to want to park up there, on your right, in front of the Starbucks."

"There aren't any spaces."

"There will be in a moment. Slow down."

As if on cue, the lights of a gray Audi parked against the curb came to life. The driver pulled out of his spot and Sebastian pulled in and parked. It was well after midnight—and well past his bedtime—and yet WeHo was alive and kicking like it was New Year's Eve, the streets packed with people bar- and club hopping.

Someone knocked on Frank's window. He cracked it an inch, just enough to allow a white envelope to slide into the car.

Frank opened the envelope and removed a small clear baggie. It held a pair of black capsules.

"Meet Paul's new sexual-enhancement drug," Frank said. "MDMA, otherwise known as ecstasy, or molly, mixed with carrier blood—a pregnant woman carrier's blood. Supposedly it gives you the most incredible orgasms of your life."

"Does it work?"

"Hard to say. MDMA causes arousal. The sexual stimulation we heard about involving Sophia Vargas—that, most likely, was from a transfusion. All we know at the moment is that Paul has been testing his new drug out in a couple of high-end nightclubs downtown, charging about five hundred bucks for a couple of these pills."

Sebastian took the baggie and turned on the map light. The capsules were dark red, not black, and looked sloppily put together—not by a machine but by a human hand.

"Why would Paul be wasting his time with this bullshit?" Sebastian asked, more to himself than to Frank.

It didn't make sense; Paul said he had a product that was better than Pandora—Pandora 2.0, he called it—and went on about how his product offered all of the health and physical benefits of Pandora (although Paul didn't technically know what made Pandora so special, but Sebastian was sure Paul had some solid ideas about it). Pandora 2.0 came with an extremely potent side effect: making the user more sexually desirable and uninhibited. Got you off way better, too.

But the real gains—and the real money—came from whole-body transfusions. Why would Paul do this nickel-and-dime shit, creating these handmade capsules to sell at—

The answer hit him, and his eyes widened. "Infrastructure," Sebastian said.

Frank nodded sagely. "He doesn't have the necessary money to become operational—and he needs a good amount of it to buy storage units for the blood and the necessary transfusion equipment, chemicals, and medications."

"And a place to house his carriers."

Another nod, and Frank said, "Paul needs to create a revenue stream because he doesn't have a financial backer. Or he may not want one. I wouldn't be surprised if Paul's decided to do this all on his own."

Which had been Sebastian's theory all along, Paul wanting to go it alone so he could control everything. A financial partner would want to know what made Paul's blood so different from what was currently out there—the secret ingredients for his special sauce, so to speak. There was no way Paul would give that up. Once he told someone, he would run the risk of being cast aside, or killed.

Early on, after the incident at the house, Sebastian had wondered if Paul would be stupid enough to approach either the Mexicans or the Armenians and try to partner with them. Such an action would have resulted in Paul's death—which would have suited Sebastian just fine if it weren't for the fact that Paul could easily hand over Sebastian's name as that of the person who was manufacturing Pandora. Both organizations took what they wanted by force. When they found out Paul didn't have an actual product, per se, just the recipe for one, they'd torture him until he spilled the information, and once it was verified, they would kill him.

But almost four months had come to pass, and neither the Armenians nor the Mexicans had made a move. Paul, it appeared, was determined to keep quiet, do everything on his own. But he had to have people working with him—people he trusted, like Bradley Guidry.

"And this is definitely carrier blood from a pregnant woman?"

"I can't say for sure," Frank replied. "I'm going to hand those capsules over to Maya, have her test them for the gene as well as the pregnancy markers."

"Paul said he had a couple of carriers who were pregnant."

"And he's adding more to his stable. Seven weeks after your attempted murder, two female carriers were abducted. One was twenty-six, the other twenty-four."

"You don't know for sure Paul was behind the abductions."

"Actually, I do." Frank dipped his fingers into his inner suit jacket pocket. He came back with a folded piece of paper and handed it to Sebastian.

Two photographs, each taken of the front windshield of a different car—a Honda Accord and a Toyota Camry. Both photographs showed the same man behind the wheel: Bradley Guidry.

Frank said, "The photos are from traffic cameras posted near where the women were abducted. I enhanced them."

"Where'd you get these? Our LAPD contact?"

Frank shook his head. "I obtained them myself," he said. "I now have what's called root access to the servers used by highway patrol. I won't bore you with the technical details—"

"Thank you."

"—but suffice it to say, I can get in and out without being detected. After Ron sent me Guidry's picture, I went to work. I got lucky."

It was about goddamn time some luck had been thrown their way. "What about Guidry's car? You know the make and model. Got a plate?"

"He used a stolen car both times. Both vehicles have not yet been recovered, I'm told. As for gleaning any useful information about the actual abductions, my contact says they were clean jobs—no witnesses or evidence."

"Gleaning," Sebastian said. "Look at you, Mr. Walking Dictionary."

"Trying to educate you," Frank replied in his characteristic dry tone. "Through osmosis."

Sebastian cracked a grin—a rarity these days.

Frank said, "If Paul had any capital, he wouldn't be going the pill route. It's a short game and, I'm sure he knows, very risky. Raising money with these pills—I think it safe to say your original theory about him not having anyone backing him is correct."

"And probably the reason why he's been quiet these past few months. He's building his own infrastructure, and that takes time, and capital, no matter how small that infrastructure. How did Ron come by this information?"

"One of Ron's people happened to be at a club, a place called Deliverance, which is conveniently located right over there." Frank pointed out the windshield, at a building across the busy street.

It was a two-floor structure that took up nearly the entire block—sort of like a little mall plaza you'd find in a nicer part of Mexico. The Spanish architecture was clear—a courtyard behind brick pillars wrapped with strings of party lights where people sat at tables, eating and drinking; flat red roofs, doorways, and windows designed with Moorish influence. But a closer look revealed a more Tuscan aesthetic, with the exterior's intricate masonry. The windows, he noticed, were stained glass.

"Ron's guy spotted someone he was sure was Paul dealing drugs," Frank said. "Paul looks different now—wore glasses and grew out his hair. No more military buzz cuts. Ron's guy tried following Paul, to get a closer look, but lost him. But he approached the guy he spotted buying the drugs, and when Ron's person pretended to be an undercover cop, the kid handed over the bag you're now holding and explained what it was."

"I take it there's a reason behind tonight's field trip."

"The guy selling the blood pills? I've received word he's here tonight, at the club. We're watching him as we speak."

Frank's phone chirped twice. He looked down at the screen.

"We have him. Let's go. I've already got a place nearby where we can have a nice, friendly chat."

CHAPTER 19

THE KID'S NAME was Enrique Sabino. He was small, a hair shy of five foot seven, and built like a drinking straw, with thin arms and legs and a mop of thick black hair that hung in long bangs over his forehead and eyes. With the exception of his crotch, nearly every inch of his olive skin was smooth and hairless. Sebastian knew this because he could see nearly every inch; Ron's men had stripped Enrique to his birthday suit before tying him down, with plastic zip ties, to a battered and dirty rolling desk chair held together by duct tape.

Sebastian didn't like it when Frank stripped guys down for interrogation. Their junk shriveled up, and more often than not they pissed and shit themselves—sometimes from fear, almost always when Frank went to work on them. Torture was Frank's domain, and he insisted on setting the stage and mood right from the very beginning. People felt vulnerable when they were naked, Frank liked to say, and were more inclined to tell the truth.

Enrique was definitely on the right path. Head hung low and eyes slammed shut, he shivered from fear and from the cold and from the sobbing, an ugly and heartbreaking mewing that echoed inside the tiny bay of the auto garage. It was a sound Sebastian recognized all too well: *I don't belong here. I can't die—not now, not in a place like this.*

Sebastian stood in front of him, reading, by flashlight, the detailed file

Frank had prepared on the boy. Sebastian took his time; there was no need to rush. The garage had gone into foreclosure, so no one would be stopping by, and Frank had disabled the alarm system installed by the bank. If the kid screamed, that was fine, too. The place was in a strip mall that had tanked. Frank, as always, had done his homework.

Sebastian handed the file to Frank and said, "How about giving us some privacy?"

Frank didn't argue. He nodded to Ron's three men, and they filed out the side door, into the night. The door shut with a bang that made Enrique jump in his seat.

Sebastian sat down in the stiff plastic chair brought in from the tiny waiting room off the front door. He crossed his legs and sighed, seeing his breath plume in the air. The garage smelled of grease and the kid's sweat and cheap cologne.

"That file I was just reading," Sebastian said, bundled in a warm Patagonia jacket and a pair of thin black leather gloves. "It says you've got a kid. What's his name, again? Your son's."

Enrique mumbled something under his sobs.

"Sorry, I didn't catch that," Sebastian said.

"Jonathan." Enrique snorted, blinking away tears. "His name is Jonathan. He'll be four. In February."

"Great age." Sebastian looked behind Enrique, at the wall of shelving and pegboards holding a wide assortment of auto parts and tools. "What's the deal with your girlfriend? Carmella. You love her?"

The kid's head bobbed up. Snot and tears ran down his lips and chin, dripping onto his lap.

"Do you love her?" Sebastian asked again.

"Yes," the kid replied, his voice clear. "With all my heart."

Sebastian believed him. His eyes were bloodshot and wet, but Sebastian could see the emotion in them.

"Where'd you guys meet? High school?"

"Middle school," Enrique replied.

Sebastian's eyebrows jumped. "Really?"

Enrique sniffed, trying to wipe his mouth and nose against his bare shoulder since his forearms were tied down to the chair's armrests. "We've known each other since we were kids."

"Was it one of those things where you looked at her and you just knew?"

Enrique nodded. Snorted.

"I had one of those, a long time ago," Sebastian said. He groaned as he got to his feet, his knees popping, and he moved to the tools. "That type of love doesn't come around too often. If it does and you're anything like me, you'd sell your soul to the devil to protect it. To keep it."

When Sebastian came back, he reached for the kid's head. Enrique flinched, bucking against his restraints, and screamed.

"Relax," Sebastian said softly, and used the dirty blue rag he'd found to wipe the snot away from Enrique's face. "I saw a picture of her. In the file. Carmella's a very pretty woman. I'm sure you want to give her the world—am I right? Her and your son."

The kid didn't answer.

"You an alcoholic?" Sebastian asked, tossing the rag aside. "An addict?"

"No, sir. I'm clean, I swear."

"I'm not judging. I'm one. An alcoholic. Although, if I'm being honest, I'm probably an addict, too, even though I've never done coke or any of the other hard stuff. But if I tried it even now, even with all the sobriety I have? I'd be hooked"—Sebastian snapped his fingers —"just like that."

Sebastian picked up his chair and moved it closer. "What I'm trying to say is, I know myself. I know my true nature. It will never change. That's what recovery has taught me. That and probably the single most important life lesson: the importance of accountability."

Enrique swallowed several times, his throat working.

"No one can make me drink or use, Enrique. *I'm* the one who decides whether to pick up a drink or a drug. Sure, I can blame it on people, places, and things—a divorce, death, accident, what have you—but when you really stop and analyze it, those things can't make me drink or use. It's *my* decision. Which brings us to you and your current situation."

Sebastian sat a few inches away and leaned forward. He could smell the sour odor rising from the kid's armpits, the product he used in his hair.

"File I have on you says you work full-time at a Best Buy selling electronics or some shit," Sebastian said. "Carmella is a waitress at that Italian place that's in walking distance from your apartment. I'm guessing that's not really paying the bills, which is why you got into selling those blood pills—am I right?"

"My son—he's—" Enrique cut himself off. His jaw trembled, his eyes filling with fresh tears.

"What about your son?"

"He needs me. He's got issues."

"What's wrong with him?" Then, when Enrique didn't answer, "Go on, tell me. I want to know."

"We think he's autistic. Pretty sure he is. The health insurance I've got is for shit. Specialist we want him to see isn't covered and he's expensive, but he's the best in the state."

Sebastian nodded in understanding. "So you're trying to make some extra money to do the right thing by your kid, your family. I can respect that. Would do the same thing if I were in your shoes, probably.

"I appreciate your candor, Enrique, so I'm going to extend you the same courtesy. Truth is, I'm not really all that interested in you. Now, the man you work for, the one who gave you those pills—that's who I'm after."

Enrique opened his mouth to speak. Sebastian said, "Before you answer, let me tell you how this works, since you're new to this. I've got a file on you. My people have been following you for about a week now, so I know things about you. You with me so far?"

"Yes, sir."

"Good. Now, if you answer my questions truthfully, you'll get to go live your life with your girlfriend and kid, get him to that specialist, see him grow up. Flourish. If you lie, well, then that's on you. You do that, then you're forcing me to open that door behind you and let those animals back in and have their way with you until I get the information I want. It's that simple, okay?"

"Yes. Yes, ask me anything."

"We'll start with an easy one. These pills—what are they?"

"They've got carrier blood in them. Supposed to get you super horny and get you off."

"Have you tried them?"

Enrique shook his head. "I just sell them for extra money. At the nightclubs."

"And who supplied you with these pills?"

"Gee-Gee."

"And that would be . . . ?"

"Guy I grew up with, Gerry Gambles. We call him Gee-Gee."

That name wasn't in Frank's file. Ron's people had shadowed Enrique for a little over a week, said the kid pretty much went to work and then straight home to be with his kid and girlfriend. But Frank had taken the kid's phone and would no doubt be working his magic on it, sucking out all the contacts.

"Me and Gee-Gee go way back. We're tight," Enrique said. "I tell him everything. I told him about my kid, and he told me how I could make extra money, and I said yes."

"How many people are selling these pills?"

"I don't know exact numbers. I know Gee-Gee sells 'em, and that's it. He hits the nightclubs, too. The ones downtown."

"Okay. Good. This is very helpful. Do you know who I am?"

"No, sir, I do not."

"Enrique, look at me." Then, when Enrique did: "What did I say about lying?"

"I don't know your name or the other guy's."

"What other guy?"

"The one who was standing next to you. The guy holding my phone."

"Frank?"

"I don't know his name or your name or the names of the others. When I agreed to sell, Gee-Gee showed me pictures, a whole bunch of 'em, of about ten, maybe fifteen guys. Told me that if we saw any of them, we were to leave whatever it was we were doing and call him."

"Call Gee-Gee?"

"No, the guy running the thing. Paul."

The name raised the hammers in Sebastian's heart and flooded his veins with adrenaline.

"I don't know his last name, I swear," Enrique said.

Sebastian felt a peculiar thirst in the back of his throat. His limbs were humming now, ready for a fight—the way he'd felt, back in the day, when he'd step into the boxing ring, ready to knock someone right the fuck out.

His silence, or maybe the look on his face, maybe both, made Enrique shudder. "I don't know his last name," Enrique said again, his voice trembling with fear. "I swear to God I don't."

"What's he look like, this guy Paul?"

"He's all swole. Like a bodybuilder. He's tall, black hair and—"

"Black hair," Sebastian said.

"Yeah. Black as ink. He's got all these really weird, or really cool, tattoos, depending on your point of view. And he—" Enrique cut himself off, straightening. "I can tell you."

"Tell me what?"

"Where he is." Enrique's face brightened with triumph. "It's not too far from here. Half an hour, maybe forty-five minutes."

"Where?"

"Cudahy."

Sebastian knew the area, of course. Cudahy, located in southeastern Los Angeles County, was the second smallest city in Los Angeles, the place named after some meatpacking magnate or some shit. And Enrique was right about Cudahy being close by.

"Gee-Gee couldn't pick up the new supply of pills, asked me to do it," Enrique said. He was speaking clearly now, the fear having been temporarily pushed aside by the excitement of holding what he believed was a winning lottery ticket—not for money but for his life. "Paul was there, and he gave me the pills."

"We talking apartment, house, what?"

"House. Yellow stucco. Red clay roof, and a garage—an attached garage. I know the address." Enrique eagerly gave it up without any prompting.

As a real estate agent, Sebastian had access to an app that could pull up the details for any house in the state of California. He used it now and typed in 143 Cypress Drive. It had been listed for sale until the middle of July, when it was pulled from the market, for reasons that weren't noted.

The listing came with pictures. Sebastian tapped on one showing the front of the house. He enlarged it until the photo filled the screen and then showed it to Enrique.

"That's it," Enrique said. "That's the place."

Here it was, finally, everything he, Frank, Ron, and his men had been searching for all these months. Sebastian felt a joy that bordered on rapture. He wanted to jump to his feet and rush out the door, sprint straight for US Route 101 North and run all the way to Cudahy. He could do it, too. His blood was caffeine.

Sebastian patted the kid's knee. "You did good. I need you to hang tight for a little bit until I get this sorted out, okay?"

"Could I get, like, a blanket or something? It's freezing in here."

Sebastian took off his coat and draped it around the kid's shoulders. "I'll see what I can do about a blanket, too," he said. "You hungry?"

Enrique hesitated.

"This isn't a trap, my man," Sebastian said. "If you're hungry, say so."

"I could use something to eat, sure, if it's not a bother."

"It's not. What would you like?"

"Anything—I'm not fussy." Enrique looked up, craning his head back. "Thank you," he said, eyes filling with tears of gratitude. "Thank you so much."

Sebastian placed a hand on the kid's shoulder and smiled. "You're welcome," he said, and grabbed Enrique in a headlock. As he strangled the kid, Sebastian made a promise to himself to send some money to Enrique's widow so their boy could see that specialist. And if she did something else with the money, well, then that was on her.

The air outside seemed warmer than earlier, as though the temperature had risen another ten or fifteen degrees in the last hour—which, obviously, it hadn't. Sebastian had been sweating underneath his down jacket—sweating from excitement. Finally, after all these months, he had the son of a bitch.

He had a powwow with Frank and Ron's men, and then, by phone, with Ron himself.

"I'll put together a team," Ron said. He was still at the hospital, waiting for his daughter to give birth. "We'll start surveillance tonight. Then we'll—"

"Surveillance?"

"We don't know how many people he's got working for him, what kind of hardware he and his crew are carrying, how this place is laid out."

"It's a house, not some goddamn military installation."

"And that's the fatal flaw in your thinking. Paul and Guidry are military," Ron said. "If they're bunkered in that house, using it as a lab, keeping their carriers there, whatever, they've taken steps to secure it. They've got people watching it—people who are probably ex-military, too."

"As are your people. Guys with me right now, I've already talked with them. They said they're trained for this exact kind of midnight op—get in and out without making a peep."

"I know you've got a major hard-on for Paul. I get it. But you're going to need to keep it in your pants until I—"

"We're doing this now."

"No, we're—"

"I'm running a democracy all of a sudden? 'Cause last time I checked, you work for me. You *and* your boys." Sebastian's voice was clear, but his face was flushed with heat. "Make it happen. Tonight."

A long silence followed.

"Where do you want them to bring Paul?" Ron asked, barely keeping his anger in check. "The Bungalow?"

It was Frank's pet nickname for his den of torture, a funeral home Frank owned, under some dummy corporation, on the other side of the city. It was a one-stop shop for all your diabolical business needs: a private torture chamber with easy cleanup and cremation in less than half an hour.

"Long Beach," Sebastian said. "It's closer—and I'm going to take the next few days off, spend some one-on-one time with Paul until I get him situated in a more permanent living situation. Bring Paul there."

"What about Guidry?"

"I don't give a shit about Guidry or the others."

"Let me speak to Marty."

"Which one's that?"

"Tall guy with the beard, has a face and head that look like they belong in a caveman exhibit. Before you hand off the phone, know that you're not going along with Marty and the others. They can't do their job if they're also babysitting you."

Sebastian bristled at the word *babysitting*. He was about to argue the point when Ron said, "This isn't up for debate. You go, I pull the plug. Now, put Marty on the phone."

Marty grunted his way through a fifteen-minute conversation with Ron. After Marty hung up, he returned the phone to Sebastian and explained that he would stay in close contact with him.

"No," Frank said to Marty. "You'll be in close contact with me." Then, before Sebastian could argue: "You're too emotionally involved. This requires finesse. Patience and detachment."

If anyone but Frank had publicly dressed him down like that, the guy would have been on the ground, sobbing, picking his teeth out from blood and vomit. Frank knew it, too, and to add insult to injury, said, "No, don't shoot me that look. You know I'm right."

Hot, bright white stars exploded across Sebastian's vision. "When this is over," he said, his limbs shaking, "we'll have a meeting, me, you, and Ron, talk about who's running things." Sebastian turned to the three men. "Get rid of the body in there."

Sebastian stormed away. He needed to keep busy, stay out of his head. He paced in the shadows, his skin tingling and itching in places as though it were covered with ants. He knew the real reason behind his discomfort: He hated giving up control, the problem of every alcoholic and addict. In the past, he had treated it with a bottle of Scotch. Now he had to go through the problem instead of drinking his way around it.

Christ, how he missed booze.

That bottle of rare Scotch Paul had brought to the house, the one with the gold crown, was still there. Paul had left it behind, and Sebastian hadn't thrown it out. Should have, he knew, but he couldn't bring himself to do it. He had been nursing a fantasy of drinking it nice and slow in front of Paul until the old Sebastian came back to life. That person was still there, locked away and maybe a little dusty from disuse, but Sebastian 1.0 was still there, backed up, ready and waiting.

And the strange, messed-up thing? He *wanted* that previous version. Needed it. Sebastian 1.0 was still plenty angry, and that was a *great* thing, actually, because what the so-called experts on the subject of rage didn't want you to know was just how clarifying anger was, how it reduced all the bullshit in your life to ashes and left behind what truly mattered to you. Anger didn't allow you to hide. It kept you sharp.

Footsteps approaching. Sebastian turned and saw Frank nibbling like a rabbit on one of his organic, no-gluten, no-preservatives, all-natural, and zero-taste protein bars. Frank didn't partake of junk food, no matter the occasion. Sebastian, the true alcoholic he was, both admired and despised Frank's self-discipline.

"Are you through sulking?" Frank asked.

"It's not wise to poke the bear."

"I won't apologize for taking the reins on this. Finding Paul has become your new drug."

Sebastian stopped pacing. "Say that again?"

"You're an alcoholic. All you see is what you want, and you go after it with the subtlety of a bulldozer. I don't fault you for it. All alcoholics and addicts are wired only one way."

"And which way is that?"

"To self-destruct."

Frank, Sebastian knew, was right. Still, it did little to mollify his anger.

"Our new celebrity center," Frank said. "I found someone we can use to run the front office, keep an eye on things."

Sebastian said nothing.

"She's one of Anton's stickmen," Frank said.

That got Sebastian's attention. "Since when did Anton get all woke?"

"He's always had an eye for talent. And this woman, Faye Simpson, is quite talented. I spoke with her. I was impressed."

"Inviting someone in from Anton's crew. What a great idea."

"I think it's an *excellent* idea, as a matter of fact. Anton has taken quite a shine to her. I can see why. She's very attractive, but also she's very . . . unique. Tough. I suspect she can handle herself, keep her wits about her. Anton trusts her, and if he uses Ms. Simpson to gather information on our operation, feed it back to Paul—well, then we'll know for sure if he and Paul are working together."

"Of course, the question will be moot if we get our hands on Paul tonight."

"We will," Sebastian said.

Frank's phone buzzed. He took the call, listened for a moment, then hung up.

"That was Marty," Frank said. "They're entering the premises."

Sebastian paced the cracked, sunbaked asphalt, his shoes crunching against the broken glass of beer and liquor bottles and, he was sure, crack vials. He'd spotted a couple in the car headlights when Frank had driven around the back of the garage.

"What the hell is this?" Frank said under his breath.

Sebastian stopped pacing, turned, and saw Frank staring down at the screen of his phone, his brow furrowed in thought.

Frank showed Sebastian the message on his phone. It was from an unknown number and contained one word:

Ka-boom!!!

"What the hell does that mean?" Sebastian asked.

His phone vibrated. He took it out, saw a text on the screen. It was also from an unknown number, and the message contained three words:

Nice try, asshole.

Paul. This text was from *Paul*. Had to be. But how had he gotten this number? They had purchased new encrypted Enigma Black phones—

Another text: You guys walked right into it!

Sebastian felt as though his stomach was packed in ice. *It was a trap. Either that kid Enrique led us into a trap or Paul had somehow anticipated our movements and—*

Another text: I'm coming for you, old man. ☺ ☺ ☺

Sebastian didn't know what had happened, not yet, but he knew Paul had been one step ahead of him. Paul had somehow engineered a trap and Sebastian had sent—no, forced—Ron's men to march straight into it.

CHAPTER 20

T HE GENERAL PUBLIC didn't know much in the way of specifics about the actual workings of the blood world—how it was run and who ran it, how transfusions were performed—and for very good reason. Law enforcement agencies, private investigators, legitimate journalists, and hacks were constantly out in the field, digging for information to lead them to an actual blood farm, looking to talk to people who had undergone a successful blood transfusion. Not surprisingly, few people were willing to talk on the record, because carrier blood was illegal. True carrier blood was as rare as the Hope Diamond, and ridiculously expensive, so only the überrich could afford it. They got their blood in secret, the transfusions performed by experienced medical professionals. If you weren't part of the elite, then you had to take your chances on finding what you prayed to God was legitimate carrier blood that fit your budget. This second-tier level was peddled mainly by the Mexican cartel.

These were the prevailing theories on the Internet, where people took to social media and discussion websites like Reddit to post their opinions and experiences. People were more comfortable sharing both the truth and bullshit there, because they labored under the delusion that they could hide behind a username and remain private, which was why Ellie spent much of her time on the deep, dark web, in chat rooms on restricted websites that didn't show up in Internet searches. These sites were harder to find and, generally speaking, unknown to law enforcement. There, Ellie had spent thousands and thousands of hours searching for her elusive white whale—stories from people who had received successful transfusions using what was generally considered *the* single best blood product available: Pandora.

The problem was, there was no way to know who was telling the truth. Still, Ellie combed through each post carefully, trusting her gut instincts as to which users were telling the truth or clamoring around it.

Ellie recalled a post from one user named PandoraAngels333. She remembered the username because the person who had written the message, a woman who claimed she was in her early fifties but easily passed for thirty, said something that had always stuck with Ellie: "Getting Pandora is like welcoming the entire Kingdom of Heaven into your heart. Your skin glows like an angel & you feel beautiful & warm & safe & confident, like God Himself is with you, wrapping you in His Almighty Love. God is real, and I am no longer afraid. I am now complete."

Ellie carried those words with her when she started working at Frank's so-called Celebrity Center. To the public, it was known as the Los Angeles Health and Wellness Center, a legitimate business that did, in fact, cater to a number of celebrities. The Center, as it was called, wanted to be a one-stop shop for all your physical, mental, and spiritual needs. It was a hybrid of legitimate Western medicine and what Ellie called typical hippie-dippie LA bullshit. The place also offered a line of ridiculously expensive skin care products enhanced with collagen and a whole bunch of other so-called natural and organic ingredients that helped you look younger, fresher, and rested. The Center couldn't keep them in stock. Business was booming.

If transfusions were taking place on the Center's premises, Ellie saw absolutely no signs of it.

But she knew *something* blood related had to be happening here, because Frank was involved, and Frank was involved in the blood world and wanted her to work with high-end clientele. If transfusions were taking place on the premises, she was sure they were going down on one or both of the top two floors. The newly renovated building on Santa Monica Boulevard had a total of ten. The key card issued to her allowed access to every single room on floors one through eight, but nine and ten were strictly off-limits—they didn't have a key card reader.

"They have to be doing the transfusions there," Ellie told Roland a week later. She had met him at traffic court, where they waited with other people waiting to go before a judge to argue a speeding or parking ticket. Roland's people had planted one on her car, to get her to meet him here, early this morning. To an outsider, they looked like two people who happened to be sitting next to each other, indulging in polite chitchat.

Roland said, "But you haven't seen any signs of a transfusion taking place anywhere in the building."

"No. Nothing. Patients who come in are out within an hour—not enough time for a full-body transfusion."

"Maybe they're getting a pint."

"I thought of that and checked their arms for needle marks. I'm telling you, it's not happening during normal business hours. Maybe they're bringing blood patients there at night or on the weekends." Roland, she knew, had people watching the Center.

"No one is coming there on nights or weekends," Roland said. "At least not yet."

"What's going on with that carrier I tagged for you?"

"It's a dead end."

"Why?"

"That liquid GPS didn't work out quite the way we wanted it to."

"You lost him."

"We prefer the term *temporarily out of pocket*. Sounds better. We're investigating some angles. I'll let you know if anything develops. Hang tight."

Roland was about to stand when Ellie said, "I think Frank changed his mind about having me work with his high-end clientele."

"It's only been a week. They're probably watching you, see how you work—see if they can fully trust you."

"Or they've dug deeper into my background and found something."

"Your cover story is rock-solid." Roland caught her doubtful expression and added, "You seriously believe we'd send you into an undercover situation without making sure you were one hundred percent safe?"

"What if they're looking for Ellie Batista?"

"Ellie is skipping around the globe, providing security for a self-help celebrity. If anyone asks for her, makes any inquiries, we'd know, and no one has. If that changes, I'll let you know—"

"I'm worried about pictures. I know you said your people scoured the Internet, removed any pictures of me, but what if they found one? What if your people missed something?"

"We've taken care of everything. Stop worrying."

"Something's wrong. I can feel it."

"That's impatience, what you're feeling."

She had to admit, he had a point. She felt like she was trapped in limbo. She wasn't used to inertia. When she experienced it, she found a way to break it.

"I'm going to talk to Frank."

"*No,*" Roland said, drawing out the word, "you're going to keep doing what you're doing."

"I'm not doing *anything*. My job title is 'senior administrator of hospital personnel,' which is a long-winded way of saying 'babysitter.' I'm watching a staff of four ridiculously good-looking young men and women stand there looking sharp and pretty while answering the phones, confirming appointments, and making sure they smile and act polite while talking to clients and delivering them herbal teas, kombucha, and bottled mineral water from some volcanic spring on the other side of the planet. My main job, though, is to make sure they don't bring their phones into the Center."

"Frank say why?"

"To protect the privacy of his patients," Ellie replied. "Each morning, he has me frisk the front desk staff and search every purse. I've got to wave a wand over them, see if they have any, you know, bugs or listening devices. We've got a lot of famous people coming in there for skin treatments, other shit, and he doesn't want anyone selling anything to the tabloids."

"Sounds reasonable. And it sounds like they're doing actual medical work there."

"As far as I can tell, they are."

"What an excellent cover," Roland said, more to himself than to her.

"I haven't talked to Frank since I first started working there."

"You're overthinking this. Just give it some time." Roland checked his watch. "I've got to get to work on getting Faye Simpson a boyfriend."

"What? Why?"

"Because you have an ungodly amount of people following you, and I need to find an easier way to deliver messages. Just keep doing what you're doing. I'll be in touch." Roland stood and left.

Ellie stayed the course. She was no closer to finding out anything about Frank's blood business—or the fate of her brother.

Her boyfriend's name was Max Evans. She didn't know his real one, just knew he was a Fed around her age and, for the time being, worked as a physical trainer at a swanky fitness club called Imperial, a place where the staff catered to every client's need, including wiping away their sweat with the finest Egyptian cotton towels imported all the way from France. He lived with his single mother, also a Fed, in a modest suburban home in Glendale.

Max delivered her information from Roland. Sometimes, when Max was hugging her, he'd whisper quick instructions in her ear. Mostly, Max, like her gambling sponsor, Jon Carlo, who she also met with on a weekly basis, would slip her instructions written on scraps of paper. Paper was old-school but safe in this world where everything except your inner thoughts could be captured by technology. Paper could be burned or flushed down the toilet, even swallowed.

Max reminded her, on a daily basis, that the two of them were constantly being shadowed. Watched. It wasn't safe for her to meet with Roland.

That changed during her fifth week on the job. Late Saturday morning, Roland was smuggled in an SUV driven by Max's mom. Once she drove into the two-car garage, Roland entered the house. The blinds had been drawn in advance, in case someone was watching.

And someone was watching. Like during those first months with Anton, Frank had put people on her to make sure she checked out. Like Anton, Frank had moved her into a place closer to where she worked, a beautiful sunlit apartment she suspected was bugged. And like Anton, Frank had given her a copy phone, which she also suspected came equipped with all sorts of hidden software that tracked her movements, listened in on her conversations, monitored each and every email, call, and text she sent and received.

Roland was in a gregarious mood, his dry wit on full display as the two of them ate Chinese takeout on plastic plates in the upstairs bedroom. "He's an interesting guy, our Frank," Roland said. "On paper, he's pretty vanilla. Forty-eight, lives in Beverly Hills, drives a Buick. Owns a conservative mix of stocks and mutual funds, decent balance, nothing that will raise any alarms. He's funded his portfolio using income from his job, which is in IT—you know, computer servers and cybersecurity, shit like that."

"And he can afford to live in Beverly Hills?"

"He works for a real estate company called Kane and Associates. He's got a deal in place where he lives there. They don't outsource the company servers. Everything's in-house—literally. The real estate company operates out of a converted house."

"He using the company to launder his blood profits?"

"Hard so say at this point. To find out, we'd have to conduct a proper forensic accounting audit. That will come later. We're more interested in the guy who owns the company, Sebastian Kane. They're close friends, he and Frank. Grew up together in the same shitty neighborhood in East LA. Both were raised by single mothers. From what I've read, Frank never met his old man. His mother died when he was twelve—heroin overdose—and Kane's mother took Frank in so the kid wouldn't be kicked into the foster care system."

"And this Kane guy? What's his deal? Anything interesting?"

"Oh yes, most definitely." Roland wiped his mouth on the back of his hand. "When Kane was nineteen, he killed an undercover cop working in one of the big taco gangs running guns and drugs in East LA. It was self-defense—guy was protecting his girlfriend, this smoking-hot Latina."

"Good to know."

"Don't go all 'Me Too' on me now. I like to be thorough and descriptive." Roland grinned as he dipped a dumpling into a container of soy sauce. "The judge assigned the case had to play along with LAPD and side with the cops, and Sebastian got handed life without parole. Two years into his sentence, some pro bono liberal lawyer who worked for the Innocence Project thought nineteen-year-old Sebastian Kane got a raw deal because of being brown, and decided to take up the cause, do a little digging, and discovered someone on the jury was married to a cop. Showed bias. The real kicker was that the judge knew the deal about the juror and turned a blind eye. Case was overturned, and Sebastian was free to go."

"I'm more interested in his connection to the blood world."

"Oh, I'm sure Kane is involved."

"What about the woman who owns the Health and Wellness Center? Maya Dawson."

"You didn't google her?"

"Are you serious? I don't google anyone, just in case Frank is tracking everything on my phone."

"It was a trick question. You passed, by the way." Roland plopped another dumpling into his mouth. "Dr. Dawson had a kid who was a carrier, her son, Bradford. He was six when he was taken. She was away at a dermatology conference in San Diego when someone, maybe a group of people, broke into her house during the early-morning hours. Kid was snatched from his bed and the husband was dead asleep when someone pumped a round from a .38 into the back of his head and turned his brain into scrambled eggs. This was twelve, maybe fifteen years ago? She's at the conference, wondering why her husband hasn't returned any of her phone calls or texts for the past few days, when San Diego PD came to the hotel and broke the news to her. She still doesn't know what happened to her kid. No one does."

Ellie thought about her brother and wondered if the woman had, like her, purposely gone into the blood world in order to find her son. Had she discovered Bradford was dead, or was she still looking for him now, fifteen years later?

"Dawson had some sort of nervous breakdown," Roland said, "and squirreled herself away for a few months inside a private psychiatric facility in Denver. Then she decided to come back to LA, where she went from popping zits to running a high-end luxury facility that specialized in tit and nose jobs and laser peels and all that other fancy shit—and, I'm sure, blood treatments for discreet clients with deep pockets. You've met her, I take it."

"Just in passing. What about the people shadowing me? You haven't said anything."

"They're from a private security outfit owned by a gentleman by the name of Ron Wolff. Mr. Wolff, it seems, has found a good number of carriers who have been abducted. He also works with—or for—Frank and Sebastian Kane."

"That's . . . interesting."

"It's *genius* if my theory holds true. Would you like to hear my theory?"

"If Sebastian, Anton, whoever, abduct carriers, have them missing for a bit, and then Ron Wolff finds them, it gets Wolff in the good graces of the criminally overworked, underpaid, and overstressed LAPD. Cops are grateful for any help from the private security companies that are springing up all over the state. Ron Wolff offers to help the cops working the Blood Unit on other cases—maybe the carriers Frank and Kane have. Wolff can keep tabs on any developments in those cases."

"Look at you, being a detective, putting all the pieces together," Roland said. "I also have a solid theory as to why there's all this security on you and your boyfriend, Max. He a good kisser, by the way? I tried to get you a good kisser."

"Speaking of which, when am I going to see Cody?"

Roland waved his hand and sighed theatrically. "I need you to keep your mind on the job and not on sex. Think you can do that for ten minutes?"

"I'll try my best."

"Good. Now, let's talk about that explosion in WeHo. You hear about it?"

"I read about it online."

"What did you read?"

"Police said the homeowners were out of the country—Asia or something—and that some local drug dealers knew that, because the owners posted all their travels on Facebook, and then broke into the house, used it as a temporary meth lab, and had an accident."

"One of those shake-and-bake deals, supposedly."

Roland swiped a napkin across his mouth, then said, "That explosion happened hours after you had dinner with Frank. The next day, you start working for him, and you've got teams of people on you. I thought that was odd, so I made some phone calls. First off, it wasn't a meth explosion. Residual testing from the lab came back yesterday—no traces of meth anywhere."

"Then what caused the explosion?"

"ATF is leaning toward a bomb made of fertilizer. The three people who were killed in the explosion—they practically had to scoop up their remains using spatulas, what I was told. Anyway, it took some time to ID the bodies. Here's where it gets interesting. The three vics were men, all employed by Ron Wolff. You started work the next day after the explosion, and Ron's doubled the amount of people on you—*and* Anton. They're watching him very closely, too, and I believe it all has something to do with this fine gentleman."

Roland reached into a suit jacket pocket, came back with a four-by-six photograph, and handed it to her. The picture showed a white male with a squared-off jaw dressed in a Marine uniform.

"That the same guy in the photo Frank showed you?" Roland said.

Ellie nodded. "Gingerbread Man. Can't see the tattoos, though."

"But you're sure this is your shooter?"

"One hundred percent. You got a name?"

"Paul Young. He was a military man, once upon a time. Then he went back overseas, back to camel country, only this time as private security, which pays much better than the government. I guess you could call him Sebastian Kane's stepson."

"You guess?"

"Kane never officially adopted him. He did, however, live with Paul's mother, Trixie—yes, that's her legal, God-given name—for a long time. Paul was four when he and Mom moved into Kane's home. Paul doesn't live there. We don't know where he lives, honestly, or where he currently is."

Roland plucked another dumpling up with his chopsticks. "So, we know Paul is your shooter, and that he is most likely the one behind the death of the two carriers you saw in the house. So it stands to reason that Paul is involved in the blood world—more specifically, Frank and Sebastian's business. Our operating theory is, Frank and Sebastian are actively looking for Paul because he has become a liability or a threat, for reasons that have something to do with Brentwood."

"Was Paul behind the explosion in West Hollywood?"

"That has yet to be determined."

"Have you bugged Frank's car?"

"No. We can't get close enough to do the actual work. We need twenty minutes, minimum, to do it, and it has a car alarm, which is another complication. Every night he parks it in the garage of his home, which is the real estate office. We can't get to the car, and we don't want to ask a judge to sign off on a wiretap warrant, because we're afraid that it will get back to Frank, Kane, or Wolff. We have, however, installed a tracker on Frank's car."

"So where was he that night?"

"With his BFF, Sebastian," Roland said, beaming. "The night of the explosion, they took Sebastian's car—he drives a Jag—and drove to West Hollywood."

"To do what?"

Roland tapped his chopsticks against his paper plate. "When you agreed to go undercover, I gave you my word I'd always level with you. So here's the deal: we're having what you could call staffing issues. I don't have to tell you there are a lot of moving parts. The organizational chart we've created—it takes up two walls and gets bigger by the day. We're collecting a lot of information on this Ron Wolff guy, the people who work for him—the list of people keeps growing and growing and we've run out of bodies on our end. It's costing us a pretty penny, this operation, and it keeps getting bigger, along with the government's tab."

"And the federal bean counters got their panties in a bunch and are complaining to the top guys."

"Not just our bean counters, but also the LAPD's. Remember, this operation is supposed to be a joint expense. What's happening now is a lot of people on the top of both food chains are arguing about who's paying for what instead of splitting the tab fifty-fifty, as was agreed. You going to eat that last dumpling?"

"Help yourself," Ellie replied, distracted. She wasn't a stranger to bu-reaucratic infighting—she had dealt with it, albeit on a minor level, as a patrolwoman, and she had heard her fair share of stories around the sta-tion about the penny-pinching ways from the desk jockeys whose sole job was playing around with Excel spreadsheets. But this was the first time she had been involved in something that directly affected her—not just her career, but possibly her life.

Roland said, "It's a minor hiccup, happens all the time."

Ellie nodded.

"Hey, look at me. You're our prime asset. I won't let anything happen to you, okay? Me, the team—we've got your back. We watch over our own."

Ellie wanted to believe him—*had* to believe him. What other choice did she have?

Roland said, "Let them argue who's gonna pick up the tab. We've got more important matters—like celebrating. Remember the choker Anton took from you?"

"How could I forget?" For weeks Ellie had lived in fear that Anton had taken it apart and discovered it was bugged.

"The cheapo son of a bitch gave it to his Russian girlfriend as a gift. She's been wearing it, and she's been bragging a lot to her girlfriends about how Anton is going to be making some big move soon that'll make him—and her, she believes—ridiculously rich."

"Details?"

"Not as of yet. But we're watching your boy Anton—and Frank and his crew are watching him, too. Keeping a *very* close eye on him, as a mat-ter of fact. When's the last time you spoke to him?"

"About a week or so. He keeps asking about the job—just general 'How's it going?' stuff—and reminds me that I can come back to work for him if I want. I'm giving it some serious thought." Roland shot her an *Are you out of your mind?* look and Ellie said, "I'm bored out of my skull.

Frank's got me doing paperwork and babysitting a bunch of Barbie and Ken dolls."

"It will change. At some point he'll invite you into the inner circle, have you working with the actual blood clients. Just don't push him on it."

"I haven't."

"The three guys who were killed in the explosion—these guys had military training. So it stands to reason they went into that house, at that hour, to find someone. I'm guessing that someone was Paul. Only the house was rigged. So Frank and Sebastian are spooked, playing it safe, taking no chances. The surveillance on Anton and, therefore, you, since you worked for him—Frank needs to know if he can trust you, see if you're feeding information to Anton. I think, by the way, Frank is sort of hoping that happens. The building where you work? A lot of Ron's people are watching it—especially at night. I think they're hoping Paul comes there, you know, maybe tries to sabotage it or something—which is why you need to keep your eyes and ears open, keep reporting everything you see and hear to Max. Speaking of which, I need you to be—how can I say this?—more intimate with your make-believe boyfriend."

"I'm not sleeping with him."

"Wasn't asking you to," Roland said. "Although if you kids did, neither I nor Uncle Sam would stand in the way of young true love."

"I'm being serious."

"So am I. The way you kiss him, a quick peck on the lips, the way you hug him and hold his hand, it's like you're afraid you're going to catch a major case of the cooties. Is that what you young kids call it? The cooties?"

"Nobody has said that. Ever. And I want to see my real-life boyfriend."

"And I assure you, my good woman, I am currently working on that. In the interim, with Max, it's important to keep up appearances. You're not Ellie Batista; you're Faye Simpson, and Faye Simpson has got a love interest, and you've got to act the part—and look natural while you're doing it. You've got a lot of eyes on you, and I'm not the only one who has picked up on the way your body stiffens when you're in physical contact with Max."

"I had to do it once, for Anton, for the blood carrier."

"McDouchebag," Roland said.

"It left me feeling . . . Carrying lies for Faye Simpson is one thing. But kissing another man, fooling around with him, even if it's job related— no matter which way you cut it, it's cheating. Cody didn't sign up for that, and I'm having a hard time sitting with it."

"Of course you are. If you didn't feel that way, you'd be a sociopath." Roland's eyes searched hers for a moment. "We talked about this before you went undercover, that you'd have to find a way to put Cody to the side."

Ellie nodded. They had talked about it. At great length.

"You're playing a part, no different from an actress," Roland said. "But right now, you've got to keep your head in the game, and that means keeping up appearances. It means allowing Max to stay over at your place every once in a while."

"And in my bed."

"Ellie," Roland sighed, "all I'm asking you is to sleep with him in the same bed. I'm not asking you to have sex with him. It looks odd, you never having him stay over at your place, is what I'm saying."

He sounded frustrated, but she saw a lot of compassion in his eyes. "Look," Roland said, "this is a curveball, adding Max into the mix in order to deliver you messages and asking you to pretend you're really into him. I get it. Frank moved you into that nice apartment, so it stands to reason he probably owns it, and that it's bugged with mikes and cameras. Just up your game with Max, okay? Pretend he's Cody, some movie star, or football stud, whoever—I don't care. Just act like you're excited to see him—to *be* with him. Frank and his buddy Sebastian are paranoid by nature—they have to be, in order to have survived this long in the blood game. Now, though, three guys dead from a bomb—it screams setup. It says someone is after them. Maybe it's Paul or the Armenians or the Mexicans, maybe all three. Frank and Sebastian are in a watch-and-wait mode, putting everyone under the microscope, so let's not give them any reason to suspect you might not be who you say you are, okay?"

Down the hall, Ellie heard her phone ring—the one Frank had given to her. She had paired the phone with her smartwatch, and her watch vibrated against her wrist, the name of the caller displayed on the tiny screen: Anton.

"Ah," Roland said, seeing Anton's name. "The game's afoot, as Sherlock Holmes would say."

Ellie got to her feet. "Actually, it was Shakespeare who said that. *Henry the Fifth.*"

"You young kids. You think you know everything."

CHAPTER 21

THE NIGHT SEBASTIAN received the text from Paul—and he knew it was Paul, because no one else but that cocksucker would have sent him that message—he ditched his expensive smartphone, with its fancy CIA-level encryption, and went the old-school route still used by drug dealers working the streets: cheap, disposable burner phones.

Sebastian had four, each one assigned to a certain key person in his operation: Frank, Ron, Maya, and his executive assistant at the real estate company, Gabriella, who was handling all of his business calls. Sebastian couldn't tell her the truth of what was going on—she had no idea what he really did for a living—so he sold her a story about how he had been a victim of identity theft, his bank accounts nearly wiped out, the police suspected, by Russian hackers. Until the culprits were found, he had been advised by his accountant not to open up any new accounts—hence the need for a cheap disposable. Sebastian didn't owe Gabriella an explanation, but revolving numbers—he used a new phone every day—were odd, the things of drug dealers, and he didn't need Gabriella talking.

Every day at noon, Sebastian changed out his burners for new ones. It was a major pain in the ass, this process—he had to call each person and exchange new numbers (they themselves were all using brand-new burner phones each day)—but it had to be done. Sebastian and Frank still had no idea how Paul had gotten ahold of the number for Sebastian's previous smartphone, which made Sebastian wonder if he had a mole in his organization. If he did, it was one of four people: Frank, Ron, Maya, or Gabriella.

Fresh from the shower, he grabbed a new burner, and was working it from its blister pack when one of yesterday's burners rang. He walked over to the bureau, where he had set them up. Maya Dawson was calling.

As usual, Maya skipped the pleasantries and got right to the point. She spoke cryptically, afraid that Paul might be listening in. "I need to see you. I have something to show you."

Sebastian knew what this *something* was. "Come to the house."

"No. You need to see it. In person."

Maya was asking him to come to their new Celebrity Center. She sounded nervous—or was that a tinge of excitement he detected?

"Okay," Sebastian said. "I'll be there as soon as I can."

Since the attempt on his life, both he and Frank had operated on the assumption that Paul, Guidry, or a group of people had eyes on them at all times, hoping he and Frank would continue business as usual and lead Paul and his crew to the key places of their operations—the treatment centers and blood farms. For that reason, neither Frank nor Sebastian had visited the Celebrity Center. Fortunately, a plan had been put in place months ago, in the event he or Frank had to travel to any of his key buildings without being followed.

When Sebastian left his home, he drove to the Sherman Oaks Galleria and parked on the top floor of the private garage, where he traded his Jaguar for a Toyota Camry with tinted windows. All the substitute cars had tinted windows dark enough to prevent his face from being seen.

Sebastian drove and parked at two more locations. His last car, a Honda Civic, was the one he used to drive to the Celebrity Center. He was making his final approach to Santa Monica Boulevard, in West Hollywood, when one of his burners rang—the one labeled "Frank."

"Anton reached out to Faye Simpson about twenty minutes ago," Frank said. "He wants to take her out to lunch so he can pick her brain on—and I'm quoting here—why women are such ungrateful bitches."

Sebastian didn't have to ask how Frank had found out about the call, nor did he need to ask about the contents of the Simpson woman's conversation with Anton. Faye Simpson's phone, like that of every other employee they brought into their blood world, was bugged, along with the employee apartments and every single thing inside them.

"Lunch," Sebastian said. "Should I call the press conference, or are you going to take care of that?"

"Reason I'm calling you is to figure out coverage."

Which had become a major problem and a major headache since the house explosion.

Three of Ron's men had died in the explosion, and there was no way to cover up that fact. Their remains would be identified at some point, so it was best for Ron to get ahead of the problem—and he did, using a story they had locked down in the event something catastrophic happened. He called a detective on the Blood Unit, Mark Alves, and explained that he had received a credible tip on his toll-free hotline about a sixteen-year-old carrier named Jonathan King, who had been abducted five months ago in Orange County. King, the caller said, was in a home in Cudahy. Ron had men in the area, working on an unrelated security matter, and he sent them to check out the lead. When they approached the house, Ron's team leader, Marty Straton, heard what he thought were gunshots, and decided to enter the premises. That was the last word he'd received from Marty.

But an explosion in a residential area that had left three dead and many injured and hundreds of thousands of dollars in property damage was another matter. A reporter had a source who had confirmed the explosion wasn't caused by some amateur junkie chemists trying to make meth but by "a sophisticated improvised explosive device utilizing fertilizer—the kind of IED used by terrorists." The terrorism angle was about to invite even more scrutiny, on a federal level, to Ron and his employees, who were already under the microscope, being questioned, possibly even watched. Ron had to divert his resources away from blood world matters until things quieted down. It was the safe play for everyone involved.

Frank said, "You know the guys Ron gave us, the ones who aren't on the books?"

"The guys we have keeping an eye on the Celebrity Center."

"Right. I say we divert them from the Center and have them follow Anton for the day, see if anything develops. I can remotely turn Faye's phone into a listening device. My tablet has all the software I need to listen in. All I need is to be somewhere in a radius of seven hundred and fifty feet."

"Here's an idea: how about turning the dial down on the paranoia?"

"Paranoia is what's going to keep us alive, Sebastian."

"Look. You're the one who's been all Team Anton since the beginning— and everything keeps pointing to he's still on our side of the fence. As for Faye Simpson—and I'm using your words here—she hasn't done a single thing to indicate she's working for anyone but us."

Frank said nothing. *What can he say?* Sebastian thought. *He knows I'm right.*

"Besides," Sebastian said, "Faye doesn't have access to our blood clients, and she has no idea where our donors are housed. In other words, she doesn't know anything valuable."

"She knows the building belongs to us."

"Which is all the more reason why we're to keep the guys we have at the Celebrity Center. That's our prime asset. You want to go play spy, you'll have to do it alone."

"I'll come by and pick you up. It'll do both of us good to get out."

"I have to go see Maya."

Frank didn't ask what it was about; he knew.

Sebastian hung up, thinking about the explosion. Again. It was always there, what had happened, a thorn stuck in the brain.

Early on, he and Frank had considered the possibility of Paul trying to take them out with a mail bomb delivered to the home or office. Such bombs were easy to make, provided you knew what you were doing, and it stood to reason that Paul and Guidry did, given their military training. Sebastian had taken the necessary steps, diverting all of his mail to a post office box, where one of Ron's men picked it up and brought it to a place where the mail was x-rayed. They had never once considered the possibility of Paul leading them into a trap, one involving an IED.

These past few months, he'd assumed—arrogantly, as it turned out—that Paul was simply a boy, and not a bright one at that. Sebastian had underestimated him. He wouldn't make that mistake again.

The Celebrity Center's official, public name was the Los Angeles Health and Wellness Center. The building sat tucked back from the main street, another boring, vanilla structure of light gray concrete. It had ten floors, with nice views of the city and the ocean, but its main attraction was the private parking garage, with its private elevator access. Celebrities and other high-profile clients looking for a nip/tuck or to treat dermatological issues could come here and not risk being spotted by the paparazzi or anyone else; they were guaranteed privacy.

The same would be true for blood clients. They would be driven here and brought up separately, to the tenth floor, where they would wake up in private, hidden treatment rooms to receive their Pandora transfusions.

The master key he carried was the size of a credit card and fit neatly in his front suit pocket. It also acted as a garage door opener. As Sebastian approached the private, locked garage, the door opened automatically and, after he entered, slid closed. The only car he saw was Maya's Jeep Grand Cherokee.

It was Saturday. The Wellness Center didn't see patients on weekends.

He parked next to the private elevator, and then rode it up to the tenth floor. He made his way through the circular-shaped hallway, the walls made of glass, the heels of his shoes clicking across the spotless white floor until he stopped at the door of Maya Dawson's private office. He didn't need a magnetic key card to unlock it. The master key automatically did that. But it wouldn't help him with the next part.

Once inside Maya's office, he secured the door with a good old-fashioned dead bolt, even though Sebastian knew he and Maya were the only ones in the building. It was more out of habit than out of paranoia. Medical offices, like schools and other facilities, weren't immune to gunmen looking to abduct carriers. Medical offices, though, were also targeted with alarming frequency, especially for break-ins, people looking for information on carriers or, even better, discovering which facilities stored carrier blood.

Sebastian moved behind the immense glass deck and pressed his right hand flat against the section of touch-sensitive glass. It scanned his handprint and matched it to the only three stored in the database: his, Maya's, and Frank's. Sebastian typed the password on the keyboard—Frank always insisted on dual security measures—and turned his attention to his left, where three bookcases took up an entire wall.

A soft click of latches springing free, and then the middle bookcase opening noiselessly. It hid the treatment rooms behind the walls, not only to give the clients ultimate privacy but also to prevent them from being discovered in the event of a police raid. It had never happened to him, but it had happened to the Armenians. Sebastian had survived—and flourished—by staying off everyone's radar. And now Paul had put his life's work in jeopardy.

Sebastian hurried inside the small hidden alcove and with four quick steps found Maya Dawson seated in an office chair in the compact square room, staring at three privacy screens. Each one took up a wall, and each one looked inside the treatment room using the same one-way glass the police used when interrogating suspects.

The middle screen was black, but not the other two. In those rooms he saw two clients, both middle-aged women, one of whom was a successful TV actress on a sitcom called *Life with Howie*, where the woman played a mouthy former beauty pageant contestant from Long Island turned trophy wife of an older guy who'd won the lottery. They both sat in comfortable chairs—the actress watching something on TV, the other woman reading an actual, physical book—while a transfusion machine slowly withdrew their blood and replaced it with a carrier's, a process that took most of the day. Clients weren't allowed to bring their phones or any other electronic devices they owned. They were meticulously searched for everything, including GPS trackers that could be injected under the skin, before being transported to the center.

Unlike the treatment rooms in the previous building, the rooms here resembled luxury suites—fresh flowers, beds with linens made of the highest-quality merino wool woven with a silk jacquard and small amounts of gold; catered meals featuring caviar; bottled water collected from a spring off the coast of Hawaii and hailed as having amazing health benefits; and a whole host of other bullshit trappings expected by the rich and famous.

"Why's the screen turned off?" Sebastian said.

"I'll show you in a minute." She picked up a computer tablet.

In addition to overseeing the new Celebrity Center, Dr. Maya Dawson was responsible for the health of all of Sebastian's carriers. When she discovered Jolie Simone's pregnancy, Maya had immediately removed Jolie from the donation roster. Donating blood while pregnant depleted a woman's iron, made her susceptible to anemia and other health risks.

During the time when no one except Simone and her baby daddy knew she was pregnant, Jolie had donated only two pints—not enough to perform a whole-body transfusion but certainly enough to test out Paul's theory about the power of a pregnant carrier's blood.

Which was why Sebastian had Sixto Ferreria, the second person Paul had texted, handed over for testing. *But not before breaking the kid's bones,* he thought. Sebastian had ordered Frank to do that first, before taking Sixto here for testing. Sebastian wanted to see how pregnant carrier blood would affect healing, among other things.

"Mr. Ferreria," Maya said, "is up and walking."

Sebastian chuckled. "Bullshit."

Maya's expression remained stern.

Sebastian felt a quickening in the pit of his stomach. *That can't be true,* he thought. Pandora could heal broken bones and fractures, but it would take way longer than seventy-two hours to be up and walking.

"He's still a bit stiff," Maya said, "and he's not going to run any marathons, but the bones are healing quickly—much, much quicker than with Pandora."

"Did you mix Jolie's blood with our drug combo?"

"I did. If Paul knows the medications we use—"

"He doesn't."

"Did you ever find out what he's using with his transfusions?"

"Viramab."

Maya sighed and rubbed her forehead. "Those people . . . they're as good as dead."

Sebastian nodded with his chin to Ferreria. "Side effects?"

"None."

That, too, surprised him. Almost every client complained of dizziness and nausea, experienced fever and chills during and after a Pandora transfusion. People who had an allergic reaction broke out in hives. There were more serious problems, things like a hemolytic reaction in which a patient's immune system attacked the red blood cells of the donor.

"Actually," Maya said, "there is one major side effect."

"What?"

"He masturbates. Frequently."

"On camera?"

"Anywhere. He's totally uninhibited."

Sebastian recalled the story Frank had shared with him about Sophia Vargas and the policeman in her backyard. Sophia had been on Jolie's blood.

Maya unlocked the tablet using a series of complicated passwords, all of which changed on a weekly basis. "I gave him only half a pint of Jolie's blood. I wanted to use it as a baseline. Take a look at these before pictures."

Maya handed him the tablet. She always took pictures of clients before a transfusion—close-up shots of clients stripped down to their underwear. They were used for comparison purposes, to show the clients how their skin and body compositions reacted and changed.

Only Sixto Ferreria hadn't come into the Wellness Center looking like the typical client. Like Link, Ferreria had been tortured, starved, and deprived of sleep over several months.

A series of small photographs, each one half the size of a playing card, was loaded on the screen. Sebastian tapped the first picture, enlarging it, and then used his finger to swipe through them.

In each one, Ferreria, stripped down to his soiled boxer shorts, looked like someone who had been pulled from a major car accident. Beneath twisted limbs, swelling bruises, and open wounds, Sebastian could see the traces of how the kid had looked before—a grossly overweight Hispanic twenty-something male with at least three chins, thinning black hair, and a pair of man tits with nipples the size of pepperonis.

"Okay," Sebastian said, placing the tablet on the counter. "Let's see him."

Maya flipped a switch.

Twenty-three-year-old Sixto Ferreria stood in the middle of the treatment room, drying himself off with a towel as he watched baseball highlights on ESPN. At first Sebastian thought the man had stepped out of the shower; a lot of clients opted for one instead of using heavy cooling blankets to cool down after a transfusion as their core temperature shot up. Ferreria had on a pair of gray boxer briefs. They were dark with sweat.

Maya said, "He has a slight fever from the transfusion, which, as we know, is normal, as is his excessive perspiration."

What wasn't normal—what made Sebastian's eyes widen with shock and awe—was just how different the Ferreria kid looked *now*. Not only was the man up and walking—a miracle in and of itself—but the wounds covering nearly every inch of his skin in the photos were either completely healed or on their way to being fully healed.

On top of that, nearly all his excess fat was gone. The kid wasn't going to be a bathing suit model, but he might have been twenty pounds away from it.

Sebastian snapped his attention back to Maya and said, "*This* is after one pint?"

"*Half* a pint, and seventy-two hours."

Sebastian wanted to call bullshit. To achieve Pandora's optimum benefits, a client would have to be given a full-body transfusion and then wait at least two weeks for it to work its magic. After that much blood and that much time, you might see an amazing transformation take place: wrinkles reduced, skin tightened, everything firmed up.

But this, what he was seeing right here, right now . . . it couldn't be possible. The man looked like an entirely different person. Like he hadn't been beaten nearly to death.

"Vitals?" Sebastian asked as he watched Sixto run the towel across his hair.

"His blood pressure is a bit higher than I'd like, but blood pressure usually spikes after a transfusion, because of the stress the body is put under. Again, that's normal. He may experience some mild flu-like symptoms in the days to come. We'll see."

"And his heart?" Heart attacks were always the biggest risk factor in carrier transfusions, the new blood putting the heart under strain.

"Normal," Maya said. "I performed an EKG, just to be sure. No complaints of heart palpitations or dyspnea—breathlessness—and no loss of consciousness or reported dizziness."

Sebastian couldn't keep his eyes off of Sixto.

"That is goddamn remarkable."

"That's one word for it." Maya didn't hide her disgust. Sebastian had filled her in on Paul's business plan of abducting female carriers and raping them until they were pregnant. He had also given her the pills Paul was crudely manufacturing.

"Paul was right," Sebastian said, and turned to her. His throat felt unusually dry, and his heart was tripping inside his chest the way it had at night years ago, after he'd had too much Scotch, like it was pumping sludge instead of blood. "Pregnancy blood is much more potent." Then, as an afterthought: "It will put us out of business."

She looked at him sharply. "I will have no part in allowing current or future female carriers to be—"

"I wasn't suggesting that. Jesus, Maya."

"If he goes through with this, gets this stuff to market . . ." She didn't finish the thought. She shook her head and rested a hand on her throat as she swallowed, and when she turned away, facing the window, she suddenly looked old to him, as if she'd aged ten years in the last ten or so minutes.

CHAPTER 22

BACK WHEN SHE worked for Anton, Ellie had always made sure she was on time. Her health depended on it. The first week she went to work for him, learning the ropes, one of his stickmen ended up being five minutes late for a meeting. The guy had a valid excuse: a flat tire. He had even taken a picture of it on his phone and had texted it to Anton. Anton nodded in understanding and then broke the guy's nose.

Ellie was waiting for him outside of her building at ten to one when, across the busy street, she saw Anton's black BMW, with its tinted windows, slide to a stop and double-park. The guy driving behind him had to pump the brakes a bit and voiced his displeasure by planting his hand on the horn. Ellie darted through the traffic, the guy in the Audi not letting up on the horn, and when she got into the passenger seat, Anton threw his door open, about to storm out and put the fear of God into the driver. She grabbed his arm, his bicep as hard as granite.

"It's not worth it," she yelled over the horn. "Come on—let's go."

Anton shut the door but kept his hand on the handle, his attention pinned on the rearview mirror as he debated whether or not to go out and unleash holy hell. He wasn't dressed for it: Prada loafers without socks, and tight, dark designer jeans with an even tighter black V-neck shirt. Anton put a high regard on his clothes, doted on them like children. He wouldn't want to get them wrinkled, let alone bloodied, which she took as a good sign.

The Audi peeled out from behind Anton and darted back into traffic. Anton stared after it, quiet, grinding his teeth. He wore a pair of mirrored Oakley sunglasses, and the skin of his face was red with anger.

Working with Anton, she had learned quickly to forecast his mood swings, which were often as chaotic and unpredictable as summertime in New England. Sometimes the storm lasted minutes, sometimes days (especially if he'd gotten a blood transfusion), replaced by gray clouds or, God willing, sunshine and clear blue skies. Whatever was eating at him, it had nothing to do with the Audi.

She knew better than to ask. Anton hated when his employees asked him personal questions of any kind. It would set him off.

Then again, Faye Simpson wasn't his employee, not anymore. Faye Simpson now worked exclusively with Frank. Faye Simpson wouldn't ask Anton questions, but Officer Ellie Batista would because she needed to know what Anton was after, his thoughts, his game plan, everything.

Still, she'd need to be careful. On a good day, Anton was about as stable as a live grenade.

Anton got a call. His phone was connected to the BMW's computer system through Bluetooth, so the caller's name was displayed on the console: Galina. Anton took it.

The woman spoke only in Russian. Anton spoke in Russian, too, and while Ellie didn't have the slightest idea what they were talking about, she knew it wasn't good. The woman screamed at Anton, but he didn't scream back—didn't do much of anything except sit there and rattle off a few Russian words, looking like he wanted to take the world's longest vacation. The call ended ten minutes later, when Galina hung up.

"What is it with you broads?" Anton asked, throwing his hands in the air. "You act nice, treat them right, take them out to nice dinners and shit, and what do they do? They squeeze your nut sack and smile because you're not giving them more. But if you treat them like dirt, wipe your feet all over them, shit on them, they smile and come back and ask for more. You're all insane."

Then, when Ellie didn't reply, he turned his head to her and said, "What? You got nothing to say?"

"I wasn't aware you wanted my input."

"Let's hear it. I need your help with this."

"That's a sweeping generalization, your view of women."

"You saying I'm a liar?"

"You ever think you're picking out the wrong kind of woman? That maybe instead of going after the ones who have brains the size of a chickpea and beach-ball-sized boobs—"

"I'm a tit guy. It's in my DNA—I can't help it."

"How about finding a woman of substance? They are out there, you know."

"Yeah, and they're fat and collect cats." Anton sighed.

Then, much to her surprise, he opened up to her about his problems with his girlfriend, Galina. She was Russian, Anton explained, and they had met at the wedding of a mutual friend, and after dating for eight months she thought they should move in together. Galina had become "too Americanized," he said—had become a spoiled brat of a woman who expected to have the latest this and that, top-of-the-line cars and clothes, a beautiful home that would be the envy of her friends. Only she didn't want to work for any of it. That was the job of a man, and she didn't like how cheap Anton had become. She deserved the finer things in life, and if Anton couldn't provide, then she'd find someone who could.

"I should kick her out on her ass, is what I should do," Anton said.

"So what's stopping you?" Ellie noticed they weren't heading to Culver City. Were, in fact, heading in the opposite direction. And Anton had spent a lot of time subtly checking his rearview mirror, just a slight tilt of the head.

"She's pregnant," Anton said.

"Judging by your tone, I'm guessing I shouldn't say congratulations."

"She said she was on the pill. Told me she didn't want kids, right? Had no interest in them. This morning she tells me, Look, you want me to keep this thing growing in my belly, then you've got to show me how much you love me, and that means opening up my wallet, 'cause that's all she cares about, what makes her happy."

Anton pulled right, into the entrance to a BMW dealership. "And if I don't—how you say it?—pony up these things for her, she's going to get an abortion." He made the sign of the cross. "The woman is an animal, is what she is. I should put a bag over her head, put her out of her misery."

"I thought we were going to lunch."

"I'm bleeding my heart out to you here and you're worried about lunch? That is the problem with you women, how you mess with a man's pride. You take that away from a man and he can't be responsible for his actions. Don't matter if you're a woman or man, the person who screws with your pride or tries to steal it, and you put up with that? A man without pride is not a man. He's a *pizda*."

"A what?"

"Forget it." Anton drove behind the dealership. "I got to pick up a part for my car. It'll take five, ten minutes tops. Can your little stomach wait that long, or are you going to faint from hunger?"

"I'll be fine."

"You sure? I can get you a snack from a vending machine or some shit, tide you over."

"I said I'm fine." Ellie's head ached. She'd forgotten what it was like to talk to him, trying to follow his thoughts, his violent mood swings. She wondered if he'd had a blood transfusion. She didn't see any marks on his arms.

The back of the dealership contained a warehouse-like area where BMW cars and SUVs were serviced. Several bay doors were open. Anton surveyed them for a moment, then headed toward the one on the far right, Ellie's gut instincts telling her something was up even before Anton picked up a small folded piece of paper from the console and handed it to her. It read:

Leave purse & phone in car. no questions.

Ellie stared at Anton's block-lettered handwriting, thinking: *He's afraid my phone is bugged, my movements being tracked. And he would be right.*

Ellie still had the piece of paper in her hands when he drove into the bay. The door began to slide down, a big, clanking sound that rattled inside her skull. The bay door didn't have any windows—there were no windows in here at all, she noticed, just a long row of cars being serviced by mechanics, and she had a moment of panic, feeling like she was trapped, like she had been brought here because Anton had found out something about her, possibly her real identity, and planned to take her out.

The thought, and the accompanying feeling, she realized, was insane, and she pushed it aside. Still, the feeling wouldn't go away, brushed against the walls of her heart when Anton turned in his seat and grabbed something that didn't go with his tough-guy image: a Gucci backpack. He took it with him as he got out of the car. Ellie followed, leaving her purse and phone behind as instructed, and saw him walking across the bay, the mechanics ignoring him. She followed, stopped when he turned to her.

"You drive," he said, and pointed to a silver SUV with tinted windows.

Ellie got behind the wheel. Anton tossed the backpack in the rear seat, and when he slid into the passenger seat, he programmed an address into the console's built-in GPS system.

"When the door goes up," he said, "start the car and drive."

Anton adjusted his seat all the way back. He folded his hands on his stomach and said, "I need to meditate, clear my mind. No talking."

The door went up.

Ellie drove out of the bay, heading for the highway.

They drove north on California State Route 99 for two hours in silence. Well, not *total* silence. When the British female voice wasn't announcing her turn-by-turn directions, Ellie listened to Anton snoring softly beside her.

The address Anton had plugged into the GPS was in Fresno.

What would bring Anton all the way out here, two hundred plus miles from LA?

Clearly Anton was afraid of being followed, which was why he had switched vehicles at the dealership and ordered her to leave her phone in his car. Clearly he suspected Frank or his people might be tailing him. Ellie was more concerned about her people.

Roland used her phone's cell signal to track her movements. His people, Roland had told her, were watching her at pretty much all times, but they didn't get too close, as they didn't want Anton, Frank, or anyone else to get even the slightest whiff of being under surveillance. Ellie had no idea who Roland's men (or women) were, because Roland wanted her to act natural and focus on her job, not spotting a familiar face and risking Anton or someone else she was working with picking up on it. The phone was the device that allowed the task force members working surveillance to hang back, and her phone was in LA. Had Roland's people found out they had been duped? Probably Frank's people, too, if they had been following Anton.

One thing was clear: there was a good chance she was on her own.

The uptight British GPS lady stiffly announced their destination was a mile ahead, on the right. Anton stirred awake. He sat up abruptly, and for some reason it reminded her of an old black-and-white horror movie she had seen a long time ago, when she was a kid—Dracula sitting up in his coffin, wide-awake and ready to feed on blood.

Where, exactly, are we going? Ellie wondered. Not a residential area—that was for sure. So far, the only things she'd seen on this long street were of the commercial variety: strip malls, big-box stores, and a couple of gas stations.

The address was for an expansive mall-like parking lot. It didn't belong to a shopping mall but to an old Toyota manufacturing plant. She'd caught the sign in the front, long since faded by the sun and neglect, a couple letters missing.

"Drive around to the back," Anton said, yawning.

"I think it's time you tell me what I'm walking into."

"You're not walking into anything. You're going to stay in the car." There wasn't a trace of anxiety in his voice—or on his face, for that matter. He yawned again, his jaw popping. She could see his eyes blinking behind his sunglasses. "And stay frosty, okay? Eyes and ears, eyes and ears—especially on your six. You don't want anyone to smoke check you."

It annoyed the shit out of her when he spoke in military slang, as if he had been a real soldier instead of a thug who did blood, shot 'roids into an ass cheek, shopped at Barneys, and had a five-thousand-dollar espresso machine in his condo. The tough-guy talk sounded like it had been plucked from video games and bad movies; still, he *did* have the ability to back up the tough-guy talk, because Anton *was* tough—ferociously so. She had seen him in action several times, with her own eyes.

They were in the back of the building now. She saw a bunch of gray-and-brown interconnected buildings, all the street-level windows gone, replaced by wood boards spray-painted with graffiti, like the rest of the plant.

"See that wide-open bay up there?" Anton said, pointing out the windshield. "Park in front of it."

Ellie had to drive around oil barrels, shopping carts, and more than a few soiled mattresses scattered haphazardly on the ground. "How many people are you meeting?"

"That remains to be seen." Anton snorted and leaned forward in his seat, scanning the area. "There's a Glock in my backpack. Keep it handy but not out in the open. Put it in this side compartment here, or under the seat."

Ellie's back was slick with sweat.

"You ever fire a gun?" Anton asked.

Ellie Batista had, but not Faye Simpson. "Held a couple but never fired one."

"You point and pull the trigger—that's it." She could feel his gaze on the side of her face. "Relax, will you? This is just for your protection, in case this shit goes sideways. I don't think it will, but like you Americans say, it's better to be prepared than to get caught with your dick flapping in the wind—am I right?"

"I don't even know what this situation is."

"Stop right here."

The floor inside the bay was concrete. It was stained by decades of rust and grease. The afternoon sun lit up a good amount of the space directly in front of her, and she saw part of what appeared to be an assembly line, robotic arms of different shapes and sizes frozen in midair and stiff with rust, practically all the paint in there having fallen off. Ellie shoved the gearshift into park and left the engine running.

"Don't forget the nine," Anton said, and then got out.

Ellie turned in her seat and grabbed the backpack. It was a basic thing, more stylish than practical. It had a pair of outside leather flaps with snap buttons, and inside the flaps she found vials of both steroids and human growth hormone (no big surprise there), and packs of Dentyne gum guaranteed to keep your breath fresh for hours.

In the main compartment, she saw a bunch of burner phones, a leather journal of some sort, and a thick manila folder. She hunted for the Glock, finally found it buried at the bottom—a Glock 19. The backpack went onto the passenger seat, in case she needed to use one of the burners, and then she cracked open his window and hers so she could hear, and watched as Anton made his way inside the abandoned plant.

He stopped thirty or so feet away from the entrance, then abruptly turned right, stuck his fingers in his mouth, and whistled. From somewhere inside the plant she thought she heard a car engine start. Anton didn't wait around; he walked back to the Beemer, but he didn't get inside. He leaned against the hood, directly in front of her, and folded his arms across his chest.

A single car emerged from the plant—a black Mercedes SUV with tinted windows, Ellie wondering what it was about gangster types always needing to drive top-of-the-line cars. The Mercedes parked at an angle in front of her, along the left side. The driver didn't cut the engine or step out of the car, but the passenger-side door opened. Ellie felt her mouth dry up.

Gingerbread Man looked different from the last time Ellie had seen him. The first thing she noticed was his hair: It was longer, the crew cut having grown out, and covering the tops of his ears, and it was parted razor sharply on the side. It was also dyed black—the same color as his beard. He wore a pair of stylish eyeglasses with thick black frames and a black suit that had been expertly tailored, or possibly made from scratch, in order to accommodate his muscular build.

But the other physical characteristics she remembered were still there, untouched by a surgeon's knife: the broad nose that looked like an inverted triangle, with flared nostrils; the thin, wormy lips commonly seen on certain elderly women.

Gingerbread Man—*Paul*, she reminded herself, *his name is Paul Young*—carried himself with confidence as he walked around the car. He slowed a bit when he eyed Anton, and took his measure. Paul didn't come forward and shake Anton's hand. He stood there with his hands in his pockets, jingling his change and looking a little consolatory, she thought, like a boy who had been caught red-handed and couldn't lie his way out. His tone confirmed it when he spoke.

"Appreciate you coming out, Anton."

Anton said nothing. His face, Ellie saw, was slack—which was a bad sign. It meant some internal pilot light had been turned on, his blood warming up, getting ready for a fight. It was the look he got when the shit was going to hit the fan.

Eyes on Anton, Ellie reached for the nine resting on her lap. She released the safety and held the Glock as her gaze cut to Paul. She watched from behind her sunglasses and from behind the tinted windows, the man who had killed her partner and had tried to kill her at the start of this past summer now standing on the opposite side of the door, less than ten feet way.

Paul looked Anton up and down.

Anton snickered. "You think I'm packing?"

"Wouldn't put it past you. And I certainly wouldn't blame you."

Anton said nothing.

"Thought you might not show up," Paul said. "Then I said to myself, No, he will. He *has* to. Anton has no place to go. He can't work for the Armenians or the Mexicans. They don't want him."

To Ellie's ears, it sounded like a threat. Anton, though, let it wash right over him. Which surprised her. Usually a threat caused him to start using his fists. But he didn't move, and that made Ellie wonder if Anton was afraid of Paul. Paul had a good amount of size compared to Anton, but if it came down to a fight, she'd put all her money on Anton. In her experience, guys who were heavily into bodybuilding relied solely on their size to make their opponents back down, because they didn't know how to fight.

Anton nodded with his chin to the Mercedes and said, "Looks like you brought along some company."

"Just my driver."

"He shy or something?"

"He's just my driver."

"Maybe he should say hello."

Paul looked over his shoulder, to the driver, and nodded. The window came down. The driver was a white guy who was nowhere near as tall as

Paul, and nowhere near as big, although he did seem to have a good amount of muscle on him. He wore sunglasses and a black collared shirt with the sleeves rolled up, and he had both forearms draped on top of the steering wheel to show he wasn't carrying. He was somewhere in his late twenties to early thirties, Ellie guessed, and had a military-style crew cut and teeth that were too big for his face. He chewed gum methodically, trying to give off the vibe that he wasn't nervous.

Only he was. Ellie caught the tight way he swallowed. Guy was probably not even conscious he was doing it. He was a pretender. Didn't mean he wasn't dangerous, though. Could be quick with a gun. Like her, he probably had one within reach.

"Anyone there in the back?" Anton asked.

The driver looked to Paul. Paul nodded and the driver rolled down the back window. The backseat was empty.

"You want to check the trunk, too?" Paul asked. "Pat my boy down?"

"Not a bad idea," Anton replied.

"Then please, be my guest. While you do that, I'll introduce myself to the person you brought along. Or maybe he'd like to roll down his window and introduce himself?"

"You don't get to make the rules. Not with me. Not after that shit you pulled."

Paul opened his mouth to speak, then paused, as if second-guessing himself. He sighed—a bit theatrically, Ellie thought—and then he hung his head for a moment, his lips pursed.

"You know what? You're right," Paul said. "You've got every right to be pissed about what happened in Brentwood. I know they've put you under the microscope."

"*Under* it? They kicked it up my ass." Color was creeping up Anton's neck—a sure sign he was getting ready to explode. "They've followed me for *months* since Brentwood 'cause they thought you and I were working together, had some sort of plan in place. They *still* think that."

They, Ellie thought, had to be Frank and the real estate guy, Sebastian Kane.

Paul said, "I take it they're back to watching you."

"Day and night. And I'm guessing you have something to do with that."

"Let's talk about insurance for a moment."

"I look like Blue Cross to you?"

"Not the medical kind," Paul said. "I'm talking the other kind—you know, like a liability policy. A smart man always protects his investments. He hopes he never has to use it, but he knows it's there if he needs it. It gives him peace of mind in case disaster strikes."

The anxiety Ellie felt made her want to shift in her seat, take a look behind her. Anton didn't move. He showed nothing, said nothing.

Paul said, "You're super pissed off, and I get that. I do. And I wouldn't blame you if you or your person there in the car wanted to come after me. But I'd advise you not to do that, because I took out a liability policy in the form of a friend who's handy with a sniper rifle. He's watching us right now, so let's everyone keep calm, cool, and collected, okay?"

Ellie felt the skin of her face flex against the bone. She wanted to grab the gearshift, throw it in reverse, and hit the gas, then peel right out of here. It would be the reaction of a normal, sane, and sensible person. But a normal, sensible person wouldn't have agreed to come here to meet alone with a killer—wouldn't have agreed to go undercover to glean secrets from a gang of psychopaths.

"Brentwood," Anton said.

"I asked your boy Tyree if he could hook me up with some of those new stickers you're using. Said I would pay him, too."

Paul, Ellie knew, was referring to James Tyree, the surfer-looking kid with the man bun who had packed an Uzi in his canvas bag. Her mind's eye coughed up the picture of the kid, his limp body splayed on the concrete near the pool, blood everywhere, as Paul said, "Tyree called me that morning. I told him where I was, and he came by to—"

"You go behind my back, use that kid to deliver my sticks to you—and that Uzi. My stickmen don't go around armed."

"I had nothing to do with that, Anton, I swear. I've got my own hardware—I didn't need to buy any from him."

"But you admit to going behind my back."

"Yes. Absolutely. One hundred percent."

Anton hadn't been expecting an admission of guilt. It threw him off guard just a bit, Ellie could tell.

Paul said, "I had something in the works—something major. I'm talking life changing. That's the reason why I asked you to meet, so we could—"

"You mowed him down."

"I didn't ask him to hang out, go for a swim. He was supposed to leave."

"You killed him. *My* guy."

"He got caught in the cross fire when the cops arrived—which, as I mentioned in that note I gave you, I had nothing to do with." Paul studied Anton for a moment. "It couldn't be helped, what happened to Tyree. An unforeseen consequence. As someone who has survived in this business a long time, you should under—"

"The next words outta your mouth better be about helping my bottom line."

"How much to settle it?"

"I'm thinking a million," Anton said.

"That's a lot of scratch for an orphan kid who was living on the street and giving out hand jobs."

"That's what Sebastian's offering for you."

"I thought it was half a mill."

"He bumped the reward up. It's half a million now for your head, a million if you're brought in alive."

"Wow. I'm surprised the cheap bastard bumped up the bounty."

"Tyree," Anton said.

"I'm not going to give you a million," Paul said. "But I'll give you two."

Anton stood in profile; Ellie could see his eyes narrow in thought behind his sunglasses, Anton searching for traps hidden in the bullshit.

Paul said, "But why settle for two million when I can give you more money than you can possibly imagine?"

"Yeah? I can imagine quite a lot."

"Then go ahead and pick a number and it's yours."

Anton snorted. "Whatever plan you've got cooking, Frank and Sebastian are not going to hand over their business to you."

Their business, Ellie thought. Were Frank and Sebastian equal partners?

Paul smiled. He had the look of someone who knew every single answer on a final exam.

"They will," Paul said. "I guarantee it."

"How? What are you going to do, rat him out to the Armenians? You do that, he'll turn around and rat you out. They won't stop looking for you."

"Sebastian is going to hand over everything to me. He's—"

"He'll never hand over his donors."

"I don't need them. He can go live with them, for all I care. I just need his infrastructure. The product I have is—"

"Better than Pandora. Right, you mentioned that in your little note."

"And that, my friend, is God's honest truth. Come on—let's take a walk."

"What's wrong with right here?"

"Nothing," Paul said. "But, all due respect, I asked you to come alone, so we could discuss those business matters I mentioned in my note, and you brought along someone—someone I don't know."

"That's my business."

"And now you're making it mine, which, I'm sure you can respect, puts me in an awkward position, as I don't want to bring an outsider into this."

"She's not an outsider," Anton said.

Paul's eyebrows rose at the word *she.*

"She's my insurance policy," Anton said, and then turned his head to her. "Roll down your window and say hello."

Ellie wore sunglasses, and her hair was different. Her clothes were different, too—*she* was different. *There's no way he'll recognize me,* she reassured herself as the window rolled down. *There's no way.*

Paul smiled at her the same way he did when he came out of the house in Brentwood, acting all natural and asking if there was a problem before taking out the AR-15 and turning the backyard into downtown Beirut. He pushed himself off the car and came closer—too close, Ellie thought. He leaned forward, hands on his knees, and from behind her sunglasses Ellie watched as Paul studied her face.

"Hello, there," he said brightly.

"Hello." Ellie thought her voice sounded normal—astounding given the fact that her heart was jackhammering against her breastbone like it wanted to explode from her chest and get as far away from here as possible. She couldn't stop wondering if he was looking at her the same way she was looking at him.

Again she told herself no. It was impossible. She looked radically different now, and there was no way he recognized her voice. Well, that wasn't entirely true—she *had* screamed at him to lower his weapon before the shooting started.

"You got a name, hon?" Paul asked. *"Habla usted inglés?"*

Anton answered the question. "Her name is Faye."

"Faye," Paul said, as if he were rolling the word around in his mouth like wine, seeing if he liked the way it tasted. "Faye what?"

Anton said, "Faye works for Frank."

Ellie couldn't stop the surprise from reaching her face. Her skin tingled and her brain felt like it had actually cramped. *Tell me he didn't just say what I think he said.* Paul, too, was experiencing his own WTF moment. His eyes widened, and his face stretched tight across the bone like that of someone experiencing his first prostate exam.

Anton said, "Now ask me why I brought her."

It was both interesting and terrifying to watch the transformation happening on Paul's face. Ellie had read her fair share about psychopaths, had even met one or two during her brief time on the streets, but it was always after the fact—after the creature or whatever it was that lived beneath their skin had been let out and done its damage. This was the first time she had seen one in the wild, so to speak, and the raw, brutal ugliness she saw in Paul's face reminded her of a home surveillance video of a pit bull that had mauled a four-year-old boy to death—which was what Paul wanted to do to Anton right now, lurch forward and maul him with his hands and teeth.

Anton didn't notice or didn't care. He cupped a hand around his ear and leaned forward a bit. "Sorry, what was that?"

Paul's face . . . it didn't relax, but it looked reasonably human again. At least for the moment. "Why did you bring her?" he asked, his tone cold. Clipped.

"So glad you asked," Anton replied. "Faye works at the new place where they perform the transfusions. She has access to the client database, where the blood is stored, everything."

No, I don't, Ellie wanted to scream. Why was Anton feeding him this complete and utter bullshit?

Paul said, "What about his donors?"

Anton's smile was like a fist. "You ready to have a serious talk?"

Paul said nothing. They stared at each other in a way that reminded Ellie of those old Clint Eastwood Westerns, two gunslingers measuring each other up. Only Anton's head was in a sniper scope, Anton acting like he'd been in such a position before, no big deal.

Paul eased himself off the car. Was he leaving?

No. He motioned for Anton to join him. Anton straightened and followed Paul into the plant. As Ellie watched the two of them disappear somewhere in the shadows, she rolled up the window, the BMW motor purring softly through her seat.

It was risky, the idea she had in mind. She could waste time debating it in her head or she could listen to her gut instincts. She went with her gut.

Ellie grabbed a fresh burner. As she dialed Roland's number, she turned on the radio, adjusting the volume so it was just loud enough to drown out the sound of her voice.

Roland picked up. Ellie didn't realize how dry and tight her throat felt until she spoke.

"It's me. Don't speak—just listen."

She gave Roland a quick rundown of where she was and what had happened. He gave her instructions, and an address where she was to meet him as soon as she could. The call lasted less than a minute, no way to trace it. She removed the SIM card and battery from the burner to prevent the signal from being traced anyway. Both components went into her pocket, along with the burner. Now the backpack.

From behind the tinted windows, she made a careful study of its contents while keeping a watchful eye on the front window. Anton could come back at any moment.

The leather planner was something called "The Best Self Journal." In addition to having an area where you could list your appointments, the planner had areas for goals, daily targets, morning and evening gratitude lists. It would have made an interesting read if Anton had written in English instead of Russian. The manila folder contained sheet after sheet of commercial properties available for sale all over California. Real estate listings, she thought. She saw something called an MLS number, and while she didn't know what that was, the rest was easy enough to read—costs per square foot, amenities, detailed descriptions and pictures of interiors and exteriors—everything a potential buyer would need to know.

Toward the back of the stack, she found a listing for a sprawling residential property in Ojai, a city in Ventura County, north of Los Angeles. Known for its hills and mountains, it was a popular destination for tourists who were into hiking, spiritual retreats, and buying the best organic produce grown by local farmers, no big boxes or chain stores allowed. The pictures of the house made the place seem more like a fortress than a home, but what made it interesting, beyond its eight-figure price tag, was what Anton had written along the bottom of a sheet, in blue ink: "Chauncey Harrington, 72, 87.6 mil, paper."

The sheet contained no other writing.

Ellie replaced the backpack exactly where she had found it. She glanced up and saw Paul standing outside again. He had traded his eyeglasses for a pair of sunglasses with dark green rectangular lenses—a style she associated with military and special-ops guys. He stood with his hands in his pants pockets, looking in her direction, smiling.

CHAPTER 23

THIS GUY YOU saw, Paul," Roland said. "You're sure he's the Brentwood shooter?"

Ellie nodded. She had just finished telling him about Anton's meeting with Sebastian Kane's stepson-but-not-legally, Paul Young.

"No question in my mind," she said.

"And you're sure he didn't recognize you."

"Am I one hundred percent positive? No. But I don't think he did. If he did, he would have told Anton, and I wouldn't be sitting here talking to you, would I?"

"Tell me about the ride home with Anton," Roland said.

"There wasn't much talking. For a good half of the ride, Anton was quiet—told me he wanted some time to think, process everything."

"So, Anton's in business with Paul now."

"Maybe," Ellie corrected. "Anton hasn't committed to anything yet. It's only recently that Paul started reaching out to Anton through a series of dead drops."

"How twentieth century of him."

"Paper is much safer than technology. I don't know the specific locations of these dead drops, how often they communicate, but suffice it to say the sum of these conversations amounted to Paul saying that Frank and Sebastian would be handing over their business. Today's meeting—"

"Back up," Roland said. "You said 'handing over.'"

"Those were Paul's exact words, so, yes, Frank and Sebastian are going to be handing over their business to Paul. Today's meeting—and this was the first time Anton and Paul met—was about this." Ellie reached inside her dress pocket and came back with a small baggie, the kind dealers used to sell drugs. It contained two capsules filled with a dark red liquid.

"According to Anton," Ellie said, handing the bag to Roland, "this is what's going to put Pandora out of business."

Roland's eyebrows rose. "Pandora," he said. "Anton used that word?"

Ellie nodded. "Frank and Sebastian are the ones behind Pandora."

Roland's eyes turned electric with excitement. This was the first time the elusive Pandora had been mentioned.

"Well, hot diggity dog," he said, and held the baggie up to the light.

Ellie sat on a couch upholstered in stiff white leather inside the living room of penthouse apartment number 32 at the Ritz-Carlton Residences at LA Live on West Olympic Boulevard. After Anton had dropped her back at her boyfriend's house, Ellie had used a series of federal agents posing as Uber drivers to safely deliver her here for a debriefing. Roland had insisted on a face-to-face.

The floor-to-ceiling windows offered stunning aerial views of downtown LA. The sun was setting, casting bars of deep gold and red light inside the room. Roland held the bag back up to the window.

"I take it the red stuff in these capsules is carrier blood."

"That's what Anton told me."

"And what's a blood pill supposed to do?"

"Turn a nun into a nympho, for starters," Ellie said. "Anton wants me to try them, report back to him."

"What else?"

"Anton wants me to help him get *female* carriers."

"Why?"

"He wouldn't say other than Paul wanted only female carriers—the younger, the better. Anton also wants me to give him a full report on how the Celebrity Center is set up, floor by floor, room by room. He also wants me to get access to their client list."

"You don't have access to their client list."

"Which is what I told him."

"How did he react?"

"He told me to try harder."

Roland slid his hands in his pockets and paced, his head tilted downward as he digested this information, thought, and planned their next steps.

Ellie quietly sipped her bourbon, felt it going to work on her nerves. In the distance she could make out one of those 747 planes the news called "SuperTankers" flying over the mountain, dropping thousands of gallons of fire retardant on the wildfires. Everywhere you went in LA, you could smell smoke, see it billowing from far, far away.

"When is Anton going to meet Paul next?" Roland asked.

"I have no idea."

"But the plan is for them to partner up, manufacture these blood pills?"

Ellie shook her head. "The pills, Anton told me, are a preview of what Paul's blood product can do."

"Which is . . . ?"

"Anton didn't get into specifics."

"You didn't press him?"

"You don't press Anton."

Roland picked up his drink, a glass of straight vodka, no ice, and took the chair across from her. It was also upholstered in white leather. Nearly all the chairs and sofas were white, designed more for appearance than for comfort, the kitchen cabinets, countertops, and appliances black, giving the place a very cold, modern feel. Sterile and antiseptic.

Roland stared into his drink. "If Paul recognized you, there's a good possibility he may call Sebastian or Frank, tell them you're a cop."

"They're not talking. Sebastian's got a bounty on Paul's head."

"But they worked together. Have some sort of history. And who's to say Paul might not call him to gloat, say, *Hey, dipshit, you've got a cop in your organization*—you know, rub it in his face? Or maybe he's waiting to use it as some sort of leverage. You see where I'm going with this?"

"You're assuming Paul recognized me," Ellie said. "He didn't."

"What if Paul decides to call Anton instead and tell him who you really are?"

"You've got people watching Anton. If that happens, we'll know."

"My job is to protect the asset. If your cover gets blown or, God forbid, you get killed, I—"

"That's not going to happen."

"You don't know that."

"You don't know that, either."

"But I *do* know that these people are like us," Roland said. "They can dismember someone and then go out to dinner, come home, and kiss their kids good night and sleep like a baby. If they're not outright psychopaths, they're sociopaths or suffering from some other personality disorder."

"I'm aware of that."

Roland's face twisted with concern. "I can—and will—put more people around you, have them stake out your place and your car, see what turns up. The reality is, I can't guarantee your safety. You may want to give that some thought."

"I did. The whole way home with Anton."

"And?"

"I feel like I'm on the edge of something—a major breakthrough," Ellie said. "I'm staying."

"Even knowing the risks?"

"Even knowing the risks."

Roland sighed. "The pills Anton gave you," he said. "I'll take one with me to give to the lab. The other one—I want you to give it to Frank."

"Frank?"

"Tell him who gave it to you and where you got it. Tell him everything you told me."

"They'll kill Anton."

"Not right away," Roland said, Ellie surprised how matter-of-fact he sounded, like they were discussing a board game and not a human life. "The smart play will be to use you as a mole, have you stick as close to Anton as possible, monitor everything he says and does, and report back to Frank. Then they'll make a move to get Paul for reasons I'm sure you'll soon discover."

Ellie was surprised at how fiercely she wanted to protect Anton. He was a kidnapper and murderer, and yet she wanted to tell Roland, *No, I can't sell him out, not like that.*

"This is a good way for you to get closer to Frank—to get closer to his inner circle," Roland said. "It shows you're loyal to him."

Roland began to explain exactly what Ellie had to do. She barely heard him, a part of her brain still working out her feelings about Anton. If the tables were turned, he'd throw her to the wolves in a heartbeat. So why did it bother her so much? Because she liked him? Because he was good to her? Not to everyone else, mind you, but to her. It made Ellie think of interviews she'd read of people who had known Hitler, the heinous acts he and his men had been committing, these bystanders justifying their lack of action by saying, *Well, he was always nice to* me. *Hitler and his goon squad never did anything to* me. But these people had distance; they weren't directly involved in the atrocities. She was involved—had a front-row seat.

Under that thought was another one: coming into this, she had believed she could do her job and find her brother without getting her hands dirty. Without causing suffering to herself or anyone else, unless they absolutely deserved it. Did Anton deserve this? She couldn't answer the question.

No, that was a lie. She didn't *want* to answer the question, even though she already knew what the answer was.

Roland said something. Ellie struggled to recall it, couldn't.

"Could you repeat that?"

"I asked if you understood how you're to approach Frank," Roland said.

She stared out the window.

"Ellie?"

"I heard you."

"Then hear this," Roland said. "If Ron Wolff's people were shadowing Anton—and it's reasonable to assume they were—then Frank knows that Anton and *you* gave him the slip. You left your phone behind, so Frank and/or his crew couldn't track you. If you don't go to Frank, he'll come to you."

"I understand."

"Anton may act all nice with you, but don't forget there's another side to him, a guy who has no problem slitting someone's throat or putting a bullet in someone's head. You're not an exception to the rule."

She knew he was right. But the emotional part of her refused to give any ground, and there was something else that was bothering her: Roland was asking her to use Anton as a human chess piece to further an agenda—something politicians and bureaucrats did. It didn't sit right with her, crossed some invisible line.

"Anton sealed his fate a long time ago," Roland said. "Remember that and you'll be fine. You'll get over it."

Roland checked his watch. "I've got to get going. Your next appointment will be here soon."

"My next appointment?"

"Cody."

Hearing his name was thrilling, and a much-welcomed relief given the long day. Still, a part of her mind wouldn't let go of Anton—and Frank, and Paul, all of it.

"How much time do we have?" Ellie asked.

"Couple of hours. That enough time for your conjugal visit?"

"Conjugal visit? That's for prisoners."

Roland smiled, but it didn't reach his eyes. "Aren't we all?"

CHAPTER 24

ELLIE CAME TWICE. She was on top—her preferred position, giving her the most control—and steadily working her way to a third orgasm, a new personal record, when she felt Cody's fingers dig into her hips and ass, the signal that he was getting close to having his own. She leaned forward and placed her hands on his chest, feeling the strength there, the muscles contracting, and started to ride him harder, wanting selfishly to get to the finish line before he did.

Then Cody arched his back and let out a gasp of pleasure that to her ears also sounded like a cry for help, a plea for her to come back home, back to him.

Cody hadn't said any such words to her—hadn't said much of anything since she'd walked through the door to her hotel room twenty minutes ago. It took him a moment to get over the shock of seeing not only her after their months apart but also how different she looked, with her haircut and dye job. She had also answered the door naked, except for the black stiletto heels. Cody loved it when she wore heels.

Cody was all over her, Ellie nearly ripping off his shirt as they inched their way to the bed, where she tried to lose herself in the way he touched her, the way he smelled and tasted, the sight and feel of his body— anything to divert her mind from her conversation with Roland, Anton, Paul, the entire day.

"Whatever you do," she whispered to Cody, "don't be gentle."

He wasn't, going at her like she had stolen something from him—kissing her flesh and licking it, drinking her in like she was an oasis. He was rough, and she liked it, and she almost came when he forced her legs apart and pinned her arms against the bed, acting like he wanted to tear her apart and put her somewhere inside him—someplace where he'd know she'd be safe. His.

When it was over, Ellie was about to roll off of him when he said, "No, wait," and then he brought her close to him, wrapped his strong arms around her back, and pressed her damp flesh against his, Ellie feeling his heart galloping along with her own, both of them trying to catch their breath, catch up to each other. He kissed her cheek and he threaded his fingers through her hair, and he kissed her again, on the mouth. "I love you," he said, his voice cracking. "I love you so much."

Cody was the only man she'd ever been with who felt free discussing his emotions; she was used to his saying such things. What she wasn't used to was hearing how torn up he sounded, as if the words had been wrapped in barbed wire. It made her feel guilty, hearing him like this. She had known her departure had hurt him, but she didn't know just how deeply it went until right now.

"That's all you've got to say? What about my hair?" she said, a lame attempt to break the awkward tension ballooning inside her chest.

Cody chuckled. "It's beautiful. You're beautiful."

Cody wouldn't let her go—wouldn't, in fact, stop squeezing her.

"I'm sorry," she said. "For everything."

"It's fine."

Although clearly it wasn't, the way his body tensed. He tried to sell it, though, put a bow on it, when he kissed her again and said, "I love you."

"I love you, too." And she did. Ellie smiled into his chest and lay on top of him, the room warm and drowsy with the fading sunlight. She dozed off, and woke when he gently slid out of bed. Light was still in the room, and she saw Cody squat on his haunches. He picked his jeans up from the floor, slid a hand in the right-front pocket. What was he—?

And then she remembered: the ring. All these months, and not once had she thought about it. She didn't want to think about it now, either. She said, "Hey."

He started a bit, surprised by her voice. "Thought you were asleep," he said, withdrawing his hand.

"Just dozed off. You leaving already?"

"No. I was just looking for my phone. Wanted to make sure I had it turned off. Didn't want to wake you up."

He came back to bed, his hands relaxed. If the ring was in his pocket, he'd left it there.

Cody lay on his back. She snuggled up next to him, his arm around her, his fingers tracing the slope of her hip.

"So," he said, "what happened today?"

"Nothing. Why?"

"Something went down. I can feel it."

Ellie sighed. "You know I can't—"

"I know. I was hoping to catch you in a moment of weakness."

"I'm feeling pretty weak." She craned her face up at him, smiled. "Well done, sir. Well done."

"Just tell me . . . I need to know you're okay and not in any danger."

"I'm okay."

"But in danger."

"I'm fine. Everything's fine," Ellie said, wondering if she was trying to convince Cody or herself. "I've got good people watching over me."

"You honestly believe that?"

"You know something I don't?"

Cody shook his head. "It's just . . ." He didn't finish the thought.

Ellie propped herself up on an elbow. "What?" she prompted.

He took a moment to collect his thoughts. "These people watching you—they don't have your back. They won't take a bullet for you. And it's not because they don't care; it's because they can't. It's hard enough for someone you love to carry that burden, but a total stranger?"

"You want me to get out?"

"I didn't say that."

"But if I was asking?"

"Then yeah, I'd say leave. Come back home."

"And do what?"

"You can go back to patrol."

Back to patrol. Back to playing referee in domestic disputes. Back to writing speeding tickets and catching drunk drivers.

"You could get a desk job," he said.

"I don't want a desk job."

"What if you did something else?"

"You mean, other than being a cop?"

"You ever think about it?"

She had always wanted to be a cop, and now she was; there was nothing else to think about other than the job in front of her. "No," she said. "You?"

Cody shrugged. "There are other things to do in life."

"You mean the whole white-picket-fence thing, two kids and a golden retriever?"

Cody chuckled, but it sounded cold to her. "You make it sound like a prison sentence."

In her mind's eye she saw herself hosting holiday parties and living in the suburbs, where you talked about kids and dogs and schools and shared recipes and gardening and lawn care tips. She saw herself trapped.

Cody said, "Is that so bad? Us having a life together?"

"No. Absolutely not." And she meant it.

"But that's not what you want."

"Kind of preoccupied right now, you know, with the job."

"Have you thought about it?"

"Sure," she said, although she hadn't, not really. She loved Cody—she truly did—and while she could imagine a life with him, saying yes to marriage meant accepting his feelings and opinions about the course of her private and professional life. Saying yes meant accepting no longer being able to think about just herself, and she wasn't ready for that—especially now, not in her current situation. She loved him but didn't want to feel owned by him, and she wondered if Cody knew the difference.

"It's hard to think about the future right now," Ellie said gently. "I've got to keep my head in the game, you know?"

Cody nodded and flicked his gaze back up at the ceiling. He rubbed her back absently, Ellie seeing how the worry was tearing him up. And it tore her up, too, seeing how it ate at him.

"You don't have to wait around for me," Ellie said.

Cody stopped rubbing her back.

"It's not fair, asking you to do this," she said. "I don't want you to suffer because of a decision I made."

"And you think that'll, what, just stop if we break up? Great plan."

"I'm not saying that."

"Then what *are* you saying? What aren't you telling me?"

Ellie knew what she wanted to say, but she didn't know how to put the words in the right order. She wanted to start by telling him how knowing that he was worrying about her would distract her. It was exhausting enough worrying about what was in front of her and guessing what was around the corner, and she wanted to tell him about today—not the particulars but how she had never felt more excited or alive, her life's purpose so clearly defined.

Sharing this, though, would only hurt him, and he was hurting enough—hurting *too much*. Cody put up a great front, but what people didn't know was that behind all that muscle was a sensitive guy who was in some ways still a boy. A boy who thought love lasted forever, that it was special and could weather any storm. Cody was like a pop song, eternally optimistic, a catchy tune that took you out of the darkening swell of your own thoughts and made you believe, if only for a few minutes, that there was a lot of good stuff in this world, and it was yours for the taking, but only if you had the courage to surrender your heart.

"Don't shut me out," Cody said. "Talk to me."

Ellie didn't want to get into it. She was emotionally and physically spent, and now that she had gotten what she wanted from him—his flesh and his strength and the bruises she was sure he had left on her limbs and hips—she wanted his solidarity. She wanted him to say, *Yes, whatever you want to do or whatever you need is fine by me. I won't ask questions or put any demands on you. I am here for you and I won't ask anything from you, and I won't tell you I'm scared or hurting.*

She knew her thinking was naïve and childish. Selfish. But weren't all wishes, hopes, and desires, when you got right down to it, childish and selfish?

"I love you," Ellie said, hoping to put the matter to bed, at least for tonight. "That hasn't changed."

"But clearly something *has* changed."

Ellie felt a spike of anger. It died quickly when she reminded herself that Cody was hurting because of her. She had caused this, and truthfully, wouldn't she be feeling the same way if the shoe were on the other foot?

"Just hang on for a little while longer. Can you do that?"

Cody moved closer to her. Stared at her for a moment before he said, "I'll always have your back."

Ellie nestled herself in the crook of his arm. She rubbed his chest and stomach, hooked her leg over his waist.

"Why is this so important to you?" he asked. "Can you at least tell me that?"

She thought about telling him about her brother and then decided against it—and not because she didn't trust him, because she did. She didn't want to share it with him or anyone else and run the risk of being talked out of her desire, maybe even obsession, to find her brother. She didn't want to give that power over to someone else. She wanted to keep it close, tucked inside her, where it could grow, be protected.

"It just is," she said.

"Does it have something to do with—?"

"No more questions, okay? Please? I just want to lie here and enjoy you. Us."

Then, when he didn't answer: "Okay?"

"Sure."

Ellie turned and kissed his chest, wanting to lose herself in his flesh again but unable to stop thinking about the crack in their relationship—and it was there, no question. She could feel it splintering, and if she wasn't careful, it would grow into a crevasse that would swallow them both.

CHAPTER 25

WHEN SEBASTIAN GOT sober, what surprised him the most was how his body betrayed him. Instead of being grateful that it no longer had to metabolize excessively large amounts of Scotch, it got good and pissed off. Those first awful months, he would hit the pillow every night, mentally and physically exhausted from dragging himself through yet another day of fighting off his insane craving for booze, and when he shut his eyes, the doctor-prescribed Ambien already floating through his bloodstream, his body stubbornly refused to shut down and rest.

People who weren't alcoholics—"earthlings," in AA speak—couldn't understand that addiction was a living, breathing entity. It was like you were possessed. It lived inside a damaged part of your brain and it talked to you constantly and it could, and did, use your body against you, without your permission. Those early days when he hit the pillow, his addiction, which he came to view as a spiritual entity, like a demon, constantly whispered in his ear: *Sorry, my man, no sleep for you. Not unless you give us what we need.*

What the demon wanted—*demanded*—was a glass of Scotch. And not the cheap shit, either; only the top-shelf stuff would do. Sebastian refused. His addiction laughed. *You can take as many sleeping pills as you want, amigo, but it's not going to make a lick of difference. I control things around here, not you, and I'm going to prove it.* And prove it his addiction did. His body had been hijacked, and it, along with the demon living inside his skull, introduced him to a new level of hell called insomnia.

Sebastian still suffered from bouts of it now, all these sober years later, only the insomnia was triggered by extreme mental stress. God knew he had a shit ton of it, so it didn't exactly come as a surprise that he found himself lying wide-awake at two in the morning. He knew the reason why, too. He also had a strong idea about how to fix it, but had been putting it off for months now because the remedy was . . . well, insane.

So he had two choices: lie here in bed and continue to stare at the ceiling, or get up and do what he needed to do now, in the quiet of the night, when no one was watching.

Sebastian pulled back the sheets. He dressed quickly, making sure to grab what he needed from the downstairs closet, and then headed for the garage.

Traffic on the 405 was light. He made it to Westwood in good time.

In the daylight, the Parker Brothers Memorial Park resembled a peaceful, meditative retreat more than a cemetery—a beautiful and immaculately landscaped area with a rich, deep green lawn, abundant flowers, trees, and sunshine. Sebastian suspected Trixie picked this place because of the number of celebrities who were buried there. Trixie once dreamed of being an actress. That dream got put on hold when she discovered she was pregnant. She lived the life of a single mother until she moved in with Sebastian, four years later. Trixie went back to acting, got bit parts in re-creations of murders in true-life crime shows, and then eventually left it for what she felt was her true calling: being a stay-at-home mother.

The Park, as it was called, was obviously closed at such an ungodly hour. Sebastian drove past the entrance to visit the dead—a pair of wrought iron gates secured by a chain and padlock—and pulled onto the next side street and then parked in a neighborhood less than half a mile away. He walked with his head lowered, his jacket collar turned up, and his LA Dodgers baseball cap pulled low across his forehead. He also wore a pair of eyeglasses. A bit of overkill, he supposed, but every little bit helped when you were trying to disguise yourself.

Trixie had opted for a simple gravestone. It sat flat against the earth and contained her name and the dates of her brief time here on earth. His destination was two spots over—the grave site of an immensely popular yet troubled female singer who had died young of a heroin overdose. Her grave site was decorated with a haphazard mess of half-lit candles, flowers, cards, drawings, and assorted trinkets (he saw a Matchbox car and a perfume bottle, of all things) from fans who came from all over the world to visit her. If he was being recorded, he wanted to appear like some nut who had been touched by her haunting songs. *I'm probably nuttier than those people,* he told himself, *doing what I'm about to do.*

Sebastian kept his head bowed and his hands in his jacket pockets. He took in a deep breath, the night air cold by California standards—in the low forties.

"My mother believed in the power of prayer. Believed that you could talk not only to God but to your loved ones. But she told me if you wanted to say something really important—like ask for forgiveness— then you had to do it at that person's grave site."

Sebastian felt silly, a grown-ass man talking to himself. The dead couldn't hear or feel, because they were dead. But that didn't prevent people from talking out loud, believing their loved one's soul or spirit was in hearing distance, looming somewhere close by, watching and listening.

Sebastian had been raised in—or, he would argue, indoctrinated into—Catholicism by his Bible-thumping mother. And while he hadn't stepped inside a church for decades, he supposed he still clung to the spiritual concept of a soul. Or maybe, deep down, he was terrified *not* to believe it. His adult self suddenly felt a lot like the little boy who believed the night-light his mother placed in his room kept the monsters under the bed and locked inside the closet.

"When I got out of prison, I went to her grave and apologized to her.

Not for going to jail—that wasn't my fault, as you well know—but because I wasn't there for her when she got sick. Frank was, and while I'm sure she appreciated that—God knows I did—still, it wasn't me. And that bothered me for a long, long time. But it felt good to go visit her and get it off my chest. Then, when I got sober, I went to see her again, and this time I asked for her forgiveness for everything I put her through—and I put her through a lot. Things I never told you about."

Sebastian snorted. The sounds of the highway traffic filled his ears, and in the far, far distance he could see a faint orange glow, like that from an active volcano—the wildfires tearing their way through Northern California. He thought he could smell smoke, too, but surely he was imagining it.

"I don't know if I believe in heaven, in that whole 'You're looking down on me' thing, watching my every move. The nuns and priests drilled that into me at school and at church, and I found the whole thing creepy, to say the least. Anyway, if it is true, then you know what's been going on. My mother, too. You both know why I'm here. Still, I've got to say it out loud. That's what they teach at AA—not to carry shit but to let it out. We're as sick as our secrets."

Sebastian took another deep breath. This time he *did* smell smoke.

"I'm going to kill him. I'm going to kill your son," Sebastian said. "I don't expect you to understand or to forgive me, although I'd be lying if some part of me didn't want that, because otherwise why would I be here? It's been weighing on me, what I'm going to do—so much so that I haven't been able to sleep. But I'm still going to do it. I *have* to do it, for reasons you understand, or don't. Like they say in AA, I can't control people, places, or things. Souls, I'm guessing, fall into that category. I will say that I'm sorry. That I wish there was another way.

"I loved you the best way I could and respected you, and now, even after your death, I wouldn't want to do anything deliberately to hurt you. But he's sick and he needs to be stopped."

Sebastian paused, expecting to feel her spirit or presence or essence move through him and protest, maybe give him some sort of sign. What he felt was nothing. No stirring, no thoughts. Actually, that wasn't true. He did feel something: he felt silly. Ridiculous. Reduced to a childlike state where he had once believed an angry, invisible man who lived in the sky would protect him from the monsters that lived in his closet and under his bed. Still, the woman who had shared his bed for nearly two decades was now lying six feet below him, sealed in a coffin packed in dirt. He felt *that*.

"It will be quick and painless. That's the best I can do. The best I can promise."

There. It was done. He had said everything he had come here to say. He had told the truth. Unburdened himself. It was time to go.

Sebastian walked away, expecting to feel at least a bit lighter, like he had on that hot August afternoon when he'd stood at his mother's grave site, making amends for his drinking and alcoholic behavior, what he had put her through. Right now, though? Right now he felt troubled. He felt some new burden weighing him down. And why did he feel that familiar itch along the back of his tongue and throat—the one that could be scratched only by a good bottle of Scotch or, back in the day, by using his fists?

By the time he reached the highway, he'd had an epiphany.

Sebastian didn't drive home. Instead, he took a detour to the Hollywood Hills.

To Ava's house.

Sebastian killed the lights and parked across the street. Her sprawling home looked like some sort of dark, futuristic monolith under the blanket of stars. He stared at the dark windows, listening to the ticking of his cooling engine, thinking about Ava sleeping in there, along with eight words he had said to Trixie back at the Park:

I loved you the best way I could.

It was true. He *had* loved her and respected her to the best of his ability. But if he was being honest, Trixie had been his consolation prize.

Trixie, with her blond hair and blue eyes and Barbie doll physique shaped by Pilates and eating low- or no-carb meals, was the anti-Ava—and hadn't that been her appeal? Hadn't he allowed Trixie and her kid into his life so he could forget about Ava? To keep his mind occupied with the reality of his life rather than constantly wishing for the one stolen from him? Trixie was a stand-in for the real thing, a placeholder. He supposed he'd realized that on some level, for all these years, but it had slept quietly, this truth, on the deep seafloor of his mind, and it had taken his getting shot—by her *son*—for him to get to this place to confront it. And if at any point during his time with Trixie Ava had knocked on the door or picked up the phone and said, "I want you back," he would have said yes. Wouldn't have hesitated.

The truth shamed him, yes, but it also freed him, made the air seem that much sweeter, the colors more vibrant. He had almost died, and he wasn't going to waste any more time. Come tomorrow morning, he was going to reach out to her and, God willing, get his real life back, the one that had been stolen from him.

CHAPTER 26

CODY WAS STILL very much on Ellie's mind as she woke up in the drowsy morning sunlight. She didn't want to think about him, couldn't stop thinking about him and their conversation from last night, Cody pretty much saying that if she gave up the undercover job, he'd be fine with it.

She'd never given up on anything in her life.

She felt bad for hustling him out of her room, but she needed to keep her head in the game.

Ellie got out of bed. It was half past seven, and she felt surprisingly refreshed and energized. She took a long shower, and by the time she finished she was no longer thinking about Cody.

It wasn't much of an effort, either. Her need to solve the mystery of her brother far outweighed her feelings for Cody, or the nagging, guilty thoughts she had of him worrying about her and suffering from that worry.

Did that make her some sort of sociopath?

Make her, God forbid, in some way evil?

She didn't want Cody to suffer, had, she reminded herself, given him an out last night when she told him he could see other people, as much as that would hurt her—and it would. But if she was being honest with herself, didn't a part of her want him to say that yes, they should take a break? If they did, she wouldn't have to worry about him. She could temporarily pack him up and put him away, examine Cody later, after she found her brother. That was far more important right now than Cody's feelings.

And wasn't that the definition of evil? Ignoring someone's suffering for your own benefit? She did it with Cody, and now she was about to do it to someone else.

By the time she finished dressing, she was back to being Faye Simpson, back to business.

Ellie stood by the window, with its panoramic views of downtown Los Angeles and Southern California, the mountains and ocean, and called Frank. He had given her his private cell number, in the event of an emergency.

He picked up.

"It's Faye."

"Good morning, Faye."

"Good morning."

Ellie closed her eyes, and as she took in a deep breath she thought of Danny. Danny, dead and buried and all alone inside his casket. Danny, who had gone through an ugly, bitter divorce, his only salvation his dog, Boomer. The words spilled out of her.

"I was hoping we could talk," Ellie said.

"We're talking now."

"I meant face-to-face."

"Why?"

"That picture you showed me the night you took me to dinner." Ellie was pleased at how confident she sounded. "I've come across some information I think you'll be very interested to hear."

"I'm listening."

Her plan would work only if they spoke in person. It was a gamble, what she had in mind. Then again, Faye Simpson was a gambler by nature.

"I want to talk to you in person," Ellie said. "Where would you like to meet?"

Frank told her to stay put; he'd come pick her up. She gave him the address for the Ritz-Carlton—the hotel, which had the same address as the private residences—and waited for him in the lobby.

An hour later, she saw his Buick pull up to the front of the hotel—the same SUV from the photo hanging on her office wall. She pushed her way through the revolving doors, dressed in the same clothes she had worn yesterday.

Frank got out of the car. He wore a nicely cut blue suit jacket with a crisp, dressy white T-shirt that, along with his sockless loafers and Ray-Ban Wayfarers, gave him a breezy, casual look.

Only there was nothing breezy or casual about him. Frank buttoned his jacket as he opened the door for her, his pale skin almost as white as his tee—Dracula dressed by Christian Dior. She could see his eyes behind his sunglasses, studying and assessing her, probing for weaknesses.

He held the door open for her. Ellie climbed in, waited for Frank to join her. When he did, she took control and spoke first.

"The man in the photograph—he looks different now. Dyed his hair black and grew it out, and he's also wearing black-framed glasses. But there's no doubt it's him. His name is Paul. At least that's what Anton called him."

"Anton?"

"He took me to see Paul."

From the corner of her eye she saw Frank squeeze the steering wheel.

Ellie said, "I thought we were going to lunch. Anton went to a BMW dealership, said he had to pick up a part, and the next thing I knew, we had switched cars. He thought he was being followed. He had me leave my phone behind."

"And why did Anton bring you along?" Frank's tone remained flat, the way it always did when he spoke—or at least when he spoke to her.

"He wants me to help him acquire young female carriers. He didn't say why."

Next, Ellie mixed facts with what Roland had shared with her last night. "They were discussing the guy you work for, or with—I'm not sure. Sebastian. Are you two partners, or do you work for him?"

"What were Anton and Paul discussing?"

"I hear Sebastian's offering a sizable reward for anyone with information on his stepson."

"And where, exactly, did you hear that?"

"From Anton and Paul. It was one of many things they discussed together yesterday. They're going to make a move against you."

No reaction from Frank.

"And when, exactly, is this happening?"

"I'll tell Sebastian," Ellie said. "Only Sebastian."

Ellie's words hung in the air like a bad odor. Frank's mouth parted slightly. Then he drew in a long, slow breath as his tongue dug into a back molar.

"The reward he's offering would solve my debt problems—all of my debt problems," Ellie said. "I wouldn't have to take out a personal loan from you—from anyone."

"Tell me what you know, and I'll tell—"

"This isn't a negotiation."

Ellie's tone was polite. Still, Frank's eyebrows jumped in surprise, and his face flushed.

"I'll share everything I know," Ellie said, "but only with your boss."

Ellie had seen plenty of men get angry over the course of her life, but she had never witnessed full-blown rage until the day when Anton, pumped full of carrier blood, flipped out and crushed a stickman's hand in a car door. Anton's rage, though, was a primal response. Like fire, it burned for a brief period of time until it either died on its own or was extinguished. What Ellie saw in Frank's eyes was a cold and clinical detachment—the soul of a man who, after slitting your throat, would sit back down at the dinner table to resume eating while you lay at his feet, bleeding.

Ellie was glad she was wearing dark-lensed sunglasses. They hid the fear in her eyes, her rapid blinking. "I mean no disrespect," she said. "This is just business. I'm sure you'd do the same thing if you were in my position."

Frank opened his mouth to speak. He immediately snapped it shut and abruptly pulled over to the side of the road and double-parked. He kept his hands on the steering wheel, squeezing it, and for some reason she thought he was going to backhand her, right here in the car. He didn't seem like the type to hit a woman, but then again, how many women had come before who had made that mistake?

"Call me when Sebastian wants to talk," Ellie said, and turned to the door.

Frank grabbed her roughly by the wrist.

"Hold on," he said.

He took out his phone and began punching in a number.

"In person," Ellie said. "Not over the phone. In person."

Frank's gaze burrowed into her face as he spoke into the phone. "I have someone who insists on meeting with you. Faye Simpson. I'm sitting with her right now. She just informed me she met Paul yesterday. Anton arranged the meeting."

The conversation that followed was short, less than a minute. Ellie had no idea what it was about, since Frank didn't speak. He listened to whatever Sebastian was saying, Ellie unable to make out a single word.

Frank hung up and placed the phone on the console. As he slid back into morning traffic, his features morphed into a waxy stillness. He didn't speak.

Ellie stared out the windshield, trying to collect herself and her thoughts. Her heart wouldn't stop racing, and she wanted to rub her wrist. He was surprisingly strong, Frank was. Then again, most men were. She realized—and not for the first time—she was at the mercy of men. It frightened her, yes, but she didn't let it overpower her. She knew how to fight, wasn't afraid of fighting.

Fifteen minutes of silence was enough.

"Where are we going?"

"To get some pancakes," Frank replied.

Frank sat in monklike silence as they ate a leisurely breakfast at a cash-only diner located less than a mile from the hotel. The only time he addressed her was to tell her how much she owed for her half of the bill.

She followed Frank back to the car, her stomach full to the point of being uncomfortable. She had stuffed herself on purpose so she would not only be alert but also have enough fuel to help her get through whatever was going to happen next.

What *was* going to happen next? She didn't know, and not knowing was making her second-guess her earlier decision to force Frank's hand. He didn't appear angry, but with Frank it was hard to say, the guy as expressive as a chunk of unmolded clay.

Ellie slid back into the passenger seat, reminding herself that she wasn't alone. Roland's people were watching. They wouldn't let anything happen to her.

Frank remained quiet and appeared relaxed during the hour-plus drive out of the city—acted as though she wasn't in the car. Ellie kept a close eye on her surroundings, especially when Frank took the exit for Long Beach.

Ellie followed the street signs all the way to their destination: 184 Palermo Avenue. A wrought iron gate covered the end of the driveway. The gate opened, and Frank drove toward a spacious Spanish Revival house with plantation shutters and meticulously manicured shrubs. It sat alone on top of a hill overlooking the Pacific Ocean and Alamitos Bay, more of a small compound than a home, she thought—the sort of place where power brokers could meet and discuss things openly without having to worry about the prying eyes and ears of neighbors.

Has to be Sebastian's house. Ellie had no way of knowing. The bay door of the three-car garage on the west side of the house was already open.

There wasn't another car parked in there—there wasn't anything—and after Frank pulled inside and came to a smooth stop, the garage door was already closing behind them as he killed the engine, Ellie looked around the garage, wondering why it was so empty. It made her reconsider her choice to meet Sebastian here, on his home turf, instead of a more neutral location.

Frank had already gotten out of the car. He moved around to the other side and opened the door for her. He didn't ask her to get out. He reached inside and viciously grabbed her by the arm, his fingers digging deep into the meat of her bicep and finding bone as he yanked her out of the seat.

She had never fought a man. Ellie had trained for it at the academy, and while she had gotten into her fair share of scrapes when arresting dopeheads, domestic abusers, and drunk drivers, she'd never had to go mano a mano with one. Frank was twice her size and three times as strong, and he was fast—and she was wearing heels. She slipped out of one, twisting her ankle in the process. The pain disappeared, replaced by a new one when he grabbed her arm and jerked it behind her back. He jerked it again when he forced it upward, toward her shoulders, in a hammerlock. He grabbed her hair, knotting it in his fist, and he marched her up the small set of stairs, to the back door, which was now open. She fell out of her other shoe and he pushed her forward through a hall, past a massive, airy kitchen and into the foyer, and he tightened his grip on her hair so hard, she was staring up at the vaulted ceiling, at a crystal chandelier. Her throat was exposed; that was all she could think about, that Frank or someone else was going to cut it—and there was at least one other person in the house, Ellie catching a shadow from the corner of her eye just before he moved her up a long set of stairs. Her feet kept tripping and Frank kept applying pressure to her arm, Ellie sure he was going to snap it and rip it from its socket, when he let go and shoved her into a bedroom bursting with sunlight.

CHAPTER 27

THE BEDROOM WAS wide, with large windows and a sliding glass door that opened onto a shaded balcony enclosed with balustrades. The only furniture in here was a cheap folding chair. The man standing in the room with her had brought it with him.

The guy looked like Elmer Fudd on steroids. He was white and young and built like a tank, with wide shoulders, a massive shaved head, and a neck as thick as a tree trunk. He wore a visible earpiece, the kind the Secret Service used, and he had dressed for the part—a navy blue suit with black shoes and a white shirt without a tie. His jacket was open, and as far as Ellie could tell, he wasn't carrying.

The bedroom door was closed. He stood next to it, leaning back against the wall, hands tucked in his pants, and as she paced the room, sometimes rubbing the tender area on her arm where Frank had grabbed her, he tracked her movements as though she were a field mouse—a possible nuisance but by no means a threat. He didn't move or say a word when she turned to the sliding glass door to the balcony, not surprised to find it locked.

Not that opening it would have done her much good. The drop from the balcony to the backyard was steep; she'd probably break an ankle. Still, she would have risked it. Even with a broken ankle or leg she could have hobbled her way down the slope, to the shoreline, to the scattered people in the not-too-far distance who were walking the beach, pausing to look up at the sky, at the smoke billowing in the far, far distance from the wildfires that seemed to want to consume the entire state, burn everything to the ground.

Two hours passed. Elmer Fudd took her to the bathroom once, and then back to the room, and shut the door. More waiting. She paced the room, barefoot. Her right ankle hurt, but the pain was manageable, thanks to the adrenaline humming through her limbs.

Her adrenaline spiked when the screaming started.

It came from somewhere downstairs and roared past the closed door, causing Ellie to come to an abrupt stop. The floor swayed under her feet and her organs turned to water. Elmer Fudd suppressed a yawn.

The screaming went on for approximately ninety-eight minutes. She knew the time because she tracked it on her watch. Out of those ninety-eight minutes, the last twenty-two were those of someone experiencing the type of pain associated with the lower rings of hell.

That someone, she knew, was Anton.

When he wasn't screaming in agony, he was cursing in Russian, and every now and then, when she willed herself to be still and strained to listen over the blood exploding against her eardrums, she thought she heard a faint whining sound—the kind made by a power tool motor. She heard it now, that faint whine, heard Anton howl and curse, and Ellie thought she was going to be sick, maybe even faint.

She had caused this. Whatever hell Anton was experiencing, she had caused it.

And at some point Frank would come for her. Frank or one of his men, or maybe Frank would contact the man in the room with her over his earpiece, tell him to drag her downstairs.

Where she'd be tortured.

Killed.

The stark, terrifying truth she'd been ducking for the past few hours came at her and hit her in the heart like an arrow:

She was alone.

On her own. Roland and his men hadn't followed her. If they had, they would have been covertly watching the house. They would have known she was being held prisoner here and they would have known Anton was being tortured. They would have known she was next. If they were here, they would have intervened by now, and they hadn't, because for a reason she didn't know, they weren't here; they weren't watching. She was alone.

What could she do?

She could tell Frank who she really was. She could tell him about Brentwood and about Paul and Sophia Vargas and everything she'd seen. She could tell him she was working with Special Agent Roland Bauer of the Federal Bureau of Investigation and his team, that they had been listening and tracking him for months.

And Frank would then torture her and kill her.

Ellie turned her back to Elmer Fudd and faced the sliding glass door. A window was cracked open, and she could hear the frenzied squawk of seagulls and waves crashing against the shoreline. Death was waiting for her downstairs, here in this beautiful house with its sweeping ocean views and bright sunlight. You weren't supposed to go out in a place like this. This house, its location—this was where you came to build your future, not end it.

Movement behind her. Ellie spun around and saw Elmer standing next to the door now, a meaty hand gripping the knob. She heard approaching footsteps. Frank was coming for her.

Fear blurred the edges of her vision. Ellie wanted the floor to turn into quicksand, suck her down past this room, to a warm womb where she would drown peacefully and not have to face the consequential horror of her choices.

Elmer opened the door.

The man who entered was tall, a good six feet, and had skin the color of cardboard. His thick black hair was cut short, and he wore a black suit, the jacket buttoned, with a lavender-colored tie and a matching pocket square. He smiled warmly, as though she were a guest and not a prisoner.

"Faye, right?" he said, extending his hand.

Ellie straightened, nodded confidently even though she didn't feel confident. His hand felt warm and dry and strong in her limp, damp grip.

"Nice to meet you," he said in a jovial tone, like they were meeting at a cocktail party. "I understand you wanted to speak to me."

"Are you Sebastian?"

"I am. Sorry to have kept you waiting. Some unforeseen circumstances, as I'm sure you heard. Billy here treat you okay?"

Ellie nodded and swallowed dryly, her limbs shaking. She hadn't known who to expect, but she hadn't expected to meet a middle-aged Latino who looked like the older version of some guy who might have posed shirtless for the cover of a romance novel. He had a square jaw and sultry lips and the most piercing green eyes she had ever seen in a human being. He also had a drop of blood smeared on his smooth cheek.

He saw where she was looking and, puzzled, touched his face. He examined his fingers and said, "That reminds me," and then reached into his pocket and came back with what looked like a sealed bag the size of a deck of cards.

"For you," he said, and handed it to her.

The bag felt light in her hand, the contents as clear as the bag.

"It's a poncho," he said. "I don't want you to get all wet, ruin your clothes."

Ellie didn't know what terrified her more—whatever horror was waiting for her downstairs or his cavalier manner, Sebastian acting as though torturing another human being was an ordinary, boring activity, like waiting in line at the supermarket.

"I was hoping we could talk here. About Paul," Ellie said. "I saw him—"

"Let's have this conversation downstairs. It will be far more productive

and a much better use of everyone's time." He stepped aside and motioned to the doorway with his hand. "After you."

Ellie stared at it as though it were a portal to hell.

Sebastian said, "If you're having trouble walking, Billy here can assist you."

Ellie walked, her legs shaky and weak, and when she moved into the
hall, Sebastian closed the door behind her. She didn't have to ask where
to go; she knew the way.

The hall ended and she rounded the corner, to a winding staircase that
ended in a foyer of travertine marble, the front door so massive it could
have been a drawbridge. And this home might as well be a castle. She was
trapped inside with the king and his guards, and at the king's mercy. She
gripped the banister, and as she took the steps one at a time, the packaged
poncho gripped in her other hand, Ellie felt as though her soul had departed her body, felt as if she were watching her corporeal self trudge reluctantly downstairs, heading to her doom—a prisoner on her way to
meet the firing squad.

Even with her limited time as a street cop, Ellie had seen the myriad
ways people hurt and killed one another, and yet there had always been a
part of her that clung to the age-old belief that good always found a way
to triumph over evil. She remembered something someone had said about
how when you found yourself in hell, the key was to keep going, and for
a reason she couldn't fathom, let alone explain, she felt a momentary
calmness. She would get through this. She had to get through this in
order to find her brother.

That fragile, scraped-together calmness shattered when she reached
Anton.

The odors hit her first—wet, coppery blood and the unmistakable
stench of excrement. Anton, stripped of his clothes and bloodied and
beaten and God only knew what else, sat in the center of the main living
area, bound to a high-backed dining chair with plastic cuffs that had cut

into his wrists and forearms and ankles from thrashing in pain against the restraints. His head hung forward, and he was drooling blood and saliva, his face unrecognizable. There was no question it was him. She recognized the tattoos—the ones that weren't covered in blood. His blood. God, there was so much of it.

Her stomach lurched and she looked away, across the room at the perfect blue afternoon sky lying beyond the windows and French doors. A man with thinning hair and wearing dress pants and a blue shirt, the sleeves rolled up, stood by the door, hands folded across his chest, a nine strapped inside a leather shoulder holster. Sebastian pointed at the man as he charged past her and said, "The hell's wrong with you, Jack?" The room was empty of furniture; Sebastian's voice echoed through the wide, cavernous space. "You want my guest to pass out? Open a couple of windows, will you? Get some fresh air in here."

The man named Jack opened the pair of French doors for the large viewing deck that overlooked the ocean. Ellie could see only the sky, but she could smell the ocean, the salt and seaweed, riding on the cool breeze blowing from the water—bright, clean, and peaceful scents that belonged in this vaulted room, with its beautiful architecture, and now suddenly didn't.

Sebastian turned to her. "Come, come," he said, beckoning with a hand. "He's not going to bite, I promise."

Ellie didn't move, staring at the floor. She'd spotted a couple of Anton's teeth scattered in blood pooled on the floor around the chair.

The man from upstairs, Billy, was suddenly standing next to her. She hadn't heard him come down. He placed a hand on the small of her back and urged her forward.

"Have her stand in front of him, Billy," Sebastian said. "And be careful of the blood—I don't want her to slip and fall." Then, to Ellie: "Sorry to have you get so close, but Anton's having a little problem in the sight department. You okay to stand, Faye? Or would you like a chair?"

Anton's head twitched when he heard her name. A low, guttural moan escaped his throat. Strings of red saliva poured from the torn, swollen mess of what remained of his bottom lip. He tried to look up, couldn't because of the pain or effort or both, and his head slumped forward again, his chin resting on his chest, near a tattoo of a heart wrapped in barbed wire.

"You look like you could sit," Sebastian said when Ellie didn't answer his question. "Billy, go upstairs and fetch that chair."

Ellie now stood less than five feet away from Anton, gagging from the stomach-churning stench and god-awful carnage when Frank came in from the kitchen, holding a large glass bottle of Pellegrino. He drank deeply from it as he strolled across the room and moved behind Anton's chair. He leaned forward to put down his bottle, and when he straightened she saw a cordless drill gripped in his hand. The drill bit was long and thick and covered with blood and bits of skin—Anton's skin. Anton's blood.

Frank hiccupped. "Excuse me," he said, then pressed a fist against his mouth as he sucked in air through his nose and held it.

Billy set up the folding chair behind her. Ellie sat, grateful to no longer be standing, but she continued to sway, like she was on a boat going through choppy water. She gripped the edges of the chair with her sweaty hands as Sebastian got down on one knee beside her. He draped an arm across the back of her chair.

"Now," Sebastian said to her. "The gentleman he met yesterday, the person you said he called Paul—Anton here tells me he has no idea where Paul is. Says he hasn't seen Paul or his muscle-loving butt buddy, a guy named Bradley Guidry. Was he there yesterday, Faye?"

Ellie's eyes never left Anton. "I . . . I don't know. He . . ."

"He what?"

Ellie swallowed, feeling cold all over. "There was a guy there, a driver, and some other guy who was watching us. A sniper."

Out of the corner of her eye Ellie saw Sebastian exchange a glance with Frank.

Ellie said, "I'm telling you the truth."

"Oh, I believe you."

"I never saw him. I don't know his name."

"That would be Mr. Guidry. Like you, Anton says he's never even heard the name before. I respectfully called bullshit, and Anton respectfully disagreed, leading to the mess you see here." Sebastian sighed, shook his head. "He should get an Olympic medal for being a stubborn bastard. He comes by it naturally, though, him and his Communist people. Isn't that right, Anton?"

Anton moaned, then began to gag, spitting up blood. Ellie couldn't look anymore, didn't know where to look.

"I know this is quite a shock," Sebastian said to her. "A beautiful woman like yourself isn't used to seeing such grotesque things, I'm sure. But, quite frankly, you have no one to blame but yourself. You wouldn't be here—*we* wouldn't be here—if you had simply answered Frank's questions."

Ellie's heart was hammering, blood pounding in her temples.

"We could have looked into the matter, conducted business like civilized people, then taken the appropriate actions," Sebastian said. "Instead, you turned stubborn yourself—which probably explains why Anton likes you so much. You're like two peas in a pod."

Figure out a way to get through this.

"My hope—and I sincerely mean this, Faye—my hope is you'll be more forthcoming than Anton. If not—if I think you're holding back something—well, I don't think I have to explain to you what will happen."

"Fresno," Ellie stammered.

"What about Fresno?"

"Where he met Paul."

Tell him about the blood pill.

Christ, she had totally forgotten about it. She hadn't told Frank about it, hadn't given it to him. She needed to tell Sebastian about it now, get control of the situation before it—

Something hard banged against the floor, to her right. Ellie whipped her head toward the sound, saw the distinctive shape of a flash-bang grenade, the kind used by LAPD SWAT, skidding across the floor, toward her.

CHAPTER 28

SEBASTIAN HAD SEEN grenades in TV shows and movies but never in person. The moment he saw it hit the floor, he had two simultaneous thoughts: first, the grenade was oddly shaped—a long cylinder, like a can of Mace—and entirely black instead of a military green; second, he had to duck and seek cover somewhere, and do it fast or the shrapnel would kill him.

Faye Simpson tackled him, like a lineman, grabbing his shirt and pushing him forward. He fell against the hardwood, Faye still on top of him, and the back of his head smacked against the floor so hard, he was sure he had cracked his skull. His lungs froze and his stomach lurched, and Faye clamped her palm against his eyes and kept it pressed there as the room filled with an earsplitting boom he felt deep in his bones.

Someone screamed something in Russian. Faye scrabbled off Sebastian and his eyes flew open and he saw his men clutching at their faces and he saw them blinking and stumbling like they were blind. He saw flashes of men entering the far side of the room and his gaze landed on a guy with a blond ponytail, dressed in jeans and a white-collared shirt, standing near the front door, a compact submachine gun with a banana-shaped magazine gripped in leather-gloved hands.

Sebastian's right hand flew into his suit jacket, reaching for his nine, when Ponytail fired. Ron's man Jack collapsed, and Ponytail fired a killing round into Jack's head and quickly turned his weapon to Frank, who was still standing behind Anton's chair. To Frank, who seemed disoriented from the flash-bang but had his hand on the nine clipped to his waist.

"Not the girl!" Anton howled. *"I want the bitch alive!"*

Sebastian had his Glock out and the safety off. He fired at the shooter holding the submachine gun and hit him high in the shoulder as a short burst of gunfire erupted from the far right corner of the room. Sebastian's eyes automatically flicked in that direction, past the moving bodies, past the limbs and furniture, and got a glimpse of the shooter.

Paul.

Paul was here and was getting to his feet and he fired again and Frank dropped to the floor, his limbs as limp and useless as a doll's. Half his head was missing.

Sebastian froze, unable to process what had just happened. *No,* he thought to himself, a scream rising in his throat. *No, this isn't happening. Frank and I are the good guys. We're supposed to win. We're supposed to—*

Billy, the man Sebastian had assigned to watch Faye, was fast. The man who had been standing beside Billy, a guy Sebastian had never seen before, lay dead on the floor, in a pool of blood. From the corner of his eye he saw Faye army crawling across the slick red pool. He saw Billy withdraw his weapon in one smooth motion, flick off the safety with his thumb, and fire a double tap that took down the man with the submachine gun. Paul ducked for cover.

Faye had a handgun—someone must have dropped it, and she had gone after it—and now she was firing, too. Billy dropped to one knee and began firing into the room, Faye coming out of her cover, Sebastian counting one, two, three other shooters—

Paul. There he was, by the French doors.

Take him down.

End this.

Now.

Sebastian scrambled to his feet, the adrenaline making his legs feel as though they were as fragile as glass. He raised his Glock and Paul raised his nine and Paul was smiling, and Faye shoved him back, toward the hall, and Sebastian lost sight of Paul. She pushed him again and this time he pushed back. The fear he had seen in her earlier was gone, replaced by a grim determination he rarely saw in women.

Ava flashed through his mind as Faye said, "There are too many of them. We need to leave. Now."

Sebastian realized she was right. They were outnumbered, outgunned.

Eyes on the room, Faye fired again. Again. "Car?"

"Garage," he replied.

"You got the keys? Then move."

He nodded, panting. When he realized Faye hadn't followed, Sebastian looked over his shoulder, saw her firing into the room, laying down cover fire. Then she swung her handgun to Anton and fired.

Sebastian bolted down the hall, legs and limbs burning. Faye darted in front of him, clutched the doorknob, her hands and fingers slick with blood. Her entire front, even parts of her face and hair, was covered in it.

"Need to clear the garage first," she said as gunshots erupted from the belly of the house. She threw open the door and cleared the area directly in front of her, Sebastian noticing how she paid close attention to her blind spots.

The Jaguar was parked next to Frank's car—the only two things in there.

They cleared the garage easily.

Sebastian turned to the garage door opener mounted on the wall, punched the button with his fist. He barely heard the motor and gears working, his eardrums ruptured from all the gunshots in such close quarters.

Sebastian got behind the wheel. Faye had barely shut her door when he threw the gearshift in reverse and hit the gas.

The Jaguar launched backward like a rocket. It sped past the brick area in front of the house, the two of them bouncing in their seats. The back tires ran over the edge of the lawn and the car dipped and then tore down the small slope of grass.

Sebastian knew he was heading toward the stone wall securing the perimeter. *Don't crash,* he thought, slamming on the brakes. The car skidded and then stopped. Faye bounced back against her seat and then lurched forward, her arm coming up at the last moment to protect her face from smashing against the dashboard.

A shooter came running along the side of the house. Sebastian heard gunfire and saw Paul running out of the garage, loading a fresh clip into his nine. A bullet slammed into the side of the car. The armor plating absorbed it, but it took Sebastian by surprise how powerful the impact was.

A nine-millimeter round didn't have that kind of kick. But a round from a sniper rifle did.

Guidry is a sniper, Sebastian thought. *He must be here, too.*

Sebastian imagined his head in Guidry's target site when he heard another report. Faye Simpson jumped at the sound and the windshield splintered but didn't shatter because of the bulletproof glass. Sebastian heard another report as he hit the gas again, the tires kicking up dirt and grass and skidding across the lawn. When he got closer to the gate, he righted the car and, turning, heart twisting in his chest, saw Faye Simpson slumped against the door, a softball-sized exit wound in her back, near her shoulder.

CHAPTER 29

Real estate had been Frank's idea. After being released from prison, Sebastian had moved in with Frank, who already had his real estate license. Frank took him under his wing, and after Sebastian got his license they began working together, selling homes in shitty neighborhoods and pooling their proceeds to save up for a place where they could house their own carriers and then begin making real money in the blood world.

When a mortuary in Northeast LA that specialized in low-cost cremation services came on the market, Frank wanted to jump on it. "Mortuaries and funeral homes—they're always around us and people don't like to pay attention to them; they pretend they don't exist until they're forced into it," Frank had told him while eating shitty Chinese food in their even shittier apartment. "We can house a handful of carriers there, use it as our preliminary blood farm. It's a good starting point, Sebastian—plus, it'll come in handy down the road. It's a hell of a lot easier and more convenient to cremate our enemies than it is to bury them."

It was less risky overall, too, in terms of leaving behind evidence. Fire destroyed nearly everything.

Sebastian had lost count of the number of enemies they had killed and reduced to ash in the crematorium—people who had, effectively, vanished from the planet without a trace. And now he had to do the same with Frank.

The mortuary was no longer open to the public, and it didn't advertise its services. Frank had been the only one who had keys to the place. Now Sebastian had those keys in his possession. He entered through the door in the private garage that had once housed a hearse.

The crematorium area would have looked like an old high school locker room from the turn of the twentieth century—gray industrial tiled floor and walls, the white ceiling yellowed from time and covered in decades of soot and grime—if it weren't for the three ovens set up in the center of the room and, to the far right, a wall-sized refrigeration unit that could store up to nine corpses.

There was only one body in there now. Frank's corpse had been resting in it for the past three days, and Sebastian had finally screwed up the necessary courage to take the next and final step.

After Sebastian fired up an oven, he sat on the floor, the machine rumbling against his back, coming to life. In all their years together, he had never imagined either himself or Frank going out this way. He didn't know how they would die, but it wouldn't have been like this. Not like this.

This was the second time death had stolen an important person from his life, and what struck Sebastian was how quiet his mind still was. Like the smooth surface of a pond. In prison, when he'd been told his mother had died, he had experienced a piercing loss, but he didn't cry—couldn't, even if he wanted to, because showing any weakness in that hellhole would single you out, make you a target. He bottled it up, which turned out to be an easy thing to do since his grief had quickly been replaced by rage at the injustice of being denied his God-given right to attend his mother's funeral. He tucked away the rage, too, focused his time and energy on staying vigilant, on finding a way to get out of here and then properly deal with his enemies.

With Frank's death, the only thing he felt was alone. Marooned. Alien. Sebastian also had the additional burden of dealing with the practical matters of the death of a man who, arguably, was as close to him as a brother. He had already told the people at the real estate office that Frank had decided to take a vacation, but that would work for only so long. At some point he'd have to come up with a legitimate reason why Frank hadn't returned. Thank God Frank didn't have a family or any close friends who would be coming around, asking questions.

"You deserve a proper send-off," Sebastian said to the empty room. "I wish I could give you one. I wish I could do a lot of things differently."

Sebastian rubbed at his face, not knowing what to say but knowing he should say something. He wished Ava were sitting next to him right now. Ava had known Frank. If she were here, she would know what to say, tell him how he should handle this moment.

But she wasn't here. No one was. He was alone—weren't we all, in the end?—and he had to handle it himself and he didn't have the faintest idea what he should say, because, really, what could he say? Frank was dead. It wasn't fair, and it wasn't right, and there was nothing he could do to change it. How did that prayer go, again? *Grant me the serenity, God, to accept the things I cannot change, and the courage to change the things I can, and give me the wisdom to know the difference.* A lot of truth in those words, sure, but that's all they were: just words. And words were meaningless.

I'm sorry, he thought. *Start with that.*

"I'm sorry for everything I've done, what I've put you through. Reason you're dead is probably because of me. No, not probably. I caused it." It was true. Frank had wanted to take a subtler, more cautious approach to dealing with Anton's disloyalty—possibly to use Anton to lure in Paul. Sebastian didn't want any part of it. He was sick of waiting, and his anger had, once again, blinded him.

"I'm sorry," Sebastian said again. "I wish I could give you something more. But that's all I've got. That's all any of us get in this life."

Sebastian got to his feet and pushed the gurney to the refrigerator, holding back the tears that wanted to come. He would grieve properly later, after this matter with Paul was put to bed. First, business. Frank, he knew, would understand—would be proud of him for forging ahead.

CHAPTER 30

Ellie usually took for granted the way her memory worked, the speed and ease with which she could recall even the minutest details.

Ellie could recall, in clear, vivid detail, everything that had gone down at the house, but, incredibly, she had no memory, even now, of being shot. But she *had* been shot. The last thing she remembered with any clarity was being in the car and driving away and Sebastian on the phone, yelling to someone about how shit had turned sideways, that he was on his way to the checkpoint and to make sure the doctor was ready, because he was bringing in someone who'd been shot. Sebastian, she assumed, had been referring to her. She remembered feeling light-headed, sure she was going to pass out and die.

And now here she was, alive, lying in a bed, her arm tucked in a medical sling and an IV taped to the back of her hand. The room she found herself in was small and boxy and had bare white walls and soft lighting and a dull gray linoleum floor and a white door that looked thick and as impenetrable as steel, like the door of a prison cell. A fish-eye camera looked down at her from the corner of the ceiling near the door, and directly across from the foot of her bed was a wall of one-way glass, like the kind used in police interrogation rooms. She wasn't bound or gagged but her clothes were gone, replaced by gray sweats.

And she didn't feel any pain, just slight discomfort in the form of a throbbing and nagging tightness coming from the gunshot wound. She knew she wasn't on any narcotic, either. She felt clearheaded and amazingly well rested and she wasn't the least bit nauseated.

In fact, she felt the exact opposite. She was ravenous, wanted to drive to the nearest In-N-Out Burger and order two of everything on the menu.

An electronic buzz filled the room, followed by the distinct sound of a latch clicking free. The door opened and Sebastian, dressed in dark-wash jeans with black driving loafers and a crisp white collared shirt, came in holding a paper cup of coffee with a lid and a brown paper bag stained with grease.

Seeing Frank die, shooting Anton, everything she had put into motion—all of it strangely evaporated like a puff of steam. All Ellie saw was the bag of food. She was seized by the crazy idea of pulling back the sheets, lurching from her bed, and tearing the bag from his hands.

Sebastian handed her the coffee. "I also brought you this," he said, holding up the bag. His voice was stripped of emotion, his face haggard. "An assortment of croissants, scones, and muffins."

"Thank you."

He placed the bag on the nightstand, along with a couple of creamers and sugar packets he'd removed from his pocket. Ellie exchanged the coffee for the bag, opened it, and grabbed the first thing that caught her eye—a chocolate croissant. She took a large bite, resisting the urge to shove the entire thing in her mouth.

Sebastian stood beside the bed, his hands on his waist. "How are you feeling?"

Ellie finished chewing and swallowed. "Surprisingly good. I don't know what drugs you put in my IV drip, but they're working wonders."

"It's just saline."

Ellie devoured the rest of the croissant in two big, unladylike bites, not feeling the least bit self-conscious. Sebastian's presence didn't bother her, either. She didn't feel anxious or afraid, and she didn't know why and she didn't care. She didn't know why Sebastian was being kind and gracious to her, and she didn't care.

Actually, she did know why: she had saved his life. And he, in turn, had saved hers—not because of some moral obligation but because he needed something from her. Ellie had a good idea what it was.

Ellie held up the bag. "Want one?"

He shook his head, his eyes puffy from lack of sleep.

"You sure?" she asked, picking out another croissant. "The way I'm feeling right now, I'm inclined to eat everything you got in here."

"Increased appetite is a normal side effect."

"A normal side effect of what?"

"An infusion of carrier blood."

Ellie stopped chewing.

"You were shot in the clavicle—a clean shot—but you lost a good amount of blood, so I gave you two liters," Sebastian said. "It will help speed along the healing."

The food in her stomach suddenly felt like it was going to come back up. "You gave me Pandora?"

Sebastian nodded. "In a couple of weeks, you'll be as good as new."

Ellie felt as though she were stuck at the bottom of a deep well, Sebastian's words somewhere miles above her. *He gave me Pandora.* Her mind seized on that fact, couldn't accept it, and yet she knew she had to accept it, was struggling *to* accept it.

"You'll experience all the other benefits as well," Sebastian said. "Your skin will look tighter and fresher, and you'll have firmer muscle tone. Not that you need any of those things." He offered up a weak smile. "How old are you, again?"

"Twenty-six." Ellie felt very, very still. The prized blood product that she had read about on dark web forums was now coursing through her veins, healing her body. It had been given to her without her permission, which, oddly, made her feel somehow violated, even though it had saved her life.

"Twenty-six," Sebastian repeated softly. He stared at the wall behind her, lost in some private memory, his face drawn with grief. Right. He had seen Frank die.

And Sebastian had survived. *That's the important thing,* Ellie thought as she snapped her attention back to the room, to the present. She went to work on her second croissant, thinking strategy. She had risked her life for him and saved him. *Figure out a way to use that.*

Ellie swallowed, then said, "Paul gave Anton these blood pills. I have one. It's in my purse."

"Why do you have it?"

She told Sebastian about her conversation in the car with Anton, how Anton wanted her to try the pills out with her boyfriend. She told him everything, Sebastian listening attentively, nodding, encouraging her to keep talking. She couldn't get a read on him. *It's probably grief over Frank,* she thought.

Sebastian turned back to her.

"How much do you remember?"

"You mean after we drove away from the house?" Ellie asked. She took another bite.

Sebastian nodded.

"I remember you on the phone, talking to someone about a checkpoint, making sure everything was ready. After that? Nothing."

"You were bleeding pretty bad."

"And you decided to save my life."

"Not me. A doctor."

"You always travel around with your own personal physician?"

"I keep her close by when I have to engage in certain . . . activities."

"You mean torturing someone with a cordless drill. How'd that work out for you, by the way?"

Sebastian didn't answer. Ellie held his eyes with her own, wondering where this sudden newfound confidence had come from. Then she remembered what she had read online from users who said Pandora made you feel on top of the world, invincible. Apparently, Pandora loosened one's tongue, too, made one speak frankly and directly and truthfully, regardless of the consequences.

Ellie finished the last bite of her croissant. She wanted another one but thought it would be better to give the food a chance to settle, ride out the inevitable sugar rush and crash. "You could have let me die," she said, reaching with her good arm for the coffee. "Why didn't you?"

"Last week at the house, you thought I was going to kill you?"

Ellie looked at him, puzzled. "Last week? I'm not following."

"Right. Of course. My fault—I should have explained. We had to put you in a medically induced coma, so you've been out of it for—"

"What day is it?"

"Tuesday."

She had called Frank and told him about her intel on Anton on Friday. She had been out for, Jesus, almost four days.

"You're in good hands," Sebastian said, and kicked over a nearby swivel chair on rollers. "The doctor who treated your gunshot wound is here. She's been keeping an eye on you the entire time."

"And where am I, exactly?"

"One of the private treatment rooms we use for transfusions." He sat and leaned back in the seat, his hands clasped and resting on his stomach. "Don't worry—you're safe."

"Did your people get him? Paul? He was there."

Sebastian drew in a long breath through his nose.

Shook his head.

"But I do have some good news," he said. "The auto plant you told us about—I had some people go there. They found Paul's blood product— the blood pills and some carrier blood. It's now in our possession."

Our. Ellie liked the sound of that, Sebastian talking to her like she was now a part of his team. His inner circle.

"You handled yourself well at the house—amazingly well, as a matter of fact," he said.

Sebastian was appraising her carefully. But Ellie didn't feel afraid. Her heart beat at its normal resting rate, as though they were two friends catching up over trivial matters instead of discussing life and death.

"When that grenade hit the floor," he said, "most people would have frozen up."

"You mean most women."

"You threw yourself on top of me."

"I did."

"You knew it was a flash-bang and not a regular grenade."

"I guessed."

"How did you know?"

"It wasn't shaped like a grenade."

"You have some sort of military training I don't know about?"

"Cops use flash-bangs all the time on TV shows."

"I was referring to your shooting skills."

Ellie had rehearsed this part with Roland in case the subject ever came up. "My mother had a longtime boyfriend who was a cop," she said. "He taught me a lot. About guns, how to shoot."

"Huge difference between shooting at a stationary target and handling a gun in close-quarters combat."

"When the shit hits the fan, what choice do you have?"

Sebastian, she could tell, wasn't sold yet. Ellie said, "It's not rocket science. You click off the safety, aim, and pull the trigger. I'm sorry about Frank, by the way."

Sebastian nodded his thanks and turned his head, she guessed, so she couldn't glimpse his pain. She never understood why men were so uncomfortable with feelings, why they saw them as a weakness. She had also sensed, perhaps incorrectly, that he was embarrassed, maybe even ashamed, of his performance in Long Beach.

"I take it you two were more than just business partners."

"What makes you think that?" he asked.

"The way you looked at him at the house."

"Oh? And how exactly did I look at him?"

"Like the single most important thing left in your life had suddenly been stolen from you. It didn't have to go down that way, you know."

"You're right. It didn't." Sebastian turned his attention back to her. "If you had given Frank the information when he asked, then—"

"Sell your bullshit to someone else."

"Excuse me?"

"You heard me." Ellie's voice was calm but firm. "I insisted on speaking to you and only you because I wanted you to hear everything from me and not thirdhand. Things easily get lost in translation that way, and sometimes people forget to pass along important information. You would have had questions, and I was the only one who could answer them."

"And pick up the reward, while you were at it."

"A reward that *you* were offering. So, yeah, I wanted an audience with you, to make sure I got credit. That's just smart business. What isn't smart, what was downright stupid, was that show you put on at the house."

"Where you saved my life."

"Again, smart business."

"Thank you, by the way."

"You're welcome." Ellie sipped some of her coffee. Her brain was alert, firing on all cylinders—firing smoothly, in fact. Yet another benefit of Pandora, she guessed. "We should discuss next steps."

"You'll get the reward when I get Paul. I pay all my debts." He leveled her with a cold glare. "Each and every last one."

"I wasn't referring to the reward."

Sebastian said nothing, waited for her to explain.

Ellie drank some more coffee. Standing before her was the man who had created Pandora—ran the whole operation, from stem to stern. He had donors—maybe a dozen, maybe two dozen, maybe a whole lot more—and he knew where they were. He knew their names, maybe, and if he didn't, they were listed somewhere. Maybe her brother was one of them, maybe not. Regardless, she wasn't about to let him out of her sight.

"Way I see it," she said, "your main problem right now is Paul. He's a major threat not only to your life but also to your operation. We've got to deal with him now—the sooner, the better."

Sebastian said nothing, which didn't come as much of a surprise. She had told him things he already knew—basic, commonsense facts. Ellie said, "Anton knew where I live, so it's safe to assume Paul does, too. So I can't go home, and I can't go back to work. Are we at the Wellness Center?"

"We are."

Which solidified her original theory that the transfusions did, in fact, take place at the Wellness Center. *I must be on one of the top floors,* she thought.

"Anton knew I work here, which means Paul does, too. Since he's still alive, this place is a target."

"I'm very well aware of that, thank you."

"Point I'm trying to make," Ellie said, "is that I want Paul gone just as much as you do. I don't want to live my life constantly looking over my shoulder."

"Which is why you killed Anton."

Ellie didn't hesitate. "You're goddamn right, I did. You heard what he said back there, at the house. I couldn't let him live—couldn't risk having him come after me."

"Smart business," Sebastian said flatly.

"And now I have to worry about Paul. I can't go on with my life, and neither can you, until he's properly dealt with. I'd say our interests are aligned, yours and mine."

Sebastian said nothing. Ellie tried to get a read on him, couldn't.

"I want to help you find him. I've seen Paul, and I saw the guy who drove him to the auto plant in Fresno. I know what he looks like, too, got a good look at him."

"Make your point."

"Let me stick close to you and watch your back."

"And then?"

"I'm not following."

"After Paul is dealt with, what do you want? Clearly you want something."

"Absolutely," Ellie said. "I want to learn the blood business—the *actual* business, not this boring front desk shit at the Wellness Center. You let me work *with* you, I'll take only the money I need from your reward to pay off my debts, and you can keep the rest, use it as an investment in my future. With you."

Sebastian slowly got to his feet.

"I'm sure you've got questions about me, maybe even some doubts," Ellie said. "Give me a chance to prove myself, show you how valuable I can be."

"You've given me a lot to think about."

"One last thing. Where are my clothes? I'd feel more comfortable in them than this hospital gear."

"I had them incinerated. They were covered in blood."

"We need to find Paul, and we need to kill him. It will be quicker and easier—safer, too, for the both of us—if we do it together."

"Get some rest," he said, and then left the room.

CHAPTER 31

WHEN SEBASTIAN ENTERED the area that served as a hub for monitoring patient rooms, he found Ron Wolff reclining in one of the brand-new Herman Miller office chairs, sipping his coffee and staring straight ahead, at the one-way mirror looking into Faye Simpson's room. Ron didn't speak, which didn't come as much of a surprise. Ever since the explosion, Ron had gone into full quiet mode. He did that when he was royally pissed off—and Ron was still royally pissed off at Sebastian for forcing his hand that night. Ron, Sebastian was sure, also blamed him for the deaths of his three employees.

And now Frank's.

Ron and Frank had been tight. In a lot of ways, the two of them were cut from the same cloth. Like Frank, Ron kept his true emotions well hidden. Unlike Frank, Ron had emotions.

"Any thoughts?" Sebastian asked.

"I think it's a great idea, having her stick close to you. Paul's probably shitting his pants, wondering what she's told you about him, his plans." He scratched his chin. "Speaking of Paul, if I were a gambling man, my money's on him investing whatever resources he has to put you down—the sooner, the better. Once you're out of the picture, he won't have to be constantly watching his back. He knows we have people out there looking for him."

"You think he has people watching me?"

"I've wondered about that," Ron said. "He knows we're watching you, so in order to avoid detection he's got to hire solid professionals who have experience in this area. If he doesn't, he runs the risk that we'll spot one of them. Which brings me back to my previous point about getting you out of the way as soon as possible. When that happens, he can relax."

"You think Paul might come after her? For retaliation?"

"More like it's smart business. If you have her stick close to you, it'll make our job easier, covering you both."

Sebastian settled into the chair next to him and watched Faye Simpson eat a softball-sized blueberry muffin like it was an apple, taking great big bites. She used a remote to thumb through cable TV channels, her face relaxed, maybe serene.

"How much do we really know about her?"

"I ran the background check myself, when Anton hired her," Ron said.

Sebastian said nothing.

Ron took the silence as an accusation. He tilted his head to him, ready for a fight. "If she wasn't one hundred percent clean, I wouldn't have told Anton to bring her on. Everything on her checks out."

Sebastian nodded absently, watching Faye and reviewing what had gone down at Long Beach. "When the flash-bang grenade hit the floor, she didn't hesitate. She turned and wrapped her arms around me and threw me to the floor."

"Like she said, it was a smart move. If you were dead, she wouldn't be able to collect the reward."

"But when things escalated into a full-blown shit show, she didn't scream or cower or cry or try to run away or find someplace to hide. Then, when Paul killed—" Sebastian's voice caught, the images of what had happened to his childhood friend constricting his throat and squeezing his heart. "When Frank went down, she didn't so much as pause. She grabbed a handgun from the floor and returned fire."

"Sometimes people can surprise us when the shit hits the fan."

Sebastian rubbed a finger across his bottom lip, thinking, watching Faye on the screen. "Way she acted—that's muscle memory. She's had training. If she isn't military, she's something else."

Ron's eyes turned hard. "You think she's a cop?"

"How many women you know who can handle a gun?"

"If she is Miss Undercover for LAPD or the Feds, then people are watching her, and they would have put a stop to what went down at the house. They wouldn't have let it escalate. They would have intervened because they knew she was in trouble."

Maybe Ron's right, Sebastian thought. *Maybe I'm overthinking this.* The bane of every alcoholic.

Still . . .

Sebastian reached into his pocket. "There's also this," he said, and handed Ron a folded picture of a young boy of three or four sitting in front of a Christmas tree; the camera captured the look of wonder and expectancy on his face. The photo had been folded and unfolded so many times, the white crease marks were beginning to fray.

Sebastian said, "Maya went to throw out her clothes and saw it peeking out from underneath the insole of her shoe."

Ron looked up from the picture. "Her shoe?"

Sebastian nodded. "She must've used a knife, something sharp, to cut out a space so she could hide it."

"I know she doesn't have any siblings. She's an only child."

"What about cousins?"

"I don't know. I didn't dig that deep. But I can, if you want me to." Then, when Sebastian didn't answer: "Do you want me to?"

Sebastian had made his living being able to read people. It had made him a lot of money in the real estate business, and it had kept him alive, safe, and well protected from his competitors in the blood world. His initial instincts about Paul had been correct, but he had allowed Paul to enter the business as a promise to Trixie, and he had paid for that dearly.

But he didn't need to consult his instincts on Faye. The only reason someone went to great lengths to hide things was to keep a secret about their true, inner self from being discovered. It was basic human nature. So why was Faye hiding a picture, of all things, inside her shoe? More important, why was carrying around this picture so important to her?

What are you hiding from me, Faye?

"Dig deep," Sebastian said. "As deep as you can without putting us at risk."

Ron nodded. "I'll also work my LAPD contacts, see if I can find anything."

"Be discreet. We don't want to tip our hand."

Ron slid the photo into his shirt pocket. "What are you going to do with her?"

"She's already on our side of the fence. Let's keep her in the fold."

"Keep your friends close and your enemies closer?"

Something Frank would have said. Frank had loved all that Sun Tzu *Art of War* shit. "Paul has a driver. Why shouldn't I?"

Sebastian got to his feet and took one last look at Faye. Her secrets would come out eventually. In his experience, they always did.

In Heaven as It Is on Earth

CHAPTER 32

A FEW MINUTES shy of eleven, Grace decided to call it a night. She said goodbye to her girlfriends, all of them drunk and happy and begging her to stay. Grace held firm. She didn't want to drive home drunk. Delirium, one of LA's hottest nightclubs, was one of the safest places to party. You didn't have to worry about someone pricking you to find out if you were a carrier, and you didn't have to worry about a bunch of wackos trying to storm the place to take a carrier. The club was, as one reviewer called it, "a maximum-security prison featuring outrageously overpriced drinks and outrageously beautiful people doing outrageously uninhibited things."

The security line was long, Grace wishing she could just leave. While she appreciated the security measures the club took so everyone could party in safety, they were still a major pain in the ass. You wanted to party at Delirium, the first thing you had to do was submit an application for a background check. If it came back clean, you were then placed in a lottery where people were (supposedly) picked at random and assigned a night. If you were willing to attend on said night and could cough up a ridiculously high cover charge, you were brought inside to the security center, where you handed over your phone, wallet, and purse. There, you were given a special electronic bracelet that was hooked up to the credit or debit card you had on file. The bracelet also acted as a GPS, tracking your movements inside the club in case someone had to find you.

The next and final step was the body scanner that treated you to a visual strip search. The scanner could detect metal as well as drugs, plastic explosives, even a polymer gun; but what it was really looking for were prickers, the devices used by stickmen to identify carriers.

After Grace traded in her bracelet for her purse, she hung in the lobby while the valet went to collect her car—a good thing, too, since the area outside the club was packed with paparazzi. Flashes were going off like machine-gun fire, the cameras pointed at a woman standing by her limo. Traffic outside was backed up, horns honking in every direction. Grace took out her phone and called her mother.

"Hey. I'm about to leave."

"Okay." Her mother's relief was palpable.

Grace said, "I'm waiting for my car, but it might be a while."

"What's going on?"

"She Who Shall Not Be Named is standing outside the club, posing for pictures."

That was what Grace, her mother, and her friends called this sex tape porn star turned reality TV star turned feminist entrepreneur. She Who Shall Not Be Named had become world-famous for a viral sex video of her getting tag-teamed in high school by two football studs at a hotel.

Grace said, "She's out there with her new boyfriend."

"Some rapper, right?"

"Da-Nutz."

The two were idiots, no question, barely a brain between them, but what really pissed Grace off about the Dipshit Twins were the ridiculous "No Blood" buttons they wore, the two of them pretending to be a part of the whole #noblood movement—which was *so* hypocritical, because one look at She Who Shall Not Be Named, and you could tell she was on the blood, her skin flawless, tight, and youthful looking even though she was way past forty.

Grace said, "I just got a text. My car is ready."

"Remember, I gave you money for the—"

"The premium service, yes. It's all set."

"Call me when you get to the car, okay?"

Grace was very close with her mother and, like most children, was able to read the subtle shift of her parents' moods, even over the phone. Her mother sounded tired, which wasn't that much of a surprise since she was an early bird. Tonight, Grace heard traces of fear in her mother's tone—fear and, Grace thought, grief.

"Okay?" her mother asked again.

"Yes. I've got to go. Security is here."

Her escort—humongous, with a shaved head and a pissed-off expression—looked like a soldier dressed by Ralph Lauren: nice black suit mixed with a body camera, a bulletproof vest, and a belt that held a handgun, Taser, cans of Mace, and what were called "flash-bang" grenades. Grace felt safe—which was the entire point. His job was to walk her to her car, make sure she was safe.

As Grace exited the club behind her escort, she reached into her purse for the newest piece of technology designed to help protect carriers in the event of an abduction.

The panic button was the size of a matchbox. Grace held it between her thumb and index finger as she walked, keeping a close eye on her surroundings. If something happened, all she had to do was press down on the button and break the seal, and it would activate the GPS device she had surgically implanted in the webbing between her thumb and index finger. The size of a grain of rice, the GPS device would immediately send a distress signal not only to the police and local FBI but also to a special recovery team employed by the private security company that manufactured what it called its state-of-the-art "Carrier Retrieval System."

Grace arrived at her car. Once she got inside, she made sure the doors were locked. Then she took out her phone and dialed her mother. The car's Bluetooth synced with her phone. Grace heard her mother's voice on the speakers.

"Did you have a good time?"

"Yeah, I did."

"What was it like?"

It was like visiting some erotic petting zoo, Grace wanted to say. Her friend Jamie had had a private table with bottle service in the VIP section of the club. There, topless, acrobatic women made of pure muscle floated high above the dance crowd, dangling effortlessly and gracefully from gymnastic rings. Muscular, good-looking men and beautiful women dressed in black thongs were elaborately tied to crosses and torture racks, unable to see the hands exploring their bodies, because they were blindfolded. Cocktail waitresses wearing dark red lipstick and dark red lingerie with matching stripper heels moved with their drink trays through the dance floor and VIP areas. Some carried whips. Some made the customers get down on their knees and lick their shoes before they would serve them their drinks.

It was all harmless theater, Grace thought, although a great number of people seemed to actually enjoy being uninhibited. She wasn't one of them. Seeing the naked lust on display made her feel too self-conscious. Uncomfortable. And maybe that was the whole point—confronting those puritan parts of you that were uncomfortable and shy and wanted to look away.

"It was loud," Grace told her mother. "I can still hear the EDM music thumping in my ears."

"I was never a fan of nightclubs."

"I don't think I am, either."

"I'm just glad you're on your way home." The fear again.

Grace said, "Did something happen?"

"You mean you haven't heard?"

"Heard what?"

"What happened in Thousand Oaks," her mother replied. "It's all over the news."

Which Grace fully admitted she avoided at all costs. Turn on cable or fire up the Internet and go on any social app, at any time of day, and you were treated to a smorgasbord of terror. Her life was already an exercise in fear management. She didn't need to add fuel to the fire.

"You should really stay informed," her mother began.

"Just tell me what's bothering you."

"Seth Boynton. You went to grade school with him."

"Name's not ringing a bell."

"He moved when you were seven, maybe eight. He lives in Thousand Oaks now," her mother said. "*Lived*, I should say."

"What happened?"

"He was a carrier."

"I didn't know that."

"I didn't, either, until I read the story. Seth was coming out of a bar and a group of blood snatchers went after him. The bar security got involved, and a couple of patrons were also carrying, and there was a shoot-out and Seth was killed."

It shouldn't have shocked her. Carriers were constantly getting snatched off the streets or dragged from their homes or taken when they were coming out of a store or a bar. It was insane, the way the world was now. And even if you weren't a carrier, you were still in danger. When professional blood snatchers went after someone, they went in hot and heavy and had no problem hurting or killing anyone who got in their way.

Grace said, "You should really stop watching the news."

"Why?"

"Because it isn't healthy."

"Ignoring the world isn't going to stop me from worrying about you."

"I'm sorry. For Seth." *And for me,* Grace added privately. *I'm sorry for what I've put you and Dad through since I was born—for what I'm still putting you both through.*

Grace sat idling at a set of lights on Wilshire. It was a four-way stop. "I'll be home in half an hour, maybe forty minutes," she said. Up ahead, she saw a truck tearing its way through the intersection, heading west.

Another drunk driver, she thought. LA was full of them—especially at this time of night.

"Tell me more about the club," her mother said.

A van pulled up alongside her. Grace turned as her mother said, "I read about it online. It seems . . . different."

The side door slid open and she saw three masked men, covered from head to toe in black.

She saw handguns.

Assault rifles.

"Oh my God."

"What?" her mother asked, alarmed. "What's going on?"

A man with a crowbar smashed her side window. Grace had already turned away, searching for the panic button—*Where is it? Where did I put it . . . ? Oh my God*—and screaming for help as gloved hands flailed at her hair, her mouth and throat.

CHAPTER 33

If FAYE SIMPSON was right about Paul and his crew, whoever they were, deciding to go after her because he thought Anton might have shared valuable information on Paul's organization, whatever plans he had in place, it made sense to keep Faye as close as possible, which was why Sebastian had her move into his house.

Space wasn't an issue. Two of Ron's best, most trusted men were already living there and were running security operations out of Sebastian's spacious home office. That left an extra bedroom for Faye. Having her under his roof, Sebastian reasoned, would allow not only him but also Ron's people to keep a close, watchful eye on her.

Ron agreed. Before he left for Vegas, he had bugged Faye's bedroom, even the bathroom she used down the hall, with hidden mikes and cameras.

In the two weeks she'd been his driver, neither Sebastian nor Ron's people had caught her snooping or making any phone calls other than to her boyfriend, Max. Sebastian heard recordings of their phone calls and gathered that Max was getting frustrated that Faye was no longer available to him. Faye informed him that she had been given more responsibility at her job, which meant she had to work longer hours, and if Max didn't like that, well, sorry. Her career came first.

Faye didn't tell Max that her new job was being a driver. Max still believed she worked at the LA Health and Wellness Center.

Sebastian didn't think the two of them would last.

It was Sunday, the morning bright and glorious. Sebastian stood in front of his bathroom mirror, finishing up shaving, while he talked to Ron over a wireless earpiece connected to a burner. Ron had been in Vegas over the week, posing as a vanilla government wonk saddled with the sad-sack task of performing a fastidious background check on Faye Simpson, who had recently applied for a federal job that required midlevel security clearance.

"The next-door neighbor was a boatload of information," Ron said. "Told me Faye was an only child and pretty much a tomboy until around thirteen or so. She also got into a lot of fights. Didn't have much in the way of family—the mother, the neighbor said, was kinda tight-lipped, didn't really like to talk about her past. Neighbor had the impression there was a lot of sadness there, so he never pried all that much. He did, however, remember one time the mother had a birthday party when Faye was really young—maybe about three or four—and the mother said she had family there, some cousins and stuff. One of them might be the kid in the picture."

"What about the story she told us about the mother's boyfriend teaching her how to shoot?"

"It's one hundred percent true. The neighbor remembered the guy's name—Daryll Parson. I tracked him down yesterday. Lives in Seattle now, retired. That's why him and Faye's mother broke up. He got a job for Seattle PD, but the mother didn't want to move, so they split up. Anyway, I got him talking about firearms, and he told me Faye took an interest when she was about fifteen. Had a real skill when it came to shooting, he said, so he took her under his wing. For a while there she had shown interest in becoming a cop, and then she got real good at cards, namely blackjack, and we know what happened there."

Sebastian rinsed off his blade and picked up the towel. "What about the photograph? You show it to him?"

"I showed it to everyone. Nobody here knows anything. Could be a cousin."

"What about the boyfriend, Max?"

"I told you, he's clean. We've done our due diligence on the both of them, and then some."

Sebastian moved out of the bathroom, thinking.

"There's a flight leaving in an hour," Ron said. "Would you like me to waste more time out here, or would you like me to come home and focus on our top priority: Paul?"

"He's gone dark again."

"No, he's gone quiet. It's not the same thing. He's marshaling all his resources and planning some big move—I guarantee it. And he'll do it soon. Has to, after what happened in Long Beach. When he does, he's going to come after you—after us—with full force."

"You may be right."

"All due respect, I don't want a repeat of what happened at Long Beach and Cudahy. I can't be effective if I'm out here."

Sebastian agreed. "Come home," he said. "But keep your people on Faye and the boyfriend. Paul might make a move on them."

He finished dressing and headed downstairs. Faye sat at the kitchen table, sipping coffee, ready for the day. She was no longer wearing her sling. The gunshot wound on her shoulder was healing quite well, Maya had told him—a thin pinkish scar that had quickly turned white and would fade in less than a week.

Faye got to her feet. "Coffee?" she asked.

"I'll get some at the office." Sebastian had been spending a lot of time at his real estate company, pretending to be busy. His employees were glad to see him, anxious for some face time. A lot of people asked about Frank, where he was vacationing, if he was enjoying himself. Asked when Frank was coming back.

Sebastian followed Faye outside. Across the street, at the corner of

Stapleton, he saw a navy blue sedan with tinted windows slide to a stop. The tint was so dark, the windows looked black.

Sebastian thought of the handgun tucked comfortably in the shoulder holster, underneath his suit jacket. He told himself he was being paranoid. Foolish. A hit wasn't going to go down here at his home, in broad daylight.

The car turned onto his street. Sebastian spotted a pair of hockey puck–sized antennas on the roof. No hubcaps. A government car, definitely.

And it was heading toward him.

The Ford sedan pulled up against the curb at the bottom of the driveway. The engine died. The driver's-side door opened, and out stepped a tall black guy dressed to the nines. The suit jacket had been tailored to accommodate the nine clipped to his waist, and he wore mirrored sunglasses.

He's not here for me, Sebastian thought. The guy was opening the passenger's door. Sebastian saw a flash of dark, shoulder-length hair. The woman walking around the front of the car, dressed in jeans and stylish sunglasses, looked like Ava.

Holy shit.

It *was* Ava.

What was she doing here?

His thoughts were scrambled. He had a flashback to the night he had pulled up in front of her house, promising himself that he would reach out to her. That promise wasn't fulfilled because life got in the way, and now here she was. . . . Why?

The answer came to him, and he felt his throat close up and his stomach drop. *She knows I've been watching her. Somehow, she found out and she came here to put a stop to it.*

No. Ava wouldn't have come all the way here to deliver that message. Or maybe she would. The Ava he had known had no problem with confrontation.

But she wouldn't have brought a Fed with her.

Faye had come around from the other side of the Jaguar.

"Go inside," he said to Faye. "I'll come get you when I'm ready."

Then he walked away, down the driveway, to meet Ava. The Fed—and Sebastian was sure the guy was a Fed—lingered a few paces behind her.

Sebastian felt an odd collection of feelings flapping around inside his chest, like bats trapped in an attic. He wanted a chance to catch his breath, take a few minutes to process what was happening. Shore up his mental defenses, maybe. He wasn't quite sure why, other than that seeing her up close felt more real and more intimate than watching her through a pair of binoculars.

Ava came to a stop. Her face went slack, and she seemed unsteady on her feet, maybe a second or two away from crumbling.

"What is it?" he asked, rushing to her. "What's wrong?"

The last time he had seen Ava cry was the day he got sentenced to life in prison. She was crying now.

Sebastian reached for her. She didn't flinch or pull away, and when he took her in his arms and rubbed her back and told her whatever was wrong, it was okay, he was here, he would help her fix it, she sobbed hard against his chest and he held her, thinking back to how, once upon a time, it was just the two of them, blessed.

Sebastian didn't want to invite Ava inside—the agent would come in with her, too, and he'd have to introduce Faye, and Ron's men, which he didn't want to do—so he took her out back, so they could have some privacy. The agent, who Ava introduced as Trevor Roosevelt, mercifully stayed in the driveway—at least for the moment.

As Sebastian waited for her to speak, he reminded himself that he was safe, out here in the open. The house where Bradley Guidry had positioned himself was now occupied by some of Ron Wolff's men. Still, Sebastian couldn't shed the feeling that he had a target painted on his back.

Ava cleared her throat.

"It's my daughter. Grace. She's a carrier."

Sebastian felt a hollow core in the pit of his stomach.

"They took her," she said. "Bloodnappers."

The hollow core in his stomach expanded, pressing against the soft tissues of his heart and lungs, making it hard to breathe. He felt for her, yes, no question, but he felt some . . . *excitement* was the wrong word, but it was something close to it. Ava needed him. He didn't know what for, not yet, but she *needed* him, and that filled him with hope.

And gratitude. It was as though God, the universe, whatever, was putting them back together.

"When did it happen?"

"Friday night. Late," Ava said. "She was on her way home from the club. I was on the phone when it happened. I heard everything." Her bottom lip trembled, but she breathed it back. "The good news is that they've reached out. The kidnappers."

That *was* good news. People kidnapping carriers from wealthy families were a part of the new blood economy, and while some were, in fact, returned, others were killed, the money gone.

There wasn't any need to share this with Ava. She had read the same stories.

"How much?"

"Twenty million," she replied.

"You have that sort of cash on hand?"

"No, not on hand. Not even close."

But I do, Sebastian thought. A couple of mouse clicks, and within a few minutes he could have the money wired into an account.

He said a silent prayer of thanks to God, his Higher Power. God was giving him this opportunity to do right by her so he could get back the life that had been stolen from him. This was his chance. But for it to happen, he had to find a way to bring Ava's daughter back alive, because if she died or, God forbid, was already dead, drained, and dumped, Ava would be forever lost to him.

"Whatever you need," he said, "I'll help you."

Ava took off her sunglasses. Her eyes were bloodshot and puffy from crying, but there was a fire in them, and she looked like the woman he had fallen in love with all those years ago—someone ready to do battle. Her voice, too, was clear and strong.

"Sebastian," she began.

Hearing her say his name turned his blood into gasoline. It surged through his system, making him focus. He went into problem-solving mode. "I know someone who specializes in this area. He does a lot of work with the LAPD Blood Unit."

"They're already involved."

"Who's in charge there?"

"Alves. I don't remember his first name."

Mark. Detective Mark Alves, Ron's contact in the Blood Unit. Perfect.

"The FBI is really in charge," Ava said. "Kidnapping, I'm told, is federal territory."

Sebastian knew that. "And Special Agent Roosevelt is heading up your daughter's case?"

Ava shook her head. "He just drove me here. He's driving me to all the people I'm going to ask for money. The lead agent is . . . Parker. Harold Parker. The others, I . . . I'm not sure." She sighed, frustrated, and rubbed her face. "They're all blurring together. I haven't slept since Friday."

"How many people know your daughter's a carrier?"

"Me, my ex, and her primary care doctor, as far as I know."

"You never told anyone about Grace?"

"No," Ava replied, her voice firm. "Absolutely not."

"Grace? She tell anyone?"

"I'd be surprised if she told any of her friends, even the close ones. We taught her from a very early age how important it was to keep that information private, but . . ." Ava swallowed, her face taking on that look he'd seen on so many parents over the years—a mask of denial, and hope that was slowly crumbling. "Charles—he's my ex—he said he never told anyone, not even people in his family."

Sebastian thought he detected a note of uncertainty in her voice.

Ava said, "Charles got Grace into this new company that surgically implanted this rice-sized GPS chip in the webbing of her hand. It was broadcasting perfectly. The bloodnappers somehow found out about it, where it was, and . . ." Ava didn't finish her thought.

Sebastian finished it for her: "They cut it out."

Ava wrapped her arms around herself and looked at the pool—at the same spot, coincidentally, where Sebastian had stood when he was shot.

"The police aren't telling us much," Ava said. "Same with the FBI."

"And focusing their attention on you, I imagine."

She turned her head to him, startled. "They are," she said flatly. "How did you know?"

"Standard procedure, from what I've heard. They have to rule you out. Some families of carriers—not a lot, but some—they stage these fake kidnappings, hoping to make a big score."

"We are not one of those families."

"Wasn't suggesting you were. I just wanted to—"

"They're just going through the motions, collecting information, doing paperwork. To them, Grace is just another case, another statistic, and they can't— These cases—there's too many of them, these kids being snatched—"

"Slow down, Ava. I'm going to—"

"They took her by force. At *gunpoint*. Dragged her out of the car by her *hair*."

The day the judge sentenced him, Sebastian felt as though his entire midsection had disappeared. Then he was floating, no longer in his body. He was free, running away from his nightmare, and then cruelly he was snapped back inside his skin, the reality of what had happened crashing down on him like every awful thing, making him feel trapped. Powerless. He felt that way now as he watched Ava break into fresh tears.

Sebastian placed a hand on her shoulder and gently tried to move her closer to him. She resisted, so he slid his hand to her back, felt the muscle constricting in fear.

"Listen to me," he said gently, but with some force, too.

Her gaze skittered around the ground, the pool, looking for a soft place to land.

"Ava, look at me." Then, when she did: "You're not alone in this. I'll help you. I'm here to help, okay? I'm glad you came to me."

She searched his eyes, as though his choice of words contained some hidden meaning. And maybe they did, with all the stupid and crazy things he'd done for love. For her.

"We," Sebastian said, "are going to find your daughter."

Sebastian saw something in her eyes that for some reason brought to mind an image of a speeding train heading his way.

"Our," she said. "Grace is our daughter."

CHAPTER 34

SEBASTIAN'S THROAT CLOSED up, and his insides . . . he didn't know what was happening inside. His body had left but his mind was still active, and for some reason it was playing a clip from an old Bugs Bunny cartoon he'd seen as a kid—Bugs needing to make a quick escape and, when he did, speeding away like a bullet, a ghost version of himself remaining behind, hovering, before starting to waver, then drifting away, like smoke. That was exactly how he felt right now, this ghost version of himself sitting in his chair while his real self—his soul—had already departed.

Ava had turned in her chair, giving him her full attention.

"I'm sorry," she said, "to hit you with this."

Hearing her voice brought him back to the present. He was aware of his racing heart and the tightness in his chest and throat.

"I'm sorry," she said again. Her tone was consolatory but also hesitant and cautious, and it made him think of a bomb squad guy he'd seen in a movie. Ava had seen him explode, knew how quick he was to anger.

But the anger didn't come, even when he begged for it. He was in the right here, no question—she deserved to feel his full wrath for keeping something like this from him for so long—but he couldn't summon his rage, or any other feeling for that matter, and it made him wonder if he had gone into shock. He probably had.

He opened his mouth, swallowed. Opened his mouth again and tried to speak but didn't know where to start, what to ask first.

Ava wiped at her face. "Let me tell you when it happened," she said gently. "How everything happened. Okay?"

Sebastian looked down at his hands, wishing he had a drink there, because this was a time when he should be able to drink. He listened to her explain how, on the night he ended up accidentally killing an undercover cop playing gangbanger, her period had been over a week late.

"I planned on telling you earlier in the day, when we went to the Jack in the Box," Ava said, Sebastian remembering how they'd gone there to fill up on three-for-one tacos before hitting the house party. "I thought I might be pregnant, and I wanted to tell you, but I also wasn't sure, and I was terrified of, you know, taking a test. When we sat down to eat, though, I couldn't get the words out, so I decided I'd wait till later, at the party, after I'd had a few glasses of wine."

But she realized she couldn't drink if she was pregnant, and while she was at the party, sipping a Coke, the constant "Am I or am I not?" ate at her to the point where she thought she was going to scream. She ducked out, walked five blocks to a convenience store, and bought a test and took it with her into the store bathroom, the tiny space reeking of urine because someone, maybe more than one person, had pissed all over the floor and toilet seat. Squatting over the toilet, she peed on the stick as instructed, and then she paced inside the tight space, her heart pounding with dread and her gaze bouncing back and forth from her reflection in the scratched-out mirror to the crude drawings of genitals and names and numbers for blow jobs and hand jobs, Ava praying to God to please let it not be true—it *couldn't* be true, because she had been careful.

Ava said, "I took the test with me outside and walked around the corner. I was so scared, I couldn't breathe."

Standing next to a dumpster that stank even worse than the bathroom, she looked at the plastic stick and discovered God's answer. She couldn't remember walking back to the party, but suddenly she was there, looking around, and when she saw him, she—

"Crying," Sebastian said. His mouth was dry, his voice hoarse, hollow sounding. "I found you, and you were crying, and you said that you wanted to go home. That you weren't feeling well."

Ava nodded, her eyes down, Sebastian thinking how maybe their lives would have turned out differently if she'd told him at the party. How maybe he wouldn't have walked her back home and that car wouldn't have pulled up in front of her house.

"I knew something was wrong that night," Sebastian said, still feeling separated from his feelings, a wall there. "You were upset, and you wouldn't tell me."

"I was trying to—I *wanted* to. Saying it out loud . . . it would make it *real*. Force me to acknowledge that every breath I took, cells were dividing and multiplying, forming limbs and a head. A heart." She swallowed, eyes still downcast. "And then the car came and, well, we know the rest."

"No," he said. "Not really."

"What do you mean?"

"You could have told me."

"When? After the fight?" Her voice was sad now. "Cops were there in minutes, and they separated us, remember? They took you to the side and they—"

"You had plenty of opportunities to tell me afterwards."

Ava took in a deep breath and held it for a moment. Then she said, "You're right. I realized that later. I'm not making excuses, but at the time I was nineteen and scared out of my mind—terrified because I was pregnant, and terrified because they arrested you and the judge refused bail."

"You tell my mother? That you were pregnant?"

"Of course not. Why would I do that to her?"

It was a valid question. But he wondered if knowing she'd be a grandmother would have kept his mother around for a while. Maybe if she'd known about her grandchild, she would have fought harder, instead of so willingly surrendering her fate to God.

The pieces from that time of his life—the things that troubled him, the ones he had no explanation for—were coming together. "That's why you stopped visiting my mother, why you stopped visiting me in prison. Because you were showing."

Ava nodded. "I didn't want you to . . . Seeing me pregnant, me telling you it was yours—I couldn't do that to you, what you were facing. Having you go away for life and knowing I was pregnant—"

"I would have found a way to help you."

"You were nineteen."

"So you kept it all to yourself. Shut me out, my mother—and Frank."

"I thought that was for the best."

"A clean slate." Then he added, bitterly: "For you."

"At the time, telling you . . . it seemed wrong. Cruel."

No, Sebastian thought. *It would have given me hope. A purpose.*

"And," Ava said, "the pregnancy was difficult, very touch and go. The doctor said I might lose it. If I came there and told you I was pregnant, and then I lost it? I kept thinking about how that would affect you." She sighed, rubbed her face. "I thought breaking it off, it would hurt, yes— God knows I knew it would hurt you, because it *destroyed* me. I don't expect you to believe that, given what I did, but my thinking was, if *I* broke it off, then you could hate me, and I thought hating me would make things easier for you."

"And you."

"Maybe."

"No, not maybe," Sebastian said, some steel finding his voice. "You got engaged pretty quickly."

"I did."

"Accident or planned?"

"A bit of both. I met Charles when I was out with a few of my girlfriends. Charles was nice. A gentleman. He was stable, and he had a good job, and he was and still is a very kind man. And when he took an interest in me, I felt . . . it was like I had an opportunity to have a huge burden lifted from me. I wouldn't have to raise the baby alone. We wouldn't be poor. I felt relieved—and grateful. I don't regret my choice."

That was the thing he loved the most—and hated the most—about Ava, her ability to never look back, because the past was the past, and the future was the future, and there was no point in discussing either, because the only thing life guaranteed you was the present.

"Charles," Sebastian said. "He knows Grace isn't his."

Ava nodded.

"But he doesn't know about me," Sebastian said.

"No. I never told him who the father was. I wanted to keep that— I know this isn't going to make sense, and I don't expect you to believe me, but not telling him—not telling anyone—that was my way of holding on to you. To keep a part of you to myself." Ava swallowed. Rubbed at her face, swallowed again. "I'm not doing a good job explaining this."

"Grace?" Sebastian asked, his voice pinched tight. "Does she know the truth?"

Sebastian saw her pained look and knew the answer.

He said, "And you're telling me this now . . . why? To give me an incentive to give you money to help find her, in case I turned you down?"

Ava shot him a look that said he was above such pettiness.

She said, "You mentioned earlier that the police focus their investigations on the families. They're going to find out Charlie isn't Grace's biological father. They're going to ask me questions. If I tell them about you, they're going to come here and ask *you* questions. Given your . . . background, they might make your life a living hell. That didn't seem fair, or right. And you deserved to hear the truth from me, not them. That's why I came. To tell you the truth. I don't want your money."

"So," Sebastian said, his gaze flicking to the driveway, to Agent Roosevelt, "the FBI doesn't know."

"No one does."

"Then what's he doing here?"

"He's driving me," Ava said. "Charles and I came up with a list of people who might be able to help with the ransom."

"And how are you going to explain me?"

"I don't know. An old friend, maybe. But I felt it was important to come here—and I couldn't do it on my own. They insist on driving us everywhere."

Sebastian exhaled as he leaned forward in his seat and, elbows propped on his knees, rubbed his face with his hands.

"A daughter," he mumbled into his palms.

"We all make mistakes when we're young," Ava said. "Some mistakes you can't come back from when you're young and scared—and I was *terrified*, Sebastian. I was pregnant, and you were in prison. I wanted to give my baby a good life, not the one you and I had. And I did. I made that decision, and—"

"Stop. Just . . . stop."

She did. They sat in silence, Sebastian trying to wrap his mind around everything she'd said. In the midst of the confusion and the rising anger and loss and grief and everything else he was feeling, a small but powerful voice kept whispering to him, *You have a daughter. With Ava.*

Grace. Her name was Grace.

A daughter with Ava. Mother, father, daughter. A family. The life he'd wanted but not the life he had. His real life consisted of a psycho quasi stepson who had tried to kill him and was, without question, going to try to do it again. Then he would turn around and take everything he had worked and sacrificed for and burn it to the ground.

"Please," Ava said. "Tell me what you're thinking."

"The kidnappers."

"They called Charles the following morning, using some device or piece of software that changes their voice. Don't know if it was a man or woman. The person said they had Grace and they wanted twenty million dollars in unmarked bills, some other things."

"When did they ask for delivery?"

"They haven't given an exact time yet. They said they would be in contact."

"How much do you need?"

"Charles is in the process of liquidating his portfolio. That'll give us, by the end of the business day tomorrow, roughly six million, which leaves us fourteen million to—"

"You'll have it."

"Sebastian," she began.

"It's done. I'll have the money in a couple of hours. All I ask is two things. First, when we bring Grace home—and *we will*—I want to get to know her."

"You can take that as a given."

"Second, I would rather not invite the police into my life at this point."

"I understand."

No, I don't think you do, he added privately. The police would start poking around, asking questions not only of him but of the people around him, and that would lead them to wanting to talk to Frank, who was "on vacation," and to Paul, who was hiding. All a cop needed was to catch the slightest whiff that something was off, and Sebastian would have every aspect of his life put under a microscope.

"Don't tell them yet that I'm going to give you the money," Sebastian said. "I need to think about how I can do it without it coming back to me. Have someone else do it."

Ava nodded. "They want us to take a polygraph. The FBI. To rule us out as suspects."

"They *want* you to, or they *asked* you to?"

"Asked. Said it's normal procedure—I get that—but still, it makes me nervous. What if they start asking questions about Grace's biological father?"

"Has Charles told them he isn't the biological father?"

"No."

"Then keep it that way." Suddenly Sebastian found himself on his feet. "I need to get to work on this. How many other people are on your list to get money?"

"Four more. Maybe five."

"Go speak to them. Better to have as much money available as possible when the time comes. Sometimes banks screw up."

Sebastian felt his phone vibrate in his pocket, reached for it. A text, from Ron: candice jackson flying to la later tonight.

Candice Jackson? Then Sebastian remembered: Paul's last girlfriend. Ron had wanted to talk with her for a while.

"I need to take this," Sebastian said. "How can I get in touch with you?"

"I wrote down my number for you." Ava reached into her pocket, came back with a scrap of paper. He took it, and she placed her hands against his chest, leaned up, and kissed him on the lips—not a quick peck, and not the long, sultry kiss of two people madly in lust, but something more mature, more permanent. It was a kiss that said, *You're still in my heart*. It said, *I still love you*. He inhaled the smell of her skin and hair, and in that moment, he felt like the before Sebastian, the original version, the boy who believed he was in possession of the kind of once-in-a-lifetime love that held the power to shape his destiny any way he wanted.

CHAPTER 35

ELLIE STOOD IN the kitchen, watching Sebastian and the woman he had called Ava through the windows above the sink. Ellie had no idea what they were discussing, even though she had cracked open the windows; Sebastian and Ava sat too far away, at the table on the other side of the pool, the two of them huddled together and speaking in the sort of intimate, hushed tones of a husband and wife confronting the sort of life horrors every human being feared but few ever faced.

Whatever their conversation was about, it involved the FBI. The guy lingering near the top of the driveway, by the basketball hoop, was a federal agent—he had that look and air about him. Ellie didn't recognize him and wondered if he was one of Roland's.

Why *was* the FBI here? Did the agent know what Sebastian really did for a living? Did Ava? If so, why would she bring a federal agent to Sebastian's house? And why had the woman burst into gut-wrenching tears?

Ava kissed Sebastian. Not a "Nice to see you" peck but a kiss full of emotion—conflicting emotions, Ellie thought. Clearly, the woman had some sort of romantic feelings for him. Clearly, Ava—

"I didn't know spying was in your job description."

Ellie started, then turned, saw one of the security guards or computer geeks or whatever their title was standing at the island, grabbing a handful of grapes. There were two at the house. She didn't know their names because they hadn't introduced themselves. She knew they were watching everything she did.

"I work for you?" she asked politely.

He shook his head and popped a grape in his mouth.

"What I thought," Ellie said. "So how about you go outside and play hide-and-go-fuck-yourself?"

He chuckled and winked at her as she turned back to the windows.

Ava was gone. Same with the federal agent. Why would the agent leave without speaking to Sebastian? Her gaze cut to him, pacing the backyard, his phone mashed against his ear, listening. She fetched the car keys, and when she was sure he wasn't looking, she shut the windows and moved out of the kitchen, rubbing her shoulder. Pandora had healed the gunshot wound quite nicely—the scar was growing fainter by the day, and she no longer had to wear the arm sling—but she still had some muscle tightness there. Sebastian assured her it would disappear.

One thing she noticed about being on Pandora: all her senses were alive, as if they were on steroids. Her sense of smell was strong, intense, as was her sense of taste. No matter what she tasted, even something as ordinary as Starbucks coffee, something she had tasted hundreds if not thousands of times, it was as if she was experiencing it for the first time.

She could see why people wanted Pandora so badly. To feel this way day after day—it was easy to understand how people would turn a blind eye to the ethics. Still, she couldn't help but remember that someone else's blood was in her system—the blood of some young man or woman who had been kidnapped, forced to give up their blood.

Knowing this made her want to work even harder to find her brother.

Her phone rang. She fished it from her pocket. Max was calling her again. Max could wait. She opened the sliding glass door and entered the backyard. The cool morning breeze ruffled her hair and blew past her ears, but she heard Sebastian say, "Call me as soon as you get this."

He pulled the phone away from his ear, read something on the screen, then made another call. He turned and saw Ellie standing on the other side of the pool.

Glared at her.

Ellie held up his car keys as if to explain her sudden presence. He pointed at the driveway. Ellie got moving, heard him say into the phone, "I got your message." When she reached the gate, she heard him say, "I'm on my way."

Ellie knew they weren't heading to the real estate office today.

Sebastian confirmed that when he got into the car. "Wellness Center," he said. "Head straight there."

Meaning they weren't going to play the whole change-cars-all-over-LA game today. Sometimes Sebastian ordered her to do that to prevent Paul or his people, whoever they were, from following him. The Wellness Center was the only place she went with Sebastian. He had conversations with someone there—Maya Dawson, she assumed, who she also assumed was the doctor who had treated her gunshot wound and administered Pandora. Sebastian always made her stay in the car.

She kept wondering about his carriers. Where were they? Who was taking care of them? Clearly Sebastian wasn't the one doing it. She had overheard him saying that all blood operations had been shut down. Okay, but someone had to be taking care of his carriers.

And when was he going to bring her closer to him, trust her with his secrets? With Frank dead, she had hoped she could fill his absence. She had hoped Sebastian would have brought her into the fold by now.

Be patient, she reminded herself. *Keep looking for openings to show him you're someone he can trust.*

It was a Sunday, so traffic was reasonable. Sebastian stared out the windshield. When he wasn't rubbing his finger vigorously over his pursed lips, he was tapping his phone against his leg.

The phone, she knew, was a burner. She also knew he kept changing his burners on a daily basis. Ellie watched everything like a hawk, committing everything to memory, and shared it with Max when they got together, which wasn't all that often now that she was pretty much glued to Sebastian.

"The car is safe," he said. "He can't get us while we're in here."

He had told her about how he had taken the Jaguar back to a company that outfitted cars with various security measures for celebrities and politicians—had the bulletproof glass replaced and added hidden armor that could withstand a bomb blast, tires that wouldn't deflate for several miles if punctured by a bullet.

"Everything okay?" Ellie asked.

Sebastian gritted his teeth as he sucked in air, straightening in his seat.

Ellie held up a hand and cut him off from speaking. "I'm not trying to pry," she said, her voice confident because she felt confident, from sunrise to sunset, thanks to Pandora. "I'm asking because I saw what happened in the driveway, with the woman who visited you, and it looked like it shook you. What can I do to help?"

He seemed to be mulling over the question. Or maybe he didn't want to talk; she couldn't tell. He was tough to read—much tougher, Ellie thought, than Frank. Sebastian was more emotionally available, as a therapist would say, and more willing to talk. But sometimes he would retreat behind a wall, his words clipped and cold, like now.

Sebastian's features relaxed. She got the sense that he was ready to let her in a bit—all she needed was an inch in order to get to work on him—when her phone rang. She didn't answer it. She knew Max was calling, and Sebastian did, too; her phone, automatically synced with the Jaguar's system via Bluetooth, displayed Max's name on the dashboard console's screen.

"Go ahead," Sebastian said, distracted. "Answer it."

"I can call him—"

"No, it's fine."

Ellie had learned to read the tone and rhythms in his speech. His tone said, *Do it. Don't argue with me.*

It was against the law in California to speak on a phone while driving, except for hands-free calling. She took the call, and spoke before Max could say anything.

"I'm in the car, and I'm working," Ellie said sharply. "Make it quick."

Max knew all her calls were being monitored and possibly recorded. He played the role of the aggrieved boyfriend perfectly. "I'm sorry to bother you," he said, sounding disappointed and miffed. "My friend Cody is coming into town, and I was hoping the three of us could get together, grab some dinner, and hang."

Ellie's heart surged in equal measures of joy and dread. Max was telling her he had arranged a call, maybe even a visit, with Cody. As much as she wanted to see him, she needed to stay on target, keep close to Sebastian.

The main reason for the call was that Roland wanted a status update. He wanted her to get together with Max and share information about the investigation. Ellie never spoke about operational matters on the phone with Max, only in person.

"When?"

"Tonight," Max replied. "I know it's short notice, and I know you're incredibly busy, but it would really mean a lot to me. He really wants to meet you."

Ellie didn't get a chance to answer; Sebastian answered for her.

"She'll be there."

Ellie opened her mouth, about to protest, when he held up his hand to quiet her. Sebastian said, "What time?"

"I'm sorry," Max said. "I didn't know Faye was—"

"No apology necessary. In fact, I should be apologizing to you, having kept her so busy. What time do you need her?"

"I was thinking around seven? Eight? Does that work for you?"

"Seven it is," Sebastian said. "I'll make reservations for you at Belle Âme, in Chinatown. Fantastic French restaurant. Dinner, everything, is on me. Afterward, you and Faye can spend the night at the Four Seasons. In fact, make it two. I'm giving Faye the day off tomorrow. Enjoy."

Max terminated the call. Ellie took in a deep breath.

"You've been working hard, doing a good job, and you deserve a break," Sebastian said. "To live your life."

Ellie didn't want to be away from Sebastian—especially not now, given whatever was happening. "I'm thinking of breaking up with him," she began.

"So go and have a nice dinner and sleep in, and we'll talk tomorrow."

A lot could happen before then. "I'm more worried about Paul," Ellie said.

"I'll be fine."

Another call came through, this one from Sebastian's sixty-two-year-old secretary at the real estate office, Mary Jo. The woman called Ellie because Sebastian's number kept changing.

Ellie answered the call, and Mary Jo's cheery but raspy voice echoed over the speakers: "Paul called."

Sebastian straightened in his seat, leaned closer to the console.

"It was so nice to speak to him," Mary Jo said, clueless to the drama unfolding in the car. "How is he doing, by the way? I haven't seen him in so long."

"He's doing fine," Sebastian replied, his voice measured. "What did Paul want?"

"Your new phone number. He said he was having trouble getting in touch with you, and I explained what was going on with the identity theft. Anyway, he said he'll send you the information you wanted by email."

"He tell you what information?"

"The introductory information on how to meditate with grace."

Sebastian's face stretched tightly across the bone, his skin paling in shock or fear, or both.

Mary Jo chuckled. "I had no idea you were so *Zen*, Sebastian."

Ellie saw Sebastian swallow twice, three times.

"I'm trying," he said, his voice stripped of color. "I'll be on the road for a good part of the day. Thanks for letting me know."

Sebastian terminated the call and stared out the window. He looked like he was coming apart at the seams. Ellie saw him blinking behind his sunglasses. His left hand gripped the raised storage compartment between them so fiercely that his knuckles formed white half-moons. Ellie was about to speak when he said, "Drive faster."

CHAPTER 36

SEBASTIAN DIDN'T REALIZE they had arrived at the Wellness Center until Faye asked, rather timidly, "Where would you like me to park? Out front or in the garage?"

"Garage," he replied distantly, his attention locked on his phone, on what had consumed him during the entire drive here: a photograph of Grace published on a web page for the *Los Angeles Times*, a story head-lined BLOOD WORLD CLAIMS YET ANOTHER VICTIM.

What had seemed like a routine kidnapping, complete with a ransom demand, was actually Paul's way of getting a message to him.

And now my daughter's life is on the line.

But how had Paul known about Grace? About Ava? *Paul must have followed me one of the times I went to Ava's house and . . . watched her.* That was the only logical explanation. And how had Paul known Grace was a carrier? Or was it just a sick coincidence? Knowing Paul had Grace made him want to—

No, he told himself. *Don't think about that. Stay focused.*

Grace looked so much like her mother. Same beautiful black hair and angular face and fierce "Don't hand me your bullshit" eyes. Only Grace's eyes were blue, not brown, and the color stood out against her light brown skin, not a blemish anywhere. And, Sebastian was willing to bet, she was smart, like Ava, and determined.

Hang on, Sebastian thought, eyeing Grace's smiling face. *Find a way to hang on until I bring you home—and I will, no matter what it takes, no matter what it costs.*

Faye slid into a parking spot next to the private elevator.

"Stay here," he said, in a tone that left no room for discussion.

She nodded, kept quiet, looked straight ahead. After he'd hung up on his secretary, Faye kept asking him if he was okay, if there was anything she could do. "Yeah," he told her. "You can start by shutting up."

Sebastian pressed the elevator call button, and again his thoughts spiraled back to the day the judge sentenced him to life in prison. Again he reminded himself he wasn't a frightened nineteen-year-old kid. He wasn't trapped and he wasn't powerless. He could fix this. He didn't know where Grace was, but he sure as hell knew who had her.

First, he had to deal with Maya Dawson. She had called moments after Ava had left, and told him he had to come to the Center right away. It was about Sixto Ferreria, Frank's former IT guy and the second person who, like Link, had received a text from Paul. Maya said it was urgent but she didn't want to get into it over the phone.

Sebastian knew why; he was using burners that weren't encrypted. He wanted to toss his original phone into the garbage; then he remembered his secretary had given Paul his number. Best keep it for when the prick called.

As Sebastian rode the elevator to the top floor, he saw his reflection in the mirrorlike stainless-steel door.

"Grace," he told his well-dressed reflection. "My daughter's name is Grace."

CHAPTER 37

SOMEONE IS ALWAYS *watching or listening or both.*

Roland's first words to her, the day she'd met him for undercover training.

No matter where you are, no matter what time of day, even when you're sleeping. You always have to be Faye Simpson. And sometimes Faye Simpson will have to say or do things that Ellie Batista would never say or do. If you can't commit to that, then tell me now, spare me, the bureau, all the people who will be working for you, the time and expense.

Ellie gave Roland her word that she would do whatever it took.

When she walked into the restaurant a few minutes shy of seven and saw Max, she acted excited to see him. She kissed him, pretending he was Cody, her real-life boyfriend, and not her make-believe one.

After she broke away from his kiss, Max slid his arms around her waist and pulled her close to him. "It's so good to see you," he said, and then kissed her cheek. His lips slid to her ear and he whispered, "Last stall."

Ellie knew what that meant.

Her tastes in cuisine were limited to taco trucks, Five Guys double bacon cheeseburgers, and, when she really wanted to celebrate and let loose, a buy-one-entrée-get-the-second-free coupon special at a local restaurant. She never understood the fuss of getting dressed up all fancy to go out to eat, but as the hostess brought them to their table, Ellie had to

admit Belle Âme was pretty damn impressive. First, there was the matter
of the building—the historic building, she had read on the restaurant's
website, that had once been home to the Bank of Italy. The gold-domed
ceilings looked luxurious instead of Las Vegas tacky; the booths were
upholstered in rich, dark leather; and the tables had candles, the flames
twinkling like stars in the gloom.

A bottle of Château Lafite Rothschild sat on their table, opened, to
allow the Bordeaux to breath—compliments, the hostess told them, of
Kane and Associates.

"You must be doing one hell of a job," Max commented after consult-
ing the wine list. "That bottle costs five hundred bucks."

Ellie excused herself to use the restroom. It was downstairs, housed
inside an actual bank vault. She seemed to be the only one inside but
checked the stalls, just to be sure.

The stall door locked, she removed the toilet tank lid. The burner
floated in the water, sealed inside a pouch. She removed the phone and hit
the redial button.

Roland answered, his voice loud, almost explosive, against her ear.
"Sebastian's security guy, Ron Wolff, is in Vegas, trying to dig up information on Faye Simpson."

That explains why Sebastian has so many people watching me, Ellie
thought, fear blooming in her heart. "Did he—"

"No, absolutely not," he said. "Your cover story is flawless. He's been
going around asking questions, showing people a copy of this picture of
a boy of maybe seven or nine sitting in front of a Christmas tree."

Ellie felt unsteady on her heels.

"Any idea what that's about?" Roland asked.

"I don't know." Although she did. The photo of her missing brother had
been tucked inside her shoe. Sebastian—or someone in his organization—
had found it before her clothes were incinerated. If Sebastian hadn't found
it, someone had given it to him.

"Don't bullshit me," Roland said. "If you've deliberately hidden something from me, something that will jeopardize this operation, I swear to *Christ* I'll—"

"Sebastian had two visitors come by his house this morning, a Fed and a woman named Ava." She kept her voice low, barely above a whisper, but it still echoed off the cool marble walls. "I don't know her last name."

"Lewis. Her maiden name is Martinez. She and Sebastian grew up together, were heavily involved. She was there when he killed that undercover cop."

Wonderful. Thanks for reminding me, Ellie thought wryly.

"He went off to prison," Roland said, "and she went off and got married."

"She seemed upset."

"I'm sure she is. Her daughter was recently kidnapped. She's a carrier."

That explained why the woman had broken down in tears. But why had she come to Sebastian? Did she know he was in the blood business?

"There's a ransom—twenty million," Roland said. "She's going to several people, including Sebastian, looking for additional money. We're keeping a close eye on the situation."

"Paul also reached out to Sebastian earlier today, while we were in his car. He didn't reach out to him directly; he called Sebastian's secretary at the real estate office, looking for his new phone number. She told Sebastian that Paul had sent him an email—and I'm quoting here—on how to meditate with grace."

"That's it?"

"I didn't read the email, and Sebastian hasn't mentioned anything to me about it."

Roland sighed. "Interesting."

"What's interesting?"

"Grace is the name of Ava Lewis's daughter. Maybe Paul phrased the email that way as code, to let Sebastian know he has the young girl."

"And use her for leverage. Now put Cody on."

The bathroom door opened. Ellie heard the click of heels and terminated the call. That was the rule. You never knew who might be listening.

She flushed the toilet, drowning out the sound of her removing the battery from the phone. The phone went into her purse, along with the bag.

Ellie sat on the toilet lid with her eyes closed, and thought about Ron Wolff going around Vegas, showing people this picture of her brother. Ron wouldn't find anything out there, but that didn't mean he—or Roland, for that matter—wouldn't keep digging.

And digging.

CHAPTER 38

R ON RETURNED SEBASTIAN's call the moment he touched down at
LAX. Sebastian kept the conversation brief. He gave him the broad
strokes on Ava and Grace Lewis, and then he told Ron what he wanted to
do. Ron said he'd get to work on it right away and promised he'd be in
touch as soon as he knew something.

Sebastian was left saddled with needing to find Grace now.

Anton supposedly had had contacts with Armenians who were stickmen. But it was a moot point now, with Anton dead. Sebastian couldn't
make any inroads with the Mexicans. The cartels rewrote the handbook
on fear on a daily basis. The Armenians were more pragmatic and private,
took genuine pleasure in the torture their people had perfected over cen-
turies of war.

Sebastian couldn't do anything, had to do something. He spent the
next few hours dealing with Ron's men, tasked them with finding people
in the late Enrique's network. Ron's men made detailed surveillance reports and were more than glad to answer his questions. The problem was,
despite all the manpower and technology, they hadn't found anything of
real significance. The interesting fact Sebastian found out was that Enrique's friend, the one he called Gee-Gee, the one who sent Enrique to
Paul's house—his full name was Gerald Gambles, and he was dead. His

body had been found the day after the explosion. The police report said he had been beaten to death.

Paul, it seemed, was tying up any loose ends.

When five o'clock rolled around with still no word from Ron, Sebastian sent a text. Ron responded a few minutes later, said to meet him at nine at Paradise City on West Sunset. Sebastian knew the place. The dive bar, in Echo Park, was well-known for offering cheap drink specials before Dodgers games.

Sebastian arrived at quarter of, found the bar area surprisingly quiet. The billiard tables were doing brisk business, each one occupied by what looked like bikers—big guys with beards and leather vests, a lot of tats on the necks and hands, even the faces. The sound of pool balls smacking against one another filled the air as Sebastian slid into a red vinyl booth in the corner. He ordered a seltzer water with a lime for himself and, for Ron, an old-fashioned with Maker's Mark bourbon. Sebastian was staring at it when Ron slid into the booth, across the table.

Ron got right to it. "Alves is no longer in charge of Grace Lewis's case."

Sebastian felt as though the floor had tilted. "What? Why not?"

"He suffered a major heart attack this afternoon. He's in the ICU."

"Did Paul find out he's working for us? Try to take him down or something?"

"No."

"You're sure? Because there are medications, drugs you can slip into—"

"Stop. You're being paranoid. Nothing nefarious happened, I promise you. It's just bad luck."

There seems to be a lot of that going around, Sebastian thought. He sucked in a deep breath, gritting his teeth as he pinched his forehead between his fingers.

"Because of the ransom demand," Ron said, "the kidnapping is a multi-jurisdictional affair, which means the Feds are involved. FBI doesn't play well with others, and they sure as hell aren't going to allow a free-lancer to come in and help."

"What about your other contacts?"

"Worked them all afternoon, at the Back Nine, which is why I'm al-ready half in the bag."

Now Sebastian understood why Ron suggested they meet here. The Back Nine, another dive bar, was only a few blocks away, a popular water-ing hole for the LAPD.

Ron picked up his drink. "They wouldn't share any case details with me."

"Because the Feds are involved?"

"Because Paul practically blew up a neighborhood," Ron said wearily. He took a sip of his drink. "LAPD is still investigating, along with the ATF. It wouldn't look good for them to have me involved in any of their investigative affairs, so all my overtures were politely rejected."

"After all the shit we've done for them?"

"It is what it is. Isn't that what you AA guys always say?"

Sebastian yanked his phone from the table to check his email again.

"My people are doing that," Ron said. "Monitoring your account."

Sebastian knew that, but the gesture soothed him, gave him the feel-ing of some sense of control—which, deep down, he knew was complete and utter bullshit. Paul had Grace. Paul controlled her life, could do anything he wanted to her.

"The tech guys explain to you how it'll work? Tracing the message?"

Sebastian nodded. "When Paul reaches out, they'll trace the message back through the ISP, and get an exact location within a minute, or less."

"Don't hold me to that. There are a lot of factors involved that can prevent—"

"I know—they told me."

"And if he sends it from a phone, then powers it off, we're shit out of luck."

Sebastian stared at his screen, saw real estate–related emails.

"Still nothing."

"This afternoon, when we spoke," Ron said, "you didn't tell me how Paul found out about Grace."

"I have no idea."

"You never discussed that topic with him?"

Sebastian cocked his head to the side, frowning. "How shit-faced are you? I told you earlier I didn't know I had a daughter until"—he glanced at his watch—"nine hours ago."

"I was referring to Ava Lewis. I'm trying to understand how Paul found out about her."

"The hell should I know?" Although Sebastian did. Ron, though, didn't know about his biweekly pilgrimages to watch Ava.

But somehow, despite Sebastian's caution and safeguards, Paul had found out. Either Paul or someone else had been following him.

"What time does Candice Jackson land, again? Ten?"

"Flight got delayed. Technical issues," Ron replied. "She won't land until sometime after one."

"It keeps turning Paul's way, doesn't it? Son of a bitch has the luck of the devil. We should put people on her."

"Candice? Why?"

"Maybe she knows something. If Paul finds out she's back here, he might make a move on her."

"Sounds reasonable," Ron said. "You should get her to talk to Candice."

"Faye?"

Ron nodded. "Be better if a woman does it. Broads like to confide in other broads."

"She's at dinner with the boyfriend."

"I know. I just got word they're getting ready to leave."

"Anything out of the ordinary?" Sebastian knew Ron had bugged the table, and the hotel room.

"She is who she says she is." Ron sighed, Sebastian catching the sweet odor of bourbon and cherries on his breath, wanting to inhale it.

"If Paul does, in fact, reach out—"

"He will," Sebastian said.

"What then?"

"What do you mean?"

"What are you prepared to give him?"

"Whatever he wants."

"The keys to the kingdom?"

"If that's what it takes."

"Donors?"

"Everything."

"And then what?"

"Then I'll get to know my daughter," Sebastian said. "I plan on—"

"I was referring to Paul. After you offer him everything." Ron licked his lips, his eyes suddenly looking glassy from booze. "What do you think makes him tick?"

"Money. And power."

"Over *you*. Only *you* didn't die. As long as you're alive, you're a liability. Now that he's discovered your Achilles' heel, he can torture you . . . indefinitely. You really think he's going to give you her?"

"We *will* find her," Sebastian said. *We have to,* he added privately. "I'll take you home. You're in no condition to drive."

"I'm way out of your way."

"You can stay at my place." As Sebastian slid his hand into his jacket pocket to grab his car keys, Grace's smiling face flashed through his mind.

I will find you no matter how much it costs, no matter what it takes.

"Day before Frank died," Ron said, "you know what he said to me? He said when this was over, he was going to cash out, go to some island and drink, eat, and screw his brains out from sunrise to sunset, and hope he went out in the saddle."

Sebastian couldn't picture Frank saying those words, let alone living them. "Didn't know you guys were that tight."

"We were," Ron said. "We were," he said again, the loss finding his voice this time. "We talked about a lot of shit. Especially books."

"Books?"

"Yeah, he was always giving them to me, encouraging me to read and, you know, broaden my mind." His eyes filled and he sucked air sharply, blinking. "You've been real good to me, Sebastian. Made me a lot of money, more than I can spend in a lifetime. Hell, *three* lifetimes."

Sebastian froze. "Are you bailing on me?"

Ron cleared his throat. "Sebastian," he began.

"Stay with me on this. Until we find my daughter. Once we do that, we can go on and live our new lives."

Ron picked up his glass and looked away.

CHAPTER 39

SEBASTIAN HAD NO memory of falling asleep. He was jolted awake by someone shaking his shoulder, saw Ron, and bolted upright in the chair.

"Paul make contact?"

"Two minutes ago," Ron said. "He sent a picture, and a phone number."

Sebastian didn't get a chance to ask any questions; Ron had moved out of the living room and darted upstairs, to Sebastian's home office. Sebastian could hear footsteps above him, Ron and his men talking, as he looked around for his phone. *There, on the coffee table.*

Sebastian checked his watch. Three thirty-five a.m.

The email's subject line read, "Proof of Life?" The body of the email contained no text, just an attachment. Sebastian tapped a finger against the screen, and as the attachment opened, he prayed to God that she was alive—*Please let her be alive.*

The attachment was a headshot of Grace.

The first thing he noticed was the left side of her face. Her cheek and jawline were scraped raw, the skin slightly swollen, like she had been in a minor car accident. Her eyes were closed, her features slack from sleep.

Yes, sleep, he told himself. Grace was sleeping, not dead. There was color in her face.

Sebastian scrolled to the bottom, found a phone number written in black on a piece of paper beneath her chin.

Ron came halfway down the steps. Sebastian was already on his feet, moving. He was wide-awake. His blood was caffeine.

"We're ready to trace the call," Ron said. "Keep him on as long as you can."

"Your people?"

"We're ready."

"Email?"

"Working on it now."

As Sebastian dialed the number, Ron's words from last night about Paul flashed through his mind: *Now that he's discovered your Achilles' heel, he can torture you . . . indefinitely. You really think he's going to give you her?*

He's wrong, Sebastian told himself as he dialed the number. Ron didn't know Paul. Sebastian did. Sebastian knew what Paul wanted, what fed him.

The phone on the other end of the line was picked up.

Silence.

Sebastian broke it. "I have your money."

Silence.

Wait, Sebastian told himself. *Make him come to you.*

Sebastian waited, pacing, watching the second hand on his clock.

Twenty-two seconds passed.

"What else do you have for me?" Paul asked.

"My donors. All of them."

Paul chuckled. "I don't believe you."

"You should. Let's arrange a trade. Where and when do you want to meet?"

"You sound anxious, Sebastian. Nervous. Is it because I have the daughter of your childhood sweetheart? You're still in love with her, aren't you?"

"We need to discuss your product."

"Aren't you going to ask me how I found out? Aren't you dying to know?"

Sebastian looked at his watch. Fifty-three seconds.

"Stop looking at your watch," Paul said. "Ron and his people aren't going to be able to trace this call."

How did Paul know he was looking at his—?

Sebastian turned around, the hairs standing up on the back of his neck when he faced the windows at the front of the house.

"That's right—I'm watching you right now," Paul said. "Through a sniper scope."

Not Paul, Sebastian thought. *Guidry.* Guidry was the sniper. But a round wouldn't penetrate the windows. The original glass in all the windows had been replaced with a flexible polycarbonate designed to stop even high-caliber rounds.

Or maybe Paul was simply messing with him. Maybe Paul had installed his own cameras in here, in the house, way back when, before the summer, before everything turned to shit. Maybe Paul had been listening in for months, collecting intel.

Heavy footsteps echoed across the ceiling. Ron's people, Sebastian knew, had binoculars equipped with thermal-imaging technology that could the detect heat signatures of people crouched behind cars, even walls. They were no doubt rushing to the windows to search the area. Sebastian heard muted conversations, Ron talking to the men positioned outside, in and around the neighborhood. They had sniper and combat scopes equipped with thermal imaging and night vision and—

"I've changed my mind," Paul said.

"About what?"

"Everything," Paul replied, suppressing a yawn. "Frank inspired me. Frank's death. I kept thinking about the look on your face when I blew Frank's head off his shoulders, and then I started asking myself, Why give up Ava's little girl when I can do so many wonderfully creative things with her? Like, say, drop a finger every now and then in the mail to her mommy. Or you. Do you think Grace could hold her baby without any fingers?"

Sebastian kept the terror from reaching his face, his voice. "I've been running tests using Jolie's blood. You were right. The results are remarkable. Spectacular. But it's never going to work."

"Oh? And why is that?"

"The test subject we used died a few days after the transfusion. His blood wouldn't clot properly—more or less turned into a hemophiliac, so he bled out."

It was true. Maya had shown him the results the day Faye Simpson had driven him to the Wellness Center: Sixto Ferreria had hemorrhaged.

"You can see the results for yourself," Sebastian said. "It's all on video."

"Speaking of which, I have something special planned for Grace tonight. Do you prefer video, or would you like me to send you pictures?"

"I know you gave Sophia Vargas a transfusion using Viramab. I don't have to tell you that won't deliver long-term results. You're not going to build an empire that way. And that's what you want—an empire. You can have mine. Pandora, the donors and infrastructure, all the money and the secret cocktail combination to—"

"But you've already given me what I need—something far more important," Paul said. "I've hurt you. Knowing that you're out there, suffering, in agony; knowing that you've become one of the walking wounded, going through your days with a noose around your neck; knowing that I can, at any time, tighten the noose—well, you can't put a price tag on that kind of love."

One of the front windows spiderwebbed. Intellectually, Sebastian knew the round couldn't penetrate the bulletproof glass, but his nervous system overrode his brain, and he hit the floor. He dropped the phone and it skittered across the hardwood, his blood pounding in his ears as the adrenaline surged through his system and told him to run and seek cover. Sebastian knew the son of a bitch was laughing even before he heard it echoing from the phone's tiny speaker.

"I'm going to pick them off one by one," Paul said. "Ron. His people. That bitch you've got sleeping in what used to be my bedroom. I know where everyone lives, what kind of car they drive, their wives and kids . . . I know everything, Sebastian, and I'm going to pick them all off one by one, destroy everyone and everything you love, and there's not a god-damn thing you can do to stop it."

Sebastian grabbed the phone.

Click.

Paul was gone.

CHAPTER 40

ELLIE CAME AWAKE to her phone ringing. The room was dark except for the alarm clock, with its bright green numbers. Four forty-six a.m.

Where was she? Right, the hotel room. Max was sleeping beside her.

Sebastian was calling her. She scooped up the phone and hurried off to the bathroom.

"I need you to come to the house," Sebastian said as she eased the door shut.

"Of course." Ellie heard the tightness in his voice. "Is everything okay?"

"There's been a development, and I need your help."

"Paul?"

"Just get to the house," Sebastian said, and hung up.

She'd had a good amount of alcohol last night and had less than six hours of sleep, but she didn't feel hungover or the slightest bit tired. Another benefit, she figured, of Pandora.

As she showered, she kept thinking about the photo of her twin brother. Ron Wolff had circulated it around Las Vegas and found nothing, but that didn't mean he would stop digging. The man was a seasoned investigator, and he had all sorts of resources at his disposal—and computer experts. Who knew what they could turn up in some database?

Maybe Ron found something, she thought. *Maybe that's why Sebastian summoned me to his house, to confront me about it.*

And then there was Roland Bauer. His entire operation was now riding on an undercover agent who had deliberately withheld information—had lied, essentially. He had the full power of the Federal Bureau of Investigation behind him. Sebastian's people might not be able to turn anything up, but the FBI *would,* and then she'd have to come clean about everything. She'd have to admit she had lied about who she was when she applied to the LAPD. That in and of itself was a crime. After this operation was signed, sealed, and delivered and went to trial, Sebastian, who could easily afford to buy his own "dream team" of litigators and legal experts, would find out she had lied to the LAPD, and a judge could summarily dismiss the *entire* case against him.

Maybe not, she thought, shutting off the water. Before hiring her for this operation, the FBI had conducted an extensive background check on her and hadn't found out a single thing about her brother, the aliases she'd used over the years—anything. It stood to reason that Sebastian's people wouldn't find out anything, either.

Still, Sebastian had the picture. Roland did, too.

I'm getting ahead of myself. She needed to focus on what was in front of her, and that was Sebastian. He would confront her at some point—she was sure of it—and she needed to have a story ready.

Ellie had thought long and hard about it last night while waiting for sleep. She thought about it again as she dressed and when she kissed Max goodbye, the way a good girlfriend did—passionate and excited, hungry for their next moment together.

When Ellie turned onto Sebastian's street, the first thing she noticed was the home's front window. It was a spiderweb of cracks; you couldn't miss it.

To the untrained eye it would look like some asshole neighborhood kid had thrown a small rock at the window, but not hard enough to break through the glass. Get a little closer, though, and you could see the bullet hole frozen in the bulletproof glass.

She parked in the driveway and went into the backyard. Through the sliding glass door, she saw Sebastian sitting alone at the kitchen table. His hands were wrapped around a coffee mug, and he stared down at it blankly, looking haggard. Distraught. His dress shirt was wrinkled, like he had slept in it.

He looked up when she opened the door. His eyes were bloodshot, the skin underneath them bruised.

"Help yourself to some coffee," Sebastian said. His voice was dry. Hoarse. He cleared his throat. "I think there are muffins over there from yesterday, some croissants."

Ellie surveyed the surrounding rooms. Empty and quiet.

"Where is everyone?" Ellie asked.

"Tracking down an email from Paul."

Maybe they were. Or maybe Sebastian wanted her alone so he could torture her for information on the photo.

Or just kill me. "He responsible for the window?"

"Him or Guidry."

"Guidry?"

"Paul's friend from the military," he said. "The sniper."

"The day I went with Anton to Fresno, Paul said he had a sniper keeping an eye on us. Lucky for you, your windows are made of bulletproof glass. I take it you didn't catch either Paul or this Guidry guy last night."

Sebastian shook his head as he sucked in air, color flaring in his cheeks.

Ellie pulled out the chair beside him. "What's Guidry look like? You have a picture?"

Sebastian reached into his pocket, came back with a folded piece of paper, handed it to her.

It was a picture of J.C. sitting in front of a Christmas tree. The same picture she had tacked on the wall of her home and then carried in her shoe, taking it out at times when she knew she was alone, the picture always righting her when she felt nervous or scared or doubted herself.

Ellie smiled warmly and sighed—a happy sigh, as though she'd just opened a wonderful, thoughtful gift.

"I thought I'd never see this again."

"Who's the kid?" Sebastian's tone was casual, but his eyes were cold, and he was very still, the way a dog was as it decided whether or not to attack.

"This," Ellie said, "is my brother. My twin brother, actually."

"You always carry a picture of him inside your shoe?"

Ellie shrugged. "Depends."

"Depends? On what?"

"On what I'm wearing that day. That day I was wearing a dress, no pockets, so I had to improvise."

"Why not your purse?"

"Because someone might get nosy and decide to take a look in my purse, find this, and start asking all sorts of questions that are none of their business." Ellie's tone was firm but not combative. She wanted to come across as confident and calm, not angry. People caught in a lie lashed out in anger. People who had nothing to hide met questions head-on, didn't act or speak defensively.

Ellie placed the picture on the table. She turned slightly in her chair so she could face him, her arms open as she said, "Cat's out of the bag, so please, ask away."

"First time I'm hearing you have a brother."

"Had," Ellie said.

"What happened?"

"He was a carrier, I'm told, and he was abducted shortly after I was born." Telling part of the truth, she'd reasoned, could sometimes be the best kind of lie.

Sebastian's gaze narrowed in thought; then his eyes widened, and his features smoothed out.

"Never knew him—never knew *about* him, either, until my mother was dying," Ellie said. "She was prepared to take that secret to her grave—would have, too, if I hadn't stumbled across this picture while gathering some stuff from her safe. Even then, she wouldn't tell me much."

"What's his name?"

"I have no idea."

"You don't know your own brother's name?"

"Maybe I'm not being clear. Sorry—late night. Thank you for that, by the way. The dinner, and the hotel."

Sebastian said nothing, didn't nod or look like he'd heard her. Ellie felt and looked relaxed as she blended fact with fiction. *It's not a lie if you one hundred percent believe it,* Roland had told her.

"So," she said. "My mother. She refused to tell me my brother's name—his real name—saying no good would come of it. That's when I found out that my name wasn't my real name."

"What is it? Your real name."

"That's the thing. I have no idea. Seems my mother changed it not once but several times, in order to protect me—to protect *us.* We moved around a lot before settling in Las Vegas. As for my brother, she never reported his abduction to the police. Why? you ask. I asked her the same question. She told me it was because the people who took my brother were cops. There were four of them, she said, and they came into the house and went at her pretty bad. My mother was a fighter. Anyway, they thought she was dead. She heard two of them talking, and she told me she recognized their voices—local cops who were heavily involved in the neighborhood. That's why she didn't report it, why we packed up the next day and moved."

"So that's what this is all about, why you're so driven." Sebastian said it more to himself than to her, Ellie thought. "You became a stickman so you could find your brother."

Ellie nodded. "I carry that picture—it's like he's a part of me—with me while I'm out looking for him."

"But why come to LA?"

Ellie had anticipated the question. "Because this is where he was taken."

"Where, specifically?"

"I don't know. My hope is that you'll help me."

"Now I know why you were so anxious to save my life." He smiled, but there was no warmth in it. "I don't have him, if that's what you're wondering."

"I wasn't. But since you brought it up—"

"I know all of my carriers," Sebastian said. "Every single one."

"You've been doing this a long time. How can you possibly know all the carriers on your blood farms?"

"I don't like that term. It implies that I treat my carriers as livestock, which I don't. You'd be surprised by how well they're treated."

"I'd like to see how you do things."

"Help me find Paul, and you're more than welcome to see for yourself."

"Thank you. Although, I should say, I don't think it's you who has him. The two cops I told you about, the ones my mother heard talking? She told me they were both Armenians."

"If your brother was taken by the Armenians," Sebastian said, "then I'm sorry to say he's as good as dead."

The sinking despair Ellie felt in the pit of her stomach was genuine. She allowed it to reach her face. "But I'm sure you have . . . dealings with them. Connections."

"If the Armenians knew who I was, they'd take me out of the picture."

"And take over your business."

Sebastian nodded.

"But if he wasn't taken by the Armenians?" Ellie asked. "I'm sure you know other people in the blood world—local people."

"You said *twin*. Are you a carrier?"

"I am," Ellie lied. "That's the second reason why I got into the business. So I could work my way up, get to a position where I could afford to live somewhere safe, protect myself. Know the players, know the landscape, stay a step ahead of it, so I would never be a victim again."

Sebastian was looking at her in an entirely different way, like he had discovered something in her that he admired but that made him wary. Guarded.

Ellie didn't speak. Sebastian didn't, either, just stared at her, thinking. The hum of the refrigerator filled the silence.

"While we're on the subject," Ellie said, "I should tell you I have no intention of becoming a part of your blood farm or stable or whatever it is you choose to call it. I will take any and every measure to prevent that from happening."

"You don't have to worry about me."

"I hope not. Because if that's your intention, we should part ways now."

Sebastian rubbed his bottom lip, thinking.

"Is there anything else you'd like to know about me?" Ellie asked.

She waited, relaxed, hands folded on her lap.

"I need you to reach out to someone this morning," Sebastian said. "Her name is Candice Jackson. She's slightly older than you—mid-thirties—and worked as a contracts lawyer for some prominent firm downtown. She had a short-term romantic relationship with Paul."

"When was this?"

"Sometime last year. I don't know the particulars—don't know anything, quite frankly. What I need you to do is talk to her, find out if she knows anything about where Paul might be. Or Bradley Guidry."

Sebastian handed her a photo of a twenty-something guy wearing a bathing suit and smiling at the camera. He had a blond crew cut and a tan, and while he was nowhere near as tall or as muscular as Paul, the guy had almost no body fat and looked, to use one of Cody's terms, "absolutely shredded."

"How does Paul know him?" Ellie asked.

"They worked together overseas. Contract work. Military. They were both Marines."

Ellie leaned back in her chair and studied him.

"Something on your mind?" he asked.

"I know about you and Ava Lewis," Ellie said. "I looked you up online. She was mentioned in the article about your sentencing years ago."

Sebastian said nothing.

"And I know about what happened to her daughter, Grace," Ellie said. "Paul has her, doesn't he?"

"He does. Which is why I need you to make contact with Candice Jackson."

Sebastian, Ellie felt, was grasping at straws. After all these months of being hunted, Paul still kept eluding him. "Why did it end? Their relationship."

"It's my understanding that something happened between them—something, I'm told, that scared her. She came back to LA last night, after a long time away."

"Have your people spoken to her about Paul?"

"No. No one has. But I'm willing to bet she'll talk to you."

"Because I'm a woman."

Sebastian nodded. "You're going to approach her under the guise that you were, until recently, romantically involved with Paul—in a serious relationship, possibly talking about marriage. You're reaching out to her because Paul has disappeared and won't return your phone calls or texts, and you're heartbroken."

"And when Jackson asks how I got her name?"

"You'll tell her Paul had talked about her—you and Paul had discussed past relationships—and you wanted to reach out to her because you're desperate, wanting to know where he went, why he left you high and dry."

"I'll tell her I'm seeing a therapist—a female therapist. That she recommended I reach out to her to seek closure. I need to move on but can't, not until I find and confront Paul."

Sebastian pursed his lips, nodded. "I like that," he said. "I'll give you her home address. She's there right now."

So Sebastian had people watching her. Ellie said, "You don't expect me to just show up on her doorstep unannounced, do you?"

"Under normal circumstances, I'd tell you to take your time—follow her for a bit, see what you can find out about her, approach her when the time feels right. But these aren't normal circumstances, for reasons you now know. Why are you shaking your head?"

"She's never met me. Showing up unannounced and asking questions—that's too aggressive. And frightening, especially if she's been the victim of domestic abuse." That sounded too much like cop-speak. Ellie said, "Did he kick the shit out of her?"

"I wouldn't put anything past Paul."

"If he abused her or threatened her, if she was previously abused by another boyfriend or a family member, then her house is most likely the only place where she feels safe. If I go there and start asking questions, she'll shut down. But if I talk to her first, establish a rapport with her and draw her out, suggest we meet for, say, lunch somewhere close to her, I think she'll be more likely to open up and talk."

"Tell me what you'll say."

She winged it, going with her gut. Sebastian discussed the flaws in her approach, and then they ran through all the possible conversations, Sebastian taking on the role of Candice Jackson and throwing up roadblocks. Half an hour later, they felt they had the conversation locked down. Sebastian gave her Candice Jackson's number.

Ellie dialed it and then listened as the phone on the other end of the line rang and rang; she thought the call would go to voicemail.

"Hello?" The woman's voice sounded groggy.

"Hi, Candice?"

"Who's this?"

"My name is Faye Simpson. You don't know me, but I'm *really* hoping we could talk about my fiancé. Well, the man I thought was going to be my fiancé. You know him."

"What's his name?"

"Paul," Ellie said. "Paul Young."

CHAPTER 41

S HE LET CANDICE Jackson pick the location, Ellie wanting the woman
to feel safe and in control. Candice suggested the Rooftop restaurant,
located—surprise, surprise—on the roof of the Hotel Wilshire in downtown LA.

Ellie knew the place. It was a tourist magnet—and not just for
the breathtaking city views. According to various websites, during the
summer, models and models in training could be found using the pool.
The hotel hired them to draw in men who would hang around, rent
out the expensive cabanas, and order VIP service, running up huge bar
tabs.

It wasn't summer anymore, but this December day sure felt like it was,
with the temperature in the mid-eighties. The pool wasn't in use, and the
cabanas were empty, but there were gorgeous people everywhere, the two
outside bars doing brisk business. Ellie spotted a couple of C-level celebrities from reality shows that had long since been forgotten.

Candice said she was five six and had short dark brown hair, said she'd
be wearing jeans and a plain ol' white collared shirt. Ellie didn't see anyone matching that description at or around the bars, or at the indoor

banquette, so she wandered down to the opposite end of the pool, to a set of stairs that descended to an outdoor lounge consisting of benches, chairs, and, for more intimate conversations, outdoor couches with plush cushions and artfully staged throw pillows. That area, too, was packed, waiters zipping about delivering drinks and brunch. Ellie didn't see anyone matching Candice's description there, either.

Maybe Candice was stuck in traffic, a common occurrence in LA. Or maybe, God forbid, the woman had decided to bag at the last minute.

Ellie took out her phone, about to call when, from the corner of her eye, she spotted a woman wearing a pair of dark oval sunglasses and sitting on a maroon divan get to her feet and wave tentatively.

During the drive, Sebastian had shown her a picture, taken from the company website, of Candice Jackson, trim and healthy. In the photo, Candice wore a sharp charcoal gray power suit with heels, everything about her—her clothes and the way she stood and carried herself—screaming confidence.

The woman standing before Ellie looked shockingly different—and not only because her hair looked dry and brittle in the harsh sunlight. It was the amount of weight the woman had lost—not having had much weight to lose to begin with. This new Candice Jackson, with her sallow complexion and concave cheeks and bony wrists and air of defeat, reminded Ellie of her mother's last weeks on earth at the hospital, the dementia and cancer having devoured every last ounce of fat and muscle, turning a once-vibrant woman into a balding, ghostlike waif.

Candice was sick, not with cancer but with a disease that was equally cunning and insidious and baffling. Ellie could smell the booze fumes as she offered her hand. Candice shook it, her hand as light and delicate as a bird's wing.

"Thanks for meeting me," Ellie said. "I really, really appreciate it."

Candice offered a painful smile, and then she retreated to the corner of the divan, looking like she wanted to sink past the cushions and disappear. Ellie sat next to her so they could talk privately, and because Sebastian would be listening in on her conversation through her phone, which was tucked inside her clutch. Ellie removed a credit card and then subtly positioned the clutch on the divan.

"They make excellent mimosas here," Candice said, picking up from the coffee table set up in front of them a champagne flute filled with orange juice. "You want one?"

Ellie didn't want a drink. What she *did* want was to project a feeling of solidarity, make Candice Jackson feel as comfortable as possible. She smiled and said, "I think I need something a bit more high-octane for this conversation. Like bourbon."

Ellie picked up the food menu. "What do you recommend?"

"Everything's good. But you don't need to buy me lunch."

"You're not hungry?"

"I think it's best for me to stick with my liquid diet."

The waiter was a good-looking guy, all smiles. Candice seemed to wither under his polite gaze, stared down at the table as she ordered two mimosas for herself. Ellie ordered a double Knob Creek, neat, then asked him to pick out a couple of appetizers in case Candice changed her mind, the woman looking like she could use a good meal.

Candice sighed as the waiter left. "I was doing so good," she said, and shook her head. "Hadn't had a drop in almost a month."

Ellie didn't know what to say, so she said nothing, just listened and watched the woman's eyes darting behind her sunglasses.

"Then I came back here and—I dunno. I just couldn't handle it."

"Because of Paul?"

"And this." Candice made a sweeping gesture to the crystal blue sky.

"You don't like LA?"

Candice snorted. "This city is an open-air insane asylum. That's why it attracts psychopaths and predators." She drained the last of her mimosa. "It's all going to burn to the ground, I'm sure."

"The wildfires."

Candice nodded. "Can you smell the smoke in the air?"

Ellie could, actually, and wondered if Candice was right about the city burning to the ground. From everything she'd read and heard, the wildfires were closing in from all sides, the already-overworked firefighters unable to hold them back.

"So," Candice said, "how do you know about me?"

Ellie had anticipated the question. "Paul mentioned your name a couple of times—you know, when you talk about exes and stuff."

"Oh? And what did he say?" Candice kept her voice light.

"Nothing but good things," Ellie assured her.

"I find that hard to believe."

"Everything was going fine between us—at least I thought everything was gone fine—and then he suddenly stopped calling me."

"He probably ghosted you."

"I definitely thought that at first. Then I came to find out, a few weeks back, that no one's seen or heard from him in months."

"He moved?"

Ellie caught the palpable relief buried in Candice's question. "That's the thing," Ellie said. "No one knows."

"I didn't meet many of Paul's friends."

"I'm sure you met his BFF, Bradley Guidry."

"Never heard of him," Candice said quickly.

Ellie knew the woman was lying; Candice's response was too fast. Ellie let it go for the moment.

"You talk to his mother?" Candice asked.

Ellie reminded herself to keep her answers as vague as possible; she didn't want to get caught in a lie. She was about to speak when Candice's face contorted, and then the woman said, "Shit, I forgot she died. Cancer, I think."

"I never met her."

"She was nice. I liked her. Her and his stepfather, Sebastian. You talk to him?"

"I never met him, either. All that time I was together with Paul, I never met his parents—he rarely talked about them with me. I just assumed they weren't, you know, close."

"Well," Candice said, picking up her glass, "trust me when I say you're better off without him."

"That's pretty much what my therapist told me. Called him a malignant narcissist."

"Your therapist sounds like a smart woman. You should definitely listen to her."

"I am. Well, I should say I'm *trying* to." Ellie chuckled, a part of her feeling guilty for manipulating this woman who was so clearly emotionally damaged. "She keeps telling me I need to move on—and I want to. Honestly, I do. But like I said on the phone, there's this part of me that keeps demanding to know *why*."

"It wasn't anything you did."

"You're probably right."

"No," Candice said, getting some steel in her voice, "I *am* right."

"I'm not, like, looking to get back together with him or anything. What I do need to do, though, is to confront him."

"Why? Paul's incapable of telling the truth."

"Which, again, is what my therapist said. But for me to get closure— for me to move on, get back to my life—she said I've got to confront him. Not over text or on the phone but in person. She said I need to tell him exactly how what he did affected me. Example she used was a victim of a violent crime. Victims are allowed to read what's called a victim impact statement to the court. It's gives them their power back, offers them closure."

"Good luck."

"Do you have any ideas about where I might be able to find him?"

Candice shook her head. "I haven't seen or spoken to him in . . . Christ, it's been almost a year." She grew very still, just for a moment. Then she took in a deep breath. "Confronting him is a waste of time."

"But I've got to at least try."

"No, you don't."

"Why?"

"Because Paul," Candice said, "is evil."

CHAPTER 42

SEBASTIAN SAT ALONE in his car, parked near the front of the hotel, listening to Faye Simpson's conversation with Candice Jackson over his earpiece. He had tipped the valet guy a few hundred to let him park there for an hour or so.

Faye's voice filled his earpiece: "What do you mean, evil?"

Candice Jackson didn't answer. The silence stretched on longer than he cared for, wishing Faye would say something so Candice wouldn't leave. That being said, he wasn't there, couldn't see Candice—and Frank had been right about Faye being smart. She knew how to steer a conversation, knew when to push and when to hold back.

"I can't keep this bottled up inside," Candice said—more to herself, Sebastian thought, than to Faye. "I have to come clean. Own up to what I did."

Sebastian relaxed a bit against his seat.

Candice said, "Okay, so, like you, I'm in therapy. Been going twice a week for a month now. I've got what my therapist calls an Electra complex, which is a really fancy way of saying I suffer from major daddy issues. And she's right. Unfortunately." Candice paused, took a breath. "I'm a people pleaser. Always have been."

"How long were you guys together?" Faye asked.

"We didn't . . . Can I ask you a personal question?"

"Absolutely. Anything."

"It's about carrier blood," Candice said. "You ever try it?"

Faye chuckled. "I wish. I can't afford it—I'm talking about the real stuff, not the crap people get in blood dens."

"Stay away from all of it. It will seriously screw you up."

"You've tried it?"

"Tried it?" Candice snorted. "I was addicted to it."

"What happened, if you don't mind me asking?"

Candice paused.

"I'm not trying to pry, honest to God," Faye said. "I'm just—well, I'd be lying if I said carrier blood wasn't something I'm considering down the road. Women—especially women in this town—we need—"

"What I'm about to tell you—this isn't me, okay? This isn't who I am as a person. The stuff that happened . . . I'm still not sure *how* it happened. It was like . . . The only way I can describe it is like I was possessed or something."

Sebastian thought about the now late Sixto Ferreria, sweating buckets but looking buff and healthy, as Candice said, "Paul gave me a small transfusion, said that was more than enough."

"What kind of blood?"

"He didn't give me a name, just said it was going to change my life."

"Did you know what was in it?"

"No, I— No, wait. Now I remember. This blood—he said it was some new version of Pandora. Which right away got me excited."

"That stuff is supposed to be the best."

"That's what they say. And when Paul said he'd gotten his hands on this version, I—well, I just believed him."

"He's got a supplier?"

"He wouldn't say, would never get into specifics. But back to your question, no, I didn't ask what was in it in terms of drugs. He gave it to me at his place—an injection. I thought it was going to be a transfusion, but he said no, this new Pandora was much more powerful. I got a single injection at first; then, as time went on, a series of them."

He was experimenting on her, Sebastian thought. *Trying out different dosages, seeing which one got the maximum benefits.*

"The first time was on a Saturday," Candice said. "That night we went out to a bar and it was . . . All I could think about was Paul. Having him. Right there on the bar, the floor, the bathroom—I didn't care. And I wasn't drunk or even buzzed, which I don't expect you to believe, given what you're witnessing right now."

I believe you, Sebastian thought.

"I couldn't wait to get him home, back to my place," Candice said. "When we got there . . . I was insatiable. I couldn't get enough of him. It wasn't just about the sex, although that was amazing, as much as I hate to admit that. I was somehow, like, super close to him, in a way I've never been with anyone before or since. It was like I was seeing into his soul. I know how corny that sounds, but we connected on this really, really deep spiritual level and . . ." She let loose a tittering laugh. "I know I sound like a crazy person."

"You don't," Faye reassured her. "And I appreciate your honesty."

"Deep down, I knew he was an asshole. He had that smugness about him. But he was a beautiful asshole. A gorgeous asshole with a gorgeous body who made me feel good about myself, made *me* feel worthy. I couldn't stop thinking about him. Wanting him. I'm talking weeks. He made me chase him, and I did, because that's what a broken girl like me does. We kept hooking up on and off, and it was great until it wasn't."

"What did he do to you?"

"He would supply me with Pandora, but only a little bit here and there."

Not Pandora, Sebastian corrected her. *Pandora doesn't have those effects. He gave you blood from a pregnant carrier.*

"Then Paul would . . . deny me."

"Because of the side effects?"

"No. Well, I did get some. I started getting nosebleeds, a lot of them, and one time, when it wouldn't stop, I went to the ER and they said my blood wasn't clotting properly, and they gave me some meds. That helped, but then I got sick—like a flu on steroids. My immune system was really weak. They thought I had cancer, but it turned out I didn't."

In his mind's eye Sebastian saw the video Maya had shown him of Sixto Ferreria bleeding out, then thought about what Candice Jackson had just shared. She was lucky to still be alive.

"And then Paul stopped giving you this new Pandora product."

"Well, yes. Eventually. But when I said he denied me, I was talking about, you know, sexually. I would want him in the worst way, and he'd say no. He would make me . . . beg for it. And I would. I did. I begged for him, and later, I begged for the blood, because once you have it—once you have that feeling it gives you—you never want to give it up." Candice was speaking like someone was standing on her neck. "The way I wanted him—I never wanted another man like that, and it disgusted me, and I couldn't help myself. And the blood, too. I wanted that blood."

Sebastian heard the self-loathing in the woman's voice, Candice having no idea she'd been used as Paul's personal guinea pig.

"No matter what he did, no matter what he asked me to do, I came back to him—*for* him," Candice said. "I still don't know why I did the things he asked. But it keeps coming back to the blood. That's the only thing that makes sense."

"Are we talking illegal things or . . . private matters?"

"Private. Things that turn my stomach. Degrading things." Her voice cracked, the woman sounding like she was coming apart at the seams. "I became this completely different person after trying that blood the first time. Booze is the only thing that helps."

Until it doesn't, Sebastian thought. He felt for the young woman, in more ways than one.

Faye said, "I'm sorry for doing this to you, asking you questions, dredging everything up."

"Hey, if I can save your life—your sanity—then it's worth it."

"You know who I also can't seem to find? Bradley Guidry."

"I told you, I never heard of him."

"Did he hurt you, too? Guidry."

A few beats of silence followed; Sebastian sensed Candice's reluctance to get into the details and wished Faye would push a little when Candice said, "I only met him once, but he was . . . he just gave off this creepy vibe."

"You know where I can find him?"

"No. But if you find him, you'll find Paul. They're *very* close." Candice said it like there was something more to it.

Faye, fortunately, picked up on that. "Meaning what?"

Candice was quiet for a moment. The woman had provided useful information. Sebastian was glad he'd had Ron put people on her. Still, he made a mental note to call Ron back with this new information, have his people watch Candice more closely. If Paul knew she was back in LA, she could be a threat.

"Screw it," Candice said. "We've come this far. Okay, you want to know? Okay, fine. The last time I saw Paul was at his place. This was on a Friday. I'd been thinking about him all week, begging to see him, and he agreed. He has one of those long, full-length mirrors propped up against the wall across from the foot of his bed. Paul loves mirrors. Likes, you know, doing it in front of one so he can watch and admire himself."

That sounds like something Paul would do. He had always been proud of his body, the discipline he showed in not only weight training but his meticulous diet. Sebastian could recall numerous times throughout Paul's adolescence when he'd found Paul lifting weights in either his bedroom or the workout room in the basement, always in front of a mirror.

"We were about to, you know, get into it when Paul said he had a special request." Candice spoke by rote, without emotion, a lawyer reading words from a contract. "He said he wanted to invite someone to join us. I thought he meant a woman. Not my thing, not at all, but like I said, I wasn't myself, and anything Paul wanted . . . But it wasn't another woman Paul wanted. It was Bradley, and I . . ." Candice didn't finish the thought. Then she said, "Later, at the parties, I said yes to that, too. He . . . well, he, you know, traded me out to certain people. Filmed me doing things."

"Where were these parties? His place?"

"No. Someplace way north. Ojai, maybe. No, it was Santa Paula. Yeah. This really big house—you know, one of those luxury country-type homes, but sprawling. Place was completely isolated. It had these stunning mountain views, but at night, it was . . . I mean, there was no one around, and you felt, like, totally alone. Trapped."

Sounds like a perfect spot for Paul to store his carriers, Sebastian thought. *Or my daughter.*

He knew he was getting ahead of himself, but still, he wanted Faye to ask Candice for the address. He wanted to take a look at this house, but he couldn't do that if—

"You have an address?" Faye asked.

Sebastian grinned. *Well done.*

A beat, and then Candice Jackson said, defensively, "Why are you asking me that?"

Careful, Faye.

Faye sighed. "Now it's my turn to be truthful with you." She paused, as if taking a moment to collect herself. "Paul brought me to a few of those types of parties, and it was . . . Okay, I kind of liked it. Got off on it. But I was always really, really drunk, and I can't remember the places we went."

Faye was good. *Too* good, actually. Sebastian thought back to this morning's conversation at the kitchen table, when he'd confronted her with the photo. The story about her twin brother and her being a carrier— she had delivered it as flawlessly and smoothly as the lie she had just given to Candice.

Faye was clearly good at pretending.

"I don't remember the parties much, either, just the one I told you about," Candice said. "Canyon Road, I think, was the address."

"Oh my God, I think I was there once. Guy owned it, David something."

"Don't know his name. Don't know anyone's name, really, because no one gave their names. Didn't see faces, either—everyone wore these creepy, like, Victorian masks. The guy who owned the house, though—I remember Paul saying something about how the guy made his fortune through these gossip-type websites that catered to celebrities."

"Was Paul tight with this guy?"

Candice thought about it.

"I think so," she said after a moment. "Yeah. Yeah, probably. Paul told me once how he went to this guy's place a lot, worked as his private trainer. But I'm not, you know, one hundred percent sure. Like I said, I don't remember much from that period of time."

"I don't remember much, either, truth be told. There were a few times—well, a lot of times, if I'm being honest—that I blacked out. I don't drink as much anymore. I've cut way back and— What?"

"You don't seem that, you know, broken."

"Everyone is broken in some way," Faye said. "Some of us—"

Candice started to sob. Sebastian worked the real estate app on his phone, trying to gather information on the Canyon Road property, a part of him wondering if the guy who owned it could be a backer for Paul. Sebastian figured Paul had to have one—or at least one potential backer. Paul's whole speech last night about wanting to torture him might have been true, but he knew Paul's major hard-on pointed in one direction: toward building a blood empire. Sebastian had offered him his own and Paul had said no, which made Sebastian believe someone else was already in play—someone with very deep pockets.

"Hey," Faye said gently, "it's okay. I didn't mean—"

"I don't understand what's wrong with me. What's so wrong with me?"

Faye didn't answer—didn't need to, Candice's question being rhetorical. Sebastian heard Faye quietly say, "Hey," and then she made a soothing, shushing sound, like she was trying to calm a colicky baby instead of a woman questioning her sanity. "It's okay," Faye said, and Sebastian pictured her sitting next to Candice, a hand on the woman's shoulder, maybe even rubbing her back and shooing away onlookers while Candice Jackson wailed. It was the howl of the damned—the same sound his mother had made after hearing the judge's verdict—and the sad, painful reality was that no amount or combination of soothing words or therapy or booze or drugs would ever be able to fully take away that mental anguish. Only death could.

CHAPTER 43

SEBASTIAN WAS LEAVING a detailed message for Ron, highlighting the important aspects of Faye's conversation with Candice Jackson and explaining their next steps, when he saw Faye come out of the hotel's revolving doors, looking around like Paul or one of his boys was going to pop out of a car and start shooting.

He slid out of his spot. She saw the Jaguar coming her way and hustled toward it.

"You hear everything?" she asked when they were moving.

"Every single word," Sebastian said.

"She's really—"

"Yeah, Paul did quite a number on her."

"Paul?" Faye whipped her head to him, Sebastian seeing the color flaring in her cheeks. "It's *your* blood that caused that. And now that shit's running through my veins."

"Paul didn't give her Pandora."

"Then what *did* he give her?"

Sebastian hadn't shared Paul's sick grand plan with anyone except Frank, wanted to keep that nightmare locked down tight.

Faye said, "It has something to do with female carriers, doesn't it?"

"Where'd you hear that?"

"From Anton. That day he met Paul. On the way home Anton told me

Paul needed female carriers—the younger, the better. What makes their blood so special?"

"Look, you—"

"Either he does something to it, enhances it in some way, or it has something to do with female reproduction. Which is it?"

"I don't know."

"Bullshit."

Sebastian turned his head and shot her a glare, one that made it clear it would be in her best interest to shut up.

Faye ignored him. "I'm putting my life on the line for you, in more ways than one," she said. "I've got a right to know what you did to me."

"I promise you, as God is my witness, that what happened to Candice Jackson will *not* happen to you. Pandora is one hundred percent pure. Untainted. No blood expanders or fillers or any other chemicals. Why do you think my product is in such high demand? You think I'd keep getting repeat customers and have a waiting list a mile long if I scrambled people's brains, made them do degrading shit to themselves? You think that's the type of business I'm operating here? Blowing up people's lives?"

"What, you have ethics?"

"I'm nothing like the Armenians or Mexicans."

"What makes Pandora so unique? So special?"

"Kindness," he replied. "And clean living."

She glared at him, incredulous, her gaze roving over his face.

It was true, what he'd said. Kindness and clean living were the final part of his secret recipe, what made Pandora so different, and in such high demand. He had figured it out early on, when he and Frank had started, by reading studies on cattle, how they experienced high levels of stress from overcrowding and the fear they experienced on their way to being slaughtered—the stress hormones changed the taste of the meat.

The same principle held true for carriers. Stress hormones affected blood, and in order for him to harvest the most efficient blood, to maximize its potency, his donors had to be in peak physical and mental shape.

That meant clean eating, rigorous exercise, things like meditation and being treated like a human being, a partner, not being locked up inside some cage in the dark like a veal calf.

"If you're not going to level with me—" Faye began.

"I *am* leveling with you."

Faye looked straight ahead, out the windshield. "Did anything Candice say mean anything to you? Help you in any way?"

Sebastian nodded. "That thing she said about the house in Santa Paula, the owner—his name isn't David. It's Wayne Dixon. Met him a couple of times, almost did some business together. Idea of him hosting private sex parties doesn't surprise me—the old prick always struck me as a perv. It all makes sense now."

"I'm not following."

"Paul wanted money from me in the beginning, to get started. You need a lot—tens of millions—to start a blood operation, do it right. Stay protected. Last night, he had no interest in money, which tells me he's managed to get an investor, someone with really deep pockets. You did good work back there. Really good work."

"What's the plan now?"

Good question, Sebastian thought. In a situation like this, normally he'd have Ron getting to work on bugging Dixon's house, phones, and cars, his place of business. As they waited for Paul to call, Ron would put together a small army to stake out Dixon, see where he went, who he talked to, everything.

But that kind of operation took time, and with Grace in the equation, Sebastian didn't have time. "I'll talk it over with Ron, best way to handle this. I left him a message, told him to meet us at the house."

His phone rang. Not the one he was carrying, but the new burner he had given Ava the number for. It didn't have Bluetooth, so the car's communication system ignored it, thank God. He wanted to talk to Ava privately—or in as much privacy as possible.

"The kidnapper," Ava began, her voice low, almost a whisper. "He reached out this morning, around four. He said to watch out for something special in my mail."

Mail. The word triggered a memory from yesterday's conversation. *Why give up Ava's little girl when I can do so many wonderfully creative things with her?* Paul had said. *Like, say, drop a finger every now and then in the mail to her mommy. Or you. Do you think Grace could hold her baby without any fingers?*

His blood ran cold and his breath seized in his throat and the road in front of him turned hazy. "Did he say why? The kidnapper."

"No. He called, said to watch out for something special in my mail, and hung up."

Sebastian struggled to speak. "My money guy—he's going to reach out to you this morning. I talked to him yesterday, got everything set up."

"Okay. I'm sorry, but I have to go. The police don't know I'm making this call, and I don't want them to, you know, start asking questions."

He wanted to be there with her. It was stupid and foolish, and he knew he couldn't do it, and yet he still wanted to ask, wanted her to know she was in his thoughts, always had been, even after all this time.

But he couldn't ask. Ava had already hung up.

Sebastian gripped the steering wheel with both hands as a cold, hard, and inescapable truth drilled into his marrow: Ava was suffering because of him. Grace, too. And Paul, the psycho son of a bitch, had no intention of returning her.

His daughter was in the hands of a sadist, and Paul, Sebastian was sure, had already arranged something that would kill Ava. Or maybe he wanted her to suffer a bit longer. Maybe Paul had engineered something that would make her wish she were dead.

And I'm the only one who can stop it.

He had to find Paul—fast.

He returned home, finding it deathly silent.

Sebastian figured at least one of the two guys who had been living here around the clock would have returned by now. Sebastian knew their first names, but he didn't have their numbers. He dealt only with Ron. Sebastian jogged up the steps, walked down the hall to his home office.

All of Ron's equipment was gone.

Sebastian thought back to what Ron had told him last night about how he had a lot of money, more than he could spend in several lifetimes. Ron was telling him he'd had enough, and Sebastian had told him— practically begged him—to stay on. *Only Ron didn't give me an answer,* Sebastian thought, dialing the number for Ron's burner. *Just stared at me from across the table.*

Ron didn't answer, and his voicemail didn't pick up. Had he thrown out the burner?

Sebastian called the direct number for Ron's secretary.

The number, an automated voice said, was no longer in service.

I'm going to pick them off one by one, Paul had said. *Ron. His people—*

"Sebastian." Faye's voice was calling from downstairs. Not nervous or scared or anything, just loud. "There's something down here for you."

He left the room on shaky legs, riding waves of anger and fear, rage and terror, trying to keep the emotions from reaching his face. If Faye saw a trace of anything, she might bail. She was smart, okay, but that didn't mean she'd sign up for some suicide mission. If she found out Ron and his people had abandoned him, she might, too.

Faye stood in the kitchen, coffee percolating. "I was making coffee and found that," she said, pointing to a white envelope with his name written on the front, in big, bold black marker so he couldn't miss it. "It wasn't there this morning—I'm sure of it."

The envelope rested up against the bottle of Scotch Paul had brought to the house. Sebastian had left the bottle next to the coffeemaker, wanting to see it every day and give it the finger, prove how strong he was.

He didn't feel strong now. He felt weak. Frightened.

Sebastian opened the envelope. Inside was a folded piece of paper—

the nice stationery he kept on a shelf in his office down the hall. He recognized the handwriting.

Some famous writer from a long time ago said either you're busy living or you're busy dying, Ron had written. *If you've checked your email, you'll see which one I had to choose, and why. I'm sorry.*

No, you're not, Sebastian thought, and wondered if Faye had read the note. The envelope hadn't been sealed. He'd check the cameras upstairs, on the computer.

Faye got mugs from a cabinet. "Everything okay?"

Stop asking me that. "Nothing we can't handle," he replied, his voice soft.

She looked at him, silently analyzing his words.

"The reason I got into this thing," Sebastian said, picking up a mug from the counter. "At some point the government is going to get involved, take over the blood business. Regulate it. They have to. Cat's out of the bag, people are being snatched, people are dying. The real money is going to be in real estate. In a decade, maybe even sooner, you're going to see carriers living together in special neighborhoods, with their own schools and grocery stores and doctors. And they'll be living behind these great big walls to keep the noncarriers out."

"That's why you picked real estate as your cover."

Sebastian nodded. She was smart—and quick. Like Ava.

He picked up the bottle of Scotch and poured some into her mug. "They're going to be living in these properties. I'm going to build a world where people like you are safe. Where you're not hunted."

He poured some Scotch into his mug—just a little, just a taste—and raised it to her and said, "To the future."

"The future."

The mugs clinked together.

Sebastian brought his mug to his lips. He tilted it back, about to drink a healthy amount, the booze hitting his lips when his mouth simply clamped shut. Some of the Scotch was in his mouth, and he wouldn't swallow it. He didn't know what was happening, but his brain provided an answer in the form of a picture—the one of Grace that Paul had sent him. Grace needed the best version of her father right now. She didn't need a drunk who was afraid to see what was waiting for him in an email. She needed a man, not a frightened little boy.

Sebastian covertly spit the booze back into the mug. He put it down on the counter and said, "Help yourself to whatever. I'll be right back." He headed upstairs, to his home office, and sat in front of his Mac laptop.

He found the email easily. The subject line read, "Maya."

Not a picture this time, a video.

She's not dead, Sebastian told himself. God had brought him this far. He wouldn't let him down now. He wouldn't. He double-clicked the file.

Maya Dawson was tied down to a dining room chair, her mouth gagged. She was in her home—her living room. Sebastian recognized the couch in the background.

Maya was sobbing, her eyes pinched shut and her head turned away from whoever was holding the phone, recording whatever was about to happen. It didn't take Sebastian long to figure it out. Someone moved behind her chair, and he saw a blue-gloved hand grab Maya by the hair and yank it back, exposing her throat. Sebastian looked away when he saw Paul's tactical knife.

CHAPTER 44

THE WORST HANGOVER Grace had ever experienced occurred the day after she celebrated her twenty-first birthday. When she woke up at the crack of noon, her stomach feeling like the greasy water found at the bottom of a dumpster, her throat scratched raw from the hours spent throwing up, her head pounding as though a car had backed up over it, she could still recall, without effort, almost every single detail from her birthday party.

That wasn't the case now.

She remembered the van sliding up next to her and she remembered seeing the armed men. One of them smashed the driver's-side window—with a crowbar—because she had been frantic, fumbling at her seat belt buckle. She managed to free herself, but it was pointless; a man, maybe more than one, had grabbed her by the hair and pulled her out through the window. Yes, there had been more than one; she remembered several hands on her. She remembered being thrown into the van and being pinned against the floor, screaming for help against the cold steel, and she remembered the stab of a needle in her neck, and that was all. She had no idea what had happened since, or how she'd arrived here.

Here was a blow-up mattress with a pillow and blanket in a room she guessed had once been an office—low-pile beige carpeting coated in a film of dust, the fibers dented in areas where furniture had sat on it. No windows. On the white walls small holes left by nails used to hang whatever. The door was closed and, she assumed, locked. She didn't know because she hadn't gotten up from the bed to check—knew she should but it was too much of an effort. She couldn't summon the energy.

Has to be the drug or drugs they gave me, she thought, and drifted back to sleep.

The next time she opened her eyes, her environment had changed slightly. A small lamp had been brought in and set up on the floor, and in the dim light she saw a bright yellow pail with the word *toilet* written across it in black marker. There was stuff in there; she could see a couple of rolls of toilet paper peeking over the top. She tried to reach for the pail—it was right beside the mattress, maybe a foot or so away—but she couldn't hold her arm up; it flopped back against the mattress.

What did they give me? Why can't I move?

It wasn't exactly true that she couldn't. She *could* move her fingers. She dug them into the carpet and worked her hand across the floor and up the pail and knocked it over, revealing the bounty inside: rolls of toilet paper, a bag of vinegar potato chips, a can of warm Diet Coke, and the kind of prewrapped sandwich only the truly desperate bought at convenience stores, the inside of the cellophane dripping with moisture and mayo. The thought of food repelled her.

Where am I?

Where am I where am I where am I? The question kept repeating itself over and over, trying to fire up her anxiety, to get her to act. She was fully aware that she was in serious trouble—she had been bloodnapped, her worst nightmare—but her mind calmly told her there was no reason to lose her shit, because she had a surgically implanted tracking unit. She hadn't had a chance to activate it, okay, but her mother had been on the phone with her when it all went down. Her mother would have called the police, and the people there would track her. All she had to do was wait for the police to arrive. They were probably already on their way here—maybe were already here, about to—

The door opened.

She heard footsteps.

Someone was coming for her.

The police. Thank God. She turned her head slightly.

The man standing next to her mattress could have easily been a cop—he was a big tattooed guy—but he wasn't dressed like one. He wore workout shorts, and his tank top, stretched across a chest swollen and rippled with muscle, was drenched in sweat. He was barefoot and had pale skin, and he left the door open.

He sat down in front of her and crossed his legs. Grace, lying on her side and curled in the fetal position underneath the blanket, could see his tattoos clearly now—the noose around his neck and, on his massive left arm, the gingerbread man with a knife clamped between its fanglike teeth. He had more tattoos along his arms, these colorful, bizarre-looking skulls with jeweled eyes and teeth.

The combination of tattoos and his pale skin made him look like a clown—a big, handsome, but mean clown. He had to be mean, and dangerous, to carry off tattoos like that.

And yet she didn't feel any anxiety or fear or terror. Those things were there in her mind, absolutely, but she couldn't *feel* them. She was fully and completely disconnected from all her emotions. It was as if they had packed up and gone away on a vacation or something, leaving this shell of a body that could only sleep and drool onto the pillow. She felt a whole lot of nothing, which explained why she didn't jump or scream or turn her head when he brushed the hair away from her face.

"How you feeling, baby girl?" He had a warm smile and kind, attentive eyes.

Her mouth felt as dry and rough as sandpaper, her tongue a block of wood.

"Tired," she said, the word a rasp.

"Totally natural." He nodded in understanding. His damp skin gave off a musky but not unpleasant odor—the way men smelled after vigorous exercise. Or a fight. "Give it another day or two, and you'll feel set-tled," he said. "You cold? Can I bring you another blanket?"

Why is he being so nice to me? So kind and considerate? It scared her, but she couldn't really *feel* it, and that scared her more, and she still couldn't feel it, and it was becoming difficult to keep her eyes open—she was so, so tired.

"I'm sorry about the accommodations," he said. "You won't be here too much longer. I'm going to take a—"

"You gonna hurt me?"

His eyebrows jumped in surprise, maybe anger, and he removed his hand.

"Why would you ask me a question like that?"

"Because I don't know you—"

"I'm Paul."

"—and because I don't know where I am."

"I'm not going to hurt you," he said.

She couldn't keep her eyes open any longer. She stopped fighting, gave in, and shut them.

"That's it—get some rest," he said. "Everything's going to be okay."

She believed him. For some reason, she believed him.

The man named Paul stroked her head.

"I need to ask you a quick question," he said, and Grace heard the smile in his voice as she drifted.

"Um-hum."

"Any chance you know what time of the month you start ovulating?"

Grace didn't hear him. Mercifully, she had fallen asleep.

CHAPTER 45

SINCE PAUL KNEW about the Jaguar and the other car in Sebastian's garage, a Tesla that hadn't been outfitted for security protection, Sebastian needed another ride. He called the company he had used to turn his Jaguar into a tank, got the owner on the phone, and told him he needed a new vehicle, best one he had, preferably an SUV, and the requirements he needed. Price wasn't an issue, Sebastian said.

The owner said he had on the lot a Range Rover that would fit Sebastian's needs. Sebastian didn't balk at the price. He wired the money to the man's account and then went to the garage, where the Jaguar was parked, and transferred the equipment he needed into the trunk.

Faye drove him to the real estate office, Sebastian thinking about Maya, what had happened to her. Everyone around him had left, and the ones who had stayed behind were getting picked off by Paul. It should have bothered him—should have sent him into a rage—but he had something far more important to focus his attention on, something to live for now.

Sebastian had come close to doing business with Wayne Dixon—close enough that they had gotten to the financial stage. He found Dixon's information on the office computer. A property search revealed that Dixon was, in fact, the owner of a home in Santa Paula. Sebastian wrote down the addresses of all his properties, and all of Dixon's phone numbers. He started with the private numbers, having to deal with secretaries who eventually got him in touch with Dixon's personal assistant, a young-sounding guy named Hollis Little.

Sebastian explained who he was, told him he had to get in touch with Dixon regarding a property coming up for sale, one that Dixon had had his eye on for a long time. A property that wouldn't remain on the market long.

"Mr. Dixon is unavailable at the moment," Little said. "Does he have your number?"

"The reason why I'm calling is, I want to know if he's up north, at his place in Santa Paula." Sebastian gave him the address. "I need to drop off some information he asked for, and he's not answering his phone."

"Well, I'm sure if you leave a message—"

Sebastian had anticipated this. "The wildfires have knocked down a lot of cell towers, and reception is spotty up that way, I've heard. How is the wildfire situation up there—do you know? We talking mandatory evacuation or what?"

"No, not mandatory."

"Look, I'm not trying to get you into any trouble. Wayne was insistent that I hand deliver this stuff to him, so that he can review the material and then ask me questions. I've got to do it now or he won't have a chance to get in on this property. Just tell me if he's there or not. I don't want to take a drive all the way up there for nothing."

"He's been there all week," Little said, "but you didn't hear that from me."

Traveling by helicopter would be the quickest way. He called the places Ron had used in the past—even dropped Ron's name—but all the birds were spoken for. The ones that weren't already booked for business were up north, the pilots pitching in against the wildfires, which left Sebastian with one option: traveling by car.

He took a Mac with a wireless Internet card from his office. Faye drove him to the car dealer who specialized in turning cars into nearly indestructible tanks. There, he picked up the Range Rover.

In the garage, he transferred the equipment, loaded in duffel bags, from the trunk to a special compartment in the back of the Rover. Faye, seated behind the wheel, watched him in the rearview mirror.

After he was finished, he slid into the passenger seat. "You in the mood to take a drive?"

"Santa Paula, I take it. To see Wayne Dixon."

"I'm told he's at home. And like Candice said, the property in Santa Paula is very isolated. It's the perfect place to keep carriers."

"Besides Ava's daughter, how many does Paul have? A dozen? More?"

"I don't have an exact number. Frank and I . . . we thought it might be at least six."

"Isn't a wildfire raging somewhere up there?"

"Not directly in Santa Paula. One you're thinking about—it's sixty percent contained. I went online and checked."

"Why are we going? That seems like a task more suited for someone like Ron Wolff."

"He's tied up with some other pressing matters. And we're closer."

Faye studied him for a moment. He could see her eyes working behind her sunglasses.

"Paul scared him off, didn't he?" she said. "That's why your house was empty this morning."

"This is the most solid lead I've had in a while, and I plan on looking into it. I need to find him." *And Grace,* he added privately. He had to be the one to find his daughter, deliver her to Ava.

"Showing up there, just the two of us," Faye said. "What if he's got a small army?"

"I've got us covered."

"Bullets don't work against wildfires."

"We're not driving into one. We're driving around one. Huge difference. We'll be fine. I checked the roads online, by the way. The ones we need are still open."

"For the moment."

"You said you wanted to rise through the ranks, get a top position. Well, this is the price of admission."

Faye stared off at the traffic in the distance.

"I'm offering you the chance to create your own future," Sebastian said. "And I'll do everything I can on my end to help you find out what happened to your brother."

Faye turned back to him.

"I'll drive," she said, opening the door.

Santa Paula was an hour away without traffic.

Three hours later, they were still twenty miles out.

On the radio, a female newscaster was discussing the various wildfires in California. The worst one, the Sierra Fire, named because it had originated in the foothills of the Sierra Nevada Mountains, had already burned its way past the small, quiet, and idyllic town of Paradise, located in the northern part of the state—a good five hundred or so miles from Santa Paula. The wildfire was so bad, so swift, and so crazy out of control that National Guard helicopters and military C-130 airplanes were being brought in to help fight it.

The Sierra Fire was dominating the news. Sebastian was more interested in the Creek Fire. That one had started on Mud Creek Road near Steckel Park, which was to the north of Santa Paula, five or so miles away. There was no mention of the severity of the fire, whether or not it was contained, as he had read online back at the house that it was.

Still, what he'd read about the Creek Fire being contained—that could change, thanks to the unpredictability of the Santa Ana winds.

The National Weather Service used a color-coded system for wind strength. Last night, the color-code had gone from red, the designation for high winds, to the never-before-used purple, which signified extreme. The merciless and unrelenting mountain winds had produced gusts of more than eighty miles per hour—the strength of a Category 1 hurricane. Those same winds were expected to come into the region again later tonight. They, combined with the dry land and lack of humidity, were breathing new life into all the wildfires, but especially into the Sierra Fire.

Faye turned down the radio. "Question," she said, her tone cautious, seeing if it was okay for her to talk. She had been unusually quiet over the past few hours, Sebastian figuring she sensed his bottled rage, didn't want to be the one to ignite it.

Sebastian cocked his head to her.

"MLS," she said. "That's a real estate term, right?"

Sebastian nodded. "Multiple Listing Service. Why?"

"That day I met Paul, Anton brought along a folder with him. It was full of pictures of commercial properties for sale, I think. It didn't say that, but it had something with 'MLS' written along the top."

"How many properties?"

"At least a dozen. They didn't contain much in the way of information, just pictures of the property, an address—the kinds of things I'm guessing you'd find in an online listing. There was one that was different, though. A listing for a house in Ojai."

He'd never been there. Ojai was a small city set in a valley in the Topatopa Mountains, a tourist hub for people who were into art galleries and New Age bullshit shops and spas where you got rubbed down with lava stones and given coffee enemas.

"Why I remembered it," Faye said, "is because Anton wrote on the paper. It said, 'Chauncey Harrington, seventy-two, eighty-seven point six mil, paper.' That name mean anything to you?"

It didn't. Sebastian grabbed the Mac, balanced it on his lap, and plugged "Chauncey Harrington" into Google.

The guy didn't have his own Wikipedia page, but there had been several stories about him over the years, mainly about his paper empire, which he had sold ten years ago for close to ninety million dollars. The most recent story had included Harrington's age: seventy-two.

Sebastian shared his findings.

Faye said, "Candice Jackson mentioned Ojai—remember?"

"Right, but then she said she was sure it was Santa Paula."

"She also said she was really messed up, didn't remember much. And remember, Anton was thinking about going into business with Paul. What if Paul told him the name of his investor? If he did, Anton would have checked the guy out."

Sebastian thought about Paul's last phone call, Paul telling him he didn't want the money anymore. Had Paul found his angel investor?

"This guy may know where Paul is," Faye said. "We should talk to him."

"Got to find out where he lives first."

"I know the address." Faye gave it to him.

"You always memorize random addresses?"

"It was the only residential property Anton had in that stack, which is why I remember it. That and the writing."

Was she telling him the truth? After her Academy Award–winning performance with Candice Jackson, he wasn't sure he trusted her.

But he needed her for this.

"I think we should go to Ojai first," she said, "follow up on that lead."

Sebastian decided to play along. "Why's that?"

"It just . . . feels right."

"Ojai is further northwest. Hold on a sec—I'm reading something here. . . . Okay, it says Ojai has been without power for the past two days. Electric company shut it down as a preemptive measure against the winds." Some of the worst wildfires in the state's history had been caused when the high Santa Ana winds either blew trees and branches into power lines, sparking fires, or snapped distribution poles and sent live wires onto the dry grass nearby.

"Santa Paula," Sebastian said, "still has power."

Faye said nothing, locked in thought, her face blank.

What if Paul is in Ojai—with Grace?

What if he's already moved his carriers somewhere else?

What if he's in the process of moving them not from Santa Paula but from Ojai?

What if, what if, what if—the words thrumming through his head and hammering his heart, Sebastian wanting to scream at Faye to slam her foot on the gas and barrel through the goddamn traffic.

CHAPTER 46

WHEN GRACE'S EYES fluttered open, she found herself tucked underneath a down comforter. She felt warm all over—and clean. She smelled of soap but had no memory of taking a shower or a bath.

What she did have was a vague memory of talking to the big-muscled guy who had introduced himself as Paul. She couldn't recall any of the details of their conversation, but she had the sense he had been kind to her. Or was she imagining that?

She brushed the comforter away from her face, found herself no longer lying on a mattress dumped on a dingy carpet with a bucket to use for her bathroom needs. She had been transferred to a new room—a small one, no bigger than a prison cell (not that she'd ever spent any time in one). The walls were bare, a pristine white, and smelled vaguely of paint. The wall across from the foot of her bed (no, not a bed, she noticed—it was a cot) wasn't a wall at all but a pane of glass that stretched from floor to ceiling.

No, not glass, she thought dully. You didn't use glass inside a prison cell, which was exactly where she found herself. Only this one had a stone floor and a barrier made of what had to be plexiglass. That or whatever clear, thick material was used at, say, the teller windows at banks. It made her feel like a specimen in a zoo.

It was difficult to collect her thoughts. Her brain felt like it had been replaced with glue, everything trapped inside her skull sticky and slow. Okay, she had been moved into this place—this prison cell. Okay. Right. *So why am I not frightened? Why am I feeling so . . . content?* No, that wasn't the right word. She knew she'd been taken, knew she was a prisoner, and yet she felt like her brain had been rewired, circuits fried, or something, because while she knew she should have felt worried, even panicked, she felt the complete opposite, her body telling her, *Hey, everything's okay. Life isn't all that bad, so chill.*

And her clothes were different. Her nightclub clothes were gone, replaced with a black cocktail dress. She sat up and saw that she was barefoot. Her fingernails, she noticed, had been painted a lovely shade of red. She brought her hand up closer to her face.

"I hope I did a good job."

Grace jumped at the voice. It came from above her. She glanced up, saw the speaker, then from the corner of her eye caught someone standing in front of the plexiglass barrier—Paul.

"You look beautiful," Paul said. He wore a dark suit with a blue shirt and a nice tie, and looked like some smart Wall Street banker type with his glasses, smiling like he had scored big on an investment. "Do you feel beautiful?"

She did, actually. She knew she shouldn't be feeling that, given the circumstances, but strangely, she did. Why? How? Had she been given some drug while she was sleeping? *What's going on here?*

"Why?" she asked.

"I can't hear you. You need to use the intercom. It's behind you there, on the back wall."

She turned her head, to the wall behind her. She saw the small intercom. It was to the left of the outline of a door. *But no doorknob,* she noticed. She couldn't open it, but someone on the outside could.

It was hard to stand—not because of pain but because she felt so lightheaded. Not in a dizzy way but in that free-floating way when you had a super-good buzz and you just wanted to sit and ride a wave of euphoric feelings. Her legs felt a little wobbly, though, and she leaned against the wall as she pressed her finger on the little square green button installed underneath the speaker.

"You don't have to keep your finger on it," Paul said. "Just click it once."

"Did you put this dress on me?"

"I did."

"And my nails?"

"I did those, too."

"Did I . . . Was I in a shower?"

"A bath," he said. "I cleaned you up. I want you looking all nice and pretty."

"I feel different. Like, floaty."

"I gave you molly. Have you tried it before?"

Grace shook her head back and forth. She knew about MDMA, of course, from friends who took it at rave and EDM concerts and at clubs because it made the music sound better, made them feel so tremendously awesome and uninhibited and free to express themselves, their hidden desires.

"It will help keep you nice and relaxed," Paul said. "Calm."

"Calm? For what?"

Paul didn't answer. He pressed something on the wall—a button for his intercom, she guessed—and then turned around, his back now facing her. He took a few steps forward, stopped. Grace stumbled forward, using the wall for support.

The man standing next to Paul was much older—and much shorter. And frail looking. Or maybe she thought that because he was so thin underneath his suit. The wisps of white hair were combed back wetly across a scalp peppered with what looked like age or liver spots.

"Mr. Jahed has arrived," the man said.

"Wonderful. How's the generator?"

"We'll have power for another two to three hours, but you need to make this quick."

Paul rolled his eyes. "Will you stop worrying about the wildfires? Everything's fine."

Grace wasn't paying attention to the conversation. Her face pressed against the cool, thick plexiglass, she looked to her right, at two small cells that were identical to the one she was in. Unlike her, the women inside—one to each room—wore what looked like hospital scrubs and were sleeping, or passed out, on their cots.

Carriers, Grace thought. *Like me.*

"My dear boy," the man said to Paul. "I grew up surrounded by wildfires. They're dangerously unpredictable, nothing to be trifled with."

Grace looked to her left, saw two more cells, but couldn't see if anyone was inside them.

Is this a blood farm?

"The wildfire is contained," Paul said. "Relax."

"The fire has damaged the town's water system, so the firefighters can no longer use the hydrants. Mr. Jahed doesn't know this, but nonetheless, he's spooked. On the way here, he and his entourage saw home sprinklers running, saw more than one person standing on their roofs with hoses. The embers can travel for miles, you know—and there are reports of monstrous winds moving in. Mr. Jahed heard that tidbit on the radio. That and chatter about a mandatory evacuation possibly happening in the next couple of hours."

Am I trapped in a blood farm?

Are they going to drain me?

"The presentation won't take long," Paul said.

"Good. He's very anxious to see the results. How *is* his mistress?"

"Can you stop talking like someone out of an old movie? His side piece of ass is doing just fine—wonderful, in fact."

"I hope so, for both our sakes. I'd hate to be victims of a *qisas.*"

"A what?"

"The Islamic term for revenge. An eye-for-an-eye retribution."

Why did he clean me up? Put this dress on me?

"I'll remind you again not to speak crudely in front of him," the old man said. "Miss Sawyer is a very important person in his life."

"I'm sure." Paul grinned. "He does understand that we're not in Tehran, right? That needs to be presented a certain way."

"Yes, he understands."

"And his men—"

"They'll stay upstairs. Now, what about side effects?"

"Just the ones we discussed," Paul said.

Grace felt a bolt of panic. It swiftly died, buried underneath the molly. Her thoughts, however, were running rampant, like they'd caught fire. *I'm trapped in here they're going to take my blood but for how long oh my God help me I'm never leaving this place alive—*

"I'd like to see her beforehand," the old man said, "to make sure—"

"Enough. Everything is fine. And look a bit more excited, will you? You're going to be a very wealthy man."

"I'm already a very wealthy man."

"Then you're about to be an immortal one."

"I hope your claim about your blood having the same wonderful transformative effects of Pandora turns out to be correct."

"The results are impressive. Mr. Jahed is going to be blown away. You, too."

"I hope so. This little showroom you insisted on having me build cost me a rather pretty penny." The old man sighed, looked around the cells, his gaze drifting past Grace as though he didn't see her. "My poor wine cellar," he said.

"Go collect Mr. Jahed. I'll have Bradley collect his . . . concubine. Is that an appropriate word?"

The old man made a face—not at the word *concubine*, Grace thought, but at the person named Bradley.

"After this is over, we're leaving," the old man said to Paul, "you and I, to celebrate properly. Alone. Mr. Guidry won't be joining us this time."

The old man walked away. Paul turned back to Grace, his smile at full wattage.

"There are some shoes under your cot, a pair of nice heels. Would you mind putting them on for me?"

"Why?" Christ, it was hard to think. "Why am I all dressed up?"

"To celebrate."

"Celebrate what?"

"You," Paul replied. "We're here to celebrate you, how special you are. You're the belle of the ball, Grace. Are you right-handed or left-handed?"

CHAPTER 47

Ellie glanced at the dashboard GPS. It said they were five minutes from the Santa Paula address.

"How are you going to play it when we get there?" Ellie asked. "You still haven't explained that to me."

"I told you, I'll talk to Dixon until he gives Paul up."

"Then why'd you pack the trunk with all that firepower?"

"You ever fire an AR-15?"

"No," Ellie replied, although she had, several times. The AR was the weapon you wanted if you went to war.

"Person sees a weapon like that," Sebastian said, "they suddenly become more eager to cooperate."

"And if he doesn't?"

"I'll offer him incentives." His eyes cut sideways to hers, and he added, "Don't worry—you won't have to get your hands dirty."

"I'm worried about how many people might be there."

"We'll find out any minute now, won't we?"

The house in Santa Paula was one of those sprawling modern things designed to look like country homes. It was isolated, as Candice had said, nothing around for miles.

Except the wildfires, Ellie thought.

The mountains and hills in the far distance looked black under the bloodred sky. Some surfaces glowed red and orange from burning embers. The air inside the Range Rover was breathable, but even with the air-conditioning's filters she could smell woodsmoke and burnt vegetation.

Sebastian had her park on a hilly dirt road overlooking the house. He studied the house, using a pair of military-grade binoculars equipped with both night vision and thermal imaging.

"I don't see any other vehicles here," he said. "Or any heat signatures."

"What about the garage?"

"Let's go check it out. And let's use this." Sebastian removed a compact Glock from his coat pocket and handed it to her. "I'll take the lead on this. Just watch my back."

They parked in the driveway, in front of the garage, and looked through one of the windows. Ellie saw a single car parked in there—a vintage Shelby Mustang.

An evacuation sticker had been placed on the front door, to let firefighters and responders know that no people were inside. Which, she thought, was odd. During the drive, Sebastian had kept checking a state-run website that offered real-time wildfire updates—well, at least until the unstable cell signal eventually dropped. He told her that Santa Paula was in the clear.

Then again, he could very well be lying to her. He had, so far, refused to tell her the truth about why Ron Wolff and his men had packed up and left.

It was clear that Sebastian was driven to find his daughter—and Paul—no matter what the cost. And that worried her. Desperate men didn't think their actions through. That made them unpredictable. Dangerous.

When no one answered the door, Sebastian used his elbow to smash one of the small panes of decorative stained glass built around the doorframe.

An alarm shrieked.

"What are you doing?" she asked, yelling over the high-pitched bleating sound.

"Searching the premises." He threaded his arm through the broken pane, reaching for the doorknob. "Carriers could be locked somewhere inside."

"If they left, they wouldn't have left carriers behind. They're too valuable."

Sebastian unlocked the door. He threw it open and darted inside.

Shit.

Her job was to protect the asset. Whatever came of this, Roland would want a detailed report.

Ellie hurried after him, trailing Sebastian through a maze of hallways and rooms bigger than her studio apartment.

There was no one here.

Sebastian, Ellie could see, was trying to keep his shit together.

He insisted on driving. He plugged the Ojai address into the dashboard GPS. It took a moment for the satellite to download the information, Sebastian looking like he was going to slam his fist through the screen.

The GPS said they were roughly half an hour away. *Provided we don't hit any roadblocks,* Ellie added privately.

"They said Santa Paula wasn't evacuating. You heard that on the radio, too, right?"

"Wildfires change," Ellie replied. "The winds shift. They can—"

"I checked online. There was no mandatory evacuation listed."

"Dixon decided to get out of town. It's the smart move."

He glared at her, as though she had just said something offensive.

"Get an update on Ojai," he said. "Find out what's going on there."

"No cell signal, remember?"

The evening sky was quickly turning over to night, the way it did during the winter months.

Sebastian's driving was erratic. She knew he had packed a good amount of firepower in the duffel bags he'd stored underneath the Range Rover's trunk floor, where the spare tire was kept. Ellie doubted a patrol cop would look there if they got pulled over for speeding, but why risk it?

"Slow down," Ellie said. "You're going to—"

He slammed on the brakes.

The laptop slid off the tops of her thighs and crashed onto the floor. She reached out reflexively to grab the edge of the dashboard with her hands to prevent herself from smashing into it, even though she was buckled up. The seat belt gripped her, and as she was thrown back against her seat she whipped her head around to the windshield, and saw a large dog, maybe even a wolf, charging across the street. The animal had missing patches of fur, maybe from burns. She couldn't tell. It disappeared around the side of a house.

Ellie stared after it, blinking. She thought back to that morning during the early summer when Danny had almost hit that black Lab. Her life had changed that day. And while she wasn't one to give credence to omens or superstition, she couldn't help but wonder, as Sebastian hit the gas, if her life was about to change again.

CHAPTER 48

EVEN IN HER altered state, Grace could keep track of the names of the people standing in the room outside her cell. There were only three now, and she already knew one: Paul. The old man Paul had spoken to earlier was Chauncey, and the sole focus of their attention was the third man, Mr. Jahed.

His full name was Nasser Ali Jahed. Before he came into this room— the converted wine cellar, as Chauncey had referred to it earlier—a pair of dark-skinned men with carefully trimmed black beards—Middle Eastern, Grace assumed, given their looks and the fact that they spoke to each other in what she was sure was Arabic—conducted a thorough search, their eyes blazing with urgency, looking for possible traps, the slightest whiff of danger. They conducted very thorough pat downs of Paul and Chauncey.

The men, she noticed, were armed.

Grace, half dozing and oddly content from the molly, watched them from the floor of her cell. The men didn't speak to her, barely paid any attention to her. They glanced at her as though she were some common zoo animal they'd seen before, or simply a piece of furniture, and then invested their energy in a thorough inspection of her surroundings.

For what? Do they actually think I'm hiding some weapon in here?

Paul seemed relaxed. He stood with his hands behind his back, smiling, like he was holding a winning lottery ticket and was due, at any moment now, to collect the world's largest cash prize. Chauncey watched the men furtively, acting like someone who could be subjected, on a whim, to an impromptu three-man prostate exam and then killed.

Several minutes after the armed men left, Nasser Ali Jahed appeared, alone. Given all the security fuss, Grace was expecting to see a tall, sleek-looking, and powerfully built man with a thick mane of black hair, dressed in a suit, shoes, and watch worth the price of a high-end BMW. She was right about the suit and watch, but Mr. Jahed, as Paul and Chauncey kept calling him, was small in stature and somewhat chubby—a nebbish, to use one of her father's favorite Yiddish words. What was left of his gray hair was buzzed close to the scalp.

Mr. Jahed spoke perfect English, without even the slightest trace of an accent, his voice soft. "Again, I'd like to thank you both for thinking of me to be the first to consider your new business venture."

"Of course," Paul said. "And thank you again for meeting with us."

"I do not want to rush this, but given the unusual weather circumstances, I think it would be best if we proceeded as quickly as possible. If I like what I see, then we can arrange a time, at my hotel, to go over the business side. Does that sound fair?"

"More than fair. Chauncey explained to you the reason behind our presentation method?"

"He did, yes. He explained everything to me in great detail."

"Excellent. I don't want to offend any religious sensibilities you may have regarding women's appearances. I assure you, it's for your benefit."

Mr. Jahed grinned. "Fortunately, we're not in Tehran."

"The main side effect of my blood product—"

"Chauncey prepared me about what to expect. But thank you for your concern—and your discretion." His tone said, *Enough talking—let's get to it.*

Paul took out a small walkie-talkie. "Bradley, could you please bring Miss Sawyer?"

All three turned toward the doorway. Grace had the best view of Nasser Ali Jahed. She could see his profile, the anxious look in his eyes while he waited.

The woman who appeared in the doorway looked to be somewhere in her mid- to possibly late twenties and wore a thick white terry cloth bathrobe. She was barefoot, and her long and unbelievably thick black hair spilled over her shoulders. She had piercing blue eyes, fine cheekbones, and a prominent jawline—a beautiful and exquisite woman, no question, but definitely a dime a dozen in LA. Yet Mr. Jahed stared at her, his mouth agape, as though an angel had suddenly manifested in human form before him.

"My God," he muttered.

Even the man named Chauncey seemed awestruck.

Paul said, "As you can see, my product has erased a good ten to fifteen years from her face. The skin is tight and glowing, not a wrinkle anywhere. Her perspiration is rather high, because of increased metabolism, but that will disappear over the next day or two. Please come in, Miss Sawyer."

She did, and stopped only a couple of feet away from Mr. Jahed, who was still stunned by her appearance. *She's been given carrier blood,* Grace thought, watching as the woman slipped out of her bathrobe.

Miss Sawyer wore a black bikini that showed her generous curves. Her olive skin was flawless. No part of her body sagged—everything looked tight, her muscles firm, as though she was in peak physical fitness. She had barely any body fat on her.

The woman looked only at Mr. Jahed. She stepped closer and, placing her hands flat against his chest, said, "Say something, Nasser."

"You look beautiful." Then his gaze cut to Paul and, blinking, he said, "This is remarkable. *Remarkable.*"

"I'm glad you're pleased."

"I'm *more* than pleased." Mr. Jahed turned his attention back to the woman. "You look as beautiful as the day I met you."

"I know you're ready to leave," Paul said, "but I have one small favor to ask." He turned to Grace. It sent her heart tripping. "Please stand up so Mr. Jahed can take a good look at you."

Grace didn't stand up.

"She's beautiful, as you can see, but also stubborn," Paul said. "Which is why I'm wondering if you could take her off my hands, give her to one of your associates back in Tehran, put her to work in one of your . . . pleasure centers. My only condition is that I take a finger or two."

Fear exploded in Grace's heart.

The woman, Miss Sawyer, touched Mr. Jahed's arm. "Do you still desire me?" she asked.

"Yes, of course." His voice was dry. "More than ever."

"Show me."

She began to untie her bikini top.

The streetlights in Ojai were turned off, but in the Rover's high beams Ellie saw people hosing down roofs and the vegetation around their homes. She saw sprinklers running and she spotted a handful of people armed with flashlights as they packed suitcases and other belongings into their cars.

Sebastian was less than seven miles from their destination. A black silhouette of a man or woman stood on the roof of a nearby house, watching a helicopter the size of a toy in the distance dumping a red-colored flame retardant onto a fire. The flames shrank and then seemed to die, but then Ellie saw them leap to life again.

Then the last mile came and the road was, as far as she could tell in the glow of the high beams, nothing but one long stretch of undeveloped land with a couple of ranches, not a home anywhere in sight.

"There," Sebastian said, slowing. "Straight ahead."

She saw it—a Spanish Colonial so large that it looked more like a private resort than a single-family home. What made the details easier to see was the fact that almost all the inside and outside lights were turned on—the downstairs lights in the house, the white string lights wrapped around the trunks of several palm trees, the solar-powered ground lamps that lit up a long flagstone driveway that wound its way up an incline and ended in a circle around a small fountain.

Ellie turned in her seat and reached into the back for the binoculars.

"House must have its own generator," Sebastian said, killing the lights.

A massive ornate gate made of wood blocked the long driveway leading up to the house. That, along with the six-foot stone wall that ran along the perimeter of the property, was more ornamental than built for security purposes.

The Range Rover was equipped with a bullbar. Made of welded steel, the bar, designed to protect the front of the vehicle from a collision with a large animal or another vehicle, would easily smash down the gate without damaging the Rover—a course of action, Ellie believed, that Sebastian was more than capable of performing.

"I'm counting two . . . no, three vehicles parked in the front, around the fountain," Ellie said. "One's a small limo. The others are SUVs—both Mercedes." She switched to thermal. "No one's sitting inside them."

"What about outside?"

"I'm looking right now. . . . No, the area's clear. Move a bit closer so I can get a better look at the front of the house."

Sebastian did, keeping the lights off. "This has got to be the place."

"That, or someone's throwing a party." She adjusted the magnification, locked onto the front of the house. Saw the potted plants near the front door made out of an enormous slab of wood, like something in a medieval dungeon. "I don't see anyone standing outside, but I do see two more vehicles parked near the front. If this is the place, we're going to conduct proper surveillance first. We're not going to— Hold on—the front door just opened. Three men—no, two. Two men in suits and a woman dressed . . . I think it's a bathrobe."

"Is it—?"

"No, it's not Grace Lewis. This woman's older."

The men stood on either side of her. The woman had long, dark hair and the bathrobe was loosely tied. Ellie saw what she was pretty sure was a bikini. Did the place have a heated pool? The woman didn't look wet. And why was she smiling? The large, dark-skinned man with the shaved head to her right gripped her arm.

The woman, barefoot, padded alongside him and then came to a halt.

"What's going on?" Sebastian asked.

Ellie didn't answer, watching the woman trying to unbutton the bald guy's shirt. The man didn't look happy about it; he gently but firmly moved her hands away and said something to her.

The man's suit jacket moved, and Ellie saw a flash of a shoulder holster.

The armed man released the woman. She moved closer and, while trying to kiss him, reached for his belt. The other guy, standing to the side, his thick black hair slicked back and looking stylish, chuckled into his fist.

Ellie thought about the morning she and Danny found Sophia Vargas in the backyard. She lowered the binoculars, turned to Sebastian, and said, "We're definitely in the right place."

CHAPTER 49

SEBASTIAN KILLED THE headlights and pulled the Range Rover off the main road and parked along the east-side wall, well out of view of anyone who might happen to drive by. He got out, gathered the supplies he needed from the trunk, climbed on the Rover's roof, and hopped onto the top of the wall. Crouching, he studied the front of the sprawling home through the gaps between the tree branches. He brought the pair of night-vision binoculars gripped in his hands up to his face to take a closer look.

The three vehicles Ellie had seen parked around the fountain were now down to two. The Mercedes SUV carrying the two bodyguards and the bathrobe-wearing woman had driven away. Two cars were here, and two cars Ellie had mentioned were parked near the front of the house. Sebastian couldn't see them— too much tree cover.

So who else was in the house? How many people?

Paul. He was in there; Sebastian knew it.

Was Grace somewhere in there with Paul?

The size of the home wouldn't have been a problem if Ron had given him the use of some of his men; they could have stormed the place, gotten everyone down on the floor, and conducted a proper search. But he had only one other person at his disposal.

Sebastian jumped down into the yard, behind a grouping of Chinese flame trees. He had put on a black Windbreaker and black industrial-grade nitrile gloves, the kind used by home security and mechanics. They provided superior grip even when damp. He also wore a clear plastic mask that distorted his features, in case any nearby security cameras were pointed in his direction.

So far, he had found only one, a camera pointed at the gate. Before parking the Rover against the wall, he had slid behind the camera and covered the lens with thick foam shot from a thin tube connected to a spray can containing chemicals for sealing walls against drafts. Then he waited, watching to see who would come out to investigate why the camera had gone dark, but no one had.

Sebastian jogged over to the gate, found the control box, and pushed the button to open it. When the gate opened, he turned and darted up the grassy incline near the wall for cover, heading for the dim light he'd seen coming from a grouping of windows on the first floor of the east side of the house, near the back.

There was no need to wait for Faye. He had already instructed her on what to do.

The windows were long and wide, and, maybe because of the lack of neighbors, the owners didn't feel the need to draw the blinds. Sebastian brought the binoculars up to his face.

He had once shown a house that had a "drawing room"—a seventeenth-century term for a space designated for receiving and entertaining guests before and after dinner. The room he was now looking at was nowhere near as wide and cavernous and as opulent as the one from his memory, but this space—with its tall stucco walls, fireplace, abundant furniture, and, in the far corner near the pool table, a bar large enough to seat six people comfortably—was clearly used for entertaining.

Sebastian counted six men, each one dressed in a suit, each one clearly from somewhere in the Middle East. They wore serious expressions and sipped from small bottles of Pellegrino. He assumed they were all armed. He wondered who they were waiting for—who Paul was meeting.

If Ron hadn't abandoned him, he could have grabbed a license plate and had Ron get a name with a few clicks of the mouse.

When this is over, I'm going to pay him a visit, Sebastian thought.

No. No, he wouldn't. After this was over, it was over. He was going to be living a completely different life—one with his daughter and, hopefully, Ava.

He heard Faye step up beside him, her breath coming hard and fast from behind her mask. He had also given her a black Windbreaker with a hood.

"Find anything?" she asked, after she caught her breath.

"Just more guys from the goon squad. I'm going to see if I can get a better view."

Sebastian withdrew the binoculars and moved back toward the driveway gate, which was open. He'd left it open in case, for whatever reason, they had to make a quick exit.

When he had a solid view of the front of the house, he looked through his binoculars again.

Saw Paul standing in the spacious foyer next to some old guy Frank would have called a Q-tip.

Sebastian felt a fierce stab of joy. He had found Paul. Paul was here, and Paul didn't know Sebastian was here.

Another man came into view—another tough-looking goon. Sebastian increased the magnification and said, "I've got a visual on Paul, some old white dude, and a guy who—"

Sebastian cut himself off when he saw the muscled goon holding the arm of a young woman wearing a black cocktail dress. Her hands were behind her back, as if she was handcuffed, and she was crying. The men ignored her.

The Q-tip laughed at something Paul said.

Sebastian got a clear look at her features and felt his insides turn to water.

"My daughter's in there," he said.

Faye yanked her binoculars away from her face and looked strangely at him.

"Grace Lewis is my daughter," Sebastian said, and moved away, confronted with a level of fear and a whole host of other emotions no father should ever have to experience.

When Faye joined him at the Range Rover, he was removing the weapons and other gear he needed from the compartment under the spare tire. The SUV's interior lights had been turned off, and the canopy of branches over the area where he stood cast everything in a gloom that made it difficult to see, but he knew where he had stored each item, could recognize each by touch.

He picked up an AR-15 and handed it to her.

"There's a patio off the back of that room," he said. "Has a sliding glass door. I'm going to go through there—after you lob a couple of flash-bangs through the window. After that, you're to swing around to the front of the house, get yourself behind that tree over there." He pointed to an immense oak roughly two hundred yards away, near the front of the house. "The rifle has a scope. I want you watching the front door. That's going to turn into a choke point. Once the shooting starts, everyone's going to start funneling through there, Paul included—provided I don't take him down first."

Faye was shaking her head. "He's going to fight you."

"You don't stand up to an assault rifle. Paul's a coward. He's gonna run straight for one of those cars—trust me."

"And if he does, you want me to take him out."

"I'm looking forward to doing that myself. But if you've got a clear shot, yeah, I'd sure appreciate it.

"Get down on your stomach—it'll give you more stability with the rifle," Sebastian said. "You see Paul, Guidry, anyone he brought, take them down. Just make sure Paul doesn't leave here. You do that, you're looking at a seven-figure bonus."

"Go," she said. "I've got your back."

CHAPTER 50

IT TURNED OUT he wouldn't have to break down or shoot his way through the sliding glass door. It was unlocked. Sebastian cracked it open an inch, and then he crouched down and looked through the glass at the spare, dimly lit kitchen, used, he guessed, strictly for entertaining. It was big enough to service a hotel restaurant.

Sebastian had never pulled the trigger on someone who hadn't deserved it. The people in his line of work had no illusions about the business they were in, and not once had he ever lost sleep over his actions or decisions. If anything, he slept more soundly, comforted by the knowledge that he had performed a valuable service, not only for the city of Los Angles but also for humanity.

His blood hummed at the thought of putting Paul down. But he wouldn't do it at the expense of saving his daughter. Grace was the goal.

But he needed Faye to play along, do her part. Would she? He had offered her a solid financial incentive, plus his promise to help her locate her twin brother.

Sebastian heard breaking glass.

Smiled.

Good girl, he thought, a jolt of adrenaline surging through his limbs. He jumped to his feet and threw the door open as the grenade exploded

in a deafening boom. In front of him was a swinging door. Just a bump
of a hip or shoulder, and it would open.

In the movies, chaos was a well-orchestrated affair, perfectly lit and
flawlessly executed. In real life, chaos was mean and ugly and merciless.
It stripped people of their manners and humanity. When Sebastian
charged into the great room, or whatever the owners called it, the stock
of the AR-15 wedged firmly against his shoulder, his gaze down the iron
sight, he saw the goons, many of them armed, blinded by the flash grenade. Some trampled over one another, like nocturnal insects suddenly
exposed to light, as they fought to see and fought their way to the exit on
the far right of the room. The blast had blown out the windows, and the
wind coursing through the shattered glass scattered the clouds of gray-
white smoke.

Sebastian rested his cheek against the bump stock's grainy polymer
and opened fire.

Save Grace, kill Paul—and Faye. Sebastian liked her—she was a good
kid and all, smart and tough—but she knew too much about him, and he
couldn't have that hanging over his head, not with the new life waiting
for him with Ava and their daughter. Save Grace, kill Paul and then Faye,
in that order.

Back at the Range Rover, when Sebastian had handed her the AR-15, Ellie knew, without a doubt in her mind, that he was going to go inside the
mansion, guns blazing, and mow down every single person possible in his
quest to save not only his daughter but also himself. It didn't make sense
to leave witnesses.

And that includes me, she thought. *I'm a witness.* She had found Paul
for him, and while Sebastian needed her to cover the front door and prevent Paul from leaving or, even better, take him out, the moment Paul
was out of the picture, she suspected she was, too. Why fork over two

million when, with a single bullet, he could kill her and leave with his daughter, all of his problems solved?

Ellie had taken cover behind the trunk of a valley oak so large and old, she suspected it had been there since the world's inception. She lay in the prone position favored by snipers, but she didn't have a bipod to hold her rifle steady, so she had to make do leaning the left side of the rifle's hand-guard against the tree trunk. The plastic mask felt slick against her wet face, her head damp underneath the hood.

The blast from the grenade had blown out most of the windows. When she heard muted gunfire coming from inside the mansion, she felt the lining of her stomach constrict, as though someone were holding a flame to it.

She was sure Sebastian was killing them—killing everyone he could. If she went in there, she knew she'd find piles of dead and wounded, all casualties in his quest to save his daughter, Grace.

His daughter, Ellie thought. It explained why Sebastian had been so driven, so determined to search the properties.

Her spot offered her the best cover but not the best line of sight. She was lying roughly two hundred yards away, east of the entrance, at a forty-five-degree angle, and on a slight incline. Ellie stared through the target scope, blinking sweat from her eye, at the front door, which was, amazingly, still shut. Once it opened—and it would at any second—people would funnel through it, scrambling in all directions. If Paul was among them—and if she was inclined to take him out (and she wanted to, for Danny)—it would be nearly impossible to get off a clean shot. She wasn't a trained sniper, had no idea how to hit a moving target, let alone do it cleanly, without collateral damage.

The same principle applied to shooting a vehicle, even if it was stationary. She had fired an AR-15 before, but she had no idea how the weapon she held in her hands had been calibrated, if it had been calibrated at all; if it had been cleaned properly and wouldn't jam. And then there was the wind to consider, and she didn't know how to factor that into her shooting.

The door opened, swinging into the house.

Her heart pounding and her breath coming hard and fast, the odors of grass and the arid, sunbaked earth beneath her filling her nostrils, she watched as armed men bolted outside. The entryway got choked with bodies, just as Sebastian had predicted, but mainly because three armed bodyguards were flanked around a small, chubby, and terrified Middle Eastern man.

Paul came out last, backward, with Sebastian's daughter gripped in a powerful choke hold; he was using her as a human shield. He was armed with a handgun—a nine, by the looks of it—and he fired several shots into the house; at Sebastian, Ellie assumed. Two of the bodyguards in the rear-flank position had turned to the house and fired as they moved backward, providing covering fire to protect their boss, or whoever he was. When they ran out of ammo, they replaced their spent magazines with fresh ones, all with the practiced ease and confidence of professionals used to handling weapons.

Paul fired as he whipped his head back and forth, trying to get a quick lay of the land. Ellie had the side of his torso lined up in the scope's reticle.

She thought of Danny and wanted to take the shot—and would have, too, if Paul hadn't taken a hostage. He held Grace Lewis effortlessly, like she was a doll, the woman's face turning a dark crimson and her bare feet kicking above the ground as she tried to pry his forearm away from her throat.

Take the shot.

She couldn't.

Too risky. If she was off just a bit, she might hit Grace. She was an innocent.

Paul's handgun either ran out of ammo or jammed; he tossed it aside as he moved to the nearest car—a red Lamborghini that screamed "middle-aged man with small penis having major midlife crisis." Ellie watched his hand reach into his pants pocket and come back with a key fob. He opened the driver's-side door and turned, his back facing her—

Ellie fired.

The shot went wide, the bullet exploding the Lamborghini's back window.

Paul spun around so fast, he lost control of his hostage. Grace slipped from his grip. He thought about going after her, decided against it. He slid behind the wheel of the sports car. Ellie sprang to her feet, eyes locked on Grace, and ran.

CHAPTER 51

H E COULDN'T FIND Grace. What Sebastian did find was the old Q-tip with the tufts of white hair slumped against the floor. His breathing was labored as he held out an arm, terrified, shaking the set of car keys pinched between his clawed fingers.

"That's my Bugatti Chiron parked out front," Q-tip said, his voice trembling with fear. "It's worth nearly three million dollars. Take it. Just let me live."

"The girl," Sebastian said.

"I can give you money, anything you want—"

"The *girl*. Where is she?"

The old man pointed to the front door. "Out there," he said. "He took her out—"

In his mind's eye Sebastian saw the old man laughing at something Paul had said, Grace standing next to them both and crying, and shot him in the face.

No witnesses.

He heard gunfire coming from outside—not from a handgun but the rapid fire from an AR-15. Had to be Faye, unless Paul had grabbed a similar weapon on his way out. He assumed Paul was armed. Sebastian approached the doorway, looking down the iron sight, ready to fire.

The area outside the front door appeared clear. He swung around the door, to his left, and saw the bodyguards and the small, fat man running, almost to the cars. Sebastian kept his finger pressed on the trigger, shooting at them and having no idea if he'd hit them, because he saw Faye— saw her standing, her hood pulled back and her mask gone, firing from her shoulder at a cherry red Lamborghini Aventador convertible that drove, in fits and starts, across the lawn as though the driver didn't know how to drive a standard. He caught sight of the steel pockmarks created by the AR rounds and knew Paul was driving the car. Paul was driving away, and he was going to escape.

Grace stood behind the tree where Faye had taken cover. Faye must have grabbed her. His daughter's shins and knees were scraped and cut in places, but she didn't look like she was in pain; she didn't appear even to know what was transpiring around her.

His daughter was safe.

But he had to consider Paul. Paul was alive, and the only way Sebastian could ensure the safety of Ava and their daughter was by killing Paul. If he didn't, he would spend the rest of his life looking over his shoulder, wondering if Paul was going to make another move against him, threaten everything he loved once more.

No. End this shit now.

The Range Rover wouldn't be able to catch up to a Lamborghini.

A Bugatti would.

"Take her to my house," he called to Faye. "I'll meet you both there."

Sebastian glanced at the Lamborghini—it was almost at the gate— and bolted back inside the foyer. He grabbed the keys from the floor, and when he came back outside, rushing to the Bugatti, he saw the Lamborghini's dim taillights racing in the distance, fading.

Sebastian started the car and floored the gas pedal. As he went after Paul he thought again about his daughter. What was more important? Taking Paul down or meeting his daughter and bringing her home to Ava?

They were both important, he told himself.

He *deserved* both.

Paul didn't know how to properly work the clutch and gearshift to drive smoothly, to take full advantage of the power and speed of the Lamborghini's engine, which meant he wouldn't be able to get as much distance from Sebastian and the house as he would have liked.

Worse, Paul had chosen as his escape route a winding, solitary stretch of track road, which allowed two-way travel but, in reality, was wide enough for only one car. The road was also made of dirt—not the best choice for a high-performance sports car—and it dipped and rose between rolling valleys of undeveloped land.

Sebastian kept reminding himself to drive carefully. The Bugatti had a lot of horsepower, and it was suited to driving on flat surfaces, not winding dirt roads through hillsides and mountains. If he didn't maintain control over the car, especially near one of the hairpin curves, he could spin out, drive off the road, and crash.

For the next twenty minutes, he trailed Paul under a sky glowing blood red from the nearby wildfires. The glow intensified, making Sebastian wonder where Paul was going. *Is he playing the ultimate game of chicken, thinking I'll stop following him? What's the son of a bitch doing?* Sebastian didn't have the luxury of focusing much on these thoughts; he had to bear down hard on driving, having Paul in his view one moment, only to lose sight of him as the younger man took another switchback road or hairpin curve or drove down some steep decline or up some rise, Sebastian's heart freezing with dread and loss until he caught sight of Paul again, thanks to the Lamborghini's headlights. Paul, he was sure, would have preferred to kill the headlights, but he couldn't. If he did, he wouldn't be able to see the roads and could very well crash or drive off an incline.

Paul turned right, across a sharp curve, and disappeared behind a stretch of land. Sebastian reached it minutes later, and when he turned onto the flat stretch of dirt road, he saw, maybe half a mile ahead, the road engulfed in flames that reached so high into the air, they looked as though they were touching the sky.

But where was Paul? Sebastian didn't see his vehicle or its headlights;

he didn't see any other roads. Had Paul decided to drive off-road, through the valley of scrub brush? The Lamborghini wasn't designed to handle that type of terrain. But there was nowhere else for him to go unless he turned around and—

There! There he is! Sebastian caught sight of one of the taillights through the clouds of smoke whipping across the road; then, as he drew closer, he saw that Paul had backed up, the sports car now sitting at an angle, like a sawhorse set up to block the road. But Paul wasn't moving. In the glare from the headlights Sebastian saw him furiously trying to work the gearshift and clutch.

End it here. End it now.

But how? What was the best approach?

Sebastian had an idea—risky, yes, but still promising. He reached into his front pocket and grabbed the switchblade he always carried with him. It felt slick in his sweaty palm, and after he clamped it between his front teeth he put on his seat belt. Then he accelerated, working the gears and clutch, the flames reflecting off the hood of the Bugatti, the Lamborghini growing larger in his windshield. He had reached almost forty miles per hour when he transferred the switchblade from his mouth to his fist and then intentionally drove straight into the Lamborghini's driver's-side door.

Before the airbags deployed, before the headlights smashed and his head and body were thrown violently against the seat belt and seat, he saw Paul, who hadn't put on his seat belt, thrown sideways, out of his seat.

The switchblade was still clutched in his fist. Sebastian used it to puncture the bags so he could see the road clearly.

The front part of the Bugatti had been smashed, turned into an accordion of steel, the windshield gone. The wind, as hot as the exhaust from a blast furnace, blew across his face, smoke filling his lungs and irritating his eyes. He quickly got his bearings—saw that he'd been thrown sideways from the impact, the Lamborghini somewhere behind him. Sebastian didn't turn around to look, focused on seeing if the car was still drivable.

It was. He drove back up the road, the Bugatti wounded, the transmission groaning, causing the vehicle to buck. He got just enough distance between him and the fire, and then parked the car. He had to make sure Paul couldn't escape. He had to make sure.

Sebastian was banged up, but he could move. He opened the door and got out, legs shaky from adrenaline. Where was the AR rifle? There, on the passenger-side floor. He reached back inside the car and grabbed it.

Paul was heaving himself out of the totaled car's missing driver's-side window.

Sebastian brought up the AR as Paul landed face-first on the ground. Through the smoke, he saw Paul's powerful arms push him up, but all of his strength, all his time spent in the gym, wouldn't get him to stand. His left leg had been badly fractured, the foot twisted and nearly torn off. There was no way Paul could stand, let alone run.

Sebastian had an idea. He churned it in his mind for a moment, then decided, *Yes. Do it.* He had time.

He had all the time in the world now.

Sebastian lowered the AR-15, grinning, and walked up to Paul. He stopped a few feet away and took a knee, Paul coughing and struggling to move, Sebastian close enough to see the lacerations covering Paul's face and scalp, his hands.

"Son," Sebastian said, "you don't look so good."

Paul didn't answer—didn't even look at him. He was trying to catch his breath and doing a piss-poor job of it, Sebastian wondering if one of Paul's lungs had collapsed, or maybe Paul had broken a rib or two.

"I've decided not to kill you," Sebastian said. "I'm going to let nature do that."

Paul eyed him, coughing from internal injuries, possibly, or maybe from the smoke. The heat of the surrounding fires was growing more intense with each passing moment. Soon, it would get to the point where it could melt skin from bone.

"Feel that wind?" Sebastian said. "That's the infamous Devil's Winds blowing behind you, fanning the flames. They're going to eat their way across these fields—across *you.*"

Sebastian saw the knowledge hit Paul, saw the fear explode in his eyes. The joy bursting inside Sebastian's chest was better than any combination of sex, booze, and drugs he had ever taken.

"You're going to burn alive, out here, in terrible, unimaginable agony," Sebastian said. "That's so much more satisfying than my original plan of shredding you to pieces with my AR-15. My only regret is not being able to stay here and savor the moment."

Sebastian got to his feet and jogged back to the Bugatti, the surrounding fires devouring the vegetation and trees. He glanced a couple of times over his shoulder, saw Paul army crawl limply across the dirt. There was no way he was going to make it out of here alive.

Now Sebastian had to work on a new problem: finding a way home to see his daughter. The Bugatti wouldn't make it to LA. He'd have to find another ride. It didn't bother him, because he had Grace. She was the priority now. Grace and Ava and their new—

A gunshot behind him, and Sebastian felt something hard and sharp slam into his back. He stumbled forward as he heard more gunshots, felt at least two more rounds slam into his back and one into his leg as he dropped to the ground.

The vest, he thought. The vest he'd been wearing absorbed the shots—although it sure as shit didn't feel like it. He scrambled to his feet, stumbling, and when he turned he saw Paul holding a handgun. Paul fired again, missed, as Sebastian brought up the AR. He was about to shoot when he thought he heard the crack of a rifle report coming from somewhere behind him.

CHAPTER 52

THE MOMENT SEBASTIAN drove away to go after Paul, Ellie considered her job done. She turned her attention to getting Grace safely to the Range Rover—getting her home and getting in touch with Roland.

The young woman was clearly on something. Her thighs and arms were scraped and cut and bleeding from having fallen to the ground, but her face was serene. When Ellie grabbed her arm, Grace didn't fight her. She had the first time, when Ellie ran to her. Grace screamed and tried to fight her off, relaxed after Ellie said, "I'm working with your father. Come with me."

Ellie led the woman across the backyard, heading toward a cluster of trees in front of the stone wall, when she heard a car engine racing somewhere behind her. She thought it was Sebastian—he had literally just left—but when she turned, she saw a compact black SUV tearing out of the garage.

Ellie dropped to her knees, taking Grace down with her. Placed a hand over the young woman's mouth and then watched the SUV—it was a Mercedes—come screaming down the driveway. It slowed a bit as it reached the gate, and in the interior glow coming from the dashboard controls Ellie saw a man behind the wheel—Bradley Guidry, she was sure. She caught just a flash of his face before the Mercedes turned left, heading in the same direction as Sebastian.

The SUV tore into the street, skidding as it turned, tires peeling and smoking against the pavement. The driver killed the lights—*He's got to be wearing night-vision googles,* she thought. *That's the only way he can see*—and raced after Paul and Sebastian.

With the headlights off, Sebastian would have no idea someone was chasing after him.

Let it go, she thought, taking off her Windbreaker and giving it to Grace. *You've done your job.*

Well, not all of it. She still didn't know the location of Sebastian's blood farm—or her brother. If Sebastian was killed, she'd lose her one and only connection in the blood world—the only person who could help her find J.C.

She had an AR-15 and a spare clip and more than half a tank of gas. The Range Rover, Sebastian had told her during the drive, had been modified by the same company that had turned his Jaguar into a tank.

Ellie tore onto the street. She turned the wheel hard to her right and, in the rearview, saw Grace thrown sideways against the backseat.

"Buckle up," Ellie said.

Grace sat up and stared dreamily at her, then out the windshield.

"Your seat belt," Ellie said. "Put it on."

Grace nodded slowly. She was still looking straight ahead, her eyes, Ellie noticed, tilted up at the cyclones of smoke in the red sky. There was no fear in her expression or in her voice when she looked at Ellie, the young woman's eyes clear when she said, "Is the world coming to an end? Has Judgment Day arrived?" Then she met Ellie's gaze in the rearview mirror. "Tell me the truth."

It wasn't easy to follow the Mercedes. Ellie killed her own lights, and she had to use the fiery red and orange glow in the sky to trail it across flat land and then winding dirt roads. When they dipped or curved suddenly, she worked the brakes and decreased the speed so the Rover wouldn't overturn.

Guidry, though, didn't seem concerned about any of that happening to him. He drove fast and had no problem handling the terrain. In a few minutes, she lost sight of him.

She thought the road would never stop curving, but then it did, and now she was driving across a long, mostly flat stretch. Far ahead, maybe half a mile away, she saw curtains of fire raining ash and the orange sparks of what she thought were embers across the valleys of sunbaked land.

Where was the Mercedes? Ellie had both hands on the wheel and leaned forward, eyes darting back and forth, searching for the SUV. She crested an incline and then saw it less than a quarter of a mile away, parked at an angle along the dirt shoulder to her left—and saw Guidry standing outside. She knew it was Guidry because, as she tore down the road, drawing closer, she saw him staring into the scope attached to a sniper rifle with a bipod propped on the hood. His back was toward her and he was using the SUV for cover, and she caught a quick glimpse of the rifle—a massive, mean-looking weapon probably equipped with .50-caliber rounds. And he did, in fact, have night-vision gear; she saw it mounted on his head.

Ellie saw a muzzle flash from his rifle. She flinched against her seat belt and gripped the wheel even tighter as Guidry fired off a second round. He smoothly picked the rifle off the hood like he was grabbing a suitcase, and then he turned around and brought the rifle up.

Aiming it at her.

Ellie knew Guidry could see her clearly, thanks to the night-vision goggles mounted across his eyes. Every cell in her body screamed for her to turn around, but it was too late to do that. She veered left, into the bumpy terrain full of scrub brush, and as she bounced in her seat, the top of her head slamming into the cab's ceiling and Grace behind her screaming questions, Ellie wondered what grade of bulletproof glass had been installed in the Rover. She doubted it would withstand a .50-caliber round.

Then she turned the wheel hard right, heading back to the road, Guidry trying to guess where she would turn and trying to compensate.

He held the sniper rifle like the trained marksman he was. She kept driving wildly, her foot never letting up on the accelerator, narrowing the distance between them.

Her heart seized in her chest when she saw the muzzle flash leap from his rifle.

The round penetrated the windshield to her right. She turned the wheel again, and in the rearview she caught Grace jumping against her seat belt; but Grace didn't scream, even when her frightened gaze locked on the golf ball–sized hole left by the round. The hole had splintered, but the cracks hadn't spread into Ellie's field of vision. She could see well enough, and she righted the wheel and kept her foot on the gas and charged toward him at full throttle. Guidry lowered his weapon, realizing, maybe for the first time in his life, that he might not live to fight another day. He knew he wouldn't be able to make it inside his car in time, which left him only one option: running.

The rifle was heavy and cumbersome. He should have dropped it before turning to run, but he held it tight. He was trying to make his way around the front of the Mercedes when the rifle stock slammed against the front side of the SUV and slowed him down. Then he dropped it, but it was too late. Ellie hit him full-on, with the steel bullbar.

Instead of flinging him across the windshield and tossing him over the roof and into the air, the bar slammed him forward. Ellie caught his shocked expression before he disappeared, thrown downward and underneath the Rover. Ellie didn't slow down, but she did glance in the rearview, and looking past Grace's horrified expression, she saw the crushed and twisted remains and felt her stomach lurch. Ellie looked away, back to the road in front of her, and as it dipped she saw, through the smoke, both Sebastian and Paul on the ground. Only Paul, though, appeared to be moving.

Ellie skidded to a stop. She turned in her seat and said, "Stay in the car—and don't roll down the windows. Understand?"

Grace's face had gone slack with shock. "You ran him over. You ran—"

"Do you understand?"

Grace flinched, then nodded, trying to catch her breath. Ellie grabbed her rifle and got out, slamming the door behind her.

The heat from the surrounding fires was intense. Smoke filled her lungs and her eyes watered and burned and it hurt to breathe. She moved forward, looking down the sight at Paul. She saw a handgun lying on the road and she saw him lying flat on his stomach and his fingers clawing at the dirt as he tried to pull himself forward, tried to get some distance from the road fire that was moments away from engulfing the crushed shell of the Lamborghini. Paul was heading for the vehicle Sebastian had taken. It was also mangled, the hood crushed but the car still drivable; she could hear the motor running.

The gun was behind Paul. His pants leg, she noticed, was rolled up, over the calf, revealing the ankle holster strapped to it. There was no way Paul could reach the gun, but she kept her attention locked on him as she knelt next to Sebastian's head. Ellie couldn't stop coughing.

Sebastian was coughing, too—weakly. He lay on his side, eyes blinking rapidly as he stared down at his hands. They were pressed against the entry wound in his stomach; he was desperately trying to stem the flow of blood that was leaking through his fingers.

"Guidry," Sebastian said. "I think he shot me. He's—"

"He's dead." Ellie ripped open the front of Sebastian's jacket, then his shirt, saw that a sizable round had penetrated the vest. *Only an armor-piercing round could have done this,* she thought.

The blood pooled around Sebastian looked as black as oil in the firelight.

"I can't feel my legs," he said, his voice surprisingly strong and clear.

Eyeing Paul, who was focused solely on trying to reach Sebastian's vehicle, which was never going to happen, not at Paul's current pace, Ellie craned her head over Sebastian's shoulder. The back of his Windbreaker was slick with blood and peppered with bullet holes. When she lifted up the Windbreaker and shirt, she saw that more rounds had penetrated the vest, knew that the handgun lying on the road had been equipped with armor-piercing ammo as well.

"Grace?" Sebastian asked.

"In the car."

The black fabric of the vest, Ellie saw, had been blown apart. When she saw the gaping exit wound in his back, the stomach-churning devastation caused by Guidry's sniper round, she knew Sebastian had only minutes left.

"Help me up," Sebastian said. "We need to get out of here."

Ellie lowered her head closer to the ground, to get away from the smoke, watching Paul as she said, "You've lost too much blood. Even if I could get you to the hospital, they wouldn't be able to save you. I'm sorry."

His eyes went wide with fear, Sebastian realizing, she suspected, that he was dying, all of his options used up, no way to turn back.

"Grace doesn't know," he said.

"Know what?"

"That I'm her father. Bring her. Bring her to me so I can tell her."

For a brief moment she saw a window into his humanity. "Your carriers," she said. "Where are they?"

Sebastian was looking off in the direction of the Range Rover. "I need to tell her. She needs to hear it from me." Then, when she didn't answer: "I can't die without her knowing. Please."

The desperate, terrified look in his eyes broke her heart.

"Tell me where your carriers are," she said, "and I promise I'll take care of them."

Sebastian told her. Ellie leaned an ear closer to his mouth and made him repeat it to make sure she had heard him correctly.

CHAPTER 53

WHEN FAYE HAD scrambled to her feet, she staggered up the road, coughing, heading back to the Range Rover, its bright lights shining down on Sebastian like the eyes of God.

Sebastian knew he was dying. The moment he'd reached around his back and prodded the exit wound with his fingers, his intestines coiling out from it like a nest of snakes, he knew he was going to die right here, on this dirt road.

But he wasn't alone. He had Paul for company.

The fire had caught up to him. Sebastian had Paul's agonizing, almost inhuman-sounding howls to keep him company. Sebastian turned his head and saw Paul lying on his back and frantically flapping his arms, trying to smother the flames devouring his legs.

At least, Sebastian thought, *I have this.*

Faye had heard Paul, too. Sebastian saw her whip her head around and look back down the road, past him.

Sebastian looked only at the Rover. He squinted against the harsh bright white lights, hoping to catch a glimpse of Grace somewhere behind the reflection of the flames dancing across the tinted glass. He needed Grace to know something about him. That was how you continued to live long after you were gone, by sharing the story of your life. It made you real, kept you from fading away.

But what would he tell her? Maybe start with a quick story about him and her mother, how they'd met (sophomore year of high school, when Ava and her family moved into the neighborhood); the exact moment when he fell in love with her (when Ava held his hand for the first time, at a football game); about their first kiss (on a brown couch at Kim Jackson's house party, Ava drunk on wine poured from a box, Ava making the first move). He wanted to tell Grace how Ava, at sixteen, was already so confident, so sure of her place in the world. How if he lived with her for a hundred years he would come away knowing only a fraction of the world that lived behind her beautiful brown eyes; how when he saw those eyes for the first time they soothed that rage inside him, made him feel that everything was going to be okay—not perfect but okay. He wanted to tell his daughter how he had dreamed of this moment before she was born, being married to her mother and having kids. A family. He wanted—

CHAPTER 54

AVA CAME AWAKE to the sound of the doorbell, police lights flashing across her front windows.

She had fallen asleep on the couch. Her mind was numb with fatigue and worry and too much wine, and when she saw rising from the plush chair directly across from her a thin white man with a red beard and dressed in a suit, she almost screamed.

Then she remembered: she had invited him into her house. His name was John Bace, the LAPD detective who had taken over her daughter's case. Detective Alves was still hospitalized.

John Bace was smiling now. Right then, Ava knew the police had found her daughter—*alive.*

It was like she was rising from the depths of an ocean. She broke the surface of the water, gasping, the sweet air filling her lungs and rinsing away the iron grip of fear that had laid claim to her mind, body, and soul. Her eyes clouded with tears of relief and gratitude and she held on to the doorway to keep from falling.

Detective Bace grabbed her by the arm. "Easy," he said. "Easy. Everything's fine. Your daughter is fine."

"Where?"

"At a hospital in Ojai. No, she's okay, I swear. Come on—I'll take you to her."

Ava headed to Bace's department car, a black Ford Fusion. She got into the back, and she didn't realize she'd forgotten to put on her shoes until Bace brought them to her.

"I want to talk to her," Ava said, after Bace slid behind the wheel.

He looked at her in the rearview mirror. "Cell signals up that way are spotty, because of all the wildfires. And they're running some tests—standard stuff, don't worry—and they don't allow cell phones back there. Where's Charles? I thought he was staying with you."

"He went into the office." Ava caught his confusion and said, "China is fifteen hours ahead of us. Charles wanted to be there when the markets open. I'll call him and let him know what's happening. He can meet us there. Go. Please."

Two cruisers—one in front, the other in the rear—escorted them out of the neighborhood. It was predominantly quiet, so they didn't need to use sirens. The flashing lights were enough to signal drivers to pull aside and let them through.

When she called Charles and told him the news, his voice was thick with sleep, and she could hear a woman's voice in the background. Charles had told her he was involved with someone. Her name was Emma and she was all of thirty-two. From bits and pieces of conversation with Charles, Ava had gathered that this whole ordeal with Grace had frightened Emma terribly, made her feel unsafe when she stayed in his brand-new mansion in Bel Air.

Ava didn't judge him, was no longer in a position to judge.

"What was she doing all the way up in Ojai?" Ava asked.

"I don't know the answer to that. We'll find out more when we arrive."

Ava stared out the window, trying to absorb everything, trying to get herself settled so she could think. The homes raced by her in a blur. She was more awake than she'd ever been in her entire life.

"Sebastian Kane," Bace said.

Ava turned away from the window, saw Bace looking at her in the rearview.

"He's one of the people you visited to help raise money for the ransom, correct?"

"Yes," Ava said. "Why?"

"He was in Ojai. With your daughter."

Our daughter, Ava added privately. "What was he doing there?"

"I don't know. I was hoping you could shed some light on that."

She hated the circuitous way cops spoke, asking questions around the questions they really wanted to ask. She had grown tired of it. "Why don't you ask him?"

"I'm afraid that's not an option."

His tone told her everything she needed to know. She straightened in her seat. "What happened?"

"That's the million-dollar question at the moment. What little we know came through your daughter. She said he was shot multiple times, and—"

"Grace saw him—"

"No," Bace said quickly. "No, she didn't see him get shot. But she did see his body."

"He's dead?"

Bace nodded somberly. In her mind's eye she saw flashes of the boy she'd once known and loved—Sebastian winning her the world's ugliest stuffed bear at a carnival and Sebastian bringing a bouquet of carnations to her mother. Sebastian always attentive and listening and gentle, always gentle with her.

"I'm sorry," Bace said. "I understand you two were once close."

"That was a long time ago."

"Well, I wanted to prepare you for it. I should also tell you it's going to take some time to get an official medical ruling on how he died. His body . . . He collapsed near the site of a wildfire that is still raging."

Ava nodded, somewhat surprised at the sudden loss she felt.

The night that changed their lives forever, Sebastian had been only trying to protect her. But that hadn't stopped the police from arresting him and then sending him to jail, and with the baby growing inside her, Ava had come face-to-face with the cruelty and coldness of parenthood—her life and her choices had belonged to someone else. Her new life had involved forever being consumed by making thousands of daily decisions to protect and nurture someone who didn't have the capacity to make decisions.

It had all been up to her.

Every. Single. Thing.

Ava had always been pragmatic. She knew she had to let go of her old life and form a new one, without Sebastian. She had to cut off all ties and reinvent herself, give her child (and herself, too) a clean slate. A life where her child would grow up never knowing he or she had a father serving life in prison. Once she made that decision, she never looked back. It hurt like hell, but there was no doubt in her mind that it was for the best.

"I don't know much in the way of details other than the Ojai police found your daughter and that she's okay," Bace said. "They're still at the scene, still gathering stuff, but they promised to fill me in on everything they have so far when we arrive. I promise I'll share everything with you when I know more."

Ava closed her eyes. Sebastian waited for her there, in her mind.

Her heart.

Sebastian had been her first love, and you never forgot your first. The Sebastian she had known had a lot of anger in him, yes, but she also thought he'd had a lot of potential.

And when she saw him recently, after those decades apart, she realized her instincts had been correct. She had been looking forward to getting to know him again. Who knew what would have developed?

Now she would never know.

That was probably for the best.

The ER doctor told her he had given Grace a mild sedative to calm her down. When the police brought her in, he said, she was barefoot and wearing only a Windbreaker and in a state of shock. She would not explain how she'd lost her clothes or how she'd gotten the fresh cuts and scrapes on her knees, thighs, hands, and elbows; but she did tell him a man named Paul had given her molly, and she kept asking if the entire world had been engulfed in fire. She said she wouldn't speak to anyone except her mother. The doctor didn't have the results from the lab yet, and he couldn't say whether or not she had been sexually assaulted, because Grace refused to let anyone examine her.

Ava found it difficult to slide back the curtain. She didn't know what condition Grace was in, and a part of her believed that some terrible mistake had been made.

With a held breath and with her heart slamming against her chest, Ava pulled back the curtain.

And there she was, her daughter, looking real and alive underneath the harsh overhead light. Grace lay on her back, her eyes shut and her features relaxed, her mouth parted slightly and her chest slowly rising and falling; she was lost in sleep. She wore a hospital gown, and her cuts and scrapes were covered in bandages and gauze, and she had an IV line connected to a bag of saline. The doctor said he wanted to keep her well hydrated.

Ava let out her breath, and the terror she'd been carrying dissolved like wet sand, made her knees buckle and her eyes water with gratitude. Grace had dried blood on her hands and forearms, and her toes and the soles of her feet were stained with grass and caked with dirt, and she reeked of smoke, but she looked okay. Ava was more worried about her daughter's mental health.

Detective Bace hovered close by, along with a young nurse who wore a worried expression on her face. Ava did not want to share this moment with them. She asked for some privacy, and she did not wait for their answer. She slid the curtain back and, blinking back tears, fought the terrible urge to reach out and clutch her daughter, let out all the soul-crushing terror she'd been carrying for what felt like decades.

But this wasn't about her; it was about her daughter. She needed to be strong. *Be strong,* she told herself as she sat on the side of the mattress. *Be strong for her. This is about Grace, not you. Put her first.*

And Ava would. She had been putting Grace first her whole life—had done so willingly and gladly. That was what you did as a parent. You put the needs and welfare of your child above your own, always and forever, until the day you died.

Grace's eyes fluttered opened, widened when she saw her mother sitting next to her.

"You're home, baby," Ava said, her voice clear and strong.

Grace's lips quivered, and just before she pushed herself up and gathered herself in her mother's arms, Ava caught a glimpse of the terror and pain that were now living behind her daughter's eyes. It cut Ava deeply, knowing there was nothing she could do to erase her daughter's pain, and like a child Ava wished that God would somehow magically grant her wish to remove this burden from her daughter. If Ava could trade a limb, even her eyesight, to erase her daughter's pain, she would do it.

But life didn't work that way—and God didn't work that way. God had left his own son to die on the cross, so it was foolish to think that He would meddle in her affairs. She would guide her daughter through this. Ava had gathered a lot of hard-bought experience in the area of pain management—and that's all life was, learning how to manage your pain.

Grace sobbed against her chest. Ava rubbed her daughter's back. She kissed the top of her head and her cheek, Grace's sobs loud and wet against her ear, and she kept holding on to her daughter when she felt her relax in her arms.

"They—" Grace began.

"You don't have to talk," Ava whispered. "There's plenty of time for that later. You're safe. That's all you need to think about right now."

"She made me go to him."

"Who?"

"The woman. She said she was working with Dad."

"Your father? He didn't have—"

"She kept saying he was the one who rushed inside the house to come get me. She's crazy. She made me get out of the car and kneel down in all this blood next to this man lying in the road and kept screaming at me to talk to him."

Ava felt very still.

"I'd never seen him before," Grace said. "This woman kept telling me to talk to him even though he was, like, already dead."

"What did this man say?"

"Nothing. The fires were coming and there was all this smoke and we had to leave. We had to leave him there."

"You left him there," Ava said, trying hard not to picture Sebastian.

"Yeah. In the road. We left him there and he probably, like, got all burned up."

"Who was this woman?"

"I don't know. She wouldn't tell me her name—and she wouldn't tell me why I had to talk to this dead guy. Sebastian was his name. Sebastian Kane." Grace sniffled. Swallowed. Sniffled again. "Do you know him?"

"Yes," Ava said, rubbing her daughter's back. "I've known him all my life. You will, too."

Give Us This Day

CHAPTER 55

WHEN ELLIE DROVE back to the house, she was surprised to find it lit up by a carnival of flashing blue and white and red lights from half a dozen or more patrol cars and ambulances parked along the street and in the long driveway. Someone must have called the police, but how? The cell signals here were dead.

That didn't matter, she realized, if someone had placed the call on a landline.

The cops gathered on the street took one look at the Range Rover's splintered windshield, the blood and, most likely, pieces of skin, hair, and bone splattered across the bullbar, and drew their weapons. Ellie saw shotguns and assault rifles mixed in with the department-issued nines, and within moments she was surrounded. When someone on a bullhorn ordered her to roll down her window and put her hands on top of the steering wheel, Ellie complied.

When they approached and saw an AR-15 rifle in the backseat and a terrified young woman sitting in the front, her hands and knees caked with blood and dirt, Ellie gave them the woman's name and information. She didn't have a chance to say anything else. They arrested her at gunpoint, put her into the back of a sheriff's car, and drove her to the Ojai station, where she was booked and fingerprinted.

For three hours, Ellie sat in an interrogation room with her hands cuffed to a D ring in the middle of a table bolted to the gray linoleum floor and told a detective with a handlebar mustache and a head as large as a pumpkin to call Special Agent Roland Bauer. She gave the detective Roland's number, but he was more interested in the details of what had happened at the house—why Ojai's wealthiest resident, Chauncey Harrington, had been shot to death along with four other men, and why there were three young women locked inside what appeared to be a wine cellar that had been converted into a prison chamber.

Oh, that would be Paul's blood farm. Ellie said nothing. She wouldn't divulge anything until she talked to Roland. The cops left her alone for a good amount of time, the door opening every now and then with a new detective who was determined to get her to spill all the details. Ellie had grown numb to the cops shouting and threatening her, and when the exhaustion finally got to her, she put her head down on the table, closed her eyes, and thought of Cody. Only Cody.

She was half-asleep when she heard the door open again. Roland came in alone, looking like a group of pissed-off local cops and pencil-pushing bureaucrats had taken turns kicking a two-by-four up his ass, which probably wasn't that far from the truth. The FBI had been caught playing in Ojai's backyard, without permission, and his undercover cop turned federal agent had played a large role in a mass shooting.

Roland placed both hands on the back of the folding chair on the other side of the table. His neck was mottled red and spots of color were creeping into his cheeks. This hadn't turned out to be the operation he could hang his hat on.

It's not all bad, she wanted to tell him, but couldn't. There was no doubt a big crowd was crammed together inside the tiny room behind the one-way glass, watching and listening and, Ellie was sure, recording.

"I couldn't call you—no cell service up here," Ellie said, wanting her words to be part of the record. She had heard stories from other cops about how the Feds turned into professional finger-pointers when the shit

hit the fan. She had gone into what Danny had called CYA mode: cover your ass. "And they didn't allow me to call after I was booked."

Roland studied her for a long moment. She expected to see anger, at least a flash of it. What she found, surprisingly, was sympathy.

He leaned forward slowly, as if trying to stretch out a muscle spasm in his lower back. He had an American flag pin on the lapel of his navy blue suit jacket and his ID hung from a lanyard around his neck. He cleared his throat and swallowed several times, as though he was having trouble breathing.

"You're going to be in here for a bit." His voice was hoarse, probably from yelling, but there was no heat in it, just a weary sense of defeat, she thought. "Phone calls, paperwork, all that."

"I want to talk to Cody."

Roland looked her up and down. Then he straightened and walked away, and when he opened the door, he did so slowly, as though he was entering a funeral home to say his final goodbyes to a loved one.

In her holding cell, Ellie came awake to the sound of a baton rattling against the bars. She sat up on her cot, the bare mattress stained from months, probably years, of perspiration and other bodily fluids, and saw an older patrolman with a ruddy face and a potbelly standing on the other side, his expression flat to hide the anger he felt toward her. All the cops here were pissed, and she couldn't blame them. She had detonated a bomb in their quiet city and now they had been tasked with cleaning up after her while battling the wildfires.

"You can use our bathroom to freshen up if you want," he said as he unlocked her door.

Ellie rubbed the fatigue off her face. Her head was pounding, and her mouth was coated with the early-morning paste of sleep. "Where are we going?"

"I'm going back to my desk to do paperwork. You're going home."

Home. The word had never sounded sweeter to her. "Can I use your phone?"

He pointed to the one on his desk.

She called Cody's cell.

He didn't answer.

In the bathroom, she scrubbed her hands, arms, and face with liquid hand soap and rough paper towels. She cleaned herself up as best she could.

The older cop was waiting for her outside the restroom. "Your FBI friend Bauer is in the waiting area."

He wasn't. Ellie found a Hispanic woman dozing on a stiff plastic chair. Her clothes smelled of smoke, and her dried tears had left trenches in the soot on her face.

Ellie stepped out the front door, into the cool morning air. It was shortly after five, the sky red and not as dark as last night. She could see tornado-shaped plumes of smoke in the distance.

Roland was leaning against the trunk of a white Chrysler sedan, its sides streaked with ash and dirt. He wore the same suit she had seen him in earlier. He looked like he hadn't slept.

Ellie knew why he was here. He was going to take her someplace, probably a federal safe house where, for the next few days, a bureaucratic machine composed of men and women who had never put their lives on the line would find the best way to dump as much blame as possible into LAPD commissioner Jim Kelly's lap.

Roland glared at her as she approached the car, his gaze a volcanic mix of anger and resentment, all of it aimed at her.

She turned it all to ice with a handful of words. "Want to take a ride to Sebastian's blood farm?"

"Where is it?"

"I haven't been to it yet. All I have is an address. I should also add that I have no idea if he was telling me the truth. He told me under . . . unusual circumstances."

"Where is it?" Roland asked again.

"First thing is, I'm going with you. Second thing is, I'll tell you after I see Cody. Those are my terms."

"Terms," Roland repeated, as if making sure he'd heard her correctly. He dug his tongue into a back molar for a moment, then shook his head. "You've got a set of balls on you—I'll give you that. Who's the boy in the picture?"

"His name is Jonathan Cullen. I'll tell you the rest along the way."

"No, you'll tell me now."

Ellie said nothing, looked out into the distance, at the plumes of smoke drifting above the mountains and rolling hills, thinking about Sebastian Kane's final moments.

Roland eased himself off the car. For a good ten minutes, he threatened to come down on her with the full power of the federal government, throwing in all sorts of sanctions and promises of prison time, everything he had.

Ellie held her ground, waiting for his tantrum to end. When it finally did, when he realized she wasn't going to budge, he moved to the driver's-side door, turned back to her, and then knocked twice against the passenger window.

The door opened. Cody got out, wearing a Patagonia vest over a long-sleeved flannel.

Ellie's eyes filled.

"Yes," she said.

Cody looked at her, puzzled. "Yes to what?"

"To you," she said. "To everything."

CHAPTER 56

ELLIE STILL HAD official business to conduct, and Cody wasn't allowed to accompany her. Cody drove home with the federal agent who had driven him here.

Sebastian had told her the location of the blood farm, as well as where to find the hidden access area and the code. She shared none of that with Roland. The moment she did, he would send her on her way to be interrogated by a bunch of pencil pushers while he went off to the blood farm, to claim all the glory.

She wasn't seeking glory. She wanted to see the blood farm.

"Where?" Roland snapped, his face red with anger.

"Downieville," Ellie said.

"The hell's that?"

"The guy was dying. I didn't ask for directions."

"Address?"

Ellie hesitated.

Roland glared at her, incredulous. "What, you thinking you and I are just going to waltz in there and free 'em? I need support staff, make travel arrangements. Give me the address. *Now.*"

"Our Lady of the Immaculate Conception," she said. "And if you're thinking of just leaving me here because you're pissed off, don't. You'll need an access code. I'll give it to you when *we* get there."

Roland was on his phone as they drove out of the parking lot. He didn't put the call on the car's Bluetooth, so she couldn't hear the conversation. Ellie guessed he was talking to his boss or some other higher-up; he kept saying "sir" as he brought the person on the other end of the line up to speed about the recent developments. Whoever he was speaking to must have been pleased, because Roland's voice grew lighter, and the tension he'd been carrying in his jaw and shoulders relaxed a bit.

Roland hung up, tossed the phone in the cubbyhole. "This boy, Jonathan Cullen," he said. "Who is he?"

"My twin brother."

Roland shifted in his seat, thinking. "Your file says you're an only child."

"My file is missing a lot of important facts."

"Such as?"

"Let's start with my name," she said. "It isn't Ellie Batista."

Ellie had never heard of Downieville, had no idea where it was. A quick Internet search on Roland's phone told her it was a "census-designated place" in Sierra County, which was in the northern part of the state and bordered Nevada. It had a population of fewer than two hundred people, and the town had no restaurants or grocery stores. That was all the information she got before Roland took his phone back to answer an incoming call. He spoke cryptically, so she couldn't glean anything from his conversation.

Reaching Downieville by car would take nine hours. Roland, through the FBI's LA field office, had made arrangements to borrow, under the government's law enforcement assistance program, a helicopter from the Homeland Security Division of the Los Angeles Sheriff's Department, located at the airport in Long Beach.

The helicopter, painted green and gold, was the same type of amphibious aircraft used by the president of the United States, and by the navy for search-and-rescue missions, medevac, and shipping. It was called a Sea King, and in addition to being able to handle any type of weather conditions, the helicopter was known for its speed. They made it to a landing pad just outside of Downieville in under an hour.

A black Jeep Cherokee with tinted windows drove up to them. The driver got out and handed the vehicle off to Roland. Ellie thought it was odd that no one had accompanied them during the flight, and she didn't see transport of any kind nearby as they drove onto the main road. She suspected Roland had sent an advance team to scope out the church.

The bright sunshine of Ventura County was gone; here in Sierra County, the sky was overcast, and the weather was different, chilly and windy. But there were no fires, and the air smelled fresh and clean, a welcome relief from the past forty-eight hours. It had a transformative effect, too. The physical and mental exhaustion from yesterday's events that had turned her blood to sludge—all of it had been blown aside.

But that wasn't the reason why she was sitting up straight in her seat, feeling wide-eyed and alert. A part of her kept wondering if Sebastian had been playing her. What if he had told her an elaborate lie to shut her up and get her to bring his daughter to her so he could say goodbye? She had tried. By the time she had driven Grace to him, Sebastian was already gone. But what if there was no blood farm here? And if there was, why was it all the way up here?

Downieville felt like a small rural town in Vermont—deep green valleys and hills of pines and oaks so tall, they obscured the mountains and kept out sunlight; the kind of quaint, small homes made of weather-blasted wood you'd find in New England. The only thing missing was snow. They passed through a tiny downtown area of homey mom-and-pop stores, an old theater, and a gas station, and in the blink of an eye it was gone, and they were once again driving down an isolated stretch of road, surrounded by trees.

Twenty minutes later, after not passing a single house or car, Roland turned left and made his way down a paved road that led deep into a pastoral valley that looked like it belonged in another century—the Old West, where everyone carried guns and rode horses. Maybe she thought that way because of the church. It was small and rectangular and painted white, including the roof—more of a house than a church if it weren't for the spire holding a small plain black cross. She could see a mountain range and part of a river, but she didn't see a single vehicle except theirs, and there were no people here, no homes, nothing but the church.

Roland killed the engine, and pocketed his keys as he got out. He jogged toward the church's rustic barn door, and by the time Ellie shut the car door he had already slipped inside. On her way, she saw a bronze plaque set in stone informing people about the history of the town's first Catholic church. She saw 1862 and FIRE and REBUILT (1876) before she opened the door.

The inside was tiny. Twelve pews made of knotted pine, six on each side, sat in front of a simple all-white altar. The plain stained-glass windows looked old, and the statues of the Virgin Mary and Jesus stared down toward the carpeted floor, away from the eight men dressed in camo. Their gloved hands held assault rifles and they wore military-grade tactical vests and belts equipped with flex cuffs and flash-bang grenades. They all wore helmets equipped with night-vision goggles except for the one Roland was talking to, a man twice his size and twice as tall. He had a black buzz cut and sharp features, and his eyes were set back deep in his skull and looked like two small marbles. The man kept glancing over Roland's shoulder, at her, as she approached. Everyone did. They had all stopped talking the moment she entered.

Roland turned to her and said, "Lead the way."

Ellie walked down the center aisle, the men filing in behind her, and moved past the altar, to the white-painted door with the plastic EXIT sign above it. She opened the door and moved down a hallway no longer than ten feet.

She hadn't been raised Catholic, but she had known plenty of Catholics growing up and had picked up on a lot of things. The room she found herself in was called a sacristy—the Catholic version of "the greenroom," the place where the priest waited before mass started. It was also used to store his vestments and whatever other religious items he used during the service, but those were long gone. The only items inside this windowless white room were a bare wooden desk bolted down to the floor and, nailed to the wall, a black crucifix that matched the one on the spire.

Ellie turned her attention to the old fireplace. The soldiers were filing into the room. She held up a hand.

"You can't be in here," she said. "Everyone needs to back up into the hallway."

"Why?" The question came from the guy with the black crew cut.

Must be the point man, she thought. "We won't have enough room," she replied, kneeling in front of the hearth. She had reached her right hand up, inside the chimney, her fingertips feeling for the loose brick when she saw that the man hadn't moved. "I can't do this if you guys don't back out."

Roland said, "Do what she says."

Ellie removed the loose brick. Then she reached inside the cavity, found the lever Sebastian had described, and pulled. When she moved back to the archway leading into the hall, she had to push them back.

She expected to hear the rumble of some machinery—gear workings, a hum of a motor, something. She heard a creak, and the floor directly in front of her rose quietly, stopped at a forty-five-degree angle.

A set of steps faced her now. She saw a keypad, and a vault door made of steel.

Roland grabbed her by the arm and said, "You don't know what's down there. Let them handle it."

"Okay."

"Give them the code."

She did.

The point man went down first. The others fell in line. She couldn't see him entering the code, but she barely heard the soft beep as he keyed in each number. Blood was pounding in her ears, and her breath was coming short and fast.

The vault door opened.

The men rushed inside, weapons hot.

She heard them shout orders to drop to the ground. She heard people's screams and gasps and knew she had found the farm—knew there were carriers down there. Roland kept a fierce grip on her arm as she heard a crash against the floor. She thought she heard doors slamming open and doors being kicked open, but she didn't hear any gunshots.

It got very quiet. She thought, maybe even imagined, she heard someone crying, a young girl, maybe. The sound was lost behind heavy footsteps. The point man appeared below and, looking only at Roland, said, "All clear."

Ellie didn't know what she had expected to find buried in the earth underneath the church—a prison, maybe. Some sort of dungeon or holding pen with very little light. What she found reminded her of the play areas she'd seen those giant tech companies use to lure bright minds to come work for them: a wide-open space containing comfortable sofas and beanbags and a full kitchen and classic arcade games and games like foosball and Ping-Pong. A place where you could come and relax and unwind.

This brightly lit playroom—she didn't know what else to call it—had high ceilings and was longer and wider than a basketball court. It did, in fact, have a half court at the far, far end. She found pinball machines, and a built-in fish tank that took up a good length of wall. She found shelves holding books and games, and the flat screens hanging on the walls—there were so many of them—soundlessly played movies and TV shows and were connected to Xbox and PlayStation game systems. The couches, sectional sofas, armchairs, and recliners scattered across the room were empty of people, littered with wireless headsets and game controllers. The people who had been sitting in them were all lying facedown in the center of the carpeted room, their hands clasped behind their heads, and struggling not to look at the weapons aimed at them.

"Stand down," she told the men.

They ignored her.

She looked for Roland, saw him coming out from a door that led into a neatly furnished bedroom. "Tell these guys to take it out of overdrive, will you?"

Roland didn't have a chance to answer. The point man said to him, "We checked the bedrooms, the exercise rooms and bathrooms and closets, the place they use to draw the blood. This is all of 'em."

Ellie moved to the carriers. There were eighteen of them—some as young as teenagers, others her age if not older. Five of them were males who seemed to be roughly her age, and of those, two had the same brown hair as her brother. They all looked well-fed.

The one with the rumpled white collared shirt and wearing jeans and socks had, she thought, her skin tone and also shared the same features as her brother. Same button nose and full lips.

Ellie took a knee beside him. She touched his back, felt him flinch, his muscles as hard as iron. He was physically fit, in great shape. Everyone here was—just like the two carriers she'd seen months ago at Sophia Vargas's home in Brentwood.

Looking at him—at everyone—and seeing how healthy they were, how well cared for, triggered a memory of words Sebastian had said to her that morning at his home, at the table, when she inquired about his blood farms. *I don't like that term,* Sebastian had said. *It implies that I treat my carriers as livestock, which I don't. You'd be surprised by how well they're treated.*

Sebastian had been telling her the truth.

"It's okay," Ellie told the carrier. "You're safe." Then she addressed the others: "You're all safe. My name is Officer Ellie Batista. I'm with the LAPD. I'm working with a federal task force. You're all safe now. It's over."

Roland spoke to the point man: "Tell them to bring the truck around. Back it right up to the front. Have them do a final sweep of the area first, make sure everything's locked down."

Ellie turned her focus back to the man lying on the floor. "I'm going to pull down the collar of your shirt. I just want to take a quick look at your neck, okay?"

The man didn't answer, didn't flinch as Ellie gently moved his collar down.

He had a patch of light brown skin on his neck—what doctors called a café au lait birthmark. It looked like a pair of drip marks sitting on top of each other.

Her brother had the *exact* same birthmark.

At least that was what her memory told her. What if she was wrong? What if she was—what's the word?—projecting?

"Are you Jonathan Cullen?"

He didn't answer—didn't look at her, his gaze flicking between all the weapons aimed at him and the others.

"You're safe now. I promise," Ellie told him. "Are you Jonathan?"

"No. You're thinking of somebody else."

A part of her screamed yes, this was her brother, while another part, an overwhelming part, told her he was telling her the truth, because, really, what were the chances that J.C. could still be alive after all this time? And when Sebastian had said no, he didn't recognize the boy in the picture, Ellie had believed him because, again, what were the chances?

But here was the birthmark, staring back at her.

It has to be him.

Ellie said, "Your mother always called you Jonathan, but everyone else called you J.C. You had awful earaches—so bad that you were going to get ear tube surgery. When you were little, you wore these bright orange floaties on your arms at the pool, and then even in the bath, because you were terrified of water. You wore a swimmer's mask because you hated getting water in your eyes, and you wore that, too, in the bathtub when Mom had to wash your hair."

His eyes slid to hers, and right then Ellie knew. She could tell by the way he was looking at her.

"Who are you?"

"I'm Ellie," she said, smiling. "Your sister."

ACKNOWLEDGMENTS

This book would not have been written without support and hard work from the following people: Josh Getzler and Jon Cobb of HG Literary; Joelle Hobeika and Josh Bank of Alloy Entertainment; Paul Tresler; and Rajani LaRocca. Special thanks to John and Elizabeth Badaracco, owners of CrossFit Synergistics in Ashland, and to all its members who helped keep me physically and mentally healthy and on track.

And thanks, as always, to Jen and Jackson; Kay and Jim Byram; Frank, Sandra, and Kathleen Mooney for their unwavering support, patience, and understanding.